When Alison Grange's husband was murdered, she inherited the greatest private fortune in the world.
And the most dangerous.

Golden Girl

by

Caroline Gray

This title first published in Great Britain 1992 by
SEVERN HOUSE PUBLISHERS LTD.

This edition licensed by Severn House Publishers Ltd.,
produced by Magpie Books Ltd., and published by Parragon
Book Services Ltd. in 1994

A copy of the British Library CIP data is available
from the British Library.

ISBN 0-75250-113-5

Printed and bound in Great Britain

CONTENTS

PROLOGUE

The forest steamed. Great swathes of white mist rose from the damp earth and masked the huge trees which reached upwards a hundred feet and more, looking for light. The sun had risen.

There was nothing like this forest in the world. Pat Grange had read of the Congo; he had never been there. The Congo could not compare with the Matto Grosso, he knew – and he *had* been there. But even the Matto Grosso could not compare with the green hell of the valley of the Amazon, or of its northern tributary, the Rio Branco. Now even the Rio Branco was behind them, as the three men had pushed on towards the large rectangle of land that contained the borders of Brazil, Venezuela and British Guiana.

Grange had explored this country several times, still without being able to tell exactly where he was; it was possible to walk within five feet of a man, or a hill, or a beast, or a river . . . or a gold mine, several times, and not see it, so thick was the foliage. He knew that could he climb one of these trees to the top, or find a clearing where there were no trees – equally improbable – he would see, some thirty miles to the north, the peak of Roraima, rising ten thousand feet out of the equatorial jungle. Sir Arthur Conan Doyle had written a novel about Mount Roraima, which he had called "The Lost World". In it he had depicted a plateau where prehistoric monsters had still roamed, and where fabulous riches were to be found.

Sir Arthur Conan Doyle had never been to South America. If he had, Pat Grange had often thought, he might have realised that his imagination had not been so wonderful after all. In the dozen years that he had wandered through this jungle, Grange had encountered creatures as deadly as any in the world: alligators twenty feet long; spiders as big as a man's hand and filled with poison; bushmasters eight feet long whose venom could kill in thirty seconds; ants which could eat a man within half an hour and small river fish which could tear him to pieces in less than a minute; gentle tapirs which sought only existence, and growling, tree-bounding jaguars which sought only prey; chattering sakkiwinki monkeys with the tiny faces and the highpitched squeals of pleasure or alarm; howlers, also monkeys, but capable of emitting a roar like a lion when disturbed. And water constricters, anacondas, some thirty feet in length.

In this forest, when one died, one disappeared. And it was an easy place to die. If none of the larger lords of this tropical hell found one out, then the anopheles mosquito was sure to do so.

Pat Grange sighed, and rested his hand on the forehead of the young man. Jonathan Carter was only twenty-two. He was more than six feet tall, with yellow hair and a handsome face. He dived and swam like the perfect specimen of humanity he was, and Grange had seen him take on a barroom of hostile drunks with nothing but a broken bottle in his hand, and tame them.

But the mosquito had got to him.

"What do you reckon?" Waller asked.

Waller was short, thin and anxious. For him, success meant everything; Carter had come along for the adventure of it.

"You know the drill," Grange said.

"You think he's going to die?" Waller blinked at the unconscious young man.

4

"Yes," Grange said.

He unbuckled Carter's bandolier, transferred all of Carter's bullets to his own belt, save for ten; he checked the rifle to make sure there was a full clip in the magazine. Then he took Carter's haversack, opened it, counted out ten biscuits, and also took out one of the few remaining tins of corned beef; these he placed in the boy's hat, which lay on the leaves beside its owner. Lastly, he emptied what remained in his water canteen into Carter's.

"Wouldn't it be better just to shoot him?" Waller asked.

"We made an agreement," Grange said. He slung Carter's haversack over his shoulder beside his own, stood up, looked down at the dying man for some seconds. "It's always the young ones who fall first," he remarked, with some contempt.

There was nothing young, physically, about Pat Grange. He was as big as the dying boy, over six feet tall, and powerfully built; from beneath his slouch hat lank black hair hung, uncut, in greasy curls on to his neck. He wore a thick moustache and a straggling beard, but these could hardly conceal the large, handsome features, or their ruthlessness. Twelve years of existing in the jungle had left his body as hard and strong as that of an animal. His skin was brown-yellow, less from the sun than because he too had had malaria, and survived.

Pat Grange was a legend. From San Paolo to Panama men who knew the forests had heard of Pat Grange. Now, when he jammed his hat a little more firmly on his head, adjusted the balance of the rifle slung on his left shoulder, and hefted his machete in his right hand to begin another day's hacking through the undergrowth, Waller followed him without question with just a single backwards glance at their fallen partner.

It had begun in 1923. Born at the turn of the century, Pat Grange, it was said, came from a middle-class family, had been educated at a public school, left early to fight in the last year of the Great War, and then gone to university. He had graduated – intended for the Church, some said – and then dropped everything and left for South America.

He had read of the legend of El Dorado, and he sought the richest gold mine in the world.

El Dorado, so the superficial story went, was a city in the South American jungle, where gold had been so plentiful the very houses had been made of the precious metal. The Spaniards had written of it, and told stories of it, without ever finding it. Sir Thomas Raleigh in 1618 had sailed up the Orinoco in search of it, in the disastrous expedition which had cost the lives of his son and his best friend, and his own when he had returned to England, empty-handed, to face the wrath of King James.

He had not found El Dorado.

Pat Grange had nothing but contempt for such men. He knew Spanish, and he had gone to the source, and spoken with the Indians who lived above the Rio Branco. El Dorado did not mean The City of Gold, it meant The Gilded One, which, properly interpreted, meant The Man of Gold, and the true story was this: somewhere in the vast forest that filled the borders of Venezuela, British Guiana and Brazil, there had once lived a tribe of Indians who had worshipped the sun, and who had been fortunate enough to strike a vein of gold, the metal the colour of the sun, in their territory.

There were considerable gold diggings along the rivers in the interior of Guiana; gold was one of the British colony's principal sources of income. This part of the story was entirely practicable.

Thus every year this tribe had sacrificed to the sun. A young man had been chosen, and for a year he was made the most favoured man in the tribe. He need do no hunting, no fishing, no fighting. Instead he lived off the best the tribe could procure, and was given the comeliest maidens as his mates. He was the appointed one.

On the day when the sun was directly overhead – a matter of some calculation in a land where the sun always seemed to be directly overhead – the young man was covered all over in molten gold. No doubt he quickly died. He was then placed in a canoe, and taken out into the centre of a neighbouring lake. Prayers were said, and the offering was thrown into the water, to sink immediately to the bottom. And the sun was pleased for another year.

Pat Grange had dedicated his life to finding that lake. A piece of water into which for years, perhaps centuries, gilded bodies had been thrown. A lake the entire bottom of which would be covered with gold-encased skeletons.

By this year of 1935 Pat Grange had been searching for twelve years, without success. Yet with undiminished confidence.

In those twelve years, he had been through a great many partners. Pat Grange needed partners, both because it was impossible to exist in the jungle without them, and because he could neither swim nor dive, had indeed a psychological aversion to being under water.

As he did not trust Latin Americans – amongst many others – and as no Indian would seek El Dorado, which was regarded with superstitious awe by the local tribes, his partners had always been Europeans or Americans, but as a rule he had preferred Englishmen like himself. Both Jonathan Carter and Geoffrey Waller were English, both were expert swimmers and divers. They had followed Pat Grange through the jungles for a year, with three-monthly breaks in the town of Boa Vista, drinking cheap whisky while Pat sought employment to finance his next trip.

He was readily employed, by the rich Brazilian cattle

ranchers of the savannah south of the forest. To have Pat Grange as a butler for a month was a cachet. And his fund of stories was inexhaustible. On those occasions Pat, with his beard shaved and his hair washed and brushed, was undeniably a most attractive man; wearing a white jacket and blue trousers and mixing rum cocktails with a good deal of expertise, he was unrecognisable as the ruthless taskmaster of the jungle . . . yet enough of the essential hardness of the man, as well as his almost mystical belief in his dream, always came through to leave people fascinated, even as they pulled his leg.

"You ever going to find that golden man, Pat?" they'd laugh.

"When I die, I'm going to be buried in a golden coffin," he'd tell them.

It was in the jungle that the real Pat Grange came alive. Geoff Waller watched the big man in front of him, tattered shirt and shorts both soaked with sweat, right arm swinging methodically as he hacked away vine or creeper attempting to impede his progress, compass hanging round his neck and checked every few minutes.

He worked to a plan, a series of marches in and out, radiating away from Mount Roraima. The famous peak seemed to have the same almost religious fascination for him as it had for the Indians in this area. He also seemed to have a fixed idea that this was where El Dorado was to be found. This was based on the talks he had had with the Indians, certainly . . . but he had covered this piece of jungle ten times already and never found his goal.

Geoff Waller was feeling unutterably depressed. Then he heard the gunshot, echoing through the trees.

"Pat!" he gasped. "It's him. Jonny. We have to go back. He's in trouble."

"He's woken up and fired his gun," Grange said. "Maybe he's shot himself."

"You can just stand there, and say that?" Waller cried, close to tears. "A man's dying, and you just walk away from him?"

Pat Grange stopped slashing at the bush and turned to face the frightened young man.

"Listen," he said. "We made an agreement. You, and Jonny, and me. We made it when we were sober and in perfect health. We agreed that if any one of us couldn't go on, he'd be left, with ten rounds of ammunition, ten biscuits, one tin of beef, and a canteen of water. We all recognised there's no way we can carry a sick man, and there's no way we can sit with him, maybe for weeks, trying to keep him alive. We agreed to that, Jonny as much as either of us. I've always dealt with my partners like that."

"And how many have you lost?" Waller blurted.

Grange looked at him. "I never lost a coward," he said. "So you'll survive, Geoffrey my boy."

He turned back to the forest wall.

"I'm going back," Waller said.

"You do that," Grange said. "If you can."

He was slashing as rhythmically as ever; so thick was the jungle that he had already almost disappeared.

Waller hesitated, face working in mental anguish, then he hurried behind the older man.

"How much further?" Waller asked, when they bivouaced for the night. This was simply a matter of lying on the ground, as they had no tent; when it rained, they got wet.

"With Jonny's grub to add to ours, I'd say two more days out," Grange said. "Then we'll have to turn back."

"To Boa Vista? Thank God! We'll get them to send out a party to look for Jonny."

"Yeah," Grange said. He could imagine the alcalde's

9

reaction when he was requested to send his policemen into the jungle to look for some crazy Englishman who would certainly be a skeleton by the time they found him.

"God, my feet hurt." Waller pulled off his right boot, peered at the sole. "Worn right through." He brought his foot up, peered at the sock with the hole in it. "I've a blister the size of a fried egg."

"Looks like one, too," Grange said, and rolled over to go to sleep. Waller was a pain in the ass.

"God, this is terrible." Waller was using his rifle as a crutch, limping along behind Grange. "Pat, when we get back to Boa Vista, I quit."

"You do that," Grange said, not turning his head. Rivers of pain ran through his right arm, as he cut and slashed, but he was used to that; it was part of the business. Somewhere around here was all the riches a man could dream of. Somewhere. Some . . .

He slashed another hanging vine aside, and gazed at water. He stopped moving, so suddenly that Waller bumped into him.

"What the hell . . ."

"Shut up," Grange said, and slashed some more. The foliage fell away and he stood on the banks of a lake. It was a small lake, perhaps three hundred yards across. The water was still, and dark, even in the middle of the morning.

He had never seen it before. But that was not unreasonable, no matter how many times he might have passed within a hundred yards of it. There was no feeder, and therefore no noise.

That was impossible. A lake without a feeder would evaporate in a week in this heat. Therefore there had to be an underground spring . . . a big one.

Waller pushed against him. "Heck, water. Boy, is my canteen empty."

"Shut up," Grange snapped again.

He continued to stare at the lake. It was almost entirely circular. Just a water hole. But a big one, and in all his twelve years he knew he had never seen it before.

He parted the last leaf curtain, and stepped into open air. The sun struck down at him like a live creature, drying the sweat on his arms and scorching them in the same instant.

Behind him he heard the crackling of the undergrowth as Waller joined him on the bank. Even in the noonday sun the water was utterly dark.

"Feel like a bathe?" Grange asked.

He was aware of a slowly building excitement. He had supposed he knew and had explored every body of water in northern Brazil, southern Venezuela or Guiana. But he had never explored this one before.

Waller surveyed the water. "Looks sort of murky."

"So use your flashlight," Grange recommended.

He had had special sealed torches made, which would remain dry under water.

"What about piranha?"

"Piranha live in rivers. This is a waterhole. There won't be anything alive in there."

Waller glanced at him. "You think there could be something underneath there?"

"I've never seen this lake before," Grange said.

Waller swallowed. "You don't reckon . . ."

"I said I'd never seen it before." Grange unslung his haversack, laid it on the ground, then took his rifle from the other shoulder, made sure there was a cartridge in the breech. "I'll cover you."

Waller also divested himself of his equipment, then of his clothes. His diving gear consisted of a pair of goggles and a pair of flippers; he could hold his breath for up to two minutes.

He adjusted his goggles. "Well . . . wish me luck," he said.

11

"All the luck in the world," Grange told him, sincerely.

He sat on the ground, his back against a tree, his rifle across his knees. The forest was still, and yet never silent. The noon breeze was soughing through the trees, and every so often there were sounds, the sharp crack of a twig, which was merely old age in most cases, the rustle of a lizard, which to the inexperienced might indicate a snake – those used to the jungle knew that snakes made no noise – and occasionally a distant, fearsome roar which suggested there was a lion on the loose, but that was only a howler monkey.

He watched Waller wade into the water, a strange mixture of sunburned arms and legs and dead white buttocks.

"Hey, it's cold," Waller complained.

"Underground feed," Grange said.

Waller waded up to his waist, then threw himself forward. The flippers kicked up faint splashes as he swam out into the centre. Then he dived. He was perfection in the water, where on land he was an awkward little man.

Grange found himself counting, past the hundred. His greatest fear was of drowning. But that seemed to mean nothing to Waller.

"One hundred and seventeen," he muttered, when Waller broke the surface.

Grange waited for a report, even as he felt his heartbeat become quite painful.

Waller was taking great breaths of air, treading water.

Grange could contain himself no longer. "Well?"

"I'll have to go down again," Waller said. His voice was high with excitement.

"Is there something?" Grange stood up, the rifle hanging in his hands.

"Something," Waller said, and dived again.

Now Grange went down to the water's edge and waited there, shifting from foot to foot. He dared not think, dared not suppose; he had been bitterly disappointed too many times before.

Waller broke the surface again, and swam towards him.

"Well?" Grange demanded.

Waller reached the shallows, and stood up. He was breathing heavily, and his cheeks were flushed. He came up the bank with the peculiar flat-footed slap of the flippers. As he did so, he held out his hand.

Grange slung his rifle to take the object. It was dark, but heavy.

"That came off a skeleton," Waller said. "The little finger. The whole skeleton is coated in it."

Grange stared at him, then took his pocket knife and began scraping at the piece of metal. The bone rattled inside it. Where he removed the slime and mud, he saw gleaming yellow.

"Holy Jesus Christ," he muttered. "One skeleton?"

"There were others," Waller said. "I'm sure there were others. But there's a whole lot of weed down there."

"Go and make sure," Grange told him.

Waller hesitated, then turned and waded back into the water. Grange did not watch him, this time; he continued to scrape away at the object, kneeling to wash it in the water as he did so, until the entire shining piece of metal was revealed.

He raised his head, watched Waller break the surface.

"Skeletons!" Waller shouted. "A whole lot of them. All . . ." he swam towards the shore. "All covered in . . ." he stared at the finger Grange was holding.

"Gold," Grange said. "Gold!" he shouted. "We've found El Dorado!" he shrieked.

Waller stamped out of the water and threw both arms round his waist. They cavorted together for some seconds.

"El Dorado!" Waller shouted. "We'll be famous."

"We'll be rich!" Grange corrected him, more practically. He freed himself and went to his haversack. From it he took a quarter bottle of Dom Perignon. He always carried one, and at the end of each unsuccessful venture he had drunk it. But now . . . he pulled off the wire and the cork flew into the trees. Champagne bubbled, and he took a swig, then handed it to Waller. It was hot and tasted foul, but it was a measure of his achievement.

"Rich!" Waller said, and handed the bottle back.

"How many, d'you reckon?" Grange asked.

"God knows. I only looked at a tiny area. But everywhere there were these bodies . . . gruesome, really. I'd say there are hundreds down there. Maybe thousands." He finished the champagne, threw the bottle at the trees, then was suddenly serious. "How the hell are we going to get them up?"

"Equipment," Grange told him. "Proper diving gear. And professionals. We'll drain the lake if we have to."

"It'll cost a fortune to bring heavy equipment up here," Waller objected. "Even proper diving gear."

Grange grinned at him. "We have a fortune, boy. And a lot more besides. Where d'you think the Indians got that gold?"

Grange made Waller sit down to eat. It was necessary to regain control of their emotions, channel their jubilation: the temptation just to lie on the ground and dream was too great.

When they had finished eating, they set to work, exploring the ground away from the lake. They spent the whole afternoon at it, and collapsed exhausted on the lakeside in the dusk.

"Oh, bugger the mine," Waller said. "We've enough gold down there to make us rich. Let's get back to Boa Vista."

"We're going to find the mine," Grange said. "It can't be far."

14

"Then why aren't there still Indians living here?"

Grange shrugged. "Could be any of a hundred reasons. Famine, disease . . . most likely they were just wiped out by another tribe, who had no idea what was down there. Or didn't care. But what's down there could be nothing compared with what could be in the mine, Geoff. We're going to find it."

They found it the next day, again entirely by accident: Waller trod on what he thought was a pile of leaves, the earth turned beneath him, and he disappeared with a shriek of terror. But Grange knew now that everything was running his way. After twelve years of toil and sacrifice, he had hit the jackpot.

He shone his flashlight into the hole, then slid down beside his partner in a cloud of dust and rubble. "You hurt?"

"I don't think so," Waller panted. "God, what a spooky place. You think it's some kind of a trap? Those leaves could've been put there deliberately."

"Yeah, they were put there deliberately," Grange agreed, shining the torch beam around them, and picking out the stone slab which had been laid across the hole, before being covered by leaves, and which had slid down into the cavern beside Waller. How many centuries ago had that stone been set in place? "But I don't think it's a trap."

He stood up – the roof was still three feet above his head – shone the beam into the interior. The light faded before it reached the far wall. There was water gathered at their feet, where tropical rain had come through the entrance, but that apart, the interior was dry: they were at least a quarter of a mile from the waterhole.

He took a few steps further into the cave.

"Hey, wait for me," Waller gasped, scrambling up to hurry behind him. "Could be snakes in here. Or spiders." He was more afraid of spiders than he was of snakes.

"No snakes," Grange assured him, picking his way forward. The floor of the cave was uneven, with occasional lumps of rock sticking up, and the roof was gradually coming down as he went deeper. The walls to either side were simply dark earth, but with veins of rocks showing through them, and they were remarkably even: the initial cave had been hewn out.

He knew what he had found now, no matter how far in he had to go.

There was a gradual downward slope, and every few minutes he struck a match to make sure of the oxygen content; bad air was their greatest risk. But although it got progressively more stuffy, he was still breathing quite easily when, after creeping forward for nearly an hour, his flashlight picked up a gleam from in front of him.

"Jesus! What the hell is that?" Waller whispered.

"Gold," Grange told him.

They went closer, and saw the yellow metal peeping out of the wall.

"Hold the light." Grange drew his sheath knife and prised at the rock. After some effort it came away, a nugget the size of a tennis ball.

"You think there could be more?" Waller asked.

"More? I think this place is stuffed with it. Think, man. Those Indians found this seam, probably by accident the way we did. So they started mining it. They had no equipment. They just tore at the rock with their knives. Year after year they took what they wanted, gradually eating back the cave. Then they just stopped."

"Could be because they ran out of gold," Waller said.

"Then why was that nugget waiting there? Just think what's behind these rocks, what we can find with the proper equipment."

*   *   *

They sat on the bank of the lake and ate their supper.

"Tomorrow we head for Boa Vista," Grange said.

"What's the drill? We don't make a noise about this, do we?"

"Not on your nelly. But the first thing we want is a Brazilian partner."

"Eh?"

"Must have him, boy. The government is always trying to get people to homestead in the bush. Not very successfully. But it's there. For Brazilians, not gringoes. So we want a front man who will claim a certain area on the map. We don't tell him more than we have to, to suck him in. And we don't pay him more than we have to, either. I'll work it out; I know the very man. Once that's done and registered, this land will be ours, to do what we like with."

"How much do you reckon we're going to have to pay this Brazilian partner?"

"Not more than ten per cent. That still leaves ninety for us."

"What about Jonny's share? The agreement was we split everything three ways."

"Look, Geoffrey my lad: Jonny Carter is dead. Wherever he is, there's no way he's going to be interested in gold."

"Yeah . . . but he has a family."

"We didn't make any agreement with his family. Figure it out, boy. Let's say, for the sake of argument, there's a million pounds worth of gold in the mine and the lake. It's going to cost a bit to get it out, as you said. Say fifty percent. That leaves half a million. Pedro or whoever it is gets fifty thousand. That leaves four hundred and fifty. Two hundred and twenty-five for you, two hundred and twenty-five for me. You start worrying about Carter's share and that cuts us down to a hundred and fifty grand each. Think about it."

Waller chewed his corned beef. "You really think there could be a million quid's worth of gold down there?"

"Why not? Could be a whole hell of a lot more."

"Or a whole hell of a lot less," Waller said lugubriously, and lay down to sleep.

Grange looked at him for several seconds, then resumed gazing at the water. Waller was the most miserable bastard on the face of this earth. Grange wondered why *he* hadn't caught malaria and died instead of Carter – Carter had been quite a cheerful fellow.

And now he was going to walk away with forty-five per cent of any profit. Forty-five fucking per cent, he thought bitterly. After hardly more than a year in the bush, and all of that time whinging incessantly while being led by the nose.

While he had fought and bloody near starved, been virtually disowned by his family, for twelve years . . . for the same result. He was a fool to have made the agreement so simple. It should have been a share for every year. Then Waller would get one share and he'd get twelve. On the figures he'd used earlier, that would give him more than four hundred thousand. He grinned. And Waller would actually get less than their Brazilian partner.

Trouble was, with an agreement like that on offer, he wouldn't have found any partners at all!

But it was a damned unfair world, he thought, as he went to sleep.

Grange was awake with the first light, sitting up, mind alert. Beside him Waller still snored.

Grange got up, went down to the water's edge to wash his face, and froze. Years in the jungle had given him the extra senses of an animal, and although there was no definite sound, he knew there was something hostile close by.

18

He turned his head, carefully, then stood up, and moved slowly back to where his rifle was. As he moved he watched the snake come out of the undergrowth. It was an anaconda, and as big a water snake as he had ever seen: at least twenty feet long, with a thick, mottled body and a flat, sinister head.

The constrictor had certainly seen the man, but was not interested at this stage; it was making for the water and a breakfast off the vegetation at the bottom. Grange reached his rifle, sat down, his hand on the barrel, but he did not raise the weapon, watched instead as the huge snake slipped silently into the lake and vanished beneath the surface.

He found his heart beating quite violently. Not from fear. He had encountered big snakes before, and he had the utmost confidence in his marksmanship. It was from imagining what it must be like to encounter a creature like that in the water, its natural habitat. Suppose the snake had already been in there when Waller had gone in yesterday. There was no way they could have known. There was not a ripple on the surface where it had disappeared.

"Hey!" Waller sat up. "Christ, the dreams I had. Money. Nothing but money."

He got to his feet, walked down the bank to the water. Grange opened his mouth, and then closed it again.

"You know something, Pat," Waller said over his shoulder. "I sometimes wonder if it is all a dream. Hell, it's not a dream, is it?"

Grange felt quite sick. He had to lick his lips before he could speak, while the most terrible thoughts revolved about his brain.

"It's no dream," he said. "You saw those skeletons, didn't you?"

"Yeah." Waller stood up. "So I did."

"You did, didn't you?" Grange asked. He was speaking more freely now: the decision had been taken, although

19

he would not admit it to himself. "You didn't hallucinate down there?"

Waller grinned. "Not me."

"I think you should take another look," Grange said. "Just a quick dive in the centre. Bring me up another little finger."

Waller hesitated, then shrugged. "If it'll make you happier."

He stripped off, pulled on his flippers and mask, splashed into the water.

Grange stood up, the rifle in his hands. He moved to the edge, watched the younger man swim out into the centre of the lake and then dive. Only ripples remained, as he disappeared beneath the water, and within seconds the surface was smooth again.

Then there were bubbles. A great number.

PART ONE

The Man of Gold

CHAPTER 1

Friends

With a blaring of sirens, the *SS Antilles* made its way slowly up the Para River to dock at the port of Belem.

A two-funnelled, old-fashioned ship, in that her superstructure rose amidships and separated her forward and after holds, the *Antilles* was a freighter which carried passengers, a very important communications link between South America and Europe. She had left Rio de Janeiro two days previously already loaded with coffee. Her stop in Belem was entirely for mail and fresh provisions, before starting out across the Atlantic for Southampton; she flew the Red Ensign.

Her passenger accommodation was limited to twelve, in six double cabins, all on the same deck, but not all of quite the same class. The two forward cabins, port and starboard, had *ensuite* bathrooms and windows looking out over the foredeck. The two after cabins, on each side, shared bathrooms, and had only small round portholes in the side of the ship to admit light and air. But she was a comfortable vessel, and had a good reputation. She was much in demand by British officials and engineers, businessmen and even ex-patriots, living and working in Argentina and Brazil, for their home leave.

The nine passengers currently on board had been awake since dawn for the run up the river. The Para was close to the Amazon – the two rivers were actually connected – and there was always something exotically exciting about entering the basin of the greatest river in the world . . . even if one had done it before.

Alison Bennett had done it before, but the last time had been three years ago, and she had only been thirteen; she had forgotten much of it. And now, she supposed regretfully, she might well be looking at Belem for the very last time. Thus she gazed at Marajo Island, the largest fluvial island in the world, to starboard, and then at the roofs of the buildings slowly coming into sight, shimmering in the midday heat, for Belem, situated virtually on the Equator, had an average year-round temperature of eighty degrees Fahrenheit.

They had already experienced the invariable morning downpour.

Now she could make out the twin steeples of Santo Alexandre, one of the first cathedrals in America, for it had been built in 1616, the very year Belem had been founded by the Portuguese, and was thus, in this year of 1936, three hundred and twenty years old.

Tom Bennett threw his arm round his daughter's shoulder and gave her a little hug. "Skipper says we'll be here until tomorrow morning. We might dine ashore. Last Portuguese meal and all that. Would you like that?"

"Yes," she said.

Alison was a positive girl, although she was only five feet tall; her wedge-heeled sandals added one more inch. Her hair was yellow, and curly; at sixteen she still wore it long, and loose, secured only by an Alice Band across her crown. Her clothes consisted of a white blouse and a beige calf length skirt, no stockings. Her figure was slim and she often looked as if a puff of wind might blow her away, but she possessed a surprising strength of body, as well as mind, indicated by the wide mouth, the strong little chin, the flaring nostrils, and above all the wideset blue eyes.

As her father well knew, just as he knew how upset she was at leaving Brazil. But it had to be done.

24

Tom Bennett worked for an English company which dealt in coffee; he was their Brazilian manager, and had been for the past nine years. When he had removed himself and his family to Rio, all of the children had been quite small – Alison had only been seven. Bennett's contract called for him to return to England on six months' long leave at the end of every three year tour. Thus six years ago Tom junior had been left at boarding school, to see his parents every third year – crossing the Atlantic to and fro simply took too long to be contemplated even during the summer holidays, which were therefore spent with relatives. Three years ago Harry had joined his brother.

There had been less urgency to send a girl away to boarding school. Marjorie Bennett had preferred to keep her youngest child at home; there had been a perfectly adequate English School in Rio. After all, no one expected a girl to wish to go to university.

At sixteen, however, one began to expect a girl to contemplate doing *something*, for the hopefully few years which lay ahead before marriage. Marjorie had at last determined that Alison should go to a secretarial college in London; she could stay with her Aunt Audrey.

Alison had been miserable about the decision, and remained so. She regarded Brazil as much more of a home than England, spoke Portuguese like a native, and had a lot of school friends. Now she was being thrown into a large outer world of which she knew only what she had observed on previous visits, when she had both been very young and entirely beneath her parents' wings.

Yet she had always known it was coming.

"This place always reminds me of a frontier," Tom Bennett said, looking past his wineglass at the passersby. Several of them did carry rifles, or revolvers slung

25

on their hips, rather as if they were players in a western movie, and they all sported moustaches and bush clothes and did not appear to have bathed very recently. Yet rubbing shoulders with them were very well-dressed Brazilian men and their wives, out for a stroll now that the heat of the day was fading.

"Our last night in Brazil," Marjorie said dreamily. She was very little taller than her daughter, and every bit as romantically inclined.

"Hammond the Purser told me we have a passenger for A One joining us here," Bennett said. "Do you think he'll be one of these fellows?"

"In A One all by himself? That's the best cabin on board."

It was the forward *en suite* cabin on the starboard side, so that on the voyage north it got the sun in the morning, but was cool in the afternoon and early evening.

"Well, obviously he's some bigwig, to want a cabin all to himself."

"Maybe he's married," Alison remarked, somewhat gloomily. If she was just as romantic as her mother, she was also more practical. She was at the age to be swept off her feet by some handsome Brazilian, who would defer her return to England, perhaps forever; but equally she understood that a wealthy man would almost certainly be married . . . or at least firmly attached – and travelling by liner rather than freighter.

After the meal they strolled back to the ship.

"New passenger on board yet?" Bennett inquired of the Purser.

"Couple of hours ago. What do you think of that?"

Hammond, who was a great gossip, held up a piece of metal which glowed dully in the electric light; it was the size of a hen's egg.

"What is it?" Alison asked.

"Gold, Miss Bennett. Solid gold. Weighs four ounces."

"Great Scot! I've never seen anything like that," Bennett commented.

"Here, feel it."

Hammond held it over his counter, and the Bennetts passed it from hand to hand. Alison thought it felt delightfully warm.

"Where'd you get it?" Bennett asked.

"This fellow Grange paid for his passage with it. Well, it's not usual to receive a gold nugget instead of cash . . . but the skipper said it'd be all right."

"Grange?" Marjorie inquired. "That sounds like an English name. Or American."

"English, I'd say," Hammond commented.

"Is he travelling alone?" Alison asked.

"Oh, yes, Miss Bennett. Quite alone."

The Bennett's cabins were A Two and Three, the pair immediately aft of A One, which shared a communal bathroom. Tom and Marjorie were in A Three, and Alison alone in A Two.

She used the lower bunk, and as she settled down for the night, her shoulder touched the bulkhead separating her from A One. It occurred to her that this strange man named Grange, who had paid for his passage with a gold nugget, might also have his shoulder leaning against the bulkhead. She thought that was incredibly romantic, depending on what he looked like, of course.

Then she remembered that this bulkhead separated her from A One's bathroom, not the sleeping cabin.

She still wondered what he might look like.

So did everyone else. Heads turned at breakfast the next morning when Pat Grange made a somewhat late entry.

By now the *Antilles* was on her way back down the river; she had left at dawn. But for the moment her speed was low and the surface so calm not a teacup rattled. Conversation had been quite audible until Grange entered. Then it died.

Alison thought she had never seen anyone quite so striking, and she was a keen film fan: up to a year ago she had kept a picture of Clark Gable on her dressing table.

Pat Grange was not the least like Clark Gable, except for physical size, and there he was even bigger; she put him down at six foot two, with matching shoulders, accentuated because he walked with a slight stoop, as if perpetually ducking beneath something; she had always had a weakness for very big men, probably because she was herself so very small. For the rest, he was clean shaven, and his hair was light brown rather than black. His features were sharply chiselled, but with a pronounced chin. His eyes were pale blue. She estimated his age at the middle thirties, and in that respect was disappointed; he was old enough to be her father, just.

He was conventionally enough dressed, in a well-cut pale linen suit, but he wore the jacket awkwardly, as if unused to it. His eyes, too, challenged everyone who looked at him, as if daring them to belittle him.

Hammond made the introductions; the passengers all ate at the same long table in the centre of the small dining saloon, and a space was found for Grange.

Whereupon everyone watched in consternation as the newcomer ate his fried eggs in a great haste; the remnants of an earlier breeding were there, but the food was shovelled into his mouth as if he had a train to catch.

"Grange. I believe I've heard the name. Been in Brazil long?" asked Tremlett the Consular Official, also on his way home for leave, and feeling it his duty to break the ice.

"Twelve years," Grange said, his voice quiet, but with a slight burr.

"Good Lord! Of course, you're the famous gold prospector. But you've been home in that time?"

"No," Grange said.

"Ah . . . odd we haven't met," remarked Mearns the retiring railway engineer.

"Why?" Grange asked, spilling coffee into his saucer as he stirred too vigorously.

"Well . . . have you spent much of that time in north Brazil?"

"All of it."

"I've been laying railway lines around Manaos."

"I was in the bush," Grange said.

"Prospecting for gold?" Bennett inquired.

Grange grinned; his teeth were large and white and even. "I used to prospect for gold. Now I've found it." His gaze swept the table. "Any of you gentlemen care to invest in the richest gold mine in the world?"

"Did you ever hear such rubbish," Tremlett remarked, as they had their mid-morning coffee. "I know a lot about this fellow. He has spent the past dozen years in the jungle. You know what prospectors are like. He's about the worst of the lot. They never actually find anything. The richest gold mine in the world! Ha!!"

"He paid for his passage with a nugget," Alison pointed out. She had fallen for Mr Grange at first sight, even if he was sadly in need of a crash course in manners – she was at an age when manners were not all that important.

Tremlett gave her a pitying glance, indicating that young girls should be quiet in the company of their betters. "I'm not saying there isn't some gold in the interior. Everyone knows there is, scattered about in isolated veins or river beds. But the richest in the world . . . balderdash!"

"Where exactly is your gold mine, Mr Grange?" Marjorie asked at dinner, trying to be polite and at the same time endeavouring not to look at Grange eating peas;

29

he invariably overloaded his fork so that at least one fell off on each journey to his mouth. By now they were out at sea, and the movement had reduced their numbers to just five, Tremlett, the Bennetts, and the prospector.

Grange grinned. "I may look like a fool, Mrs Bennett, but don't take me for one."

"Oh!" Marjorie said, surprised and confused.

Bennett felt called upon to come to his wife's rescue. "Meaning it doesn't really exist."

Grange regarded him for a moment, then put his hand into his jacket pocket and pulled out three more of the large nuggets. "Then I'm a magician," he said. "When they bury me, it's going to be in a gold-lined coffin."

Alison felt horribly embarrassed. If it had been wrong of Mr Grange to be rude to her mother, it had equally been wrong of Mummy to ask such a question. And Father had not come off best in the exchange.

By next morning, feelings against the mysterious Mr Grange had hardened; his appalling table manners, allied to his somewhat tart tongue, especially when anyone inquired about his gold mine, had upset everyone. "Look," he told them, "if you have money to invest, let's talk business. If you don't . . . then mind your own business."

People began to look the other way when they saw him coming, and on a small ship with only ten passengers, this had to be terribly obvious.

Alison felt sorry for him. Of course he was a rough diamond, but then he had every reason to be protective about his find. She knew nothing about prospecting, but his complexion told that he had spent long years in the bush; he might not have found the richest gold mine in the world, but he had certainly looked. And he had found something.

Equally, he had adventured. People supposed that just living in Brazil had to be an adventure. But the fact was that Brazil was almost as large a country as the United States, and living in Rio de Janeiro was rather less exciting than living in New York – under the firm rule of Getulio Vargas there was not a great deal of organised crime. All her life Alison had wanted to explore the interior, and especially the Matto Grosso and the Amazon Basin, even if it had been only a trip up the river as far as the fabled city of Manaos.

Now she supposed Belem was the nearest she was ever going to get.

But this man had spent twelve years in those forests, and lived to tell the tale.

When she found him looking at her, she smiled at him, and he grinned back. She felt at once guilty and exhilarated, as if they had somehow communicated without him having ever actually addressed a word to her. That evening at dinner she was furious at the succession of snide remarks and asides made about him, even if he didn't seem to care, so much so that by the end of the meal she had had all she could stand, and with a mumbled apology to her parents, who were as guilty as everyone else of putting him down, left the table and went up to the boat deck, where she could be alone, and seethe to her heart's content.

The boat deck on the *Antilles* was situated aft of the bridge and was not very large. She leaned against one of the steel davits, looked up at the funnel belching smoke which obliterated the stars, taking deep breaths and wishing there was some way Mr Grange could prove to them all that he wasn't just building castles in the air . . . and then, there he was.

"Warm, down below," he commented.

Alison couldn't think of a word to say, and yet found herself speaking.

"I'd like to apologise for my parents," she said.

"Forget it. Think your dad would invest in my mine?"

"I doubt it. Daddy isn't the investing kind. And he's really not at all wealthy. Is it important? I mean, if the gold is there, all you have to do is dig it up, isn't it?"

"Well, it's not quite as easy as that. I need machinery to get at the real gold. And some of it's underwater. All that costs money." He gave one of his grins. "Would you believe that I have to be about the richest man in the world, and I have to borrow money in order to prove it?"

She wished he wouldn't carry on about being the richest man in the world.

"I'd love to go into the jungle," she said.

He frowned at her. "It's no place for a lady."

"Why not?"

"Well . . ." another grin. "You sweat, and you get filthy, and you stink, and sometimes you starve and you get lice and sores where you shouldn't . . . and the natives aren't always friendly."

"Tell me about it. The jungle."

"You really want to know?"

"Yes," she said. "The real thing."

They met again the following night. There was no arrangement. They did not speak during the day, nor did they look at each other over dinner. But when Alison went up to the boat deck again, she knew he would join her.

By now the *Antilles* was well out into the Atlantic, steaming into quite a chop, and although they were still technically in the Tropics, it was necessary to wear coats on deck.

Alison didn't mind. She was lost in a world of ana-condas and jaguars, soldier ants and piranha fish, bush ticks which would attach themselves behind the knees or in even more intimate places and had to be burned off with a glowing matchhead or their heads would remain behind to fester, and chiggers which had to be dug out of the toes with a needle. Pat Grange had experienced them all . . . or he said he had. Then he told her about El Dorado. "You mean you searched for that, for twelve years?" she asked in wonder.

"It's the only dream I ever had."

"All by yourself in the jungle?"

"Well, I've had partners, from time to time. But in the bush . . . they're just a nuisance."

"And then you stumbled on it, just like that. That's a marvellous story, Mr Grange."

It had never occurred to either of them to suggest she use his first name.

"What did you do when you saw the lake?"

"Well, I kind of felt that this was it. So . . . I stripped off and went in."

"All by yourself! But suppose there had been piranha fish . . ."

"Still water," he explained. "No chance."

"Well, then, a water snake . . ."

She couldn't see his face properly in the darkness, but he hesitated for a moment before replying. "It's a risk one has to take."

"And then you found the mine itself. Oh, Mr Grange, that's just incredible."

"You do believe me, don't you?" he asked, anxiously.

"Of course I do."

"You don't," he said sadly. "You think I'm shooting a load of bullsh . . . rubbish."

"I don't," she protested.

"Nobody believes me," he said. "Not a single sh . . . louse. Listen, I'll prove it to you. Come down to my cabin and I'll prove it to you."

"Your cabin?" Alison licked her lips.

"I'm not going to bite you."

She believed him. She did not suppose a thirty-six-year-old man – he had told her his age – would be the least interested in making advances to a sixteen year-old girl. Sometimes she felt he had been so long in the jungle he didn't really know anything about women, or what to do with them or to them, and certainly not for them.

All he wanted was someone to believe in him.

33

"All right," she said. "But if someone were to see us . . ."

"No one will," he said. "We'll go in through the forward bulkhead door."

She followed him down the ladder to the promenade deck, terribly aware of her skirt whipping in the breeze, then along the side deck past the cabins. Forward of the cabins there was another ladder leading down to the well deck, and facing this there was a steel door in the forward bulkhead. Cautiously Grange opened this, and looked in. In front of him the corridor stretched past the cabin doors to the dining salon, but this was presently empty. The rest of the passengers, including the Bennetts, were all in the smoking lounge beyond.

Grange stepped inside, unlocked his cabin door, and came back for her. "All clear."

Feeling like a thoroughly delinquent schoolgirl, Alison scuttled through the door and into the cabin. Grange closed and locked the door behind them, and switched on the light. She turned, facing him, panting; she had never done anything quite so daring in her life.

He gazed at her. "There's nothing to be afraid of."

"I'm not afraid," she told him. But suddenly she was. She could not understand how she had agreed to do this. Now she was alone in a locked cabin with a man she hardly knew.

"Drink?" Grange asked, and took a bottle of whisky from his desk drawer.

"I don't."

"Oh. Just how old are you, anyway?"

"Sixteen."

He grinned. "Well, they can't get me for statutory rape."

She gulped in sudden alarm, but he apparently thought he had made a joke. He poured himself half a tumbler of whisky into his toothmug, drank some of it, and sat at his desk. "I wanted to show you this."

He opened the drawer again, and took out something

34

wrapped up in paper. This paper he now removed and laid the object on the desk.

Intrigued, Alison moved forward to stand at his shoulder. "Is it gold?"

"It's covered in gold. It's the little finger I broke off a skeleton, at the lake."

"Ugh!"

"Well, I had to have it, to prove what's down there. Hundreds, maybe thousands of them, just lying there. Take it."

He held it out, and very carefully Alison took the gold-coated bone.

"How old is it?"

"Your guess is as good as mine. Could be hundreds of years, though."

"If you showed this to the others, they'd have to believe you."

"I don't give a damn whether they believe me or not, any more," he said. "As you said, none of them has any money, anyway." He caught her hand. "I want you to believe me, Alison."

"I do believe you, Mr Grange. I do. I'd like to show that finger to my dad."

"No," he said abruptly. "I don't want you to do that. I don't want you to tell anyone on board about it. Understand?"

He was vehement. Alison nodded. "All right, if that's what you want."

"Good girl."

To her consternation he kissed her hand, then stood up. She was quite breathless as she looked up at the size of him, compared with her.

He grinned at her. "Now you'd better get back to your folks before I do something stupid."

"Oh . . . yes," she said. She went to the door. "Mr Grange, thanks for showing me the finger." She opened the door, stepped into the corridor, and faced Tom Bennett.

Someone had seen them, after all.

There was an enormous row. Bennett had to be
restrained from assaulting Grange, for his own good;
Grange was a far bigger and younger and stronger man.
The Captain became involved, and read Grange a lecture
– he couldn't actually do anything else, as the *Antilles*
didn't touch land again until Southampton.

The Captain also clearly felt that Alison was at least
partly to blame. So did the Bennetts. Tom Bennett was
so angry Alison actually thought he might hit her, for all
her protests that nothing had happened.

"Then why did you go to his cabin?" Bennett demanded.

Alison hesitated. But she had promised, and she was
not going to break her word.

"We wanted to talk."

"Talk!"

"I like him," Alison said, simply.

Marjorie managed to cool Tom down, but Alison
was absolutely forbidden to go on deck without either
her mother or father for company. Pat Grange's stock
slumped to a nadir; now no one would speak with him
at all. He didn't seem to care, ate his meals in silence,
and then either went up on to the boatdeck or back to
his cabin. Alison didn't dare attempt to catch his eye.

They did not speak again until the *Antilles* was actually
in the Solent, steaming past the Isle of Wight on her way
to Southampton Water. Everyone was on deck to see
England again after so long, and were totally preoccupied
with pointing out the sights they had half forgotten.

"Home," Pat Grange said, leaning on the rail beside
Alison.

She turned her head. "Is it really your home?"

"Oh, yes, I was born in England. I even have family
here, if they're still alive. I imagine you're glad the
voyage is over," he said.

"Yes. Aren't you?"

"A bit of yes, and a bit of no. This voyage is the first real rest I've had in twelve years. I needed it."

"I'm sorry about the fuss."

"Forget it. My fault. One shouldn't invite girls to one's cabin . . . unless you mean business. Alison, you wouldn't care to marry me, I suppose?"

She turned her head in consternation, and he grinned.

"There I go again."

"I . . ." she licked her lips, her mind a total jumble. Of course she couldn't marry him. She didn't know him, and he was twenty years older than she, and just about the most uncouth man she had ever met, and in any event, she had never thought about him that way – from her point of view – in the slightest.

But the idea of going into the South American jungle with a man like Pat Grange to dig up the greatest treasure in the world was utterly breathtaking in its excitement.

Pat grinned again. "You're just a kid, and I'm a dirty old man. Here come your parents, so I'll be away." He touched her hand, lightly, for a moment. "Maybe I'll ask you again in two years time."

"What was that damnable man saying to you," Bennett demanded.

Alison watched Pat Grange's back receding. "Only goodbye."

But it was au revoir, she thought. If he could ever find her again.

CHAPTER 2

Lovers

"Read all about it!" shouted the newsvendors. "Read all about it! Hitler enters Prague! Czechs weep as they watch the panzers. Read all about it!"

Alison Bennett stopped to buy a paper, as she always did on emerging from this Knightsbridge tube station, which was only a few hundred yards from Aunt Audrey's flat, and received her usual grin from the vendor.

"Nice day for it."

"Nice day for what?" was her invariable answer, as, buttoning her coat, she left the station and stepped on to the windswept street.

Actually, the sun was shining, but it was March and the wind whistling through the London streets was cold; also, she had just had her hair washed and set, and although her head was bound up in a scarf, she was in a hurry to get into the warmth; the solicitor for whom she worked was a sensible man who closed his office on Saturdays, but it was still necessary for a girl to go out and get things done when she could have more comfortably spent the day in bed.

But tonight Roddy was taking her to the pictures.

The two events, hairdo and Roddy, cause and effect, karma – she was a great reader of Eastern literature – always left her feeling slightly breathless, and slightly defiant too. More so with every week that passed: in just another month her parents would be arriving in England for long leave.

That alone would have been a matter for concern: she had not seen them for nearly three years. It had been a very long three years, in the context of a girl they would remember as sixteen and who was now a woman just gone nineteen. And when they had last parted she had still been under a cloud.

No doubt her disgrace had been imparted to Aunt Audrey. But Aunt Audrey was such a delightfully relaxed woman. She believed everyone should live their own lives with as little outside interference as possible, and merely requested Alison never to do anything which might bring disgrace to her family. Neither had her brothers been at all disapproving, although undoubtedly they also had heard all about the sinister Mr Grange. They regarded it as a typical teenage absurdity. Both now in their twenties, they were long past such indiscretions, apparently, and although they obviously loved their pretty baby sister, and entertained her whenever it was reasonable, they saw no reason to inflict her on their sophisticated friends – especially of the female sex – more than was necessary.

As for the hair . . . Aunt Audrey had even recommended it.

"Long hair is so old fashioned," she had said. "Especially when it curls all over the place, like yours. Short hair is so smart!"

It had not occurred to Aunt Audrey that Mummy and Daddy might object.

They were also almost certain to object to Roddy, who although very sweet, was a bank clerk with not too many prospects. But he was twenty, more her own age than the supercilious young lawyers and doctors and accountants who made up Tom and Harry's circle of friends, and who, while they undoubtedly found her attractive, were on the one hand restrained because she was the baby sister of chums, and on the other even more supercilious because of her accent – English remained almost a second language to her – and her gaucheness, even after three years, when it came to English manners and mores.

She was, she reflected sadly, the ultimate colonial. And Brazil wasn't even a colony!

It was maddening, really, because she alone of all her circle of acquaintances seemed genuinely concerned about the political situation. Tom and Harry's friends either admired Hitler – "We could do with someone like that here," they'd mutter whenever there was talk of a strike – or had not the slightest doubt that when Britain and France decided to act, Nazi Germany would be crushed out of existence.

She regarded the sandbagging of public buildings against possible aerial bombardment with the gravest misgivings. She had been utterly depressed only the previous week when she had queued up to receive her gas mask. How safe Brazil seemed at this moment, so very far away from the turmoil that was Europe. How she wished she could escape there. She had actually considered emigrating to the United States, but of course at nineteen she would have to have parental permission. It was certainly something she hoped to discuss when they arrived.

Meanwhile, Roddy. He was becoming somewhat venturesome, as he felt that she was his "girl". They went to the pictures every Saturday night, and he had early established a pattern of sitting in the back row and kissing her. She had no objection to this, providing no one was actually sitting beside them. But what her fellow stenographer Josephine called "heavy petting" – she read a lot of American books – was out, in a public place.

And she wasn't too sure about a private place either. Roddy was inclined to start breathing very hard and press himself against her when it came to saying good night at the front door, while his hands were everywhere. He had even suggested once or twice that she invite him in, sure that her aunt had gone to bed. She had always refused. But there could be no doubt that a crisis was looming.

How she *wished* she could be back in Brazil.

40

She had reached her corner, when a Rolls-Royce suddenly pulled into the kerb in front of her. The inside rear door opened, and Alison veered to the left to go round it as a man got out.

He fitted the car in which he was being driven. He was tall and well built, wore a pearl gray suit, very well cut, and a pearl gray fedora. His black shoes were highly polished, and he carried a stick with a brass head . . . or was it gold? She couldn't believe that.

But he was a very good-looking man, in a somewhat mature fashion . . . and he was raising his hat.

"Hello, Alison," he said.

Alison goggled at him, and knew she was flushing. But it was at least partly excitement.

"Mr Grange?" she asked in amazement.

"For a moment I thought you'd forgotten me." He held the door for her. "Hop in."

"I live just round this corner, thank you."

"I'm not taking you home, Alison. I'm taking you out to lunch."

"Lunch? Oh!" She hesitated. Her mind was instinctively rejecting both his rather peremptory manner and the very idea of being whisked off to lunch without any prior warning. But was that a sort of automatic negativism? Mr Grange was an old friend. And this was a superb car. And Saturday lunch with Aunt Audrey was invariably of the boiled beef and cabbage variety.

Still . . . "I must at least telephone my aunt," she said.

"You can do that from the restaurant," he suggested.

Alison got in, and Grange sat beside her. The liveried chauffeur touched his cap and smiled at her, and the car moved off.

Presumably Mr Grange had hired it.

"I love the car," she remarked.

"So do I. I only bought it last week."

Alison gulped, and tried again.

"What a coincidence," she said. "You seeing me on the street. And recognising me!"

41

"I agree that was the difficult part," Grange said. "Why did you cut your hair?"

"Well . . . it's fashionable."

"Who wants to be fashionable? I think you should grow it again."

"Do you?" She began to bridle. Of all the cheek. And then she remembered that this was the way he was about everything.

"As for actually finding you, that was simple. I employed a private detective."

She turned her head. "You employed a private detective, to find me?"

"It was the quickest way. After that, it was just a matter of waiting. I didn't want just to come to your aunt's flat. That would have been too commonplace, don't you think?"

Alison was finding it difficult to think at all. She knew she was putting her foot in it, but the questions just slipped out. "But . . . why did you wish to find me in the first place?"

"To ask you to marry me. Remember?"

Alison looked straight in front of herself, at the back of the chauffeur's head; fortunately there was a glass window separating the driver from the rest of the car, so he couldn't have heard.

"I did say I would, in two years' time," Grange pointed out. "Well, I'm a year late. I apologise. Things didn't happen as quickly as I thought they would. But as you haven't married yet, it's all right."

Alison continued to stare in front of her. She had no idea how to handle this, whether to giggle her embarrassment or make him stop the car and let her out.

"I haven't offended you, I hope?" he asked.

"Not in the least," she answered coldly, and realised that the car was making for the West End. "Where are we going?"

"The Savoy Grill."

Her head turned, willy nilly. "The what?"

"The Grill. The food there isn't half bad."

"I can't go to a place like that."

"Why not?"

"Well . . ." I never have before, she thought, desperately. And in your company it will be terribly embarrassing. "I'm not dressed for it. I have to change."

"You look perfectly well-dressed to me," he said. "In fact, you look perfect. But then, you always did."

She stared at him, perhaps seeing him properly for the first time. He had changed, if in a subtle way. His face and eyes and hair were the same – maybe there was a touch of gray in the hair she hadn't noticed three years ago, but that gave him a suggestion of distinction. He spoke with a trans-Atlantic accent, difficult to pin down but certainly inclined to be nasal. But the look of angry defiance which he had shot in every direction had gone. This man was totally self-assured, totally confident, and on the evidence of his clothes and his car, he was also totally wealthy.

He also was almost old enough to be her father, and yet had proposed marriage. The very idea! But he was taking her to lunch at the Savoy Grill. She took off her headscarf and shook out her hair.

"Why on earth did you cut it?" Pat Grange asked.

"Because I'm no longer a little girl, Mr Grange."

"Tell me what you've been doing during the past three years," he invited, as they ate their prawn cocktails and sipped a wine she had never even heard of, but which was quite delicious. And he was actually using the right spoon.

But he apparently ate here often; he had been greeted by name as they entered, and she had been immediately provided with a telephone to call home. She had merely told Aunt Audrey that she had met a friend and they were having a "bite to eat" together; Aunt Audrey had not been concerned.

"Very little," she confessed. "I went to secretarial school, qualified, and got a job with a solicitor. I've been with him for a year now."

"Yes." Obviously he would have found all of that out. "Boyfriend?"

It was absolutely no business of his. And anyway, she didn't actually have a boyfriend. "Not really."

"What do you think of the international situation?"

"I think it's frightening."

"I think you're right."

"Do you?" He was just about the first person to agree with her.

Their prawns were replaced with steaks, and a different bottle of wine. With the steaks were served peas, and Alison watched in trepidation as Grange started to eat, but he had also learned how to use a fork properly.

"I suppose you've been very busy," she ventured.

"And then some. As I said, I had no idea it was going to be so difficult. There I was, the richest man in the world . . ."

Alison winced. He hadn't changed all that much.

"And I damn near starved before I could find anyone to put up the money to work the mine. At least anyone who didn't want to take the thing over and leave me with a percentage. There was no way I was going to be chiselled."

Alison could believe that: as he spoke a look of singular hardness came over his face.

"But you found someone in the end," she said.

"Yes. I found someone in the end." Suddenly his eyes sparkled, and he leaned across the table to hold her hand. "The mine's in full production, now. And we've drained the lake – that involved sealing the spring and thus creating another lake a little distance away – and got up nearly all the skeletons. It's costing a fortune, but there's a lot more than a fortune down there." He grinned at her. "And guess what we did find in the lake – an anaconda seventeen feet long."

"Oh, my Lord!"

"I shot it myself," Grange said.

"But . . . do you think it was there when you first dived?"

"I have no idea. If it was, it didn't get me. I got it."

She gazed at him. This man had lived!

"Your family must be awfully proud of you."

The animation left his face. "Don't speak to me about my family. You'd think they'd have been prepared to put up some money. They have it, you know. It wouldn't have been enough, but it would've been a start. They just didn't want to know. They'd written me off as dead. And when I came back, they wrote me off as mad. Well, fuck them. I beg your pardon."

"I'm terribly sorry," Alison said, trying to keep from wincing again – both because of his language, in such a place, and because his fingers were eating into her hand.

As he now noticed. He released her. "Let's forget it. And them."

"You can't just forget your family," she protested.

"I can. I have. Which shows haven't you seen?"

"Shows?" She hadn't seen any West End show.

"I thought we'd take one in tonight."

"Tonight? I can't."

"Why not?"

"I have a date."

"Break it."

She gazed at him, and he smiled his crooked smile. "I intend to be the only man in your life from now on."

Alison drew a deep breath. "Look, Mr Grange, it's been wonderful meeting you again, and I'm so pleased things are working out for you. And this has been a fabulous lunch. But . . ."

She hesitated, but he didn't say anything, just smiled at her.

45

"You really can't just appear and take over my life," she finished lamely.

"I'm asking you to marry me."

"You know that has to be impossible."

"Why?"

"Well . . . I'm only nineteen, and . . ."

"I'm pushing forty. You reckon I'm too old for you?"

"I didn't say that," she protested, even if she *had* meant it.

"I'm one hundred per cent fitter than any of the pasty-faced louts I see around here."

She couldn't argue with that; Roddy, for example, always seemed to have a cold.

"We don't really know each other."

"Don't really know each other? Do you realise that I've dreamed of you every night for the past three years?"

Alison didn't know what to say, or where to look . . . she was positive the people at the next table were listening to every word.

Pat Grange grinned at her. "I'm a believer in making dreams come true."

She couldn't argue with that, either, seeing what he had achieved. So she tried her last card, but one.

"Mr Grange, you're a rich man, and I'm a secretary . . ."

"I'm going to make you a rich woman. And you're going to start calling me Pat."

But she had at last created an opening. "Don't you see . . . Pat . . . I can't marry you, just *because* you're rich. I'd be marrying you for your money."

"Meaning you don't love me."

"Well, how can I? I mean . . ."

"You hardly know me. Okay. Why don't you try getting to know me? Starting tonight?"

"I just don't know what to do," Alison confessed to Aunt

46

Audrey. "He won't take no for an answer. He's calling for me at eight o'clock. In a Rolls."

"He certainly sounds a forceful young man." Aunt Audrey was sixty. "I look forward to meeting him."

"You mean you want me to accept his invitation?"

"I think if you don't, you need your head examined. Lunch at the Savoy, a West End show and dinner . . . this is your chance to get out there and live, Alison. You'd be a fool to pass it up."

"What about Roddy?"

Aunt Audrey looked her in the eye. "What about Roddy?"

Slowly Alison got up, went to the telephone, and hesitated. "And when Mr Grange asks me to marry him again?"

"Tell him you can't, without your parents' permission."

"They're going to be here in a month's time. And they don't like Mr Grange, anyway. Or they didn't, three years ago."

Aunt Audrey smiled. "So enjoy yourself, for a month."

"Do you really have to go to work every day?" Pat wanted to know on Sunday evening, after they returned from dinner and the ballet. "Looks like being a fine day tomorrow. I thought we might take a run into the country."

"I do have to go to work."

"Can't you ask for time off?"

"Not at this short notice."

"I think you should quit," he said. "After all, as we're going to be married . . ."

"We said we wouldn't talk about that until Daddy and Mummy get here," she reminded him.

He gave one of his crooked smiles. "Sure we did. Well . . ."

They were sitting in Aunt Audrey's sitting room, and Aunt Audrey, who had clearly fallen for Pat herself, at

47

first sight, had discreetly withdrawn to leave them alone. Last night he had been terribly polite. But tonight she knew he was going to kiss her.

And she wanted him to. He remained the most exciting man she had ever met, as well as the most charismatic. To his looks and his strength and his experience he had added – or had he just rediscovered? – this veneer of sophisticated wealth.

He was the sort of man a girl might dream about. But he was so old, and so, well, she had to confess at least to herself, out of her class in every way. To surrender to him . . .

He held her shoulders and brought her against him. She didn't resist him, and it was a gentle kiss, but yet exploratory.

"I adore you," he said.

Oddly, she realised this was the first time he had ever said it.

She licked her lips.

"But you don't adore me," he said sadly.

"I . . . you must give me time, Pat."

"Of course. When do your parents get back?"

"Three weeks tomorrow."

"You'll be taking time off then, I guess."

"I have a week's leave. Their first week."

"I'm looking forward to meeting them again. And having a chat with your·father." He kissed her again, and then stood up. "I'd better go."

She was left more uncertain than ever.

As advice from Aunt Audrey was a waste of time – she would probably have suggested an elopement – Alison went to see Tom junior.

He lit his pipe, as he was fond of doing when required to think, gave her a glass of sherry, and peered at her for several minutes. At twenty-five he was all set to be avuncular.

He was also just qualified as a solicitor.

"How do you know he's rich?" he asked. "Because he claims to own a Rolls, and takes you to a few expensive restaurants, and has a couple of good suits . . . it could all be on tick."

"What about the mine?" she asked.

"You've only his word for it that it exists. That so-called finger could have been a fake. You want to have *him* investigated by a private detective, in my opinion."

"You've got hold of the wrong end of the stick," Alison tried to explain. "I am really not the least interested in whether or not he is wealthy. It's just that I find him so attractive, and stimulating . . . but he's so *old*."

"You have to make sure he isn't a fake about his money," Tom pointed out. "A man who is a fake at one thing, is usually a fake at most things."

Alison had to see the logic in that, but she kept to her point. "I want to know your opinion about someone of nineteen marrying someone of nearly forty."

"It's been done before. Once upon a time it was the accepted thing." He frowned at her. "You're actually thinking of doing it?"

"If I wasn't, and I was accepting all he's treating me to, then I'd be the sham, wouldn't I?"

"Have him checked out," Tom advised again.

Harry's advice wasn't much different, but by the time she spoke with him it didn't really seem to matter: Pat grew on her every time they were together, which was two nights a week during the week, and every Saturday and Sunday. On these days they spent the whole day together, save for the ubiquitous chauffeur, whose name was Clem. Clem was an American, was very large and powerful, and fussed around Pat almost as if were a bodyguard, but he too was excellent company, and very well-trained; he always wandered off when he felt that his boss and the girl friend wanted to be alone.

Usually they drove into the country, as the weather was now improving, and either picnicked if it was fine, or lunched in a pub if it was raining.

Of course there were things about Pat that jarred. He could be very rude to people who didn't immediately do what he wanted, he was impatient, and often angrily contemptuous of the society in which he found himself. His language, too, could be startling, and when an obscenity slipped out it was quite liable to happen in front of ladies.

But he was always instantly contrite. The important, and reassuring, thing about him was that he was genuinely trying to improve himself.

He remained a compelling companion, whose fund of stories was endless, once he had finished reminding her that he was now the richest man in the world, even if the mine had not yet produced sufficient to prove it – he was still covering his overheads. The great thing about his tales were that they were always personal adventures. As she had thought when they had first become friends, three years before, he had *lived*. And intended to go on living. She could tell that he was anxious to get back out to the jungle. He apparently had a manager acting for him, but this was the first time he had been away for more than a few weeks at a time.

She was anxious to get back out there as well.

The thought was insidious, and arrived fully-formed in her mind before she had even decided if she loved him. The point was, she *could* love him, she was certain. She liked everything about him, the way he kissed her, the way he touched her, without ever in any way embarrassing her or frightening her. The first few times they kissed, and his hand flopped against breast or knee, she tensed every muscle, remembering Roddy and expecting a crisis, but there never was one. He sought possession, certainly, but was content to wait on her permission to intrude. She liked that, even if the giving of such permission more and more seemed a formality.

Of course the age difference remained an enormous factor, but that too was growing less important with every day. Pat *was* fitter and stronger than most men half his age, and more energetic too. In addition to the theatre and the opera, he took her dancing, and if his steps were very old-fashioned, he was delightfully light on his feet. She attempted to rationalise, to remind herself that he would be sixty when she was forty . . . but she really couldn't convince herself that Pat at sixty would be any different to Pat at forty, while the thought of her being forty was just impossible.

Pat could tell that he was growing on her. "I'm going to speak with your Dad the very moment he sets foot on English soil," he told her.

"No. Please, Pat. Let me speak with him first."

"If that's how you want to handle it. But . . . you are going to marry me?"

Alison hesitated for the last time. "Yes," she said. "I am going to marry you, Pat."

She would not, however, let him come with her to meet the boat train. Tom and Harry were there of course, and so was Aunt Audrey, but she had sworn them all to secrecy as well, until she had had a chance to talk with her parents in private. So it was all rather arch, and as she had feared, neither Mummy nor Daddy really went for her hair.

"Would never have recognised you," Tom Bennett said.

"How you have grown up," Marjorie commented. It didn't sound as if it was meant as a compliment.

Butterflies began roaming Alison's stomach. But Aunt Audrey kept up a steady flow of bright conversation, all the way to the flat in a taxi, and over dinner afterwards. Tom and Harry stayed to dinner, and Daddy kept saying what a great occasion it was, the whole family united, and Mummy wept a bit, and after a few glasses of wine remarked, "It's such a shame about your hair, Alison dear."

The boys left soon after, but by then Alison had drunk too much wine, so the subject was not broached until the next day. She couldn't put it off any longer because she knew Pat was waiting for her to ring, and she also knew that if she didn't call him he'd turn up at the flat anyhow.

Aunt Audrey discreetly announced that she had to go out early, and departed, leaving the three of them alone to have a leisurely breakfast.

"So how has life been treating you?" Tom Bennett asked, as if she hadn't written to them every month.

On the other hand, she had never put anything of real importance in her letters.

"Pretty good, recently," she said.

"What do you think of the international situation?"

"I think it's terrible."

"Hm. I'm retiring after this coming tour, you know."

"Are you? But you're not coming back to England?"

"Of course we are," Marjorie said. "It's our home."

"But suppose there's a war?"

"There won't be a war," Daddy said. "Herr Hitler has more sense."

"Um." But she didn't dare start an argument, at this moment. She got up and began placing the breakfast things on the tray. "I've had a proposal of marriage," she said, casually.

"Have you?" Marjorie cried. "Your first proposal! How exciting! Do we get to meet him?"

"Well, of course. If you want to."

"How can you possibly consider marrying someone we haven't met?"

"I couldn't," Alison agreed.

"You're a little young to be thinking of marriage, anyway, aren't you?" Daddy inquired.

"Oh, nonsense," Marjorie said. "I was nineteen when *we* got married."

Daddy cleared his throat, but Alison reckoned she had won the opening skirmish.

"So tell us his name," Marjorie said, when Alison returned from taking the tray to the kitchen. "And what he does. And who his people are."

Alison sat down. "His name is Pat Grange."

"Pat Grange. There's something familiar . . ." Marjorie's head came up. "You're not serious."

"You've been seeing Pat Grange?" Daddy asked. "The prospector? When?"

"Well . . . for the past month. He suddenly turned up, and started dating me, and, well . . . asked me to marry him. He's changed enormously," she hurried on as her parents stared at her. "He dresses well, eats well, and in only the best places, owns a Rolls . . . I mean, he still carries on about his mine, but of course I take that with a pinch of salt."

"He does have a gold mine," Tom Bennett said, quietly.

"Does he?"

"It's all the talk in Brazil. I suppose it hasn't made the papers yet over here because everyone's concentrating on Europe."

"Oh!" Alison said. "Well, then . . ."

"He also comes across as a pretty unsavoury character."

"Now, that's not fair, Tom," Marjorie Bennett protested. "He won his case."

"What case?" Alison asked, looking from face to face.

"Well, it seems that on the expedition which actually found the mine," Tom Bennett said. "He was accompanied by two partners"

Alison frowned. Pat had told her he was alone when he found the mine.

"One of them contracted malaria fever, and was abandoned," Tom Bennett said. "Now don't misunderstand this. The jungle is a nasty place, and it was apparently the agreed course of action in the event of something like that happening. Jonathan Carter, the man who was abandoned, has no complaint against Grange for that. But Carter didn't die. He was found by some Indians and nursed back to health. This took a very long time, and it was pretty near a year before he regained civilisation. During this time he had no idea what had happened to Grange and the other man, a chap called Waller.

"Well, he was ekeing out a living in Rio when the news of Grange's find broke. He got in touch with Grange and claimed his third share, and Grange refused to give it to him. So Carter took him to court. His claim was that the agreement had been that anything they found would be split three ways. Grange's counter claim was that they had agreed that only the partners who actually found the mine would share; if any of them dropped out beforehand, he automatically lost his share. Of course, the agreement had been verbal. I don't suppose any of them really expected to strike it rich. The point was, that the Brazilian court upheld Grange's side of the story. They told Carter, in effect, it was bad luck you got malaria, but you did drop out. So he lost his suit."

"Oh," Alison said. "That doesn't necessarily make Mr Grange a villain."

"No, it doesn't. It does mean he's a very sharp businessman."

"You can tell that by looking at him," Alison said. "And there really is a gold mine?"

"A very valuable one. People are talking about millions of dollars. Of course, much of that is speculation, but there's something down there. As for those skeletons, they're fantastic. I've seen photographs of them. But that's another thing. Grange is apparently running his mine like some kind of prison camp. The area has been fenced off, and is patrolled by armed guards, while people are only allowed in or out with a pass. And anyone found trying to break in is liable to be shot. But Alison, money or no, you can't be serious? I mean the man is twice your age, and is an uncouth rogue . . ."

"I told you, he's changed," Alison said absently. Money

54

or no. The money really didn't matter. She had allowed herself to begin to fall in love with Pat . . . and he had lied to her. Where a man is a fake in one direction, he was a fake in every direction, Brother Tom had said. So maybe he wasn't a fake about the mine, but . . . she just had to see him.

"I think you had better let me have a word with him," Tom Bennett said.

"Now, Tom," Marjorie said. "We mustn't go jumping off the deep end."

It occurred to Alison that having her daughter marry a millionaire was certainly mattering to Mummy.

"I'll bring him to see you," she said. "Tomorrow."

She hurried from the house to use a telephone booth at the tube station.

"I was just thinking of coming round," Pat said.

"I'd like to speak with you first."

"Problems?"

"I don't know," she said. "Can you pick me up at the tube station?"

"Fifteen minutes," he promised.

The Rolls arrived on time, and she got into the back.

"Where would you like to go?" he asked.

"I just want to talk."

"Drive into the country, Clem," Pat said into the intercom. "What did you want to talk about?" he asked.

He was as relaxed and confident as ever.

"A man called Jonathan Carter. And a man called Waller."

"Ah!" Pat said. "Your parents have been telling you about the court case."

"You told me you found the mine on your own," she said, not looking at him.

"I did."

She turned her head. "But Carter . . ."

"Even Carter admits he fell by the wayside. He just

didn't have what it takes. Got a little sick and refused to carry on. Hell, I've had malaria a dozen times, but I've always kept going. Carter refused to carry on, so by the terms of our contract, Waller and I abandoned him. I won my case, Alison."

"I know. But what about Waller?"

"He died a few days later. I'll hand it to him for guts. He kept on going to the end. But he didn't make it. I was really distraught when Geoff caved in. He was one of the best partners I ever had. But it's a funny thing. I searched for that mine for twelve years, Alison, and never found it. I was wandering around in a kind of daze after Geoff's death, and I stumbled right on it. Talk about fate."

Alison gazed at him. "Is that the truth, Pat?"

"Of course it is. Why should I lie? Especially to you."

She held his hand. "I've been so upset. Do you really shoot anyone who tries to get in to your mine?"

He put his arm round her shoulders and held her against him. "I don't want you ever to be upset, my dearest girl. Yes, I certainly shoot *at* them. I've a lot to protect."

"Pat . . . is the mine really worth millions of dollars?"

"It's worth a lot more than that. And it's all going to be yours."

"I wasn't talking about that. Pat . . . if there really is so much money, couldn't you give some to poor Mr Carter? And to the relations of this man Waller?"

"There was nothing like that in the contract."

"I know. But does that matter? It would be such a nice gesture."

He looked down at her, and smiled his crooked smile. "You're too good for this planet, Alison. It's a jungle out there, and I'm not talking about Brazil. I'm talking about the whole business world. It's dog eat dog, and the devil take the hindmost."

"It would still be a nice gesture," Alison insisted. "And surely you wouldn't miss a few thousand pounds."

He ruffled her hair. "Okay. If that'll make you happy, I'll do it. Supposing I can find Carter again. He disappeared after the trial. As for Waller . . . I don't even know if he has any relatives."

"You could employ a private detective to find them, just as you did to find me," Alison said. "Will you promise me you will do that, Pat?"

He grinned. "What is this, some kind of ultimatum?"

"No," she said. "It's just something I think you should do."

But it was an ultimatum, and he knew it. He kissed her. "I'll do it. Now do I get to meet your folks, again?"

Patrick Grange and Alison Bennett were married at Caxton Hall Registry Office on Saturday 6 May 1939. Marjorie would have preferred a big church wedding, but neither Pat nor Alison wanted that. It would have required a lot of time, and Pat felt he had been away from his mine for too long. Alison agreed with him entirely, and besides, she was anxious to begin her new life, which promised to be so exciting and fulfilling.

So Marjorie swallowed her disappointment. Nothing could alter the fact that her daughter was going to be a millionairess. Now that Pat had stopped saying how he was the richest man in the world, Alison found her mother's attitude very off-putting, if only because it kept raising that tiny spectre of doubt in the back of her own mind. Could she be marrying Pat for his money? Of course she wasn't, she would remind herself. But . . . if he hadn't been able to turn himself from an ill-mannered bush lout into a gentleman, would she have looked at him twice? And that had required money. If he hadn't turned up in a Rolls and taken her to the Savoy, would she ever have dated him again? And that had required money.

It was all so confusing. But however it had happened, she had fallen in love with him. Of that she was certain. Nothing else mattered.

* * *

57

"Well," Marjorie said, the night before the wedding. "I suppose that's it."

The pair of them had not been alone a lot; Alison had rather been avoiding *tête-a-têtes* with any member of the family, but she had realised she owed her mother one.

"Nineteen seems such an early age to be married," Marjorie said.

"You were married at nineteen," Alison riposted.

"Well . . . things were different. We all felt . . . well . . ."

"Mummy, things were exactly the same. You got married in summer 1913, because you felt Europe was moving towards a crisis. You've told me this. Well, wouldn't you say Europe is moving towards a crisis now?"

"But I'd known your father for years."

"How many years?"

"Well . . . certainly two."

"I've known Pat for three years."

Marjorie began to look cornered. "Yes, but your father and I . . . we moved in the same social circles. His family knew mine."

That put Alison on the spot. She was certainly concerned that Pat had resolutely refused to invite any of his family to the wedding, or even to take her to meet his father and mother, who she gathered were still alive.

"Well . . . Pat is different," she said.

"That is the understatement of the year. Alison . . . you and I have never really had a woman to woman talk, have we?"

"There hasn't been the opportunity." She was suggesting a reproach here; if they hadn't decided to send her away to secretarial school . . . on the other hand, she would certainly have accompanied them on long leave three years ago, so she would still have met Pat, and even if she had been returning to Brazil, he would still have been able to find her if he had wanted to, and without the expense of hiring a private detective. "But please, Mummy . . . no birds and bees. I do know the facts of life."

"Um," Marjorie said. "I suppose you do."

But do I, Alison wondered, as following a long and sumptuous lunch in one of the banqueting rooms downstairs in the Savoy she kissed all of the guests goodbye and Pat escorted her upstairs into the suite he had taken on the Seventh Floor.

There Clem was waiting to dispense more champagne.

"You'll stay and drink a toast with us, Clem," Pat said.

"My pleasure, Mr Pat."

One of the most reassuring things about Pat was the loyalty, almost devotion, he seemed to have attracted from this man.

"Does that mean I'm . . ." she looked from face to face.

"Sure you are, Mrs Pat," Clem said.

"I'll drink to that," Alison said.

They raised their glasses as high as they could.

"Here's to everything in life," Pat said. "Because from here on it's all ours."

Alison drank, fervently, and became aware of an odd strap coming down the side of Clem's shirt, inside his jacket. She had drunk several glasses of champagne, so she giggled, and asked, "Do you wear a corset, Clem?"

"No, ma'am," Clem said. He had also had a great deal to drink. "It's the gun, see."

"Gun?"

He drew the Browning automatic pistol from the shoulder holster.

"Oh!" she gasped.

"For God's sake put that thing away," Pat snapped. "This is England."

"Yes, sir." Clem obediently tucked the pistol out of sight.

Alison sat on the sofa. Her legs felt weak.

59

"You'd better go off now, Clem," Pat said.

"Yes, sir. Good night, Mrs Pat."

Alison watched the door close.

Pat sat beside her. "Mrs Pat. I like the sound of that."

"Does he always carry a gun?"

"Clem? I think he'd feel naked without one. Don't tell me, it's illegal in England. But who's to know? Unless he actually has to use it, and then I'd happily pay the fine."

"Why should he ever have to use it?"

"When you're as rich as I am, darling, you have to be careful."

How she wished he wouldn't talk like that. But then, she reflected, it was something she might have to get used to. Kings and queens, prime ministers and film stars, all had their bodyguards. And presumably millionaires needed them as much as anyone.

"I'm going to have to find you one as well," Pat told her.

Suddenly she found the thought exciting. But that might have been because he was leading her into the bedroom as he spoke.

They gazed at each other as they undressed. He was everything she had hoped for, and indeed, expected. The big, wide shoulders, slender hips, and long legs of the born outdoor man had been evident in his suits, just as the obvious vigour had emanated from every stride. The heavily matted chest and pubes, the muscles which rippled in the flat belly and powerful thighs, were by way of bonuses. The powerful, erect manhood was a little frightening, but she knew she would have been disappointed had it been any different.

And what did he think of her? Catching a glimpse of herself in the full length dressing mirror as she removed her clothes she was suddenly alarmed at how small she was. It was all there, in perfect proportion, but she wondered if he'd notice. Her shoulders were narrow, as was her chest. Her breasts would scarcely fill his hand. Her legs were relatively long for the tiny body, and her hips were slender. Her pubic hair was pale, and scanty. She was not at all the sort of woman a man like Pat Grange should have married; she should have been big-breasted and large-bellied, wide-hipped and luxuriantly clad in hair . . . she faced him with half-open mouth, quite expecting him to send her to bed, by herself.

Instead she watched him approaching her, and lifting her from the floor as if she were a feather.

"I have never wanted any woman but you," he said. "Alison, no matter how much I hurt you, I love you, and will always love you."

"As I will always love you, Pat," she promised.

"I want one thing of you," he told her, as he kissed her.

"Just name it."

"I want you to grow your hair again."

She laughed. "Your wish is my command, sir."

They loved, again and again. He did hurt her, but it was part of being Mrs Patrick Grange, and that was all she wanted to be. Next morning came all too soon, especially when he routed her out of bed very early to catch the Boat Train. Then it was all wild hurry and excitement. She had especially asked her parents not to attempt to see her off. She knew she had swum out of their orbit, in every way, and while she looked forward to sharing some of her enormous good fortune with them as time went by, at this moment she needed to concentrate on being everything Pat wanted in a woman, and in looking forward to getting back to Brazil, and the jungle.

How that prospect excited her!

Besides, she was wearing Pat's wedding present to her,

a full length sable mink coat; she couldn't imagine Mummy's reaction to seeing her baby daughter in something like that.

They travelled by the *Queen Mary*, in the very best suite. Pat had warned her of this, and of the necessity to dress for dinner every night; before the wedding he had given her the money to go out and buy herself five evening gowns at Harrods, and she had accepted the gift – she was already Alison Grange rather than Alison Bennett. She had chosen slinky and somewhat low-cut and bare-backed pastel shades, rather as might have been worn by her girlhood idol of a woman, Kay Francis, even if the dark-haired Miss Francis was as opposite to her in colouring as any woman in the world could be.

She and Pat were seated at the Captain's Table and treated like royalty. There were in fact quite a few well-known passengers, and not all of these were pleased with the attention lavished on such obvious *nouveau riches*, but they were so equally obviously honeymooning that it was difficult for anyone actually to dislike them.

New York basked in spring sunshine. Pat and Alison were whipped away from the pierhead by taxi, leaving Clem to look after their luggage. They went to the Plaza, where Pat had taken a suite. Management bowed and soft-footed bellboys escorted them to their apartment, while Alison hugged her mink closer and wondered if she had ever been alive before.

In the sitting room was an ice bucket with two bottles of champagne, a bouquet of flowers from the management, and another, of red roses.

Alison picked up the card. "Who's Carlo Rubio?" she asked.

"What?" Pat took the card. "Fucking cheek!"

"Who is he?" she asked again.

"A business associate, you could say."

"Well, what's cheeky about it? I think it's a sweet gesture. And they are lovely roses."

But Pat was distinctly annoyed, and even more so when she asked at supper, taken in their room, "Am I going to get to meet him? All of your partners?"

"Carlo Rubio is not my partner," Pat growled.

Alison decided to leave it; they were on their honeymoon.

For the next week they explored New York. Pat obviously knew the city very well, and while they did all the obvious things, like riding to the top of the Empire State Building and taking the Staten Island ferry, went shopping at Macys and Bloomingdales's and B Altman, he also knew all the delightful little restaurants where they ate meals she had never suspected to exist – always accompanied by the ubiquitous Clem.

He was also doing some business however, and as apparently Clem also accompanied him to business meetings, Alison was left on her own . . . but with strict instructions not to leave their suite and not to open the door to anyone save Clem or himself.

"I wish you'd tell me why," she suggested.

"New York is a funny place, darling."

"Yes, but in the Plaza . . ."

"Will you just do as I ask?"

"Of course I will, Pat. But you can't blame me for being curious." She forced a smile. "You're making me feel like Bluebeard's Eighth wife."

"There's nothing for you to worry your pretty head about," he assured her, and gave one of his crooked grins. "I just want to know where you are. I love you, angel face."

When he spoke like that, she would have done anything for him. But she was put out all over again when, during the morning, she decided to telephone her mother in London, and was informed by the desk that Mr Grange had given instructions that no calls, either in or out, were to be connected with her apartment unless he was there.

Her anger grew throughout the day, and she had her lunch by herself, in the apartment, so that she was really in a fury by the time he and Clem arrived that evening.

"Just what am I?" she demanded, standing before her husband with her hands on her hips. "Some kind of prisoner."

"Now, honey . . ." he was clearly taken aback, never having seen her in a temper before, perhaps never having realised that this tiny, often naïve – in his terms – and so feminine person *could* appear so angry. Then he placed *his* hands on her hips, under hers, and lifted her from the floor exactly as she was.

"You put me down," she snapped. "You . . ."

Clem discreetly withdrew, as Pat carried her into the bedroom and laid her on the bed.

"No," she told him, sitting up. "Not until you tell me what's going on."

"Nothing's going on. The phone business . . ." he sat beside her. "Look, a guy like me gets lots of begging phone calls, threats from loonies or deadbeats . . . it's the price you have to pay for being where I am. And now you're there too."

She didn't want to be mollified, but then he took the little box from his pocket, and opened it, and she gazed at the sapphire winking against the platinum setting on the ring.

"You honestly think you can buy anything," she said. "Well . . ."

"Just try it for size," he suggested.

Perhaps he *could* buy anything, she thought. Even herself.

Next morning she hated herself for surrendering so easily, but next morning it also all seemed such a storm in a teacup, as they took a taxi to an apartment building on Fifth Avenue, where they were greeted by an anxious looking agent and escorted to the penthouse. Here they were shown the two reception rooms, the three *en suite* bedrooms, the magnificent kitchen, and then the roof garden, with fabulous views out over the city.

"What do you reckon?" Pat asked.

"It's just marvellous." The apartment was fully furnished, and Alison tested the white leather-upholstered sofa in the sitting room. "Whose is it?"

"You really like it?"

"I think it's out of this world."

"Then it's yours. Bring the papers along this afternoon, Townsend. I want to move in tomorrow."

"Yes, sir, Mr Grange." The agent was suddenly very enthusiastic.

"You mean we're renting it?" Alison couldn't believe her ears.

"No. I've just bought it."

She sat down with a bump. "Bought it? This?"

"We have to have a base in New York," he explained. "This will be it. You're sure you like it? You can throw out the furniture, if you wish, and start again."

Alison put her arms round his neck and kissed him.

That afternoon Mr Townsend duly came with the papers, and Pat wrote out a large five-figure cheque, just like that. Alison had never actually seen a sum that huge before.

Mr Townsend handed over the keys, and Pat took one set and gave her the other. "Put that in your handbag, honey."

Alison felt dazed.

Townsend left, and Clem hovered in the doorway. "That other guy is here," he said.

"Bring him in," Pat said.

Alison watched a very large young man filling the doorway; he was even taller than Clem, and had equally

65

heavy shoulders. He was also quite good-looking, which could not be claimed for Clem.

"Hugo Miklos, Mr Grange."

"Hugo, I've been told some good things about you," Pat said.

"Thank you, Mr Grange." Hugo Miklos stood in the centre of the carpet like a rather uneasy bear.

"This is Mrs Grange," Pat told him.

"Howdy, Mrs Grange."

Alison held out her hand, and to her consternation Hugo Miklos bent over it and kissed it.

Presumably someone would eventually tell her what this was all about, she thought.

"What do you think of him?" Pat asked.

Alison shot him a glance. How on earth could he expect her to answer that question in front of the man?

"I think he's just the man for the job," Pat said, without waiting for her answer. "Okay, Hugo, eight o'clock tomorrow morning. There's the address."

"Yes, sir, Mr Grange." Hugo gave Alison an anxious smile. "I'll be there, Mrs Grange. You can rely on me."

"You'll address her as Mrs Pat," Pat told him. "Just as you'll address me as Mr Pat. Got it?"

"Yes, sir, Mr Gr . . . Mr Pat. Good night, Mrs Pat."

He was shown out by Clem, who went with him.

"You'll need a maid-housekeeper, and a cook," Pat said. "I thought I'd leave that up to you. Hugo's the important one. I feel a lot happier now."

"You have lost me, hook, line and sinker," Alison said. "Who is Hugo?"

"Your bodyguard."

"My . . ."

"Now, honey, I told you you had to have a bodyguard."

He might have been Aunt Audrey reminding her that she had to take her umbrella when she went out.

"And that's it?"

"He's all right. You'll get to like him. He'll take care

of everything. Clem'll brief him. He comes very highly recommended." Pat grinned. "For this job. He's bent, see? So there's no risk of any hanky-panky."

"Bent?"

"For God's sake, honey, you know . . . he doesn't go for dames, right?"

"Oh." Alison had been brought up in a very conventional household, with very conventional points of view. "Then that's out."

"Eh?"

"I'm sorry. I don't want a queer as my bodyguard."

"But . . . honey, I can't leave you with a guy who's gonna get the urge to raise your skirts every now and then."

Alison frowned at him. "Leave me?"

"Yeah, well . . ." he flushed. "I have to get back to Brazil, honey. I've been away three months. That's too long."

A lump of lead suddenly seemed to have formed in her stomach. "But I'm coming with you."

"Not this trip, honey."

"Pat . . ."

"I said, not this trip honey." Without warning there was steel in his voice.

Alison stared at him. "You promised . . ."

He sat beside her, held her hands. "Honey, try to understand. There are some problems down there."

"What sort of problems?"

"Things which need ironing out. I just don't reckon it's the place for a pretty little girl like you, right this moment."

"I am not a pretty little girl," she shouted, losing her temper. "I am your wife. If you have problems, they are *our* problems. I want to share them. Tell me what they are."

Once again her explosion alarmed him. "Easy, easy."

"Tell me," she insisted.

"Well . . . we're having trouble with the Indians. There

always has been a spot of bother with those guys. You have to understand their point of view. They've roamed that forest for maybe a million years. Now along comes a guy, me, who chops down the trees to make a motor road from Boa Vista, who imports one hell of a lot of machinery, who seems to be, so far as their simple minds can work, tearing the guts out of their jungle." He grinned. "Worst of all, I guess, is the fact that I won't employ them in the mine. I can't. They have no notion of regular work, come and go as they please, can't be relied on . . . and they have a kind of communist society which says what's yours is mine. You can't have that attitude around a gold mine. There's also a kind of sacrilege involved, I guess, with me draining that lake. I don't know if any of the people around El Dorado are descended from the originals who sunk those poor kids, but they still regard the lake as holy."

"Maybe they're right."

"Honey, they're standing in the way of progress."

Alison hugged herself. "So what are you going to do? Mow them down with machine-guns?"

"It's a government matter. All I want is for the dispute to be settled. I own the land, I own the mine. That's legal: nobody can argue about it. I pay my taxes to the Brazilian Government. They have to sort it out. But I have to be there when it's being done."

"And I have to be there at your side."

"No," he said. "These Indians, they don't abide by any rules. They use blowpipes, and their darts are dipped in a poison called wourali. It paralyses the nervous system, so all your automatic functions just stop. So you die. I'm not exposing you to any risk of that."

She held his hands. "But you're exposing yourself, Pat."

He grinned. "I know the score. No Indian is going to get the low-down on me." He squeezed her fingers. "Try to understand, angel. I have a job of work to do. I can't do it, properly, always looking over my shoulder to make sure you're okay. Listen, when this little bother settles down, I'll take you out. How about that?"

"Promise?" she asked.

"Cross my heart and hope to die."

CHAPTER 3

Rumours

Alison understood that Pat felt obliged to act the father as well as the husband and lover because of the great difference in their ages, and she also knew his refusal to expose her to the risks of some kind of jungle warfare arose from his love for her; she had grown up in a very masculine world of two older brothers and a father who considered himself an empire builder, and for whom protection of their womenfolk was one of the prime elements of the white man's burden. It never seemed to occur to them that given a gun and taught how to use it a woman could be just as effective as any of them, nor did they seem to realise the problems inherent in sitting at home waiting while the menfolk went out and did; this was how it had always been, and so far as they could see, how it would always be. To attempt to rebel against such unwritten laws could only bring quarrels and misery, and she loved Pat too much to wish to risk introducing an element of discord into what was still their honeymoon.

Thus she enthused over her new flat – apartment as it was known in the States – and bravely fought back the tears as she stood on the dock and waved the Belem-bound steamer goodbye. They had loved with an utter abandon the previous night, their first in their new bed, and she had made him repeat his promise. "The very moment this business is sorted out," he had assured her, "I'll come back for you, and we'll honeymoon all over again, in Brazil. Shouldn't take more than a couple of months."

A couple of months, she thought, as she walked back to the taxi in the midst of the crowd of other non-passengers, Hugo attentively at her side. Only a couple of months.

"Home, Mrs Pat?" Hugo asked, as if she were not capable of instructing the driver herself.

Alison was suddenly aware of the strangest feeling. For the first time in her life that she could remember, she was totally, utterly free to do anything she liked. There was no one, not even an Aunt Audrey, to refuse her. There was a great deal that *had* to be done, of course; she had not yet hired a maid or a cook – the idea of doing that was equally strange to her, but Pat had insisted that she have a staff.

Even more entrancing was the understanding that she could actually go out and spend whatever she liked, not even within reason, so far as she was aware. The previous day Pat had taken her to his New York bank and introduced her to the President, who had given her a chequebook and a bank statement in the name of Mrs Patrick Grange, with a single entry in it, a deposit for fifty thousand dollars.

"Just keep that sweetened, George," Pat had said.

"Leave it with me," George had promised. "And Mrs Grange, if you have any problems at all, you know where to find me."

Alison could not remember ever actually seeing fifty thousand dollars in print before, much less under her own name.

"Mrs Pat?" Hugo asked again.

"No, I don't think I'll go straight home, Hugo," she decided. "You can drop me off at Bloomingdale's."

To her dismay, Hugo got out as well.

"There is no necessity for you to come in," she told him. "I'm just going to buy some lingerie. I'll see you at the flat . . . the apartment."

It was only a five minute walk away.

"I was hired to be with you whenever you left the apartment, ma'am," he said stiffly. "Those were the instructions given me by Mr Pat."

She glared at him, but one or two heads were turning as people passed them on the pavement, and she didn't want to make a scene, so she turned and marched into the store, with him behind her.

She went to the lingerie department and chose two satin nightdresses and some underwear. The assistant showed her into a changing cubicle to try the nighties on, leaving Hugo standing in embarrassment beside the counter.

"Oh, they are very nice, madam. They are so you," she gushed. "Would you like me to ask your young man to step in and see if he likes them too?"

"No," Alison said. "He is *not* my young man."

She felt quite out of sorts, and went straight home.

That evening, when Alison settled down beside the radio, Hugo kept popping in and out of the sitting room. "Hugo," she said. "We have got to get something straight: bodyguards have got to be better than old men's beards, neither seen nor heard."

He didn't get the English aphorism, merely looked hurt, so Alison invited him to join her for supper, which she had cooked herself. They drank some wine and she found herself realising just how far little Alison Bennett had travelled so very quickly, in that she was about to sleep in an apartment with a strange man only a couple of walls away, and was not the least bothered by it.

Heaven alone knew what Mummy would say.

But Hugo remained a nuisance. The following morning Alison got on to the employment agency, and for the next two days interviewed a steady flow of job applicants, finally choosing a black cook named Charlene, who was a delightfully practical person, and a Puerto Rican maid named Maria, who was all bustle and efficiency. Charlene almost immediately became a friend, in whom Alison felt she could confide.

"Jus' tell him to get los'," Charlene recommended.

But Alison didn't want to hurt Hugo's feelings. Then she received an invitation. It took her a few minutes to recognise the name, as it came from Mrs George Ruthven, who was having a drinks party the following Friday. Of course, Ruthven was the Bank President. How sweet of them she thought, and at a moment when she needed some sweetness: she had just missed her period, and if it was only one, it was the first time in her entirely healthy life she had ever done that.

She didn't know whether to be enormously happy or wildly unhappy. Of course she wanted to be a mother, but she hadn't anticipated it happening so soon. And she wanted Pat there. But there had been no word from Pat – well, he would hardly have reached Belem yet. Of course he would be back months before the baby was born. But that was another thing: carrying a baby, and then feeding it, put off any prospect of a trip to the malaria-infested jungles of north Brazil for at least eighteen months. Bother!

Thus when Hugo announced his intention of accompanying her to the party she blew her top.

"You will do no such thing!" she snapped.

"Mr Pat said . . ."

"Hugo," she told him, "I wish you to listen to me very carefully. I am your employer now. Mr Pat is a very long way away. If you do not do what *I* wish, I am going to fire you. And I am not attending any cocktail party with you. Got me?"

Hugo looked as if he would have liked to argue, but decided against it.

The party was much larger than Alison had expected, and she found herself being introduced to a huge variety of people, some of whom had clearly heard of her, or at least of Pat, but none of whose names she actually caught.

"I read the *Monthly Review* article," remarked one man. "That husband of yours is a real go-getter, Mrs Grange."

What article? Alison wanted to ask; Pat had never mentioned it. But she didn't want to show her ignorance.

"It must be so exciting," gushed one of the women.

What? Alison wanted to ask.

She was the centre of attention, at least on the part of the men, and this she found very pleasant, but she was relieved when people started going home. When she had first arrived Edith Ruthven had asked her to stay on and have some supper with them, and she had gratefully accepted. Now at last – it was past ten – the three of them were able to sit down while the the maids cleared away the debris.

George poured some more champagne. "How are you taking to New York?" he asked.

"New York is great," Alison told him. "I'd just love to explore it, properly. But that Hugo . . ."

"Hugo?" Edith inquired.

"My bodyguard," Alison said. "Would you believe I need a bodyguard?"

Edith looked at her husband to obtain some idea of how she should reply to that.

"Well," George said. "Pat, well . . . he feels you might be vulnerable."

"He keeps talking about kidnapping," Alison said.

"Kidnapping?" Edith cried. "Oh, my dear girl, you don't have to worry about that. Not nowadays. Since they settled with Hauptmann kidnapping is just about the most heinous crime there is in this coutnry. It's a Federal offence."

"Then what is Pat on about?" Alison asked.

"Well," George said. "He is a very wealthy man. I mean, we're talking about *millions* . . ." he frowned at the look of bewilderment on Alison's face. "But you know this."

"Pat has never really discussed his finances with me," Alison explained. "Or the business side of things at all. I mean, I know he's quite wealthy . . ."

"You could put it that way,," George agreed. "But I'm sure he'll put you in the picture when he comes back."

Alison understood that he wanted to get off the subject; he couldn't really discuss his client's affairs, even with his client's wife, without Pat's say so.

"Someone mentioned an article in *Monthly Review*," she ventured. "When was that?"

"A couple of months ago," Edith said. "You mean you haven't seen it?"

"No. No I haven't."

"Why I'll go and . . ." she stood up, but her husband interrupted.

"I threw all those old magazines out, last week," he said.

"Oh!" Edith looked doubtful, but she sat down again.

Something else George didn't wish to discuss, Alison decided.

"I suppose you know all of Pat's business partners?" she asked, brightly.

"Ah . . . not really. They're really very silent. You know the sort of thing, they put up some capital to work the mine, but Pat is the sole executive. That's how he likes things to be."

"Yes," Alison agreed.

When, half an hour later, George called her a taxi, and escorted her downstairs, she found Hugo waiting for her at the street door.

"Oh, really, Hugo!" she said. "This is too much. Come on, get in."

They sat together for the drive home.

"Hugo," Alison asked. "Do you really prefer men to women?"

"To most women, Mrs Pat," he replied, somewhat enigmatically.

Alison wondered what Pat would make of that. But oddly, she felt reassured.

Until the next day, when she went to the Monthly Review Building and asked to be shown recent editions of the magazine.

"I'm looking for an article you published on Patrick Grange, the gold-miner," she explained.

"Oh, indeed, Mrs . . .?"

"Grange," Alison told the young man with a sweet smile.

He gave a little gulp. "You do understand, Mrs Grange, that while we take every care to check our correspondents' facts, and the Editor stands squarely behind every statement made in our magazine, well . . . it is not our intention to offend."

"Just let me read the article," she suggested, feeling distinctly hot under the collar.

It was brought, and the young man left her to it, although he hovered anxiously on the far side of the room.

"MAVERICK PROSPECTOR STRIKES PAYLOAD BUT LEAVES QUESTIONS UNANSWERED" was the headline.

"'I am going to be the richest man in the world,' declared Englishman Patrick Grange at a press conference today. 'In fact, I am already the richest man in the world.'"

Alison sighed, but continued reading.

"It seems that after twelve years of painstaking search in the jungles of North Brazil, Mr Grange has actually discovered what he claims is the fabled El Dorado, a lake filled with gold-covered skeletons of former sacrifices to the Sun God. He has also located a mine nearby from

76

which the gold was taken, and which he estimates is virtually inexhaustible.

"'I always knew it was there,' Grange says enthusiastically. 'I always knew I would find it.'

"Others weren't so lucky. Grange began this final search with two partners. One has never been seen again. The other shouldn't have been seen again, as he was abandoned for dead. When he did reappear, he found himself out in the cold, after a lawsuit which was defended by Grange and his Brazilian partner. Prospecting with Pat Grange is clearly a risky business."

Alison stared at the page. They were virtually accusing Pat of murder! And a Brazilian partner? Pat had never mentioned that. Just how much of the mine did this partner own?

"Asked why it has taken him so long to raise the capital to commence work on the mine and the lake, Mr Grange merely smiles, and says, 'People didn't want to believe it.' But Pat Grange has his backing now. He won't say who it is but there's a rumour going around that it could be Rubio Enterprises. We can hardly think of a better matched pair than Carlo Rubio and Patrick Grange. Maybe they should both go up the Amazon and stay there. With their gold."

Alison got up. "Thank you," she said.

The young man hurried over.

"Was it . . . er . . ."

"I would say your correspondent does not like my husband," she said.

"He reported facts, Mrs Grange, like I said."

"And made some libellous suggestions."

"That article was checked by our lawyers, Mrs Grange. Of course prospecting in the Amazonian jungle is a risky business. No one can take exception to that. Your husband didn't when the article was published."

"Yes," Alison said, and left. She had a lot to think about.

*   *   *

77

Invitations now started to arrive with some regularity: Alison had clearly made an impression at the Ruthven's party. She was tempted to refuse them all. Everyone would have read the article. She was even more tempted when she discovered who Carlo Rubio was.

Hugo was her informant here. When she asked him, casually, at breakfast, he said, "Rubio? Oh, he's the big-time hood. Runs all the vice in New York."

"Ah!" Alison said.

Her husband was in partnership with a gangster! No wonder he hadn't wanted her to meet his associates!

And yet, her mind instinctively turned to his defence. He had tried everywhere else to raise money; he'd admitted that. But he had been turned down by his own family, and presumably by all "respectable" businessmen. Was he then never going to develop his marvellous find just because nobody would believe it was there?

And being financed by a hoodlum didn't mean he was engaged in any criminal activities himself. She believed what he had told her of Waller and Carter. The Brazilian courts had believed it. Just because some smart-ass American reporter chose not to was no reason to go off the deep end . . . however much she felt like doing so.

In the end she decided to accept most of the invitations, out of loyalty to Pat. Besides, she was definitely the lioness of the social hour, and was enjoying it. It was simply a matter of dressing in the most expensive clothes she could find, wearing all of her jewellery, and smiling sweetly at everyone. Equally everyone was very polite back to her, whatever private opinions they may have had regarding Pat.

She went to the theatre regularly. The Ruthvens put her up for their country club, and she became an enthusiastic if inexpert tennis player.

Hugo would hire a car and chauffeur her out of the city and north into Connecticut whenever she felt like escaping the bustle and the traffic.

She shopped as and when she felt like it, and she busied herself in the kitchen with Charlene, becoming quite a good cook. She wrote letters to her mother and father, and Tom and Harry, and Aunt Audrey, and Josephine . . . and seldom got replies. She gained the feeling they just didn't know what to say.

She wished Pat would come home.

There were problems, of course. Men, both married and single, made advances. These she turned aside graciously wherever possible; where not, she had a very simple, and devastating, put down: she was pregnant. She had no doubt that there was gossip about her large male bodyguard, but then, she had no doubt she was a subject for gossip in every direction. When Pat came home, she resolved, she would throw a huge return party and let them all see how proud she was of her husband, and how much in love with him she was, too.

She toyed with the idea of inviting Carlo Rubio for a drink, and then rejected it. She wanted to hear Pat's side of the story first.

But all of her plans were overtaken by events. First of all, in August there could be no doubt that she *was* pregnant. She sent a telegram to Pat, and as she received no reply, sent several more. At last one came back: HOME FOR CHRISTMAS. With which she presumed she would have to be content, although by Christmas she would be nearly six months into her pregnancy.

She also sent her mother a telegram, informing her that she was going to be a grandmother. This elicited an immediate congratulatory response.

And then, a fortnight later, England and Germany were at war.

That this was going to happen became obvious before Mr Chamberlain's fateful announcement on Sunday 3 September. Once again Alison sent Pat several telegrams, on the Saturday, without getting a reply. She also cabled

79

her parents, and learned that they would be cutting short their holiday and returning to Brazil immediately, but via Canada, owing to the shipping problem. They were sailing on *SS Athenia* the following day, and hoped to be in New York a week later to see her before catching a boat south to Rio.

The idea that she would be able to show her parents her lovely apartment and her new lifestyle quite negated the other news that both Tom and Harry were already in the army and preparing to accompany the BEF to France.

But the whole idea was at once exciting and terrifying, even if Alison could honestly say that she had known it was coming for several months. She was very relieved that her mother and father were getting out of England, but was terribly worried about what Pat was going to do. Granted he was forty, he was absolutely fit and obviously belonged in the armed services . . . but the thought of another long separation, and a further postponement of all her dreams, not to mention the fact that he would again be in physical danger, left her utterly desolated.

Meanwhile, she prepared for the arrival of her parents, and although the next day, the day on which war was actually declared, was Sunday, she had Maria and Charlene, and Hugo, working away, making the apartment as spic and span as if she were about to sell it.

That evening she collapsed into bed exhausted, but happy. She switched on the radio, and listened to the news . . . that *SS Athenia* had been torpedoed, on the very afternoon war had been declared, just west of Ireland. There were reports of over a hundred dead. For several moments Alison just sat there, hardly hearing the impersonal voice as it moved on, in matter-of-fact tones, to the first battles of the War as the Germans invaded Poland, the measures being taken by the Allies . . .

Hugo had heard the news as well, and a moment later was in her bedroom.

"What can I do, Mrs Pat?" he asked.

She was too distraught even to realise that since her marriage she had taken up sleeping in the nude.

"Oh, God," she said. "How do we find out."

Without warning tears were dribbling down her cheeks and he was sitting on the bed with her in his arms. He hugged her against himself and stroked her hair, which by now had again grown quite long.

"Only a hundred and twenty have drowned, ma'am," he said. "They might well have survived. I will find out for you."

He brought her some sleeping pills and tucked her up. She slept heavily, and awoke with a clear head . . . to catastrophe. Hugo had apparently been on the telephone all night, to various people, and had learned that Mr and Mrs Bennett were not amongst the survivors.

The day passed in a daze. Alison tried cabling Tom and Harry, but they were unavailable. So she cabled Aunt Audrey. She spoke to the shipping line herself, and had the news confirmed. She cabled Pat, and predictably got no reply. Aunt Audrey did reply, the next day, but it was a rambling and virtually unintelligible message – Aunt Audrey was clearly distraught.

But so was she. Mummy and Daddy were dead! She had been so relieved that they were getting out of England before the bombs started to fall . . . and now they were dead. Hugo and Charlene had virtually to force feed her over the next few days.

"You have to eat, Mrs Grange," Charlene said. "You's eating for two."

Hugo followed her around like a puppy. Alison felt no embarrassment over the night of 3 September . . . he *was* nothing more than a faithful watchdog. But she realised she had to pull herself together, even if she couldn't stop herself sending another sheaf of telegrams to Pat, begging him to come home, and upbraiding him bitterly for not doing so. Meanwhile, she cancelled all her engagements, and hardly left the apartment, merely sat listening to the radio in shocked horror as the Nazi armies swarmed over

Poland, and then the War seemed to come to a full stop
. . . but with Mummy and Daddy dead.

And at last, just before Christmas, Pat came home.

He held her very close for a long time, despite the size
of her stomach, which seemed to be growing every day.

"Oh, my dear girl," he said. "My dear, dear girl. I am
so terribly sorry."

In his arms all of her pent-up misery, and her anger with
him for staying away so long, seemed to melt away. He was
so strong and determined. If he was also a ruthless man,
as many seemed to think, that was what she wanted right
now. A man who would ruthlessly destroy those who had
murdered her parents.

"When can we go home?" she asked.

"Home? This is your home, darling."

"But we have to fight the Germans," she said.

"*We* aren't fighting anyone. I've spent the past few
months fighting Indians, and I've had a bellyfull. Anyway,
you want to forget about England being your home. We
have no part in this war."

"But . . . we're British."

"That's an accident of birth. Britain has never done
one damn thing for me. Or for you. Do you know what'll
happen if I go home? They'll start taxing me. And taxes
are going up all the time as they try to pay for this mess
they've got themselves into."

"Everyone has to pay taxes. Don't they?"

"I'm not everyone," Pat told her. "No crummy government is going to lay a finger on any of my money."

Like most of Pat's points of view, she just had never
encountered it before.

"It seems dreadfully disloyal, to stay away when everyone else is fighting," she protested. "I mean, Tom and
Harry are in France."

"If they're in France, they certainly aren't doing any
fighting," he pointed out. "Look, my dearest girl, your

business is to bring our child into the world, not worry about wars."

She supposed he was right about that, certainly, and it was so very good to have him home, even if she saw very little of him. She was in no condition to do any entertaining – even had she wanted to – and he seemed to have a great deal of business to attend to, so that a couple of hours together in the evenings was all they could manage. But even that was better than not having him there at all. He was so utterly sweet and attentive, brought her endless presents, would just sit staring at her, and say, "I must be the luckiest guy in the world, to have you."

It was the first time that he had made her feel wanted, as opposed to merely being desired, and she loved it. But then, she loved him. She was sure of that now.

His reappearance in New York, however, again stirred up the media.

"What, we should like to ask," remarked one tabloid, "is this self-proclaimed richest man in the world, who also loudly proclaims his British nationality, doing to help his country in its hour of greatest need? We shall tell you. He is making sure that he gets no nearer than three thousand miles to the scene of the fighting, and that he continues to extract a fortune from his mine . . . not a penny of which is being offered to the United Kingdom Government."

"Oh, the beasts," Alison shouted. "Why don't you sue them?"

Pat merely grinned. "They're like a herd of jackals, snapping at the heels of a lion. Fuck them."

"Why don't you offer to pay English Income tax?" she asked. "Then we could spit in their eye."

"Are you nuts? I don't give a damn what they print about me."

"I do," she said.

He gazed at her for some seconds, then grinned again. "Okay, you're a patriot. Tell you what I'll do. I'll offer to pay for some planes for them. Spitfires. I'll pay for a squadron of Spitfires."

"Oh, Pat!" She threw both arms round his neck. "Will you? Will you really?"

"If it'll make you happy, baby doll. And say, if I do that, they might give me a knighthood. Sir Patrick Grange. Wouldn't that be something? You'd be Lady Grange. That might almost be worth the money."

How she wished he wouldn't reduce everything to terms of value for money. But at least he was doing something.

"How did you become involved with Carlo Rubio?" she asked.

He gave her a sideways look.

"You left me here," she reminded him. "With nothing to do but listen to gossip."

"I guess I did," he agreed. "So I'm associated with a hood. He put up the money I needed. Nobody else would."

"I thought George Ruthven was your friend."

"Sure he is. Now. Like all the other bankers, he didn't want to know when I was looking for capital. Since I started putting some of that capital his way, things are different."

"They've been awfully nice to me."

"I should fucking well think so. I must be his biggest account."

"Pat . . . is there anyone in the world you don't hate?"

He grinned. "Sure. You. I love you. And don't worry your pretty little head about Rubio. Think of him as a bank with foresight. He put up the capital, and he gets it back, with interest, from my royalties. That is it. He has no stake in the mine, no say in how its run, no place in our lives."

"But the money he put up was earned from criminal sources, surely."

"That's not our problem, sweetheart. What do you

suppose you'd turn up if you started investigating how any bank or financier got his start?"

She couldn't argue with him, and the sweep of his confidence was overwhelmingly reassuring. When he told her all she had to do was be happy, it was impossible not at least to try to do just that,

Yet she remained curious about his organisation. "Who is your Brazilian partner?" she asked, casually.

Another sideways look.

"I read about it. Do I get to meet *him*?"

"When you come to Brazil, sure. His name is Pedro Alvarado. But he's only a figurehead. To own the mine, to work it, it had to be owned by a Brazilian."

"Owned?"

"It's a paper transaction. Pedro has ten per cent. He's quite happy with that, and he doesn't get in the way. It's all very simple. But absolutely legal."

"Oh, Pat, I am so looking forward to seeing it all, meeting Mr Alvarado . . ."

He lowered his head to kiss her stomach. "As soon as we've sorted junior out."

To Alison's consternation, just as she was getting over the shock of her parents' death, in February Pat announced that he must return to South America.

"But I'm due any moment!" she cried. She was at least eight months pregnant.

"I know and I'm sorry, but they need me there." He held her shoulders. "I can't spend all my time here with you, darling. Anyway, you were supposed to be coming to South America with me on this trip, remember?"

"You wretch! Don't you want the child?"

"Of course I do." He kissed her, and as usual she felt her anger melting away. "And I'll be back as soon as I can."

"I could come with you anyway," she ventured.

"Forget that. No shipping line would take you in your

condition. And what are you trying to do, commit infanticide? Look, sweetie, things are a bit fraught right now. It's all going to work itself out, believe me."

As usual, she had to accept that, because she had no choice. And as usual Pat was laying on the most lavish plans for her delivery. Her gynecologist was quite happy for her to have the baby at home, as she wished, but Pat insisted on hiring a retinue of nurses and spare doctors just in case of trouble.

Then he was off, back to South America.

Edith Ruthven came to call. "I guess Pat Grange is just about the most self-centred man in the world," she said. "But then . . . he's not so different to most other men. George was only around for the birth of one of our three. He was in France with the AEF when Billy was born. He was with me for Angie, but there was some important banking conference came up just as Al appeared. I guess that's par for the course."

"Well, Pat has had his chance," Alison said. "If he can't be there for this one, then that's it. I'm not having any more."

Edith smiled, and kissed her on the cheek.

Alison's baby boy was born on 4 April 1940. As there had been no word from Pat for over a month, she christened him Benjamin, why, she had no very clear idea.

"I think it's a beautiful name," said the nurse who had assisted at the delivery, somewhat unnecessarily, as although a small woman Alison had had no difficulty whatsoever. "I think it's terrible that his father isn't here."

Tired but happy, Alison was again in love. "Think of all the thousands of wives in Europe who are giving birth without their husbands around," she pointed out. "At least I know mine is coming back."

*   *   *

Only a week after the birth Alison was gratified when the news of Pat's gift of ten Spitfires to the Royal Air Force became public. George Ruthven had of course been in the know from the beginning, but now all of Alison's other acquaintances – all apparently fervent Anglophiles – showered her with congratulatory cards and invitations, which she had to put off for a while, as she was feeding Ben.

Predictably there were also grumbles, "conscience money" as one commentator put it, but now Alison was entirely willing to agree with Pat that this was just sour grapes.

In any event, that and all other news ceased to be of any interest at all the following month when Hitler invaded France.

Pat was home at the beginning of June, and they listened to the final stages of the evacuation from Dunkirk together.

"It has been an absolute shambles," Pat commented. "Christ, to think that I have spent a small fortune on those planes, just to have them captured by the Germans!"

"They haven't been captured by the Germans," Alison objected.

"They will be, as soon as Hitler invades Britain," he riposted.

Alison couldn't really argue with that, as most American commentators also felt that Britain was beaten, and the sooner she made peace the better for everyone. Her feelings of guilt, that she should be sitting in affluent luxury in New York while her countrymen, and women – including her own brothers – were fighting for their lives, grew, only slightly relieved by the news that both Tom and Harry had survived the debacle and were back in England, unharmed.

"What would we do, if England were invaded and captured?" she asked.

"Stay here."

"Yes, but we're British citizens."

"So maybe we'd have to become citizens of somewhere else."

"The States, you mean?"

"Let me think about that," he said. "There are a lot of other places, where I might be able to do a better deal. I'm working on it."

Alison was disappointed that Pat didn't seem more interested in Ben, but Charlene explained about that.

"Men like the boss," she said. "They don' go for kids. You wait till that boy starts to grow."

Pat was certainly interested in her, however, because he was an old-fashioned man, and hadn't wanted to have sex with her while she was pregnant at Christmas. Now he unbuttoned her blouse and unfastened her nursing bra.

"They never used to be this big," he commented.

"Don't you like big tits?" She had always been rather ashamed of her somewhat small breasts.

"You bet I do."

"Well, make the most of them. They're only big because they're full of milk."

"Show me."

She gave her left nipple a little pinch, and a drop of milk rolled down the swelling flesh. To her consternation, he immediately lowered his head and licked it up.

"Do that some more," he said.

"Pat! That's absolutely disgusting."

He raised his head again. "What can possibly be disgusting, between a man and a woman in love?"

She supposed he was right: only a month after he had returned to the Amazon, she found she was pregnant again.

Alison had now come to accept that Pat was never going to stay at home more than a month at a time, no matter what might be going on in the rest of the world. Throughout June, when he had been in New York, the Allied situation had gone from bad to worse, with France surrendering, Italy entering the War on the Nazi side, and, by the end of the month, Britain totally alone and more vulnerable to invasion than ever. But he felt his place was at the mine.

Her initial answer had been, if you can't beat them, join them. She didn't see how Pat could object to her going with him, say around the end of the year, when Ben would be off the breast and able to travel. But the second pregnancy took her back to square one. She began to think about asking Pat to use a contraceptive; but she had no idea how he would react to that.

Meanwhile life as a grass widow could be resumed in between finishing feeding Ben and starting to show with number two. She went to a lot of parties, accompanied the Ruthvens to the theatre, and listened to the news with tremendous excitement as the Battle of Britain developed: Pat's Spitfires were actually playing their part in making the world, as President Roosevelt put it, safe for democracy.

President Roosevelt was much in the news that autumn, not only because he seemed to have the measure of the crisis in Europe, but because it was an election year, and he was running for an unprecedented third term. Even Alison got caught up in the excitement of electioneering, with people apparently divided between those who did not think any president should serve three terms, and those who felt that in view of the threatening world situation it was better to stay with a tried and trusted leader.

By the time of the actual election at the beginning of November, Alison was again beginning to show although she could still be adequately disguised, and she spent the evening with the Ruthhvens, who were both committed Democrats. Roosevelt's tremendous victory was an occasion for a great deal of champagne, and Alison got quite tipsy, reflecting that if the baby got tipsy too it was in a good cause.

Next morning she awoke with a distinct headache, and Maria served her black coffee in bed. She was sitting there, idly turning the pages of the *New York Times* and listening to Ben bellowing lustily as Hannah, his nurse, bathed him, when the doorbell rang.

Hugo was in a moment later, following a very brief knock on the door; they had established an almost brother and sister intimacy during the eighteen months he had been in her employ.

"There's a guy to see you," he said.

"At this hour?"

"Well, Mrs Pat, it's eleven o'clock."

"Is it really? That's still too early for calls. What does this 'guy' want?"

"Search me. But he gave me his card."

Alison took the piece of cardboard, and frowned at it. The man's name was Jonathan Carter.

CHAPTER 4

The Exiles

Alison's initial reaction was to tell Carter to go away. But that was immediately replaced by a tremendous curiosity, not only to see what he looked like, but to discover what he wanted.

"Well," she said. "You'd better ask him to take a seat in the sitting room Hugo. I'll be out in five minutes."

There was no time to bathe or dress properly. She cleaned her teeth and made-up her face as rapidly as she could, pulled on a pair of slacks – they would just fasten – and a very loose blouse to hang outside, thrust her feet into high-heeled mules, dragged a comb through her hair – which was now as long as it had ever been, and even more curly – and went into the lounge, to stop in surprise as the man waiting for her rose to his feet.

Pat had always referred to Jonathan Carter as a boy, but then Pat was inclined to refer to everyone not actually older than himself as a boy. But Jonathan Carter *was* hardly more than a boy, she realised; she was sure he couldn't be older than twenty-five. He was a very tall young man, taller than Pat, although not so heavily built; in fact he looked somewhat emaciated, which she concluded must be the result of his long battle with malaria. The gauntness of his face, however, accentuated the very precise bone structure – he was a handsome man.

He wore the blue uniform and the insignia of a pilot officer in the RAF.

"Mr Carter?"

"Mrs Grange." He gave a quick glance at her stomach, which not even the loose shirt could entirely conceal. "I do apologise for this intrusion, but I happened to be in New York . . ."

"Shouldn't you be in England?" she asked brusquely.

"I'm on a training mission," he explained. "I'm not a fighter pilot, you see. I'm in bombers."

"Oh! Oh, yes." Of course, she recognised, he was not wearing one of the huge moustaches sported by "the few". "Would you like a cup of coffee?"

"That would be very nice."

"Well . . . please sit down." She rang for Hugo, then sat down herself, and remembered why he was there. Why he had to be there. "Forgive me for seeming so surprised. I was celebrating last night."

He smiled. It was a most attractive smile. "Roosevelt's victory? So was I. The best possible thing for Britain."

"Yes. But anyway . . . I'm so glad things have worked out the way they have. Between you and Pat, I mean."

The smile faded. "Worked out?"

Hugo came in with the coffee, and showed his usual inclination to stay.

"I'm sure you have a lot to do, Hugo," Alison said, vague worryings beginning to flicker in her brain.

Hugo left the room, shooting her a meaningful stare.

"I was talking about the settlement," Alison said. "I don't know how much was involved, of course . . ."

"What settlement?" Carter asked.

Alison poured coffee, trying to keep calm. "One lump or two, Mr Carter?"

"Three, please."

She added the sugar and handed him his cup. Her hand was trembling slightly. "My husband settled some money on you, did he not?"

"No, Mrs Grange, he did not."

Alison gazed at him, and he gazed back – and she knew he was telling the truth.

"There was no reason for him to," Carter went on. "He won his case in the Brazilian courts. Didn't you know about that?"

"Yes. I knew about it. But he was going to make a settlement on you anyway."

Carter raised his eyebrows. "With respect, Mrs Grange, but that doesn't sound like the Pat Grange I used to know."

"Well . . . he has . . . mellowed, I suppose, since his success. But . . . you haven't received any money?"

"No. Anyway, Mrs Grange, I didn't come here looking for money."

Alison was feeling slightly sick. It could have been the baby . . . but she was long past the stage of morning sickness.

"Then why *did* you come here?" she asked.

"Well . . ." he flushed. "As I say, I happened to be in New York, and I . . . well, I was curious to see what the famous Mrs Grange looked like."

"Famous?"

"Well, I suppose anyone connected with Pat Grange is famous."

She began to get angry, less with this unhappy fellow than with Pat for lying to her . . . not for the first time. But Jonathan Carter was the man in her sights. "Don't you mean, anyone *owned* by Pat Grange, Mr Carter?"

"I didn't say that, Mrs Grange."

"But you meant it. I'm afraid I have no idea why my husband has not yet paid you the money he decided to. I do know that he has been very busy this last year with labour troubles at the mine. So I will give you something on account." She got up and went to her desk, sat down, and wrote out a cheque for fifty thousand dollars – which so far as she knew was her credit limit – while Carter watched her. Then she stood in front of him, held the cheque out; she felt quite excited . . . she had never in her life written a cheque even fractionally as large: George Ruthven was going to be horrified – but Pat had told him to keep the account in credit and he would have to do just that. As for Pat himself . . . he had it coming. "I assure you that there will be considerably more when my husband returns home."

Jonathan Carter took the cheque and glanced at it, gave a low whistle. "I told you, I didn't come here looking for a handout from you, Mrs Grange."

"Oh, I do assure you that the money is Pat's. I have none of my own. As you reminded me, he owns me."

Carter tore the cheque into several strips and dropped it into the ashtray. "That makes it even more certain that I won't take it. I wouldn't accept a red cent from Pat Grange if I was dying." He grinned. "I was once, with him standing there."

"I think you had better leave," Alison said, as coldly as she could.

Carter finished his coffee and stood up. "I did have another reason for coming here, Mrs Grange," he said. "It was to see just what kind of woman would marry a bastard like Pat Grange. I'm sorry it's you. I think you're a hell of a sight too good for him. You've tied yourself to a thug, Mrs Grange. But maybe it's not all bad. One day . . . one day soon, I would say you are going to be a wealthy widow. That's worth waiting for. I'll show myself out."

Alison remained staring at the door for some seconds after Carter left. She didn't move until Hugo came in.

"That guy wasn't rude to you, was he?"

Rude, she thought. He had actually tried to pay her a clumsy compliment. But he had also threatened Pat's life. Or had he? Everyone knew Pat was twenty years older than her, and living as he did, could probably die, or be killed by a Indian poisoned dart, at any moment.

"Mrs Pat?" Hugo asked anxiously. "You okay?"

"Yes," Alison said. "Yes, I'm okay."

"Can I get you something?"

"Yes. A sherry." Baby, she told her stomach, you are just going to have to get used to strong drink.

Alison knew by now what a waste of time it was sending wires to Brazil. It was also a waste of time getting angry. She was coming to understand that her husband, for all his age and his undoubted drive and ambition and determination, was actually a small boy at heart . . . to which could be added his paranoic obsession with not parting with his money, except when and how he chose. He had made her a solemn promise, but as she had never followed it up, had done nothing about it. Presumably he had done nothing about Geoffrey Waller's family, either. Well, she thought, we shall see about that. But I shall not get angry; that would involve too much risk to the baby.

Pat returned to New York in the spring of 1941. "I've come home to be here both for your twenty-first birthday and for the birth of the baby," he told Alison. "And I've brought you a present."

It was a nugget of gold the size of a tennis ball.

"Oh, Pat! What on earth am I to do with it?"

"Put it in your safe deposit box for a rainy day. Not that there's ever going to be a rainy day, for you and me."

Definitely she could not be angry with him. She threw her arms round his neck and kissed him passionately. But that didn't mean she was going to let him off the hook for lying to her.

"Jonathan Carter called to see me last November," she said.

Pat had gone to the bar and was mixing himself a gin martini. Slowly he turned towards her. "What? You didn't actually see him?"

"Well, of course I did."

"By Christ, I am going to fire that fucking Hugo. He's supposed to protect you."

"I didn't need protecting from Mr Carter," Alison pointed out. "And it had nothing to do with Hugo. I wanted to see him."

"What on earth for?"

"Curiosity, I suppose. He's a piece of your past, isn't he?"

"What did the bastard want?"

"I think he was curious too. To see the 'famous Mrs Pat Grange.'"

"Goddamned cheek."

"However, he told me that he had not yet received any money from you."

Pat turned back to the bar, finished making his drink. "He asked for a hand-out, did he?"

"No. And when I wrote him a cheque, he refused to accept it."

Pat turned back again, the drink in his hand. "You wrote him a cheque? Why, in the name of God?"

"Because you have not yet done so."

Pat sipped his drink. "I've been kind of busy. Or hadn't you noticed?"

"Pat, you lied to me. Have you sent Waller's family a cheque?"

"No I haven't." Suddenly he was angry. "And it's none of your goddam business. Your business is running our home and bringing up our kids, not poking your nose into my affairs."

Alison was on the verge of losing her temper as well, but she endeavoured to speak calmly. "It is my business when you make me a solemn promise. Did you ever have any intention of paying those men their money?"

"Their money?" he shouted. "Their money! Jesus shitting Christ! It's *my* money. Mine, do you hear. Mine!"

Alison got up.

"Where the hell are you going?" he demanded.

"To my room. It is impossible to carry on a conversation with an hysteric."

For a moment she thought he was going to have a fit. Then he put down his glass, crossed the room very quickly, grasped her shoulder, and thrust her into a chair. "Siddown!"

Alison gasped as she fell over on to the cushions, hands immediately closing protectively around her stomach. "If you're trying to make me miscarry, that's the quickest way to go about it."

He glared at her, his big fists bunched, and she realised that for a few seconds she had actually been in physical danger. But the danger was already past. He dropped to his knees beside her, hugged her and kissed her.

"I don't ever want to hurt you, darling girl," he muttered. "Not ever. I just want you to be the happiest little girl in all the world."

Little girl, she thought. That was how he regarded her, to be sure. His very own little girl. It had been their very first serious quarrel, and she wanted it over and done with. But only on her terms.

"Pat," she said. "Don't ever lie to me again."

"Sweetheart, I told you, I've been busy . . ."

"Pat," she repeated. "Don't ever lie to me again."

He raised his head to look at her, then moved away from her and threw himself into a chair. "Okay. So I won't ever lie to you again."

"And you'll give those two men, or their families, their money."

"Well, you just said that Carter wouldn't accept any . . ."

"There's still Waller. I'm positive his family would accept it."

"I'll get a detective on to tracing them right away. Now let's see a smile. I came home to be with you for your birthday, and I'm staying till the baby's born."

He had clearly rehearsed that.

* * *

Shirley Grange was born in May 1941, a week before the Balkans exploded into flame. Since the previous September the War seemed to have settled down into a kind of stalemate, with the only fighting going on at sea and in North and East Africa.

"I don't understand why Churchill, even Churchill, doesn't make peace," Pat commented. "He's not getting anywhere."

Mr Churchill seemed to be getting even less when the Germans overran Yugoslavia and Greece. But no sooner had Pat set off again for Brazil than the invasion of Russia began, and the rest of the world held its breath.

The United States and its Government were by now deeply, and obviously, committed to the side of the Western Democracies, a term, which, originally used to refer to Britain and France, now apparently included the Communist Russian dictatorship of Josef Stalin as well. If there remained a vociferous minority who decried any involvement in European affairs, the majority were happy to provide Lend-Lease equipment to those fighting Nazi Germany, while determined to keep out of the struggle themselves. Securely ensconced in the totally supportive social circle of the Ruthvens and their friends, Alison found life very good indeed that summer. Her existence was, she supposed, utterly aimless. She played bridge, she attended parties, and, as Pat only ever seemed to come home when she was incapable of socialising, she began throwing little supper parties of her own, to which, as she always served the best food and wines, it became quite a cachet to be invited.

As with the period before Ben's birth, there were the inevitable attempts on the part of various of her male guests to flirt, with the possibility of an affair always looming in the background. And now she was not even pregnant. Rather was she blossoming into a quite lovely young woman, the gaucheness of Pat Grange's bride quite disappeared as she grew into her position, just as her confidence had grown enormously since their quarrel, and the knowledge that she could stand up to him and give as good as she got.

She regarded her victory as complete, if somewhat hollow, when she received a letter, addressed to Pat but forwarded to her by George Ruthven on Pat's express instructions, from a Mrs Waller to say that she had no desire to receive any money from Mr Grange on behalf of her dead son.

At least she had tried, Alison thought.

Pat had promised to be home for Christmas, and at the end of November Alison had the staff putting the apartment into order, with masses of decorations everywhere. Ben, who was now stringing words together, was able to appreciate the excitement, and even little Shirley sat up in her cot and clapped enthusiastically.

Alison herself had never been in a better humour. It would be the first Christmas since her arrival in the States that she was not pregnant, Pat was coming home, she had heard from Aunt Audrey that she had survived the blitz undamaged, and best of all, both Tom and Harry had been posted to the Far East, Tom to Malaya and Harry to Singapore, which satisfactorily removed them from the proximity of the fighting.

Of course the news from Russia continued to be grim, as the Germans were on the very outskirts of Moscow, but most experts expected the advance to slow down with the onset of winter, which would give the Communists time to regroup and hopefully recover, especially as masses of Lend-Lease equipment were being poured into the country.

She was just finishing her Christmas cards in time for lunch on Sunday 7 December when the news broke from Honolulu.

* * *

Edith Ruthven telephoned immediately. If she was shocked at the Japanese attack on Pearl Harbour, she was equally pleased that America was at last in the War. Alison's initial reaction was also that of relief, as she had not been able to see how England could ever succeed on her own. But then came the news of the simultaneous attacks on Hong Kong and Malaya, and she started to worry all over again.

Pat arrived a week later, and she threw herself into his arms.

"It's a big show now," he agreed. "But it's not going to worry us, baby doll."

She pulled her head back. "But I want it to worry us," she said. "I want us to do everything we can. Hell, if I didn't have the kids, I'd join up."

"Thank God you have the kids," he said fervently. "Now listen, we have a lot to do."

"Just tell me where to begin."

"First thing, start packing. I've already told Hugo. He and Clem'll see to all the heavy stuff. I want to be out of here by the end of the week."

"Packing?" she cried. "But I've just put up all the Christmas decorations. Where are we going, anyway."

"Somewhere you are just going to adore."

"*Where*?"

"Mexico."

She stared at him in total consternation. "Mexico?"

"It's beautiful down there. And we have the most splendid place."

Alison sat down. "We have a house in Mexico?"

"Yeah. I bought it in the summer, on my way back from here. Well, it's not just a house. It's what they call a *hacienda*."

"What's a *hacienda*?"

"It means a kind of ranch. It is a ranch. But we won't be doing any ranching. I've had them working on it for the past six months. It's just about ready for you. For us."

As so often happened with this man, Alison had to fight back an urgent desire to scream.

"You want to spend Christmas in Mexico?" she asked, determined to get her facts absolutely straight.

"That's right. It's beautiful down there right now. No snow."

"I see. Don't you think snow is appropriate for Christmas?"

"Snow is never appropriate, sweetheart."

"It's a point of view. Now tell me what we say to the Ruthvens and all the other people who have invited us out over the holiday, or the New Year's Eve Ball we're going to."

"We'll have to cancel."

"Just like that. Because you want to go to Mexico. Now." She was only just keeping her temper under control. "When are we coming back?"

"Ah . . . we aren't."

Alison opened her mouth and then closed it again. Then opened it again. "What did you say?"

"Listen, sweetheart . . ." he sat beside her, put his arm round her shoulders. "Things have changed. America is in the War."

"Isn't that the best news since sliced bread?"

"Not for us. Wars mean taxes."

"Oh, here we go again. I thought you had it fixed up so you didn't pay taxes?"

"I did. I had it fixed up so I only paid on the money I brought into the country. But that's going to change. They want to tax me on my world-wide income, because they say now I have an apartment here with my wife living in it permanently, this is my principal place of residence. What fucking cheek. Anyway, I've been fighting it, and we had some prospects of winning. But my lawyer tells me now there's a war on, no dice. It's every shoulder to the wheel, he says. Well, fuck him. I've done a deal with the Mexican Government. I pay them a fixed sum a year, you could call it rent, and I can live there as long as I like, tax free."

"You've been organising all of this, for the past six months or whatever, without saying a word to me?"

101

"Well, hell, darling, the business side of our life is my business. Yours is . . ."

"Looking after the home and bringing up the kids. Right. I accept that. Therefore where we have a home, and where I have to bring up the kids, happens to be *my* business. This . . ." she stamped her foot on the floor "is my home. You gave it to me. I like it here. I have all my friends here. I intend to go on living here." She paused because she had run out of breath, and because she was realising this was one battle she was not going to win . . . at least in the short term: Pat's face had settled into very firm lines.

"Honey, it has to be."

"And if I refuse to go?"

He gave a lop-sided grin. "Don't push it, for God's sake. Look, it's only for the duration. Now the Yanks are in the War, it'll all be over in a year. You wait and see."

She sighed, and tried another line of attack. "Listen, Pat . . ." she held his hands. "If you pull out of the States now, the way you pulled out of England, they'll never forgive you. My God, they'll crucify you! You'll never be able to come back here to live."

"Okay, if they want to play it rough, we'll give them two fingers. When the war's over, we'll go back to England."

"England? I thought you said England was out because of the taxes?"

"Right now. But after the War, that'll be different. I have some ideas on that. Wouldn't you like to go back and live in England?"

"Oh, Pat, I'd like that more than anything else in the world. Could we? Could we really?"

"I'm working on it. But first . . . we have to go to Mexico."

Oh, well, she thought, she couldn't expect to win them all.

George Ruthven of course already knew of Pat's intentions, although as a banker, he had kept it a tight secret, even from his wife. Now she knew what was happening, Edith was as usual totally sympathetic . . . to Alison's point of view, even if she was also a little envious. "I suppose it must be very nice to be rich enough to do whatever you feel like doing, and if a country doesn't seem right, just pack up your bags and go," she confided to Alison. "But it's going to make Pat very unpopular."

"Don't you think I've told him that?" Alison asked. "Even supposing he were popular now, which he isn't, in certain directions. But you know how unreasonable he gets whenever he feels people are trying to take his money away from him."

"My dear, I shall miss you so."

"I'll be back," Alison assured her. "We won't be ruled *personae non gratae*, will we?"

"Well . . . I don't think *you* can be. Pat may well be, if he's opting out of back taxes."

"Then I'll be back. Not even Pat is going to keep me shut up in Mexico indefinitely."

Had she not felt so guilty about Pat's behaviour, Alison would rather have enjoyed the next few weeks. Pat's overriding fear was that the courts would hurry up their processing, and serve some kind of a notice on him before he could safely escape. Thus their departure had to be both secret and speedy. They simply packed their suitcases and walked away from the apartment, leaving all their furniture.

"Don't worry about it," Pat told Alison. "You can come back to it."

"Won't they sequestrate it if they claim you owe back taxes?" she asked.

He grinned. "They can't. It's in your name."

He'd never told her that before, either.

Alison was mainly upset at having to lie to Charlene

and Maria. Pat insisted that she merely tell them they were going away for a Christmas vacation, with just the children and the two bodyguards.

"Look, you can write to them from Mexico. It isn't as if they were losing their jobs. For Chrissake, they're getting the same pay just to caretake the place. They're going to be laughing all the way to wherever else they take employment."

Presumably he was right. Yet she took a tearful farewell of the two women before they all piled into the hired limousine and headed south.

It would of course have been far quicker and more comfortable to have taken a train, but Pat remained obsessed with the possibility that somehow the US Government would learn about his intended departure and stop it if he used public transport, so instead they drove the couple of thousand miles to the Mexican border.

Hugo and Clem took turns at the wheel, while Hannah sat in the intermediate seats with the two children, and Alison and Pat occupied the back. Hannah had raised no objection at the abrupt change of plan, had not even inquired where they were going. She was a silent, introverted young woman, and indeed Alison had been wondering whether she was actually the ideal nurse, but now her ready acceptance of the new situation was invaluable.

It was all really quite exciting, almost like a second, and far more private, honeymoon, despite the presence of the children and the servants. They went straight through all the big towns, stopping for the night in out of the way hotels. Some of these, as they reached the deep south, were fairly alarming places, with equally alarming inhabitants, but the presence of Clem and Hugo, not to mention Pat himself – all of whom apart from being very large were also armed, as Alison knew – was reassuring.

More alarming was the news they heard whenever they stopped, of the extent of the losses to the US fleet at Pearl Harbour, of the Japanese victories in the Philippines and Malaya, of the loss of the two British battleships *Prince of Wales* and *Repulse*, and worst of all, of the Japanese landings on Hong Kong island itself.

"Seems it's all one-way traffic right this minute," Pat commented. "Those guys are going to take a lot of beating."

He was more concerned with the emergency measures being taken by the Administration, which included gas rationing. But this took some time to filter through and they were deep in Texas and within a day of the Mexican border before gas stations became difficult, asking for ration cards, which they didn't have, and then refusing to allow them more than a couple of gallons. Predictably, this annoyed Pat, who told his "boys" to drive on. But after a few more miles they had to stop, as the tank was getting dangerously low.

The station was set on the edge of what looked like a desert, and the single attendant refused to allow them more than four gallons.

"Are you kidding?" Hugo demanded. "This thing drinks gas like there was no tomorrow. We need to top her right up. Twenty-six gallons."

"You got a ration card?" the attendant inquired.

"No, we ain't got a ration card," Clem said. "But we gotta have gas."

"Four gallons," the attendant repeated.

Clem and Hugo looked at the back seat of the limmo, clearly expecting instructions to hold the place up.

"No trouble, Pat, please," Alison begged.

"No trouble," he promised, opened his door, and got out. "You the owner?" he asked politely.

"No, sir," the attendant said.

"Where's the owner?"

"He's in town, sir."

"Which town?"

"The one you must've just come through, sir."

Pat looked up at the overhead wires. "You got a telephone, son."

"Yes, sir."

"You get your boss on the line for me."

"Yes, sir. But I'se only doing what he told me."

"I'm sure you are, son. You get him on the line."

He bought Cokes for them all from the cool box while the boy telephoned.

"Mr Comber's on the line, sir."

"Thank you." Pat took the receiver. "Mr Comber? John Smith, here. Your boy won't sell me more than four gallons of gas. Yeah, I heard the news. Sure, I know what the Government said. No, I don't have my ration cards yet; I haven't had the time. But I sure do need that gas. Okay, okay. It's your decision. Now let me talk about something else, Mr Comber. You ever thought of selling this place? Sure, I'm serious. You can't be doing a lot of business out here, and with this rationing, you're gonna be doing a hell of a lot less. Sure, I want to buy it. Ten thousand? You have yourself a deal. Why, cash, of course. How soon can you get out here? Sure, bring a lawyer with you. We'll wait." He grinned at them. "Let's open that hamper."

They lunched.

"You seriously mean to buy this dump for ten thousand dollars?" Alison asked.

"Sure I do."

"To get twenty gallons of petrol? Wouldn't it be cheaper to pay taxes?"

"Forget it. Let's have some of that wine."

Mr Comber arrived an hour later, with a lawyer and a sheaf of papers.

"Look," Pat said. "All I want is vacant possession, now."

"Well, vacant possession will have to wait on completion of the contract," the lawyer said.

"Which is when?"

"Well . . . on payment of the money."

Pat nodded, signalled Clem, who brought out one of

the many little black valises he had packed in the the boot of the car. Pat unlocked it and flipped up the lid, while everyone, Alison included, gaped at the neat bundles of hundred dollar bills. Pat took one out and gave it to a totally bemused Comber. "A hundred hundreds, right. Now, do I own the station?"

Comber flicked the notes, looked at his lawyer.

"I guess you do, Mr Smith. May I ask where you got all of that money?"

Pat grinned. "I dug it out of the ground. Now, you guys want gas?"

"Nope. We got plenty of gas."

"Well, then, if you don't mind, you're cluttering up my forecourt."

"What about Joe, here?"

"Joe's working for me, now. That right, Joe?"

"Well . . . if you want me to, Mr Smith."

"Sure I do. Nice meeting you guys. Send the papers to Box 916, Central Post Office, New York."

Comber and his lawyer drove away, heads obviously still spinning.

"Okay, Joe. Fill her up," Pat said.

"But . . . the Government . . ."

"Joe," Pat said gently. "You're working for me, now. Right?"

Joe filled the tank, and Pat paid him six months' wages in advance.

"I'll be back to check up on how things are doing, in a couple of months," he said. "You take care." He sat beside Alison in the back seat of the limmo. "Let's go," he said, and grinned at her. "Happy?"

"You are a complete bastard," she said, and grinned back. "But I love you."

She couldn't help but mean it.

They crossed the border the next day, and continued on their way south. Now the stops were more primitive yet, and Alison became a little worried about the babies.

"When do we get to Mexico City?" she asked.

"We don't. Not on this trip. The *hacienda* comes first."

They reached it the day after they entered Mexico. They were, as they had been for twenty-four hours, bumping over a distinctly uneven surface which had Ben wailing – nothing seemed to make any difference to Shirley – when they came upon a small, rather ramshackle village nestling at the foot of some hills. They drove through this, while chickens scattered from beneath their wheels, dogs barked, and sleepy-looking Mexicans watched them from various nayas and windows, and beyond the houses they suddenly topped a slight rise to find themselves entering yet another arid valley, in the centre of which, still several miles away, there was a large patch of green and white.

"Just like an oasis," Pat said. "Hell, it *is* an oasis."

Alison craned her neck as they turned off the main road, and on to an even more potholed and stone-littered track.

"This car is going to be a write-off, Mr Pat," commented Hugo, who was behind the wheel. "What you need for this country is four-wheel drive."

"Then that's what we'll get," Pat said. "What do you think of your new home, honey?"

Alison's heart had already almost reached her sandals. Everywhere she looked was almost barren rock; the only vegetation was chapparal punctuated with yucca. Behind them the hills were undulating, as they were in the distance; to their left they rose almost into mountains, with sharp peaks; to their right they became a sort of tableland – the Spanish phrase-book she had been reading on the journey south called it a mesa. It was very hot, and the sun seemed to hang immediately over them; behind the car a plume of dust was rising into the still air. The only sign of civilisation, and it was a reassuring one, was the line of telegraph poles and the single wire strand, following the road from the village.

In the middle distance the white walls of the *hacienda* rose up like a fortress, and as they got closer she realised that it *was* a fortress: the walls were crenellated, and there were men up there looking down at them . . . she had no doubt they were armed.

"It's like stepping back a thousand years," she said in awe.

Pat decided she liked it. "Well, there weren't any Europeans here a thousand years ago. But it sure is something. I call it The Keep. You know, the sort of thing they used to have in the old Norman castles in England, the central donjon."

"The Keep," Alison muttered.

"You wait till you see inside."

Alison swallowed. The *hacienda* had obviously been built over a spring or a well, because there was some grass and a few trees outside the walls, but that did little to counter the prevailing aridity.

"What on earth did they ranch here?" she asked.

"Not a lot. The place was the country residence of some rich guy who lived in Mexico City. You won't believe this, but the city is only fifty miles away."

"You're right," she said. "I don't believe it."

But as the limousine approached the high, iron-reinforced wooden gates, these swung inwards, and Alison, who had been feeling vaguely sick when she thought of her beautiful New York apartment, gave a gasp and sat up straight.

The area enclosed by the walls was much larger than she had supposed. She looked first of all at a paved drive, on to which the car was at that moment moving with an almost real sigh of relief. To either side there were close-cut green lawns, watered by sprinklers. Further to the right was a flower garden, to the left were the stables, and she could tell there were several horses in there; further on there was a huge garage in which there were two automobiles.

There were also a great number of people, men and women, gathered to wave at her, and she could see several small and rather poor looking houses behind the flower beds.

In front of her was an inner wall with an archway, through which the limousine went, and this time she exclaimed in pleasureable consternation. Within the inner wall was a profusion of flowers to either side of the drive, together with huge shade trees. The drive ended beneath a roofed walkway, where there were white clad men and women waiting to unload them. One of these held the door for Alison, and she stepped out and looked at the swimming pool, which lay inside the portico.

She glanced at Pat, and he grinned. "You have to keep cool in this climate. We're situated over a virtually bottomless well."

The pathway led round the pool, and she entered the house itself. This was on one storey, save for a large central square upper suite. On the ground floor she looked through archways at cool marble floors, mosaic walls, comfortable chairs, a library, also open plan, a dining room and kitchen. From the main part of the house two wings stretched back towards another inner wall; the wings each contained four very large and beautifully appointed bedrooms, each *en suite*; two of them were fitted up as nurseries, and into these Hannah immediately carried the babies.

Pat escorted Alison up curving marble stairs into the master suite. The floor of the huge room was polished wood, although the bathroom was all in marble. The bed was the largest she had ever seen. There were four huge picture windows, screened to keep out insects, but all presently open to allow both the breeze to enter, and to give magnificent views of the mountains to every side.

110

Under each window there was also an airconditioning unit for when it grew too hot even for the breeze, or when the breeze died.

In the background a generator rumbled away quietly.

Alison walked from window to window, went into the bathroom, and came out again. Pat stood by the door watching her.

She raised her shoulders and let them fall again. "It's quite magnificent."

If only it were someplace else, she thought.

But Pat was happy. He swept her from the floor to hug her. "I knew you'd like it."

"It must have cost a fortune."

"A couple of hundred grand."

Money he could easily have paid in taxes to let them continue living in New York. But it seemed pointless to say it.

"Now I want you to meet David. Hey, Dave!" he bawled as they went back down the stairs. "Dave's my chief accountant. He's only been with me two years, but boy, is he is whizz."

They reached the foot of the stairs, and Alison paused in surprise, understanding why the accountant had only been with her husband for two years: he could hardly be older than his mid-twenties. Certainly, with his sharp features and his horn-rimmed spectacles he looked intelligent enough, but surely Pat's weakness for surrounding himself with very young people had reached absurdity here.

"Hi, Mrs Pat. David Brook."

He had a most attractive smile, and, unlike most of Pat's other human appendages, was not a great deal taller than Alison herself, and slender with it. She thought she might like him, and smiled back. "Hello, David."

"Dave was in charge of fixing the place up," Pat explained.

"Well, the architects did the work," David Brook said modestly. "I just paid the bills."

"Anything you want, just tell David," Pat said.

Alison smiled at him again.

"Where on earth did you find him?" she asked Pat when next they were alone.

"I wanted an accountant who'd be prepared to follow me out of the States. I advertised. Got a lot of replies. But I chose Dave. I like the guy. And he's keen. And loyal. That's what I want from my people, angelface. Loyalty!"

She couldn't help but wonder if she'd just been given a message.

That night Alison was awakened by the glare of lights. "What on earth . . ." she got out of bed and went to the windows, watched the searchlight beams criss-crossing the area outside the walls. "Don't tell me Mexico's in the war?"

"No chance of that," Pat answered from the bed. "Which is why we're here."

"But you keep men on the walls all night, and lights."

"Yeah, well, this is a poor country. There's a lot of banditry."

"And you really think this is the best place for us to bring up our children."

"Nobody's going to trouble anything belonging to Pat Grange. Those lights are just to remind people that we're awake in here."

Alison supposed one could get used to anything. Not that there was any real hardship involved in getting used to living at The Keep. If she could forget that it was set in the middle of a desert it was quite the most idyllic place she had ever known, and Pat had taken great care to stock it with her favourite music on gramophone records, and her favourite books in the library. There were servants to anticipate her every thought, or to stand by indulgently when she wished to cook something herself in the huge kitchen. There were horses and she slowly but surely mastered riding, while on her first visit to Mexico City she bought herself two Alsatian pups, both dogs, whom she named Romulus and Remus. They became her constant companions, and although she barred them from the bedroom, they slept at the foot of the stairs, and were always there to greet her when she came down in the mornings.

There was a market in the *pueblo*, where the people were all almost embarrassingly friendly – thanks to her knowledge of Portuguese she very quickly became fluent in Spanish despite some unexpected discrepancies between the two languages – and best of all there were weekly trips into Mexico City, to shop and eat at the best restaurants; often they booked into an hotel for the night in order to take in a show.

Much as Alison looked forward to such visits, they were always slightly alarming, because she knew that whoever was escorting her, whether it was Hugo, David Brook, or Pat himself, was always armed, but she was getting used to that. Her main problem was an entire lack of friends, whether male or female. David and Hugo and Clem were employees, and Pat was her husband. There was no intellectual stimulus other than listening to the radio, and that, for the first half of 1942, certainly, was a catalogue of gloom, for her as much as for anyone as Hong Kong and then Singapore fell, and both her brothers disappeared – no one knew whether they were alive or dead. She corresponded with Aunt Audrey, who was now her only living relative, at least available, but letters took a very long time to travel between Mexico and England and back again, and anyway, Audrey knew no more about the whereabouts of Tom and Harry than she did.

Alison even tried to persuade her aunt to come across to Mexico and live with her. Pat had no objection, and it would be such a treat to have someone to talk to. But Audrey would contemplate neither leaving England nor the journey.

"We *are* going home the moment the War ends?" Alison asked Pat.

113

"The very moment," he assured her.

How he was going to wangle that she had no idea, but she had to believe that he was going to manage it, practice patience, and pray for the shooting to stop.

And care for her steadily growing family. Pat paid his usual lengthy visits to Brazil, but when he was home he was as virile and in love with her as ever. Thus Patrick junior was born in 1943, and Stephanie in 1944.

The children in fact became the very centre of Alison's life, as she taught Ben and Shirley how to read and write, how to ride their ponies and how to swim, everything that she did herself. But at the same time she had to consider putting a stop to the sequence. She enjoyed a large family, but there were limits. She was not bothered about the effect it was having on her figure, which thanks to her regular exercise remained trim, and if her breasts grew larger and began to sag very slightly, this seemed to please Pat more than the original small, high mounds, while her overall health remained perfect. But she was still under twenty-five, and she knew it would have an effect if she went on too long. The trouble was, there was also a complete absence of contraceptive advice or devices in Mexico.

She broached the subject to Pat after Stephanie's birth. "Aw," he said. "I always wanted five."

She sighed. "Okay. One more. Then we're done. Promise?"

"Promise."

Her daily routine was only varied by the fact of being pregnant or not. She awoke at eight, and was served breakfast in bed. As soon as she had eaten, she was joined by the children; she fed each of them for three months but the others were always around for a romp, At nine she had a swim, dressed in a leisurely fashion,

114

and, when she was not pregnant, went for a ride, always accompanied by Hugo and several of the peons, armed with rifles, and with the dogs trotting at the horse's heels. If she was pregnant, she went for a walk instead, again with the dogs.

Returning from this, she spent an hour with the children, teaching Ben and Shirley, and, as they appeared, playing with Pat junior and Stephanie. Before lunch she sipped an aperitif on the sun porch, and after lunch she had a siesta. In the afternoons she again spent a couple of hours with the children, and in evenings she played chess or chequers with either Hugo or David, unless they were going into the city for a show.

When Pat was in residence he did as she, save that when she was with the children he was usually closeted in the office – which opened off the library and was the only totally private room in the living area of the house – with David.

Presumably it was a very odd existence for the self-styled richest man in the world, but David convinced Alison that Pat's claim was actually true. Apparently the mine had so far produced more than two billion dollars worth of gold, and there was as yet no indication of its running dry. "Of course a large proportion of that, just over a half, has gone on production costs and payment of investors." He paused, allowing Alison to understand what he was saying.

"But his share has still been more than a billion dollars," she said incredulously.

"That's right, Mrs Pat. Considerably more."

Which, she realised, even if it was producing nothing more than five per cent, would give him an income of more than fifty million dollars a year! For the first time she began to have some understanding of his reluctance to pay normal taxes on so vast a sum. Yet to go to these lengths . . .

"So he lives in the middle of a desert. What does he do with all this money?" Alison asked.

David grinned. "Invests it."

She brooded on that. "Where?"

"I'm sorry, Mrs Pat. You'll have to ask Mr Pat that."

She did, when next Pat was home. Then he grinned, and ruffled her hair. "You don't want to worry your pretty little head about things like that."

"Don't remind me, my business is looking after the kids, right."

"Well . . ."

"Pat, I want to ask you a question. Am I your wife? Or am I some kind of appendage, duly bought and paid for?"

"Now, honey, that's not fair. I told you, you want some money, just tell Dave."

"Pat, I do not wish for any money. I have nothing to spend it on. All I want to do is be your wife. Share. That's what marriage is all about. And if you tell me all we have to share is our bodies . . ."

"Of course we don't, sweetheart. But hell, there are a whole lot of men who don't discuss their finances with their wives."

"We are not a whole lot of people. We're you and me. I'm interested. Is that unreasonable?"

He gave one of his crooked grins. "Of course it isn't. Okay, I put most of it into real estate."

"Real estate?"

"Sure. Land. Property. It's the one thing in life that's guaranteed to go up, over any period of time."

"You mean you've been buying land here in Mexico?"

"Hell, no. Well, I've bought this place. But I've been buying land all over the place."

"Oh. Will I ever see any of it?"

"Sure. As soon as the War's over . . ."

"And I've stopped having babies," she said morosely. "That's when I get to see the mine too, right?"

"Right," he said enthusiastically.

*   *   *

Alison had to believe it was all going to happen, and by the summer of 1944 the future, and her release from The Keep, seemed close enough to touch. The Allies had invaded France and were streaming towards Germany, the Russians were into Poland and closing on Berlin, and the Americans were rolling up the Japanese in the Pacific. Now the news was all good. If only she had been able to learn something of Tom and Harry, Alison knew she could be totally happy.

But there was that fifth child Pat wanted. It came as something of a shock for her to realise that she was *not* pregnant, when he had been gone for two months. Now she wanted him to return more urgently than usual, so that she could complete her side of their bargain. She adored her children, and looked forward to the fifth . . . but she also wanted to enjoy being Mrs Pat Grange.

It was a very hot summer in the valley north of Mexico City, and in that respect Alison was relieved not to be pregnant. She rode every morning, and then returned for a long hour in the pool, with Ben and Shirley, who were both becoming strong swimmers. The heat was enervating, and even after a siesta she invariably collapsed into bed quite early in the evenings, to wake up in a swelter of sweat.

As she did one night in late August, to the sound of furious barking from the dogs, shots, and the glaring of searchlights. She sprang out of bed, pulled on her robe, and ran to the stairs.

David was at the foot, also wearing a dressing gown, and brandishing an automatic pistol. Beside him Romulus and Remus were highly excited.

"Someone got in," he gasped incredulously. "Someone actually got in."

He looked absolutely shaken.

"For God's sake put that thing away before you kill somebody," she told him, and went outside.

117

Here there were several of the servants gathered, chattering at each other. A moment later Hugo appeared, also carrying his gun.

"Will you please tell me what is going on?" Alison demanded.

"Some guy got up on to the wall, Mrs Pat."

"How?"

"Real old-fashioned stuff. He must have sussed the place out. Then he came along with a grapple which he threw up and lodged, shinned up the rope, and was over the battlements before you could say knife. Of course he was spotted almost immediately."

"So you all opened up as if the War had come to Mexico. Is he dead?"

"No. I don't even think they hit him. He jumped back down from the wall and disappeared into the dark. I went out to see if I could pick up his trail, but all I found was the rope and the grapple." He grinned. "He'll probably die of thirst, out there in the desert."

"You think he was just a burglar?"

"Had to be. Everybody knows Mr Pat is a millionaire. I guess they think he just leaves gold lying around waiting to be picked up."

"Hm." Alison supposed she should be reassured by the way the alarm had been handled – and also by the fact that the guards hadn't actually shot the man. "Well, I'm going back to bed."

David was still sitting in the library, his pistol dangling from his fingers, looking thoroughly dejected.

"I'm so sorry, Mrs Pat," he said. "So terribly sorry."

"You're talking as if it was your fault."

"Well . . . Mr Pat kind of left me in charge."

"Did he? I thought he'd left me in charge. And neither of us can possibly be responsible for some idiot trying to climb over the wall. Off you go to bed, and stop worrying about it."

*   *   *

118

She certainly intended to. Next day, when the police sergeant from the *pueblo* came out to nose around, photograph the place where the intruder had stood to hurl his grapple, and take the grapple itself away for "analysis", whatever that might mean, she showed only polite interest. But he had some ideas on what had happened.

"There was a stranger in the village, yesterday, *señora*," he told her.

"Meaning you don't think it was any of your people."

"Oh, no, *señora*. Our people would not do this. Señor Grange, he is too well known. The way his house is guarded is too well known. No, no. This stranger . . . he was a gringo."

Alison frowned, interested despite herself. "Do you know his name?"

"Oh, yes, *señora*. He stayed at the *pension* the night before last. His name is Smith."

"Ah," Alison said. "And is he still at the *pension*?"

"No. He had a motor car, parked along the road, and left in that. He had already checked out of the *pension*. We have sent a description and the number of the automobile to Mexico City. They will catch him."

"Señor Smith," Alison said.

Who on earth could it have been? Some enemy Pat had made during his hard years? Or since? Her mind immediately turned to Jonathan Carter. But Carter had totally rejected any idea of getting anything from Pat – when he could have picked up fifty thousand dollars from her without any difficulty.

Anyway, Jonathan Carter had not struck her as the sort of man who would try to break into the *hacienda* at night.

But if Pat did have that kind of enemy, she could understand his determination to turn his home into a fortress. And was grateful for it.

119

By the end of the week the incident was ancient history. But then a police captain drove out from Mexico City to see her. "Captain Guimard, Señora Grange."

"My pleasure, Captain. Have I committed a crime?"

"Oh, no, *señora*." His tone suggested he did not know how that could be possible. "No, no, it is about this gringo who tried to break in to the *hacienda*."

"Oh, yes. Señor Smith. Have you arrested him?"

"Alas, no, *señora*. He has got away and we think he has fled the country. But *señora*, we do not think his name was Smith."

"How odd," Alison remarked. "Neither do I."

Guimard raised his eyebrows. "Do you know this man?"

"I shouldn't think so. It is just that everyone in England or America who wishes to hide his real name, takes the name Smith. Or Jones. Or Brown."

"Oh, yes, I understand. The alias. In Spanish it is usually Garcia. But this man, we have traced his arrival in Mexico, and the car he hired, and we think we know his real name. We are wondering if you would know this name."

"Well, try me."

"It is Waller. Not a very usual name, eh?" He gazed at her. "Do you know this name, *señora*?"

Alison needed to think very quickly. There were suddenly a great many imponderables to be considered. But if the man had got out of Mexico, whoever he had been was no longer relevant – to a Mexican police officer . . . however relevant it might be to her. She gazed back. "No," she said. "I have never heard that name before, Señor Captain."

CHAPTER 5

Tragedy

When Pat came home for Christmas at the beginning of December 1944, he had with him a large, uncouth looking man, wrapped up in bandages.

"This is Tony Mayne," he explained. "My mine manager."

Alison had been anticipating this reunion with the usual mixture of anger and pleasure. Although she held Pat's double-dealing to be entirely responsible for the attempted break-in, and intended to insist upon an explanation, throughout the last year there had been no doubt that the War was won, certainly in Europe; it seemed just a matter of when Hitler was going to accept that fact. But one look at Mayne, whom she disliked on sight, upset her all over again, although she had to welcome him to her home.

"What's the matter with him?" she asked Pat when they were alone.

"He's been shot. More than once."

"Shot? You mean he's been in the army?"

"None of my people are in the army," Pat reminded her. "We have our own wars to fight. A bunch of Venezuelans came over the border to raid us, see what they could take. Oh, we saw them off, all right, but Tony stopped two in the process."

Alison took a deep breath. To think that this was

apparently going on all the time, without her knowing anything about it.

"He's actually quite badly hurt," Pat said. "They got the bullets out, but I think he ought to stay here until he's fully recuperated."

"And when are *you* going to stop one?" she asked. "Or maybe two?"

He ruffled her hair. "The bullet ain't made which is gonna stop Pat Grange," he said.

As always, his total, arrogant, confidence both annoyed and frightened her . . . but he had been proved right so often in the past. And there was too much else on her mind, as that night in bed she told him about Waller.

"Holy shit!" he commented. "You never mentioned it in your letters."

"Would it have done any good?"

"Well . . . but the thought of some madman breaking in here . . ."

"I was well looked after. Less, I may say, by hulking Hugo, than by Dave Brook."

"I told you he was a good man."

"And you were right, as usual. Now tell me why Geoff Waller's brother, or whoever he was, should try to break in here, after that letter we had from his mother?"

"How the hell should I know? Like I said, the guy was probably a nut."

"That's what the police said, too."

"Well, then . . ."

"It just stinks to me. I wrote to Mrs Waller."

"Did you now? You have her address?"

"It was on her letter. But she seems to have gone away. Mine was returned, addressee unknown."

"Yeah. Well, if she has a nut as a son, I don't blame her for moving on. If it was Waller."

"Why on earth would anyone else take the trouble to adopt the identity of Geoff Waller's brother?"

"Yeah, that's a point. Well, I sure am glad things worked out as they did. Remind me to give Dave a raise. And a pat on the head."

"Yes. I have to say I shall be very happy to brush the dust of this place from my feet. It always did give me the creeps. But now . . ."

"Hell, honey, I thought you liked The Keep."

"Oh, Pat . . . I know how much you spent on it, and how you've gone to so much trouble to make it a home for me, but . . . I'm a people person. Being stuck out in the middle of a desert isn't my idea of living. The War *is* going to be over next year, isn't it?" she asked, as she nestled in his arms.

"Sure. In Europe, anyway. Japan may want to hold on a bit longer, but I'm not sure they can do it."

"Europe's what I'm interested in," she said. "Oh, Pat . . . can we really go home?"

"That's what we're going to do."

"But how? What about the taxes?"

"That's all taken care of."

She sat up. "How?"

"Money, doll. That's the secret in this world. I donated those Spitfires to the Government, didn't I?"

"Ye-es."

"Well, that's a cachet for a start. But in addition, Churchill is committed to an election, the moment Germany surrenders. Now, what all these guys need is money. That's where people like me come in handy."

"You mean you've been subscribing to Conservative Party Funds?"

"God, no. I've been subscribing to Labour Party Funds."

Alison sat up and drove both hands into her hair. "You've lost me. You, Patrick Grange, are supporting socialism?"

"Christ, when you do that, your tits send me wild."

123

He threw both arms round her to bring her down to him.

"Pat," she protested. "Pat, we're having a serious discussion." But she couldn't resist his love-making.

Although she didn't lose the thread. "Explain," she commanded, when they lay against each other in a pool of sweat.

"I believe Labour is going to win the election."

"That's absurd. How can Churchill ever lose? After he's led the country right through the War?"

"Wait and see. Goddam, doll, you grow more beautiful every time I see you."

He was like a young boy. But she was still thinking ahead.

"And you believe you can do some kind of a tax free deal with Labour?" she asked when he simmered down.

"I can do a tax free deal with anyone," Pat said drowsily. He was forty-four, and twice in one night was exhausting even for him.

Once again, she had to believe him. What she hadn't reckoned was that he would be leaving Tony Mayne behind when he returned to Brazil in February.

"He's still a sick man," Pat explained. "This desert air is good for him. And I need him, just as soon as he's fit again."

"So I'm supposed to entertain him," she grumbled. "What are we running here, some kind of rest home? I don't even like the man."

"He'll grow on you," Pat said. "And even wounded, he's a good man to have around if any other nutter tries to get at you."

"There's something I have to tell you," she said.

"Give."

"I think number five is on the way."

"Sweetheart!"

"Just one month, mind."

"Sweetheart!" he said again, and kissed her.

The timetable for ending the European War had seemed to be upset by the Battle of the Bulge, but once that was sorted out it was clearly no more than a matter of weeks. Pat promised to be back the very moment Germany surrendered. Just supposing that didn't happen until the autumn, he would be back anyway for the birth of the baby.

Her last, Alison thought happily. Then she was going to accompany Pat *everywhere*. She now had two new nannies, Mexicans under Hannah's tutelage, and interviews immediately started for a third. She also had a Mexican personal maid named Lucia, a cheerful, happy girl, was good friends with all of the peons and their wives, spoke Spanish like a native, and felt totally in command of her surroundings. But she still looked forward to packing up The Keep and moving to England. When she remembered the callow, somewhat frightened young girl who had departed on the *Queen Mary* nearly six years before . . .

Pat had insisted upon giving her a little revolver, after the Waller incident. She had always hated the thought of guns, the more so perhaps because she was surrounded by them. But she found her new toy rather fun, and every morning would bang away at glass bottles which Hugo set up for her in the desert, thinking all the while what a ridiculous hobby it was for a pregnant woman, but becoming quite a good shot in the process.

She found herself even enjoying Tony Mayne. She did not think she could ever like the man. There was something essentially coarse about him. Of course, Pat was coarse in many ways, in his language, his outlook . . . but Alison had always felt that was a deliberate policy, a kind of juvenile "fuck you" for the years when

125

he had been laughed at for his dream. Mayne was simply, a coarse man.

Like all of Pat's employees, he was utterly loyal, and again like all of Pat's employees – except, perhaps, David Brook – he appeared to be terrified of the diminutive Mrs Pat. Alison suspected that around the campfire in Brazil – supposing they still sat around campfires – Pat regaled his staff with tales of the tough little girl he had married. She rather enjoyed the idea of that, even if she felt it was wholly false; if Brook and Hugo had proudly told Pat how unafraid she had been on the night of Waller's break-in, it had just never occurred to her that she had anything *to* fear, surrounded as she was by armed men.

Again, like all of Pat's employees – except, perhaps, David Brook – Mayne seemed to have fallen desperately in love with her. Well, she reflected, there was nobody else around. But this meant he enjoyed sitting up with her after dinner, and she soon discovered that he had a weak head: after a couple of brandies, he became extremely talkative.

"Tell me about the early days," she suggested.

"Those were great," Mayne said, leaning back in his chair, the balloon glass drooping at the end of his fingers. "Course, when I got out there the first time, Pat was already developing the mine. You have no idea, Mrs Pat, of what was involved. He had to cut a road through the bush, and then haul all of that heavy machinery up from Caracarai to Boa Vista . . . getting it to Caracarai at all was one hell of an operation."

"How did you go to work for Pat in the first place?"

"Answered an advert. He was already having trouble with Leighton."

"Who was Leighton?"

Mayne raised his eyebrows. "Pat never told you about Leighton?"

"Pat and I don't talk business much," Alison said.

"Oh. Well, maybe . . ."

"I'd like to know. Really."

"Well . . ." again Mayne hesitated. "I guess you know about Alvarado?"

"Oh, of course," Alison lied. But at least she knew the name.

"Well, Leighton was a pal of Alvarado, as I see it. Pat had to have Alvarado. He had to have a Brazilian front. So I reckon it was Alvarado who put Leighton up to be the first site manager. Leighton had some capital available, too, which was a help. So he was given shares in the Company."

"You mean there was a company?"

Mayne goggled at her. "You didn't know there's a company?"

"Pat never tells me anything about the business. Let me top you up," Alison said, and poured some more Hine Antique. "Tell me about the Company."

"El Dorado Incorporated," Mayne said.

"Makes sense. And this man Leighton had shares."

"Yeah. He got ten per cent. Same as Alvarado."

"I see. Who else had shares. Did you have any?"

"Not me, Mrs Pat. I had nothing to put in. I'm strictly an employee."

"So the rest was all Pat's."

"Well . . . I guess so."

"Right. Now, you say Pat was having trouble with Leighton?"

"Yeah. Well, they didn't see eye to eye in a lot of ways."

"So what happened?"

"Well, I don't really know, Mrs Pat. But anyway, Leighton got the push . . ."

"How could he get the push if he owned ten per cent of the Company?"

"Search me. Pat must've wangled it somehow. Anyhow, he got the push, and Pat brought me in as Site Manager."

"When was this?"

"Ah . . . end of '38."

"I see. What happened to Mr Leighton?"

"Oh, he was one of those born losers, Mrs Pat. I guess he took what happened hard. He committed suicide."

Alison drank some brandy herself; she was feeling vaguely sick. "When did he do this?"

"Ah . . . would've been late spring '39. Yeah, that's it. Late spring '39." He grinned at her. "Say, that's when you married the boss, wasn't it?"

"Yes," Alison said grimly.

"You don't want to get any wrong ideas," Mayne said hastily. "Mr Pat is tough. Well, he has to be, in his business and in that country. But you play straight with him, and he's the best boss I've ever worked for. He has guts, too. Like that time the canoe overturned on the river. Now, you know that Mr Pat has a kind of phobia about water . . ."

"Phobia?"

"He's never told you about that? Well, I guess there are some things men don't talk about. Mr Pat has this thing about getting his head under water. Some kind of claustrophobia. But there he was, straight down something like six feet when that boat capsized. But he got himself ashore. He was white as a sheet, and shaking . . . but he made it."

Alison drank some more brandy, holding the glass with both hands, because she was shaking too.

"I didn't mean to scare you, Mrs Pat."

Alison finished her drink, her nerves slowly settling. "I'm not scared," she said. But she was . . . only not of what had nearly happened to Pat. "You mean Mr Pat would never voluntarily put his head under water?"

"No, ma'am. No way."

Alison sat up in bed staring out of the windows at the mountains, and the stars, which seemed close enough to touch.

What have I done? she asked herself. Why, married a strong and ruthless man. She had known that, and admired him for it. She had wanted someone strong enough and ruthless enough to lift her out of the mediocrity she had seen all around her.

But a man with some dark secrets who was also a congenital liar. Hadn't she known that from the beginning, and always been willing to be talked out of it, for the sake of the strength and the ruthlessness?

Now it was too late. Too late even to ask him about it. If she could give a shudder of revulsion that he should have been courting her so splendidly while his erstwhile partner was descending into the pit of despair, there was yet no evidence to indicate that the fault was Pat's. Mayne knew nothing of what had actually happened between them. Leighton might have sold his shares back because he doubted the viability of the Company, and killed himself when he realised what a fool he had been. It was not a line of thought she would ever be able to understand, or even sympathise with . . . but people did do that sort of thing.

There could be any one of a million reasons for what had happened, none of which had anything to do with Pat. Necessarily.

Just as there was surely a reason why he had lied to her about personally diving to the bottom of the lake. It seemed such a childish thing to have have done.

Just as there could be any one of a thousand and one reasons, for this Bert Waller to have tried to kill her . . . if that was what he had been trying to do.

It was just that everyone who became associated with Pat – Jonathan Carter, Geoffrey Waller, the man Leighton, and how many others of whom she knew nothing? – had been left holding the short stick.

Yet was even that Pat's fault? Even Carter, who had certainly radiated dislike or even hatred for Pat, had not gone so far as to accuse him of any crime. That had been left to the gossip columnists.

From then on she didn't ask Mayne any more questions. She didn't want to know.

And it all became irrelevant when Germany surrendered.

Then it was just a matter of waiting for Pat. But Alison commenced packing immediately.

"You'll have to stay here on your own," she told Mayne. "At least until you can make other arrangements."

"You're not meaning to sell The Keep?" he asked.

"I have no idea. But *I* have no intention of living here, ever again. This was strictly a wartime expedient."

"Heck, it's just beautiful here," he protested.

"If you don't happen to like people," she agreed.

Hugo of course would be accompanying them, together with Hannah. She wasn't sure about the Mexican nannies, but she knew Hannah had to have help, especially with her now well into her pregnancy.

"I'll see to it, Mrs Pat," David said. "Once you're settled in England, we can replace them with English nannies."

"You are a treasure, Dave," she said.

She meant it. He was always so calm and collected, always knew the right thing to say or do. She could understand why Pat had gone for him from the beginning.

And in addition he was always so perfectly mannered, at least as regards her. There was never the slightest sign of male interest. Perhaps he too was "ambidextrous", as Pat put it . . . although she doubted it. In his own quiet way, Dave Brook was very macho.

Perhaps he simply did not go for small blondes. Which was at once a pity and a relief.

"You *are* coming with us?" she asked.

"Well, I don't know, Mrs Pat. That's up to the boss. I'm obviously going to be where his main finances are

130

situated, and I doubt that'll be England. Any tax concessions he wins will be for his personal income. Not his companies."

"How many companies does he have?"

David grinned. "Quite a few. One for every country in which he owns property."

Pat was home at the end of the month, full of plans, and full of aggravation as well.

"Shitting Yanks won't give me a visa," he growled. "Not even to transit. So fuck them."

He was so agitated Alison decided against any questions about Leighton or water right that minute. Besides, she was too excited at the thought of what lay ahead.

And then dejected when she discovered that the dogs would either have to stay behind or go into six months' quarantine.

"Six months!"

"Yeah, they have some real peculiar laws over there. But that's where you want to live, right?"

She had no reply to make to that.

They drove to Vera Cruz, in a motorcade of three cars, and caught a ship for Kingston, Jamaica. It took time both to organise the departure from The Keep, and to find the passage, and it was the beginning of July before they finally set out. Alison didn't mind; they were going home. She wrote to Aunt Audrey to tell her, and as usual begged for news of her brothers. But there was none, and Japan was still very much in the War.

"You going to sell The Keep?" Alison asked Pat, the night before they left.

"No way. I love this place. And so do you."

"I don't love it. It's very beautiful, and maybe if it were set somewhere civilised I'd never want to leave. But right now it gives me the creeps."

131

"You're not still upset about that guy trying to break in?"

"I never was upset, as you put it, about that. I only wish I knew what had happened to him."

"Guys like that always fade into the woodwork, where they belong," he told her. "We don't have time for losers."

His philosophy. But hers as well, now, she supposed. The important thing was, she was going home. And that didn't even mean Sao Paolo, any more.

The *SS Ciudad de Matanzas* was not quite up to the class of even the old *Antilles*. Alison was appalled to discover that there were only four cabins available. That meant David did indeed have to stay behind, but he accepted the decision with good grace. Even so, as Alison and Pat needed a cabin, and Hugo and Clem shared another – their close friendship convinced Alison that Pat had been right about them from the start – it left only two cabins for three nurses and four children. The dogs remained on deck in wooden kennels.

"For Chrissake," Pat snapped when Hannah complained. "It's only for two nights."

"This really is appalling," Alison pointed out, after she'd sampled dinner. "Aren't you the richest man in the world?"

"There's a war on, honey," he reminded her. "Still. Even money can't buy what isn't there."

Jamaica was a delight, especially after the voyage. If the sun was just as hot as in Mexico, the heat was tempered by a cooling sea breeze. Better yet, the people actually seemed pleased to see the famous Patrick Grange, and couldn't do too much for him and his wife. But Pat's simmering ill-humour intensified when he was told that neither himself, Hugo, nor Clem would be allowed to carry their guns on to the aircraft; they would have to be given to the pilot, and they would be impounded upon arrival in London.

"Does it matter?" Alison asked. "You don't need a gun in England." She had left hers behind at The Keep.

"Yeah?" Pat demanded. "Suppose that crazy guy Waller is on the loose?"

Alison supposed that a lot of people would say Pat was becoming a megalomaniac. But she understood he was nervous. She did not know, because he would not tell her, what exactly he had proposed to the Labour Party, but obviously their future depended upon the outcome of the General Election.

This took place on 26 July, two days after the arrival of the Grange *entourage*. Pat's presence in Jamaica had been noticed and passed on to England, and he was greeted at Croydon Airport by a barrage of flashing cameras and eager reporters; there was even a television camera together with one from Movietone. They were surrounded by questions, to all of which Pat gave blandly non-committal answers, much to Alison's relief, although that they were well-informed was proved when someone asked, "There's a rumour you're backing Labour in the Election, Mr Grange."

Pat grinned at him. "Aren't you?"

Alison was preoccupied with seeing Romulus and Remus into the quarantine van; they seemed perfectly happy, still excited by the trip and all the new sounds and smells they had encountered. "When can I visit them?" she asked.

"Well, not for a fortnight, madam. That's to give them time to become used to their kennelmaid," the man explained. "After that, well, whenever you choose. But we don't recommend it. It unsettles the dogs, you see. It would be best just to leave them for the six months." He gave an encouraging smile. "Don't worry, it may seem

133

a big chunk out of a dog's life, but they can't tell time, and they'll remember you."

"Um," Alison said, nott the least convinced.

Pat had taken the entire seventh floor at the Savoy, with instructions that no one save staff or members of his party were to be allowed on it, and it was possible to relax. But it was a piping hot July, and Alison wanted to explore London. She rested on the 25th, but next day took Ben and Shirley to the zoo, accompanied by Hugo and Hannah. They managed to get away without being noticed, and had an exciting if to her, somewhat horrifying day: however much she had read the newspapers and watched the newsreels, the extent of the bomb damage appalled her – it was difficult to believe anyone had survived.

"So they had a rough time," Pat agreed. "But they won in the end. That makes it worthwhile."

Alison wondered if he could possibly be right, just as she wondered that he had apparently made no attempt to discover if his family were all right; they lived in the north but London was not the only city which had been half destroyed. But when Pat developed a grudge, even against his own flesh and blood, it seemed to go very deep.

That evening she and Pat sat up listening to the election results on the radio. When they went to bed, some time after midnight, it was clear that Labour had indeed won, with a substantial majority.

"A landslide," Pat said with satisfaction.

"How on earth did you know?"

He tapped his nose. "I may never have voted in my life. But I know a bit about politics."

The next week Pat was entirely bound up with meeting people. Alison was content that this should be so. It enabled her to explore the ruined city, be with the children, and go to visit Aunt Audrey.

Aunt Audrey was looking very old; it was difficult to accept that it was only six years since they had last met.

"Why, Alison," she said. "You've put on weight."

"I'm pregnant, silly."

"Oh! Again?" She hugged and kissed Ben and Shirley as well. As usual, Alison had left Pat Junior and Stephanie at the hotel. "And this is number . . .?" she looked at Alison's stomach.

"Number five."

"You have been a busy girl." Hannah and Conchita, one of the Mexican nurses, took the children into the park across the road to play, reluctantly accompanied by Hugo, and Audrey sat beside Alison on the sofa and held her hands. "Do you always walk around with an *entourage*?"

"I'm afraid I do."

"What's it really feel like to be rich?"

Quite apart from the "*entourage*", she could tell that by just looking at the clothes Alison was wearing, so different to anything seen on the street of drab and couponed Britain.

Alison smiled. "It sometimes makes you feel guilty."

"I don't see why it should." The fingers tightened. "Although these dreadful Socialists are going to try. Isn't it awful?"

"Well," Alison said. "Pat was supporting them. *Is* supporting them."

"A man like Pat, supporting Labour?"

"He thinks it may be a good thing."

She didn't want to be drawn into Pat's reasons, and to her relief Audrey didn't press the matter. Instead she thought for a few minutes, then asked, "Are you happy, Alison?"

"Well, of course I am," Alison lied. "What made you ask that?"

"Just your eyes."

"Oh, I suppose I'm a little tired. I've had an exhausting time, recently."

135

"Of course you have. I wondered if you'd been upset by all the things that are being written about Pat."

Alison frowned. "What things?"

"Oh, they're accusing him of all sorts of things."

"They always do." Pat had refused to buy a paper since landing, as if he had known the reception he was going to get from the press.

"It doesn't bother you?"

"We get used to it," Alison told her.

But the atmosphere remained strained; Alison couldn't escape the feeling that perhaps Aunt Audrey was actually on the side of the newspapers.

She was glad to get home, and to find Pat in a high good humour.

"I'm to get a KCB," he announced.

"Oh, Pat!" She threw both arms round his neck. "When?"

"Well, the New Year's List."

"Oh, great! I'll be presentable again by then."

"Good thing too. We'll have to go to the Palace. You'll be Lady Grange."

"Lady Grange," she said, and sat down. The Palace. She'd meet the King and Queen! Oh, how splendid it would have been had Mummy and Daddy been alive for this. Or even Tom and Harry. But of course Tom and Harry were alive.

It would be one in the eye for Aunt Audrey.

"When can we start house-hunting?" she asked.

"Ah . . . in a day or two."

Alison had heard Pat speak like that before, and her stomach immediately tied itself into knots.

"Just what do you mean?"

"There are one or two small points to be cleared up," he explained. "We'll start house-hunting next week."

*   *   *

Alison remained uneasy, but he refused to tell her what was going on, and she had to be patient. For two more days. Then the predictable storm broke.

"God, what a swindle!" Pat raged when he came in. "For the past three years they've been happy to accept one hell of a lot of money from me, and now . . . well fuck them."

"Pat, will you please tell me what's happened?"

"They won't do a deal, that's what's happened. They'll give me a K, and they'll be happy to have me back . . . but I pay taxes at the going rate like everybody else, and on my worldwide income."

"Is that so very bad?"

"Bad?" he shouted. "Bad? Ninety-eight percent. Ninety-fucking-eight! Bad?"

It did seem an astronomical figure.

"All my income is unearned, in their eyes," Pat said. "*Unearned*!"

"But surely there are ways round it? Companies and things?"

"Oh, sure. We can cut it down. But it's still gonna be more than fifty per cent. You think I worked my guts out in that jungle for twelve years to pay half of it to any government? You think I need my head examined?"

Alison tried to fight back the waves of panic clawing at her mind. "What are you going to do?"

"We leave here tomorrow. They can keep their god-damned knighthood."

"Where are we going, Pat?"

"Back to The Keep."

She stared at him, unable to believe her ears.

"The Keep?"

"That's our home, ain't it?"

"No! That was never our home. It was a temporary refuge. Like an air-raid shelter. You promised me we'd leave it, as soon as the war was over."

"Well, we're gonna have to live there a while longer, until I can suss out someplace else."

"No!" Alison said again. "No, no, no!"

"Now, look, honey, there is absolutely no point in your having hysterics. We are going back to The Keep, and that's final." He grinned. "You'll be able to get the dogs out of quarantine, after only a fortnight."

"I am *not* going back to The Keep. And *that's* final. You have lied to me for the last time."

"Lied?"

She panted with a mixture of fear and anger. "Telling me you dived for that gold yourself, when everyone knows you're terrified of water. And what about Mark Leighton? How do I know you ever really tried to get in touch with the Wallers? I don't believe you did. That's why my letter was returned, addressee unknown; that letter supposed to be from Mrs Waller was just a fake, wasn't it?"

"You have been a busy little bee," he commented. "Mayne, I suppose. He never could hold his liquor."

"Pat, I am not going back to The Keep."

They glared at each other, then Pat gave her one of his crooked grins. "Okay, sweetheart, if that's what you want to do, you stay here. I'm leaving tomorrow morning. I'll just tell Hannah to get the kids packed up."

"You're not taking the children. You wouldn't dare!"

"Who's gonna stop me?" Pat asked.

Alison felt like hitting him. But he might just hit her back. Presumably she could get some kind of a court order . . . but not before tomorrow morning. If she could even then. As far as anyone knew, The Keep *was* their home. It would take too long to convince an absolute stranger of a magistrate that, having lived there in apparent contentment for four years, she now hated it. If only Tom were here . . . but he wasn't.

Pat grinned at her. "Like to change your mind?"

"I hate you," she said. "I do. I hate you."

Pat kissed her on the forehead. "Everyone does, from time to time. You'll get over it."

* * *

But she realised, as the ship ploughed them back from Kingston to Vera Cruz, she was not going to get over it. And even if she could, he wouldn't. He was too aware of his guilt. He had lied to her almost from the moment he had proposed. Maybe from before that. He had twisted facts and made up stories, and every time she had come up against something quite unpalatable, she had allowed herself to be persuaded that it was as he claimed. Now she had to accept the fact that he was going to go on twisting and telling her lies for the rest of his life.

Just as he had to face the fact that she was no longer going to believe him, about anything.

And she was bearing his child, for the fifth time. At least that prevented a crisis over sex; she had no desire ever to have him inside her again.

Yet after all the exertions it was a relief to get back to the peace of The Keep, with her horses and dogs beside her, to the quiet sympathy of David, who made absolutely no comment on the abrupt change of plans.

Her own plans were very slowly hardening, but she kept them entirely to herself. The baby came first, and Harry Grange was born in October 1945. As with the others, she fed him for three months, but in the new year, as soon as Pat had departed back for Brazil, thankfully taking Mayne, now fully recuperated, with him – he seemed to bear the manager no ill-will for his various confessions – she put them into action.

By then it was in any event obvious, at least to her, that their marriage was over. Whether or not Pat understood it she couldn't be sure, but even after the baby was born he had made no effort to sleep with her, had moved into one of the downstairs bedrooms, although he remained unfailingly polite. Presumably he was waiting for her to get over her huff, as he considered it.

"I really could do with some new clothes," she told David after Pat and Mayne had been gone a week. "And

139

a bit of a break. Do you think anyone would raise any objections if I visited New York?"

"I don't see why they should," he said. "Pat's the one who's black-listed."

"I mean, there's no chance I'll be arrested and held until Pat pays his back taxes?"

David smiled. "I don't think so, Mrs Pat. Uncle Sam does get riled up about people who don't pay their taxes, but he doesn't go around kidnapping their wives. I'll see about getting you a visitor's visa."

He raised no objection either when she determined to travel alone. Hugo was furious, and protested most strongly, but Alison refused to reconsider.

"I'm one hell of a lot safer travelling on my own," she told him. "I'm a big girl, now."

He went off in a sulk and she knew he was going to be writing or wiring Pat, but there was no way Pat could do anything about it. He was being hoist on his own petard, in taking himself off to the wilds again.

She was in any event sure he had a mistress – at least one – down there. As if it mattered, now.

But it might be important. She had to be very sure what she was doing. It wasn't the money; she wanted possession of the children.

Although there had been no difficulty in obtaining a temporary visa, in order to keep the lowest possible profile, Alison flew Economy from Mexico City to Miami, and if her heart kept going pitter-patter as she waited in the line at Immigration, while the officials consulted their huge books in which presumably all unwanted visitors were listed, no comment was made when she presented her passport, and she was through in a few minutes.

Then she caught a Grayhound Bus up the coast, enjoying the sensation of being utterly alone, and utterly incognito. Although it was February, and she knew it was going to be very cold in New York, she had brought none of her furs with her, and wore a plain woollen coat.

She had booked herself in at a cheap hotel off the Avenue of the Americas, the Universal – she couldn't remember where she had got the name but she knew it had once been recommended to her as excellent value for money – and once in her room, late as it was, telephoned one of the lawyers the Ruthvens had introduced her to when she lived in New York, at his home.

"Alison Grange?" He sounded incredulous, but also delighted. "You mean you're here in New York? Why didn't you let us know you were coming?"

"It's been rather rushed. Al . . . may I have an appointment?"

"You mean, businesswise?"

"Yes."

There was the briefest of hesitations. But obviously Al would know there was only one possible reason for Alison Grange to seek a business appointment with a divorce attorney.

"Sure," he said. "Look, I'll have to check my diary with my secretary. We'll call you."

"It's urgent, Al."

"Sure," he said again. "I'll see you tomorrow. That's a promise."

His secretary called in the morning to say that Mr Boskis's diary was full, but would Mrs Grange care to have lunch?

"Yes," Alison agreed.

Predictably Al knew a quiet little trattoria where the food was genuinely Italian and they could have a corner table and be almost as private as in his office.

"Problems?" he asked, winding his spaghetti expertly round his fork.

Alison prefered to chop hers up with a soup spoon and

141

eat it like a cereal. In between mouthfuls she told him everything she could think of, relevant to her situation.

"Not too strong a case," he commented. "You could try for mental cruelty, I guess. But . . . it'd be a toughie. And there's something else."

"What?" she asked, her heart sinking.

"Our divorce laws have no jurisdiction in Mexico." He grinned. "I don't reckon there's a hell of a big chance of you getting Pat, and all the kids, into the States. Then you wouldn't have to divorce him; the Government would lock him up."

"As you say, there is no chance whatsoever of that. Are you telling me I can't divorce him? What about in England?"

"Same would apply. You can walk away from him, and you can probably obtain a divorce . . . here at least. I don't think they go for mental cruelty in the UK. But that would be meaningless, in your context. Unless you could take the kids with you first, and simply refuse to give them back. But you'd be getting into very murky water. As for money, he could just turn off the tap as he chose."

She gazed at him. "Are you telling me I am stuck?"

"Well . . . I'm doing myself out of a fee. But seriously, Alison, running out on Pat Grange would be the least sensible thing you can do. And there doesn't seem any reason for it. So he runs his business the hard way. He's a hard man. So he's told you a few lies. Show me the husband who's never lied to his wife. So he refuses to pay taxes. Lucky him to be able to do that. But tell me this: has he ever hit you, roughed you up?"

"Well . . . no, not really."

"Doesn't he keep you in style to which any princess would like to become accustomed?"

"Let me ask *you* something, Al: whose side are you on?"

"Yours, baby. Believe me. And with that in mind, my professional advice would be, your best course is to stay married to Pat. Of course . . ." he looked at her past his glass of wine. "You could get your own back . . . so long as you did it safely."

"With you? You are a shit, Al Boskis."

Al grinned. "Seems a shame to be up here all on your own, and without a soul knowing who you are, and just waste it."

Alison reckoned he had been called a shit before.

But she couldn't think of a way round his advice. She returned to her hotel, lay on the bed and stared at the ceiling, and realised that he was absolutely right. Pat was an all or nothing man. That had been conclusively proved in his relations with his family. The world consisted of him, his friends, and his enemies. He could count his friends on the fingers of one hand – and they were all his employees. In a real sense that even went for George Ruthven.

And her. At least, once upon a time.

The moment one ceased to be a friend, one became an enemy. She had had sufficient evidence of that. If she became an enemy he would cut off her money without the slightest hesitation. And if he had never in the remotest sense been a loving or caring father – the children, as he had told her so often, were her business – he would still never give them up, just to spite her.

She sat up. She could, she supposed, rush back down to The Keep, collect them, and flee. But *could* she do that? Her account in New York had been closed just so it couldn't be sequestered. Whenever she wanted money, whenever she wanted anything, she merely asked David, who always obliged. But would David organise an escape for her? He was Pat's man. And what of Hugo and Hannah? They were Pat's people. Even more were the Mexicans.

She was quite trapped.

Staring at walls wasn't going to help. She got up and

went downstairs to the hotel bar. It was just past six and the place was packed with men having several quick drinks before beginning their journeys home. She didn't like the look of it at all, and went into the lounge instead, pressed the bell for service and got none, walked up and down in a growing fury . . . and gazed at Jonathan Carter.

For a moment Alison was too surprised to speak.

"Mrs Grange?" Carter asked. "I saw you from inside the bar."

"Don't tell me you're staying here."

"As a matter of fact, I am. I always do, when I'm in New York."

Alison snapped her fingers in dismay. That was where she had got the name of the hotel from, deep in her subconscious memory. How idiotic could you get.

But he was smiling at her. "Would you like a drink? I'm afraid the service isn't very good, but I'll fetch one from the bar."

She hesitated, then thought, why not? It would be getting one back at Pat in a slightly more civilised manner than recommended by Al Boskis. "I would love a drink. Scotch."

"Soda and ice?"

"On the rocks," she told him. "No soda."

She watched him shoulder his way into the throng. He had filled out somewhat since last she had seen him, and was now a big, strong man. And a confident one. He was back in five minutes with the drinks, and sat beside her on a rather uncomfortable sofa.

"How! If I may say so, I would never have expected to see you in a dump like this."

"I'm keeping a low profile."

"Ah! Then Pat isn't with you."

"No. Pat isn't very popular in the States."

"I get the message. So you have to sneak in and out like a thief. Is it worth it?"

144

Alison finished her drink.

"Forgive me," he said. "Sour grapes. May I get you another?"

"Why not?"

He was a handsome man, too. More handsome than she remembered.

Get your own back, Al Boskis had recommended. God, what an idea.

"Shall we share a table at dinner?" Carter suggested.

"Why not? And you can tell me about your war. And what you're doing here."

He had had a good war, come out of it as group captain with DFC and bar. Now he was into buying and selling war surplus. "There's a lot of it about."

"I can imagine."

"Tell me about *your* war."

"I spent it in a Mexican desert."

He poured wine. Coming on top of her two neat whiskies she began to feel tight.

"With Pat."

"Some of the time." She giggled. "I have five children."

"I know."

She raised her eyebrows.

"Let's say I'm interested."

"In Pat? You should've accepted the money. Hell, you earned it, even if you weren't there at the kill."

"I am not the least interested in Pat, or his money, Alison," Carter said.

They gazed at each other, and she blinked as she lost focus. But her brain was still working. "You reckon on getting your revenge some other way."

"I reckon fate is playing us along," Carter said seriously. "First time around, I deliberately came to see you. To hate you. To spit in your eye. Instead . . . I think I fell in love with you."

Alison drank some more wine, then realised she had made a mistake.

"But this meeting . . . pure chance. And yet, not pure chance. You're only here because I told you about it."

Now his face was going round and round.

"Would you take me up to my room, please," she said. "And do hurry."

He hesitated only a moment, then grabbed her arm and rushed her to the elevator. Her stomach went down, and came up again. She drew long breaths, making herself stay with it, for just another few seconds. Her key had been on the table beside her. Jonathan Carter inserted it in the latch and the door swung open. She scattered across the bedroom, her shoes coming off, and reached the bathroom, sank to her knees, and wrapped both arms round the toilet bowl. Time ceased to have meaning.

Slowly the room settled down, and she could hear herself breathing. A hand reached past her head and pressed the flush. Then a washcloth was passed round her mouth. Then the hands were in her armpits, lifting her.

"Not yet," she muttered.

He released her, and she sank back, vomited again. Once again it was flushed, and her mouth wiped clean.

"You into Red Cross?" she asked.

"You'll be okay."

This time she did not object when he lifted her to her feet and half carried her across the room to lay her on the bed. She attempted a smile. "Bang goes your evening."

"It's not over yet. Would you like me to put you to bed?"

"Would you like to do that?"

"Very much."

"Then be my guest. I don't think I'll make it on my own."

She decided he hadn't done this sort of thing very often before; he rolled her back and forth rather like a sack of potatoes as he hunted for buttons, and at one stage there was a dreadful ripping sound.

But then she had never had it done to her before, so she had no idea if other men might be more expert.

146

"I can't find any nighties or pyjamas," he complained.

"I don't wear them," she explained, and fell asleep.

When she awoke, her head was gonging and her mouth tasted like the inside of a sewer. And she was lying naked in bed beside a naked man.

She sat up and shook his shoulder. "You *didn't*?"

He sat up in turn. "No, I didn't. It just seemed stupid for one of us to be dressed."

"I need to think about that. God, I feel awful."

He got out of bed and went to the bathroom. She watched him with interest; he was only the second naked man she had ever seen, and he was ten years younger than Pat. He also may not have done anything to her while she was unconscious, but he certainly looked as if he needed to.

At some time during the night he must also have returned to his own room, she gathered, as he emerged from the bathroom with a frothing glass of Alka Seltzer.

He sat on the bed beside her while she gulped it.

"I'd order coffee," he said. "But I'm not sure what this hotel's attitude is to the facts of life. It may be cheap, but it's very respectable."

Alison was feeling better after the Alka Seltzer, and very hungry. "Leave it to me," she said.

She picked up the house phone. "I would like the biggest pot of coffee you have," she said. "And the biggest breakfast you can provide. Four eggs, hashed browns, eight rashers of bacon, mushrooms, tomatoes, and eight pieces of toast. Oh, and a jug of orange juice, fresh. Yes, you are absolutely right, I didn't enjoy my dinner: it went down the john. Thank you." She replaced the phone. "You can hide in the bathroom when it arrives," she suggested.

* * *

She staggered out of bed, put on her dressing gown, signed for the breakfast trolley, and collapsed again, on her face across the bed.

Jonathan came out of the bathroom and raised her head. "Try some juice."

She rolled over and sat up, sipped, and began to feel better again.

"What I don't understand," he said, "is why it hit you so hard. You didn't have all that much to drink. Not with me, anyway."

"I think I was just churned up. I . . . well . . . I'd just been told by my lawyer that I don't really have a hope of divorcing Pat."

She had drained the glass. Jonny Carter regarded the tray. "You going to want any more?"

"I might. Why?"

"There's only one glass."

"And one cup, and one spoon, and one knife and one fork. Do you think it matters?"

"No, I suppose it doesn't." He drank some juice himself, pulled up a chair, and sat before the trolley. "Food?"

"Do you know, I might manage some."

He pushed the trolley beside the bed, and they took turns at using the fork.

"Why do you wish to divorce Pat?"

"I suppose I've found out too many things about him. What is most annoying is that I think I always knew them, but wouldn't believe them."

Jonny poured coffee. "Why can't you divorce him?"

Alison repeated what Bokis had told her, as best she could remember.

They shared the cup, passing it back and forth.

"I'm no millionaire," he remarked. "But I'm not doing too badly. I mean, I could support you."

"Why should you?"

"I told you, I love you. I have, for five years. Don't tell me, you haven't even thought about me in that time."

"Well, I have, of course. But not . . . well . . ."

"Try doing that now."

"It's difficult not to, isn't it?" He was still naked. "But I wish you, and everyone else, wouldn't keep assuming I'm after a share in Pat's money. I don't give a shit for his money. Oh, it's been great spending as I liked. But that is no compensation for being a prisoner. It's my children."

"You think Pat'll wish to keep them?"

"You can bet on it."

"He never struck me as being a family man."

"He isn't. But he can be vicious. You must know that."

"Actually, I don't," Jonny said, surprisingly. "I reckon he cheated me out of a fortune, but then I reckon he's cheated quite a few people in his time. But that's the point. Pat is interested only in money. It's his god. He is not the slightest bit interested in children, and if it is pointed out to him that they are only going to be a drain on his finances as they grow up and have to be educated, as well as an emotional problem unless he is prepared to devote a good deal of time to them, or even if he does, I think he might well decide they're not worth it."

Alison lay down and stared at the ceiling. Would it work? It was certainly worth trying.

"I'll do it," she said.

"When are you going back?"

"I've an open return from Miami. I'd better do some shopping, as that was the ostensible reason for this trip. But I'll catch the bus back down tomorrow morning."

"Want me to come with you?"

"To Mexico? Pat would throw a fit."

"Well, as far as Florida."

"If you like." She rolled off the bed. "I just have to shower." She threw the dressing gown on the floor, went to the bathroom.

"Mind if I join you?"

She turned to look at him as he stood up. "What are you, some kind of masochist? Or queer?"

149

He grinned. "Well, neither. Just being with you is a lot of fun. But . . . I'm hoping, especially as you've made up your mind to leave Pat, that some time you might say yes."

"Yes," Alison said, and got back into bed.

Alison telephoned the *hacienda* from Mexico City Airport when she landed, and Hugo said he'd be right in to pick her up.

She had a cup of coffee while she waited. She had never felt quite such a mood, a mixture of exhilaration, apprehension, defiance . . . all overlaid with something far more important. Love?

She wanted to believe that, profoundly. There were a number of reasons. She did not wish to accept the fact that she had committed adultery merely out of anger with Pat, desperation that she might not be able to escape him. She was afraid to accept the fact that her morning with Jonny Carter had been the most stimulating experience of her life. He had made love to her with a passion Pat had never managed, and she had responded with a passion she had not known she possessed: there were parts of her body which still tingled.

But all of that was physical. She didn't want what had happened to be a merely physical experience. It had been far more exalted, far more important, far more transcendant, than that.

Or was she kidding herself? If she hadn't gotten blind drunk, would it ever have happened? How much more disgustingly physical could you get?

But it would have happened, she was certain, from the moment her subconscious had told her to book at the Universal. She wanted to believe that, and she did believe that. She was in love, and she had been subconsciously in love for five years. It was even possible to suppose that it was her karma, that she had only encountered Pat Grange, and married him, so that she

150

could meet Jonny Carter. A man Pat had once left for dead.

A man she was going to marry, and be happy with for the rest of her life. She had no doubt about that, now.

"Hi, Mrs Pat. Say, you're looking good." Hugo had apparently decided to forgive her.

"Do you like it?" Alison gave him a twirl, so that the ankle-length skirt rose and then settled again. She had chosen her new frocks in a great hurry, but at least this was in the latest style.

"Mr Pat is gonna like it too," Hugo said, as they drove out of the airport.

Alison sat beside him in the front. "Whenever next he sees it."

"Oh, he's on his way. Got a wire yesterday. He'll be here in three days' time."

"Is he? Stop the car, Hugo, I've forgotten something."

"Ma'am?"

They had not yet left the city. Alison pointed. "Pull in over there, at the Post Office. I'll have to wire the hotel."

Hugo obliged, looking sceptical. Alison ran inside, filled out the form: HOME THREE DAY'S TIME WISH ME LUCK. She'd promised to let Jonny know exactly when she would be confronting Pat.

"Think you'll get it back, Mrs Pat?" Hugo asked.

"Oh, sure," Alison said. "Oh, sure."

Everyone at The Keep seemed pleased to see her, and when she presented David with the accounting of what she had spent he nodded his head. "Very circumspect, Mrs Pat. Oh, by the way . . . do you wish Mr Pat to know about the trip?"

The question was asked absolutely casually.

"Of course," Alison said. "Why shouldn't he know about the trip?"

"You're the boss, Mrs Pat."

Did he know she'd had an affair? Was it that obvious?

She spent the entire day with the children, feeling her nerves slowly tightening. But as Jonny had reminded her, Pat was a man of strict priorities. She had to believe it was going to work out.

David went to the airport to meet Pat and Clem. This was normal. Alison remained to greet him when he arrived, and snap her fingers with anger when she saw Tony Mayne also getting out of the car. She had wanted Pat entirely to herself.

"Come to do some shooting, Mrs Pat," Mayne said, embracing her.

"I thought you did enough of that in Brazil," Alison retorted, and realised for the first time that if she went ahead with her plans she was never going to see the mine, and the jungle. Some things were just not meant to be.

Pat also kissed her, and made no objection when his bags were taken upstairs. Alison went up with them, and waited there. He appeared a few minutes later.

"Well, doll, how're things?"

"Things are fine. And you?"

"Usual problems." He grinned. "But we ironed them out. No trouble here?"

She shook her head. "How long is Mayne staying?"

"Maybe a month. Like he said, we want to do some shooting."

"Pat . . . there's something I want to talk about."

"Come on in, Clem," Pat said. "Get the unpacking done right away, will you. Shoot, honey."

"In private."

He glanced at her. "You're not gonna start whingeing about The Keep again, honey, are you?"

"It's important."

"All right. Where do you want to go?"

"That's it. There's no privacy in this place. Take me into the desert."

He looked her up and down, seemed to realise she was wearing riding gear for the first time.

"Okay, honey. Just give me time to change."

Alison put on her sombrero, tightened the strap beneath her chin, and went downstairs. "Have Mr Pat's horse saddled up," she told Clem when he appeared.

"Right away, Mrs Pat."

The horses were waiting in front of the house when Pat appeared, together with two more.

"What the hell do you think you're doing?" she asked Hugo.

"Now, you know the drill, Mrs Pat . . ."

She turned to Pat. "I said alone, Pat."

"So we'll be alone. You two guys keep off, four hundred yards minimum, right?"

"Yes, sir, Mr Pat," Clem and Hugo said together.

"God, sometimes I feel like a prisoner being let out for exercise," Alison grumbled as they walked their horses out of the front gate, watched by the ever-present guards.

"You can come and go any time you want," Pat reminded her. "Like you just went to New York."

Alison glanced at him. "Don't tell me, Hugo wired you."

"Maybe he did. But he would've missed me anyway. No, Dave told me just now."

That was quick, she thought. But she supposed David's first duty was to report on everything that had happened in the boss's absence. And it saved her having to tell him herself. She looked over her shoulder at the two young men, who were waiting patiently at the gate to the *hacienda* to let their master and mistress draw the required distance in front. "Anyway, I was going to tell you myself."

"Of course you were."

She kicked Hannibal into a canter, and dust scattered

from his hooves as he increased speed. Pat stayed at her elbow, and they rode briskly for some ten minutes, following her favourite route, which led to the *arroyo* nearest the ranch. Once there she drew rein and guided the stallion down the defile, amidst the stunted bushes, while The Keep gradually dropped out of sight. She kept on going until they were nearly at the end of the little canyon, a further mile or so, and then reined and slipped from the saddle; there was no need to tether Hannibal, who she knew would wait patiently until she was ready to remount.

Pat also dismounted. "So what's on your mind?"

Alison faced him, drew a long breath. "Pat, I want out."

He frowned at her.

"Listen to me, please," she said. "We don't have a marriage. I'm not sure we ever did. You swept me off my feet, and I fell for you. But did you ever love me, Pat? Or was I always just an appendage, the wife you wanted to have?"

He was listening with great patience, although she could tell that he needed an effort to do so. "We happen to have five kids."

"I know. But I think you mean, *I* happen to have five kids, Pat. To you they're just nuisances. You kiss them hello when you come back, and you kiss them goodbye before you leave again. Do you ever play with them, sit with them, even think of them, in between times?"

"So you reckon I should give you a couple of million pounds for the six years you've been forced to spend with me, and we call it quits, is that it?"

It was being easier than she had dared hope. Too easy. "No, Pat," she said. "I don't want any of your money. Just let me take the children and I'll walk right out of your life, forever."

"That means there's another man."

He spoke quietly, but suddenly there was steel in his

voice. And he had taken her by surprise. For a fatal moment she hesitated.

"You've been having an affair," he said.

"Pat . . ."

"In New York, by Christ! And now you think you're in love with the guy. Christ, are you a dumb little girl. Who was it?"

When he spoke to her like that she immediately began to bridle, no matter what resolutions she had made to play it cool. "Pat, I did not go to New York to have an affair. I went to see a lawyer."

"Yeah? And he told you to fleece me for what you could."

"I've told you, I don't want any money. I wouldn't accept a red cent. All I want are the children."

"You're gonna bring up five children? *My* children? Without money? You take me for a moron? I want to know the name of the guy."

"And I'm not going to tell you."

"Ha! So there *is* another man. You know what I oughta do? I ought to take this crop to your ass." He shook it at her.

Alison discovered that after all she was losing her temper. She took several long breaths. "Pat, may we please behave like civilised human beings? All right, there is another man. But that is not relevant. Our marriage is over, finished, dead. I'm asking nothing of you save to let me divorce you. Nothing!"

"Save my kids."

"My kids."

"You've been shacking up with some other guy," Pat said. "My wife! Christ, you little whore . . ." without warning he swung the crop at her, the thong unwinding as it left his hand.

Alison gasped and leapt backwards to avoid being hit, tripped over a chaparral bush, and fell heavily. Before she could get up, he was standing above her.

"I've been too good to you," he said. "Too fucking

155

good. All you've ever done is complain. Christ, you could've been that bastard Waller's sister. Now, you tell me the name of the man, or I'm going to mark your ass."

Alison attempted to get up, and he put his boot on her shoulder and pushed her flat again.

"Just who the hell do you think you are?" she shouted in a sudden fury.

"I'm Pat Grange. I'm your husband. I own you." He waved his arm. "I own this entire fucking valley. You wanna play rough? You got it. Get your britches off."

"You . . ." Again she attempted to rise, and this time he put his boot on her stomach and pushed her flat on her back.

"Get them off. I'm going to tan your ass, and then roll you in the dust."

"You're mad," she shouted. "Stark, raving mad." Her hat came off and her chignon unwound so that her hair trailed in the dust. "You let me up, you bastard!"

"You gonna get them off? Or shall I call Hugo and Clem to do it for you?" he snarled. "They'll enjoy that. It'd prove something, too, eh?"

"You . . ." she gasped as he pressed on her stomach. She had never been so angry, so outraged, in her life. But at the same time she was aware of a creeping feeling of despair. Pat might be behaving like some medieval baron . . . but he had the power, here and now, to do it. She wasn't even sure she would get anywhere bringing charges against him in Mexico City: Pat Grange was far more important to Mexico than his complaining wife.

"Get them off," he said. "And the knickers. I'm going to fill your cunt with dust, whore."

"You are a shit!" she screamed. "A shit! And a liar and a cheat, and . . ."

The whip slashed down and she shrieked and threw up her arms, but the thong nonetheless cut into her shoulder and she gave a whimper of pain, as she listened to the drumming of hooves. Hugo, coming to her rescue?

156

Pat had moved his boot, and she rolled away from him, rising to her knees as she did so, looking left and right for some weapon, a stone or a piece of wood, with which to hit him . . . and gazed at Jonathan Carter, throwing himself from the saddle.

"Oh, my God!" she shouted. "No!"

Jonny dismounted. "What the hell is going on?"

Pat stared at him. "You? *You*? Jesus Christ!" He swung the crop at Carter, but the younger man caught the thong easily enough, and with a twist of his powerful wrists tore it from Pat's grasp and hurled it into the bushes.

"Jonny!" Alison shouted. "For God's sake, what are you *doing* here?"

"I thought I'd better come down and keep an eye on things," he said. "Seems I made the right decision."

"No you didn't," Alison snapped.

"You," Pat said again. "By God, boy, but you are going to wind up crawling on your belly looking for bread."

There were more hoofbeats, and Hugo and Clem emerged through the dust. Jonny looked at them, and took a couple of steps backwards. Fit and strong as he was, he knew he was on a hiding to nothing from three big men.

Pat grinned. "Now, sonny boy, let's see what you're made of."

"You touch a hair of his head," Alison said, speaking in a low voice, "and I swear I will kill you."

Pat looked at her, but she didn't lower her gaze.

"Mount up, Jonny," she said. "Mount up and get out of here. Get out of Mexico."

"And leave you here with these thugs?"

"They're not going to hurt me," Alison said. "For God's sake, go."

Jonny hesitated, then went to his horse. "I'll be around," he promised.

"Mr Pat?" Clem asked.

"Oh, let the bugger go," Pat said. "He's a nothing."

Jonny Carter swung into the saddle and rode off. Maybe

another man would have stayed, Alison thought. But she had told him to leave, and had he stayed, he would only have complicated the issue.

"So you were messing around with Jonny Carter," Pat said. "You little shit. Now . . ."

"You lay one finger on me, Pat Grange," Alison said. "And you are going to be in court."

Pat grinned. "You reckon?"

"Oh, sure," Alison said. "You're the great Pat Grange, and I'm just a little appendage. But by God they'll have to listen when I strip off and show them every bruise on my body. And I'll do that, even if I have to create some of my own."

His grin faded into a glare. "You little . . ."

"You said that already," Alison reminded him. She picked up her hat, adjusted the strap, walked to her horse, mounted. "Don't get sunstroke," she told them, and rode back to The Keep.

She had a hot bath. She didn't bother to lock the door, and heard someone in the bedroom. But no one came into the bathroom. When she got out of the tub, Pat's clothes had been removed.

She had a tremendous urge to go after Jonny. But she didn't know where he had gone, and in any event, that would give Pat an excuse to fly off the handle again. Time enough for Jonny when she had got what she wanted. She knew Pat well enough to feel sure that his explosion of this afternoon would be followed by a complete change of mood this evening, and that would be her chance; he might think she could again be bullied or bribed or promised the earth to bring her round . . . but he was wrong.

She had a terrified Lucia – presumably all the servants knew by now what had happened – put cream on the weal caused by Pat's whip, dressed for dinner, wore her best jewellery, stepped out of the room . . . and found Hugo standing there. She raised her eyebrows.

158

"Mrs Pat," Hugo said in a hoarse whisper. "I just wanted you to know . . . I wouldn't have let the boss beat you up."

"Why, thank you, Hugo," she said, and hurried on. She didn't want any protestations of devotion, which would necessarily have to include indications of jealousy against Jonny.

As she always did, she went to see the children first, kissed them goodnight. Obviously, from the expressions on the faces of Hannah and the Mexican nannies, the story of what had happened that afternoon had also reached the nursery. But she was still Mrs Pat. They had to be polite.

David was in the sitting room, mixing cocktails. Of course he would also know, but David's manners were impeccable. He poured her a drink, and then poured for Pat and Mayne, who appeared a few minutes later.

A typical evening at The Keep, Alison thought.

"You and I have to have a talk," she told Pat.

"Yeah. Tomorrow. Let me think about it," he said.

She was utterly relieved. He seemed to have returned to normal. "Okay," she said. "Tomorrow."

Her one fear was that he might have sent someone after Jonny, and had him beaten up. Of all the stupid things for Jonny to have done, come rushing down . . . presumably that was a measure of the love he felt for her.

She reassured herself with the thought that Pat would know she would accuse him, were Jonny to be hurt. It was also reassuring to think that she had an ally actually in the house. Perhaps more than one, she thought, as she watched David, and saw him glancing from one to the other as he made polite conversation.

She went to bed immediately after dinner, and this time she locked her door. She wanted utter peace.

159

She didn't expect to sleep. There was too much to be thought about. Tomorrow, Pat would have to make his decision, if he hadn't already done so. Would he give in without a fight? Or would he wish to hang on to the children? She had to be absolutely sure what she would do in those circumstances. But she had made up her mind. She was going anyway. The future could be left to time, and not a great deal of time, she was certain. Ben and Shirley were intelligent children, Pat junior and Stephanie and Harry would certainly become so. They would size their father up, soon enough, as long as she kept in touch, and she certainly intended to do that.

No doubt there were a great many people who would describe her as a failed mother and a totally amoral woman. But to stay put as Pat's wife, especially after what had happened, would be ten times more amoral. And make her ten times as bad a mother as well, bringing the children up to his image and his ideas. She had to fight that.

She had never been more determined in her life.

She fell asleep, awoke at some time in the night, to the noise of the dogs barking at the foot of her staircase. She sat up, wondering if Pat was coming to join her after all; but after one bark Romulus and Remus were silent, indicating that although disturbed they had recognised whoever was down there.

She remained sitting up for some seconds, watching the locked door, waiting for the knock, but after a couple of minutes she lay down and fell asleep again. And awoke again to a violent banging on the door.

"Mrs Pat! Mrs Pat!"

"Just a moment." She got out of bed, pulled on her dressing gown, crossed the room and opened the door, gazed at a thoroughly distraught Hugo. "What on earth . . ."

"It's Mr Pat, Mrs Pat," Hugo gasped. "He's dead!"

PART TWO

The Pot of Gold

CHAPTER 6

Victim

For a moment Alison could not take in what Hugo had said, then she thrust him aside and half fell down the stairs.

Several maids were clustered at the foot, together with Romulus and Remus, who frisked happily as they saw her.

They had barked in the night.

"Where is he?" she shouted. "Where is my husband?"

"In his bedroom, *señora*," they told her.

She did not even know where he had slept, ran out on to the back patio, gazed at Hannah and the other nurses, standing in front of the children's bedrooms, which were all along the right wing. With them were Ben and Shirley, while Pat junior and Stephanie were being carried; behind them she could hear Harry wailing.

She turned to the left, saw Clem, leaning against the balustrade, looking sick, Mayne, standing in the doorway with his hands on his hips . . . she started forward, and David, coming up behind her, caught her arm.

"Easy, Mrs Pat, easy," he said.

His face was grim.

"What happened?"

"Someone shot Mr Pat in the head at close range, twice," he said.

Alison mouth's sagged open.

"I've just called the police," David said. "They're on their way now."

"I must see him."

"I wouldn't, if I were you."

She pulled herself free and ran along the walkway. Mayne turned to face her.

"You mustn't go in there," he said.

"Get out of my way."

He stepped aside, and she stood in the doorway, drawing deep breaths.

Pat lay on his face. His head, what was left of it, drooped over the side of the bed. Blood had poured out of the terrible wounds at the back of the skull and flowed across the floor, only coagulating after it had nearly reached the door.

She felt saliva rushing into her mouth, and turned away, went outside and leaned on the balustrade.

Mayne put his arm round her shoulder. "I told David to send for the police."

"Who did it," she muttered.

"The police'll find out," he said reassuringly.

She looked across the patio at the children. "Get them away from here," she shouted at Hannah. "Take them into the playroom. Hurry! Take Harry, too."

David was moving her along the balustrade, and she went with him. Pat was dead! Dead, dead, dead! Had she hated him enough to wish him dead? For a moment yesterday afternoon she certainly had. But to see him lying there . . .

Somebody else must have hated him far more than she ever could.

Mayne placed her in a chair, and David brought her a cup of black coffee. When she tasted it she discovered it was laced with brandy, but she didn't object.

"Who did it?" she asked again, but no one had any answers. Yet it had to have been someone inside The Keep. Nobody else could have got in. Save . . . she had been awakened, briefly, by the dogs barking. But they

164

had stopped, because they had recognised whoever had alerted them.

Anyway, how could any stranger have got over the walls, constantly patrolled as they were, any more successfully than Waller, two years ago? It had to be someone who lived here. Someone . . . she looked from face to face. Hugo had joined them by now, still looking quite distraught.

"Would you like to lie down, Mrs Pat?" he asked.

She shook her head. "I'll wait for the police. But . . . we can't just let Mr Pat lie there."

"We have to, Mrs Pat," David said. "The police will want to see things exactly as they are."

She supposed she should thank God for the presence of David, to make them do all the right things.

David had telephoned the police sergeant in the village, but the sergeant had prudently called Mexico City; the death of Pat Grange was something too big for him to handle at a local level. Yet even coming down from the city, the police were mercifully quick in arriving. As with two years before, they were smart men in khaki uniforms, peaked caps and brown boots, revolvers on hips. They took over the entire *hacienda*, shepherding the peons into a group in the outer compound, while their doctors and detectives photographed Pat's body and bedroom. Then the corpse was taken in a stretcher to the waiting ambulance.

By then it was mid-morning, and Alison realised she was still sitting there in her dressing gown. "I must get dressed," she muttered, and sent Lucia upstairs to draw her bath, while she visited the children.

"Ma?" asked Benjamin. "Who are these people?"

"Policemen, darling," she told him.

"Pa won't like them," Shirley pointed out.

"Where is Pa?" Benjamin asked. "The servants say he's gone. Is he gone, Ma?"

"Yes," Alison said. "He's gone. You be good and stay here. I'll come back to you in a little while."

At the moment it was no more important than that, to them: Pa was always coming . . . and going.

She went to the stairs, and was checked by Captain Guimard, emerging from the room Pat had occupied. "Señora Grange!" He saluted. "May I have a word?"

"Oh . . . I was just going to get dressed."

"Very well," Guimard agreed. "We will speak when you are dressed. I will speak with these gentlemen first."

He seemed as eager to please as she remembered. Alison soaked in her tub, her hair carefully gathered on the top of her head, while Lucia fussed about the room.

"They are saying someone came in from outside to kill the master, *señora*," she said.

"Who are saying?"

"The peons."

"How can they say that? Weren't there men on the walls all night?"

"Well, yes, *señora*, but . . ." Lucia lapsed into silence for awhile, until Alison was ready to get out, then she wrapped her in the huge bath towel. "What is going to happen, *señora?*" she asked.

"You will have to ask the police that," Alison told her.

"But after they have gone . . ." Lucia hesitated.

Alison had no idea. She and Pat had never discussed the possibility of his death, except in passing during his "troubles" in Brazil. And he had said, "You'll be the wealthiest widow in the world."

Had he meant that? Even after yesterday? But would he have had time to change anything, between yesterday afternoon and last night?

And what thoughts to be having when he had just been killed?

* * *

She dressed herself in slacks and a loose blouse and sandals, tied her head in a bandanna, and went downstairs. Everyone else had vanished, save for two policemen waiting at the foot of the stairs, casting anxious eyes at Romulus and Remus, who as ever greeted her with tremendous enthusiasm. One of the policemen ushered her into the library, where Captain Guimard sat at the table, together with a sergeant, examining several pages of notes.

Both stood up at Alison's entry. "*Señora!*" Guimard said. "It was remiss of me not to have offered my condolences before. This is a great tragedy."

"Thank you."

"Please sit down. Would you like a cigarette?"

"I don't, thank you. I would like a cup of coffee."

"Of course." The Captain snapped his fingers, and the sergeant hurried out.

"Will you catch the murderer?" she asked.

"Of course." Guimard also sat down. "You understand I must ask you some questions, *señora*."

"I understand."

"May I ask how long you have been married to Señor Grange?"

"Not very long. Six years."

"You are considerably younger than your husband."

That was not a question.

"I am twenty years younger than my husband."

Guimard made a note of that, his face expressionless. "But you loved him."

"When we were first married, yes."

He raised his eyebrows.

"I am sure you have spoken with the members of the staff," Alison said.

The sergeant returned with a tray of coffee, and Guimard poured her a cup, rather, she thought, as if she were a guest in her own house.

"As you have raised the matter, *señora*, yes, I have spoken with your staff, as well as your houseguest . . ."

"My houseguest?"

Guimard looked at his notes. "Señor Mayne."

"Oh. Yes." She hadn't really thought of Mayne as a houseguest.

"And they have given me certain information. Would you like to add to that?"

"I am sure I can add nothing to what they have told you, Captain. Yesterday afternoon my husband and I had a quarrel."

"During which he threatened you with physical violence."

"Yes, he did. Threatened me, I mean."

"May I ask the reason for this quarrel?"

Clem and Hugo would obviously have already told him.

"It was because I asked my husband for a divorce."

"In order to marry another man."

"Yes." My God, she thought, Jonny! She should have sent someone to tell him what had happened.

"Who was present at the time of this quarrel?"

"Yes," she said again, and realised that perhaps it was a good thing she had *not* sent to tell him.

"Señor Jonathan Carter," Guimard read from his notes. "A man, I understand, who had great reason to hate your husband."

"Of course not."

"Did Señor Carter not once bring a lawsuit against Señor Grange, in Brazil, claiming that Señor Grange had swindled him out of a third share of a gold mine, which was worth a great deal of money?"

"Well, he did . . . but that was a long time ago." Suddenly she began to feel cold.

"Seven years ago. As you have just said, not very long, *señora*. *Señora*, do you possess an automatic pistol?"

"Not a pistol. A revolver. My husband insisted I have one."

"May I ask the make and bore?"

"It is a Smith and Wesson point three-eight. It's in my bedside drawer. Would you like me to fetch it for you?"

"That won't be necessary. We have found one of the fatal bullets. Señor Grange was shot with a Browning automatic pistol, caliber point three-two, to which a silencer had been fitted. Do you know of anyone in this house who possesses such a weapon?"

My God, Clem, Alison thought. And probably Hugo as well – she had never asked to see Hugo's gun. "There are a great number of guns in the house," she said. "I think several of them are Browning automatics."

"But yours is a revolver."

"My husband gave me the revolver. He said that with a revolver you always knew what you were at. An automatic can jam, or there can be a cartridge in the breech without your being aware of it."

"That is very true. This . . . friend, of yours, Señor Carter, can you tell me what he is doing in Mexico? Did you send for him?"

"Well, no. Not exactly."

"Explain, please?"

"I was in New York last week, Captain, seeing both Mr Carter and my lawyer about divorcing Mr Grange. Then . . ."

"Forgive me, señora, but it is necessary to establish certain things. It was your intention to divorce Señor Grange in order to marry Señor Carter?"

Alison hesitated. Had Jonny ever actually proposed marriage? She couldn't remember. He had said he could support her, but that wasn't quite the same thing.

"Not exactly. I mean, nothing had been decided."

"But you are in love with Señor Carter?"

"I . . ." another hesitation.

Guimard sighed. "Señora, you must again forgive me, but if I do not know the truth I cannot solve the murder. You wish your husband's murderer found?"

"Oh, yes."

"Good. Now, señora, I must ask you an indelicate question. Have you and Señor Carter ever had an affair?"

Alison stared at him, mouth slightly open.

"I see," Guimard observed. "Did this happen during your last visit to New York?"

Alison nodded, and Guimard made a note. "Now tell me what you did next."

Alison had to draw a deep breath to get her nerves under control. "I came back here to discuss the matter with Mr Grange, as soon as he returned from Brazil. When I knew the date he was returning, I wired Mr Carter to let him know."

"Telling him to come down."

"No. Just telling him when I was going to be speaking with my husband."

"But he came anyway. Perhaps to make sure all went smoothly."

"You are barking up the wrong tree, Captain. In the first place, Mr Carter is not a murderer. In the second, there was no way he could have got at Mr Grange. These walls are patrolled and floodlit all night; you remember what happened when that Waller man tried to get in. And in the third place, even if he had somehow managed to get in, he would have had to pass the dogs."

The dogs had barked. And then stopped. They had recognised the murderer.

The same thought had occurred to Guimard. "Did the dogs not know Señor Carter?"

"No," Alison said. "Mr Carter has never been inside The Keep."

"And you yourself spent the entire night in your bedroom."

"Are you accusing me of murdering my husband, Captain?"

"Of course I am not, *señora*. I asked you a question."

"I spent the entire night in my bedroom, yes."

"Alone, because you and your husband had quarrelled. And you heard nothing?"

"I heard the dogs bark."

"At what time?"

"I don't know. After midnight, certainly. It was a quick

bark, and then they stopped. They knew whoever it was who had disturbed them."

"As you have said. Very good, *señora*. You are not planning to leave Mexico, or even the *hacienda*, in the immediate future?"

"No."

"Thank you."

Alison went in search of Hugo, found him in the paddock, gloomily surveying the horses.

"Who found Mr Pat's body, Hugo?"

"Clem, Mrs Pat. When he took him his morning juice."

"I see. Hugo, I want you to take one of the cars, drive into the *pueblo*, and find Mr Carter."

"Carter? In the village?"

"He has to be there," she pointed out. "Unless he's already left." But he surely wouldn't have done that without seeing her again.

Hugo was clearly reluctant. "Suppose I find him. What then?"

"Tell him to come here to see me. Right away. Bring him yourself, in fact."

"The police think he did for Mr Pat."

"I have just convinced the police that is impossible. As it is. Now please do as I ask."

Hugo went off to the garage, clearly thoroughly out of sorts.

Guimard and most of his men had departed by now; but two policemen were on duty at the gate, not that they made any attempt to stop Hugo leaving, after a brief chat.

Alison went inside, and found David waiting for her. "How are you feeling, Mrs Pat?"

"I haven't really decided yet. David . . . how many Browning automatic pistols are there on the premises?"

"Four."

"Four?!"

"They were Mr Pat's favourite weapon. Hugo and Clem, each had one, and so did Mayne. So did I."

"But . . . that means . . ."

David smiled. "Any one of us could have done it? That's exactly right, Mrs Pat. The police have taken all the guns away for ballistics tests. I have no doubt at all they'll come up with the right answer."

"But you at least aren't bothered."

"Why, no, Mrs Pat. Should I be?"

"I'm just thanking God that you're not."

"You look done in." He poured her a drink. "Don't worry, Mrs Pat. The police will work it all out. You mustn't get upset. You have a great deal to do, you know."

"Tell me." She sat down, the glass held in both hands while she sipped.

"Well, to start at the very beginning, there's Mr Pat's Will. It's lodged with his attorney in Mexico City. I've already informed Señor Puig, and he wishes to know when it will be convenient for him to come out here and see you."

"To read the Will?"

"Well, I imagine that is what he wants to do. Then there is the matter of Mr Pat's funeral. There is of course to be an autopsy, but Captain Guimard has promised that the body will be released to us by tomorrow. Supposing there is nothing to the contrary in the Will, where do you wish him to be buried?"

"Why . . . here, I suppose."

David nodded. "I'll put the arrangements in hand. Did you have anything special in mind?"

Pat had always said he wanted to be buried in a gold-lined coffin. But there was no time for that, even had she had any gold available. Anyway, the expense . . . he was dead and that was the end of it.

"No, thank you. David . . ." she rested her hand on his. "You are being a treasure. Pat always said you were a treasure."

"It's very nice of you to say so, Mrs Pat."

"You're not going to abandon me, I hope."

"Not if you wish me to stay."

"I am going to *need* you."

Alison spent the rest of the morning with the children. Ben continued to ask questions, but more from curiosity as to why the *hacienda* had been invaded by the police than from wondering why Pa had left after only twenty-four hours at home – there was nothing very unusual in that. Alison told them that someone had broken into The Keep. Ben at least could vaguely relate that to Bert Waller.

Hugo was back before lunch, alone.

"Didn't you find Mr Carter?" Alison demanded.

"Sure I found him, Mrs Pat. But the police had found him first. They were questioning him, and I wasn't allowed near him. I gave the message to the girl at the pension – he's staying there – and she promised to let him have it."

She had to be satisfied with that. Of course the police would wish to question Johnny. But he would come out to The Keep this afternoon. And then . . . her brain was still whirling through too many imponderables for her to think straight.

Pat was dead! She should be guilty, for feeling no grief at all. She could only feel relief that all her troubles were over, and, now that it had happened, a faint sense of surprise that it had not happened before.

He had made so many enemies. And one of them had finally killed him. No, one of his friends. She glanced around the four men at the table. One of these four had to be guilty. Clem, who had been the butt of so many of Pat's jokes? Hugo, who had also suffered in that direction and who in addition had promised to protect her from "the boss"? Mayne! He had seemed to be Pat's friend, but who could tell what he had had to put up with in the jungle, and elsewhere, from Pat's tantrums. David! The most loyal of servants, but again, who could tell what secret enmity he might have held for his employer.

The men looked at her, and she gave a guilty smile. And then realised that of course they were thinking the same about her. That of them all she had the most obvious motive. She did not know what Pat might have left her, but whatever it was, she had obviously been throwing it away by seeking to leave him. There was also the fact that he had refused to let her take the children. Now, as she had just reminded herself, all of her troubles were over. With his death.

She wondered if the police thought that too, however polite they had been. But as David had said, the ballistics tests, together with the fingerprints on the murder weapon, would prove the truth of the matter.

Save that the murderer had to know that too.

And of course she might be entirely wrong. It could just as easily be one of the peons, whom Pat might have insulted at some time, or worse, insulted the man's wife . . . suddenly she hoped that would turn out to be the case. If there was one thing on which she was determined, it was that she was leaving The Keep just as soon as it could be done. Thus she would never have to see any of the peons again.

She couldn't say the same for any of the four Americans.

But the dogs wouldn't have stopped barking, had it been a peon.

She left the table and wandered through the house. The servants were cleaning up the mess in Pat's room. She sat with the children, read to them for a while, then went out the front, played with the dogs. If only you could speak, she thought. But surely the police were through interviewing Jonny by now?

The afternoon drifted by, and still he did not come.

At five o'clock she could stand it no longer. She telephoned the pension. "This is Señora Grange speaking. I would like to speak to Señor Jonathan Carter, please."

"Señor Carter has left, *señora*."

"Left?"

"The police arrested him, *señora*. They took him away this afternoon. An hour ago."

"Arrested him?" Alison shouted.

"For the murder of your husband, *señora*. They have taken him to Mexico City."

"Oh, good God . . ." Alison slammed the receiver down. "David!" she shouted.

He came running.

"Listen, those idiots have arrested Jonny Carter. I'm going into Mexico City now. I want you to get hold of this lawyer man, Señor Puig, and tell him to meet me there in one hour."

"But . . . what are proposing to do, Mrs Pat?"

"Get Jonny out of there. What else?"

"Well . . ." David sounded doubtful. "You mean on bail?"

"Well, of course."

"They don't usually set bail in a murder case, Mrs Pat. Certainly not in the case of itinerants like Carter."

"Just get hold of Puig," Alison told him, and ran out to tell Hugo to drive her into the city.

It was dark by the time they reached the city, but the Central Police Station was a blaze of lights.

"Captain Guimard is very busy," said the sergeant on the desk.

"Tell him Mrs Grange is here," Alison suggested. "On a most urgent matter."

A few minutes later she was escorted up two flights of stairs and shown into the Captain's office. Guimard looked tired. He had taken off his jacket and loosened

175

his tie; there were sweat stains in his armpits. "I was told this was urgent, *señora*."

"It is. Where is Mr Carter?"

"In a cell. He is under arrest for the murder of your husband."

"I told you he couldn't have done it."

"But I believe he did do it."

"I told you . . ."

"Why do you not sit down, *señora*?"

Alison sat down, and Guimard did likewise.

"How well do you know Señor Carter?" he asked.

"Well . . ." Alison bit her lip.

"You have had an affair with him, is that right?"

Alison knew she was flushing.

"And perhaps you sought to use him as an excuse for divorcing your husband. But you do not really know him very well."

"I know him well enough to be sure that he is not a murderer. Anyway, what about the murder weapon? Didn't that come from inside The Keep?"

"No, *señora*, it did not."

"But you took the four pistols . . ."

"And subjected them to ballistics tests, yes. But the fatal bullets did not come from any of those four."

Alison frowned at him. "You mean there was a fifth . . . but where is it?"

"We have not found it."

"Then you have no murder weapon, and no proof that Señor Carter ever owned a Browning."

"That is true, *señora*."

"And I have proved that there is no way Señor Carter could have got into the *hacienda*."

"There is a very simple way he could have entered the *hacienda*, *señora*."

"We have armed guards on the wall all night . . ."

"He used the secret corridor beneath the wall."

"The *what*?"

"You do not know of this passageway?"

"Of course not. There isn't one."

"There is, *señora*. How long have you lived in the *hacienda*?"

"Oh . . . more than four years."

"And you do not know of this passageway? It was built by the original owner of the *hacienda*, at the same time that the *hacienda* itself was built. This was nearly a hundred years ago, you understand, and there were still wild Indians out there in the mountains, so the original owner wished to have an escape route in the event that his *hacienda* should be surrounded by hostiles and prove indefensible. The passageway runs from a secret entrance in the grounds several hundred yards to emerge in an *arroyo*."

"That is the most ridiculous thing I have ever heard," Alison declared.

"It is surprising that your husband did not show you it."

"I will tell you why he never showed it to me, Captain – because he didn't know it was there. My husband wished to turn The Keep into an impregnable fortress. What would have been the point of having men on the walls all night, with lights, if anyone could just have sneaked into the place?"

"Then perhaps your husband did *not* know of it. In which case, he was swindled, eh?"

"Because other people knew of it? You?"

"No, *señora*, I did not, until today."

"Then I don't understand how you found out."

"I received a telephone call, when I returned here this afternoon, informing me of the existence of this passage, and telling me how to find it."

Alison's jaw dropped, and she brought it up again with a snap. "You acted on an anonymous telephone call?"

"It was not an anonymous call. And the passageway is certainly there, *señora*."

"And Señor Carter knew of it? He has admitted this?"

177

"Well, of course he has not done so, *señora*. I would not have expected him to. He has denied everything."

"So," Alison said triumphantly. "You have no murder weapon, you have nothing but a secret passageway which I can assure you no one at The Keep knew about, and some telephone call . . . and on that basis you have arrested Señor Carter? Really, Captain!"

"I admit the evidence so far is a little circumstantial," Guimard agreed. "But only a little. In a murder case, there are three things a detective needs to know to determine the criminal. These three things are, firstly, motive, secondly, possession of the murder weapon by the suspect, and thirdly, opportunity to use it. Now, *señora*, Señor Carter certainly had a motive. He wished to marry you, and your husband stood in the way. You have admitted this yourself. And we have witnesses, your husband's bodyguards, that Señor Carter was present when Señor Grange threatened both you and he with physical violence. As for the weapon, we have not yet found it, but I am sure we will. And finally, he most certainly had the opportunity. He was absent from his hotel room for some hours in the middle of last night. This is attested by the clerk at the pension, and is in fact admitted by Señor Carter. Now, he says he rode out into the valley to look at The Keep, because he knew you were there, with your husband, and this thought distressed him."

Oh, Jonny, she thought. How romantic. And how foolish.

"And that proves he entered The Keep by means of this secret passageway?"

"It proves that he had the opportunity to do so."

"If he knew of it."

"Of course."

"But you can't prove that. And your whole case comes unstuck on one little point: the dogs. They barked, and then were quiet again. That means they were disturbed, and then recognised the person who disturbed them.

Those dogs had never seen Señor Carter before, and I am prepared to testify to that in court."

"They are your dogs, more than Señor Grange's, is that not right, *señora*?"

"Yes, of course."

"Therefore they would recognise, and respond to, your scent, would they not?"

Alison frowned. "Well, yes, I suppose they would."

"Amongst Señor Carter's possessions we found a scarf, which he admits belongs to you, but which he says you gave to him as a keepsake. Do you remember doing this?"

"Well . . . yes."

"The scarf is heavily scented. It is the same scent as you are wearing now."

"Oh . . ." she wanted to scream. It was all so pat, and so terribly wrong. "You do realise that this 'case' you have so carefully constructed against Señor Carter, could easily be made against a whole lot of other people. Me, for instance. Forget all this nonsense about secret passageways. Who's to say I didn't have a Browning automatic pistol as well as my revolver? The house was full of them. Who's to say I didn't get out of bed last night, go downstairs, shoot my husband, and then throw away the gun? I certainly had a motive. I wanted out more than Jonny wanted me out. I also wanted to take my children, and Pat wasn't going to allow that." She paused for breath. "And I threatened him. Ask Hugo and Clem, about that."

Guimard gave a tired smile. "*Señora*, of course it could have been you. But it wasn't. We know that."

"How on earth can you *know* that?"

"Because of the dogs, *señora*. More than one person, including yourself, heard the dogs bark, and then be quiet. All are agreed they were disturbed, and then recognised the person who disturbed them. But they were *your* dogs, Señora Grange. Would they have barked at all when you came down the stairs? I do not think so." He got up, came round the desk, rested his hand on her shoulder. "You have had a long and traumatic day, *señora*. May I suggest that you go home to bed, and have a good night's sleep? Tomorrow I will come out to the *hacienda*, and we will look at this secret passage together. Would you not like that?"

CHAPTER 7

Inheritance

Alison had to admit defeat, at least temporarily. She felt exhausted, and yet the thought of Jonny in a police cell . . . a Mexican police cell . . . When she asked to be allowed to see him, permission was refused.

"Because you are beating him up!" she shouted.

"Because it is not proper procedure, *señora*," Guimard replied wearily. "We have a watertight case, or we will have when we find the gun. There is no need to beat Señor Carter up."

Jayme Puig arrived, middle-aged, short and stout and redolent of good cigars and better wine. *He* was allowed to see Jonny, as his attorney, and told Alison that he seemed quite cheerful – but the lawyer wasn't able to arrange bail, and he too suggested Alison go home to bed.

She did, and summoned Clem and Hugo, Mayne and David, to tell them about the passageway, watching their faces carefully as she did so. But she saw nothing except total amazement and consternation.

"You mean none of you knew of it?" she demanded. "For God's sake, David, you were here with the architect when he was rebuilding the place. Didn't *he* know of it?"

"If he did, he never mentioned it to me, Mrs Pat."

"Well, tell me how this place was virtually reconstructed, new plumbing, new wiring, even new rooms, and this thing didn't appear."

"Well," David said. "It's possible, I suppose, depending on where it comes out. You see, Mr Pat didn't want too many alterations made to the main old building, what he called the donjon. Sure it was rewired and redecorated, but we used the conduits for the existing wiring. Same with the upper floor, which had been a watchtower. We made it into an *en suite* master bedroom, but there was plumbing and wiring already there. Where does this tunnel come out, anyway?"

"Oh, God knows. Captain Guimard is going to show us tomorrow. Now, we have to find the missing gun. The police don't seem to have looked very hard, but it has to be around here someplace. First thing tomorrow morning I want every peon on the *hacienda* looking."

Mayne looked as if he would have protested, but then changed his mind. None of them knew exactly where they stood, until the Will was read. But then, neither did she.

She said goodnight to the children, and went to bed herself. Despite her frustration, and her fears for Jonny, she slept heavily, but awoke early to the strangest of sensations. Being alone at The Keep with just the staff and the servants was commonplace . . . but always there had been Pat in the background, an invisible but so dominant presence. Now he was gone. Even the dogs seemed subdued.

Señor Puig arrived at eleven in the morning. By then the gardens and corrals and even the area outside the walls had been thoroughly searched by the peons, with no result.

"Of course," Mayne said at breakfast, "If someone did come in from outside, and shoot Pat, he'd have taken the gun away with him."

"By someone, I assume you mean Jonny Carter," Alison said.

"I didn't say that, Mrs Pat. I'm just stating an obvious fact."

"And you don't think it's just a little coincidental that Jonny should have chosen to murder Pat with an exact replica of the weapon Pat armed all of you with?"

The atmosphere was quite sticky, even David seeming somewhat moody, and Alison was very glad to see the lawyer.

"Who do you wish assembled?" she asked.

Puig raised his eyebrows. "Assembled, *señora*?"

"Well . . . for the reading of the Will."

"A Will is customarily read only to the beneficiary, or beneficiaries, *señora*."

"Well . . ."

"If you will step in here?"

Alison followed him into the library, and he closed the door, placed his briefcase on the table, opened it, and took out a single sheet of paper.

"Señor Grange's Will is a very straightforward document. But then, he was a very straightforward man." He stood at the end of the table and read, while Alison's brain seemed to have coagulated. "'I, Patrick Peter Rupert Grange, of The Keep, Mexico, being of sound mind etc etc, do hereby give and bequeath to my dear wife Alison my every worldly good and possession, my property wherever it may be, my shares in the Company known as El Dorado and in all my other companies, saving only that as required by Mexican law one quarter of the above shall be held in trust by my wife for my children, to be given to them, in proportion, as they shall reach the age of twenty-one. Given under my hand, etc, etc.'" Puig paused and peered at her. She had not moved, sat staring at the rows of books. "Señora Grange?"

Alison turned her head.

"I trust this is satisfactory."

"Satisfactory," Alison muttered.

"I have only a passing acquaintance with the late Señor Grange's affairs, you understand," Puig told her. "But from what I have read, I understand that he is, was, a very wealthy man. This wealth is now yours."

He seemed to want to be absolutely sure she understood that.

"Yes," Alison said absently. "You mean my husband left nothing to . . . to his bodyguards? To his accountant? To his mine manager? To any member of his family?"

"It would not appear so, señora. I will leave the Will with you to study."

"Thank you."

Alison tried to think. Pat had claimed to be the wealthiest man in the world, but he'd never actually put a figure on it. But . . . by the very lowest computation she was a millionairess. Alison Bennett . . . if only Mummy and Daddy had been alive . . . or Tom and Harry . . . without warning tears rolled down her cheeks.

"Is there anything wrong?" Puig asked anxiously, offering her his handkerchief.

Alison used it. "I'm just a little overwhelmed." Think, damn you. But first things came first. "Señor Puig, what will it cost to get Señor Carter out of that cell?"

"Oh, señora, we are talking about justice . . ."

"He is innocent."

"Well, of course, I shall defend him, as you have briefed me to do so, and if he is innocent, why, I shall get him off."

"Please do that. But can we not in the meantime offer whatever bail they require?"

"Ah . . . bail has been refused."

"This is Mexico, señor. With respect, I am sure something can be arranged."

"Oh, señora, these are difficult matters, for one so young and so beautiful to become involved with . . ."

"See what can be arranged, Señor Puig," Alison said. "I also wish to see Señor Carter at the earliest possible moment."

He was clearly taken aback by her determined manner. "Of course, señora. Of course. Now . . ."

"I would like you to attend to that immediately," Alison

told him. "Will you ask Mr Brook, Mr Mayne, Clem and Hugo, to step in here?"

"Ah . . . yes, *señora*. Of course. I will be in touch."

"I expect you to."

She picked up the Will and read it again. Had Pat felt like this when he had first found El Dorado? But how *did* she feel? Exultant? No, she wasn't exultant. Hysterical? Perhaps, just a little. Excited? Definitely. Guilty? Perhaps, just a little.

But the overwhelming feeling was one of quiet satisfaction. For all of her life she had been at the beck and call of others. Every decision had been made for her, save the vital one to marry Pat, and that had been to put herself even more at the beck and call of someone else. She had loved him. She would never deny that. He had been a dream man, come to sweep her off her feet and carry her back to the world she had wanted more than any other. He had never done that. He had swept her into the sort of world *he* wished her to adorn, while her growing knowledge of him had slowly turned her love to loathing.

But now that world, and every other world, was hers. It would take some getting used to. And yet she was already sure of most of the things she wanted to do.

The four men filed in.

"Not bad news, I hope," Mayne remarked.

"I'm a little overwhelmed," Alison said. "You'd better read this."

He took the Will first, glanced at it, frowned at its brevity, then sat down to study it.

"Jesus," he commented, and gave it to Hugo.

Hugo said nothing, and handed it to Clem.

Clem raised his head to stare at her when he had finished.

David read it last. His face remained expressionless. But then, Alison realised, David, as Pat's accountant, must have already known what was in it.

"Every damned penny," Mayne said, half to himself. "When I think of the years I slaved for that bastard . . ."

"Well," Alison said. "How would you like to slave for that bastard's widow?"

His head jerked. "Eh?"

"Did you assume I was going to fire you on the spot, Tony? I will need a mine manager, won't I?"

"You mean, you . . ."

"I intend to continue Pat's enterprises, yes."

"But you're a woman."

"I'm so glad you've noticed. Does that automatically rule me out?"

"Well . . ."

"You wanted to divorce Mr Pat," Clem protested. "You wanted to walk away from it all. You have no right . . ."

"Are you resigning, Clem?"

He gulped.

"Yes," Alison went on. "I wanted to divorce Pat. I wanted to divorce him because I found out that he was a liar and a cheat. The decision was taken long before Jonny Carter came into my life. Well, things have changed. Pat has left me his fortune. I intend to run his business, and use that fortune, and maybe, just maybe, make some amends for his wretched obsessions. To do that, I need continuity. Tony, do you wish to go on being mine manager?"

"Well . . . yes, Mrs Pat, of course I do."

"Then you keep your job, until and unless I find out that you're as nasty a piece of work as Pat was. Now, the moment this murder has been cleared away, I am coming out to Brazil with you, to see the mine and take a look at its operation."

"Mr Pat always said the jungle was no place for a woman."

"Tony," Alison said quietly. "I am not a woman. I am Mrs Pat. I am the boss. If you can't understand that, then you'd better quit, now."

Mayne swallowed.

"Now what about you, Hugo?"

"I work for you, Mrs Pat," Hugo said. "I always did."

"Thank you, Hugo. Clem?"

"I was Mr Pat's bodyguard," Clem growled.

"Well, if you wish, you can take turns at being my bodyguard, with Hugo."

"Say, you mean that, Mrs Pat?"

"Yes," Alison said.

"Well, hell, I accept."

Hugo wasn't looking so pleased.

Alison looked at David.

He smiled. "You know where I stand, Mrs Pat."

"Thank you, David. Now, I would like to know where *I* stand. Do you think you could prepare a list of everything belonging to Mr Pat, and an estimate of the current market value?"

"I'll have it for you this afternoon, Mrs Pat."

"Thank you, gentlemen."

Alison felt a tremendous bubble of confidence and excitement growing inside her. Perhaps she had always dreamed of being in this position, without ever expecting to achieve it – certainly not at the age of twenty-six. Twenty-six, and . . . the richest woman in the world?

The concomitants of her position began to emerge that afternoon, when the reporters arrived. The news of Pat's murder had taken some time to filter through to the outside world, but now it seemed every newspaper in the world wanted an "inside story". The first carloads of flashing cameras rolled up just after lunch. Taken by surprise, Alison did nothing to exclude them until it was too late, and they were inside the gates and snapping away at everything, grabbing the terrified peons to question them, and generally making a thorough nuisance of themselves. Then her determination to have them thrown off her premises was eroded by the arrival of Guimard and his policemen, to show her the secret passageway. This emerged, or began, some eight feet down the inner wall of the well, at a level just above the highest ever reached by the water. There was a ladder leading down from the lip, but this had hardly ever been used in Alison's four years in The Keep – there was no reason to use it, as the well had always provided ample water, and the house supplies had always been boiled before use. And when it had been used, apparently the peons who had done so had never realised that just to the left of the ladder there was a discoloured piece of stone which, when pressed, caused a section of the wall to swing in to reveal a remarkably well-made and preserved passageway. Guimard insisted upon taking Alison, and various reporters, along this, to where it emerged, as he had told her the previous night, in an *arroyo* some hundred yards away from the *hacienda* outer wall.

"And you say, the murderer, the man Carter, used this passageway?" asked one of the newspapermen.

"I am sure you mean the accused, rather than the murderer," Alison snapped.

"We are saying that the murderer used this passageway, yes," Guimard said. "As to whether the murderer is the man we are now holding in custody, accused of the crime, the court will have to decide. But there can be no doubt that the murderer did use this way of getting into the *hacienda*. My men have photographed every inch of it, and these photographs reveal recent footprints. Here, you can still see the evidence."

They were at the *arroyo* end of the tunnel, and the ground beyond the entrance to the little cavern, concealed by the brush from anyone who didn't know it was there, was certainly scuffed, but that could have been done by the police themselves. On the other hand, there were also some broken branches close to the entrance, and these had been broken quite recently. Again, Alison felt the police could have done it, deliberately or not, but the reporters were impressed.

Guimard then took them back along the passage-way, and showed them how the wall panel could be opened from the inside. "It is very ingenious, is it not?" he asked.

"Supposing you know how it works," Alison retorted.

She wanted only to get rid of them, but before she could do that Pat's body arrived, in a metal coffin, accompanied by a priest, and Jayme Puig.

"My husband was not a Roman Catholic," she said. In fact, she had no idea what Pat was – they had never discussed religion, nor had he ever accompanied her to church.

"A man cannot be buried without benefit of the church, *señora*," the priest protested. "May I ask where your husband is to be interred?"

"In the outer courtyard."

The priest frowned. "That is not consecrated ground."

"It is where I am sure my husband wished to lie."

The priest looked at the lawyer.

Puig shrugged. "Señora Grange is sole executrix."

The priest raised his eyes to heaven, perhaps seeking inspiration. Or support. "When is the funeral to take place?"

"The moment I can get these people off the *hacienda*," Alison told him.

The priest sighed.

Alison at last got rid of the reporters, promising them all interviews over the next few days, but stressing how exhausted and grief-stricken she was. They could all see that wasn't true, and clearly they wished to wait for the funeral, but after Guimard and his policemen had left and Alison had brought all her people together, they had to accept her decision.

Then the grave was dug, and Pat was buried in the dusk. The peons and their wives and children stood round the hole, which was beneath the east wall. Alison and Mayne, Clem and Hugo and David, stood beside the grave, with Puig and the priest. Alison had commanded Hannah and the other nurses to keep the children in The Keep itself until the funeral was finished.

When the service was over, Alison gave each of the men a glass of brandy.

"A strange end for so famous a man," Puig remarked.

"He lived a strange life," Alison reminded him, and took him to one side. "Have you arranged bail?"

"Alas, *señora*, but the judge steadfastly refuses. I have suggested that he name his own figure . . . but Señor Pat was well liked in Mexico City."

"When can I see Señor Carter?"

"Well, it is said that you may see him tomorrow . . ."

"I'll be there. When?"

"Eleven o'clock."

"Thank you."

Puig and the priest took their departure soon afterwards, both unhappy men, and Alison summoned David into the study.

"I don't suppose you've had the time to prepare those figures I wanted," she said.

"Oh, I have, Mrs Pat. Well, to tell you the truth, the figures are nearly always fully available. Mr Pat used to call for them at a moment's notice."

"So what have we got?"

He sat down and opened his folder. "Well, to begin at the beginning, El Dorado has so far produced two-point-seven billion dollars."

"Two . . . do you think I could see that written down?"

"I'm speaking in English billions, of course," he said apologetically, and wrote out the figures.

Alison gazed at them: $2,700,000,000,000.

"Now," David went on, "approximately twenty-five per cent of that has gone on production costs: these were quite high in the beginning, but now that the road has been made and the jungle cleared, and everything is running smoothly, the costs have come down dramatically. Ten per cent has gone to Senõr Alvarado, Mr Pat's Brazilian partner, and a further ten per cent has gone in repayments of interest and capital to Mr Pat's various backers. A further ten per cent has gone in tax to the Brazilian Government. The residue of forty-five per cent has come to Mr Pat."

Alison kept gazing at all of those zeroes.

"Now, a good deal of this money was immediately invested, although some was kept as ready cash. A large sum was spent on this *hacienda*, of course. But by far the greatest amount was invested in real estate, as I have said, all over the world. There are holdings in Australia, New Zealand, the Hawaiian Islands, India, several South American countries, Mexico, Canada, and of course the United States."

"The States? I thought Pat was wanted in the States for tax evasion?"

"He is, Mrs Pat. But all of this property is owned by companies, which are in the hands of nominees. You know the sort of thing, a lawyer as company secretary, five local directors – usually employees in the lawyer's office – each with a single share, apparently running the business, while Pat holds the remainder and actually calls the shots. And we're talking about real estate here. Pat has been buying, but where he's rented the company pays the taxes, and as he hasn't sold anything yet there's been no question of capital gains, so far. You must remember that Pat has never objected to paying tax in small amounts on the returns from his investments. He's only ever baulked at paying supertaxes on the bulk of his fortune."

"So what do his real estate holdings amount to?"

"I have a detailed list here . . ."

"Just give me the total."

"Six hundred million dollars."

"Six hundred . . ."

"I have these valued at purchase," David explained. "They were all bought during the last three to four years, and property prices have been depressed because of the War. Now that the War is over, I would expect that figure to double over the next few years. In addition, Mr Pat always kept a considerable amount of ready cash on hand, to facilitate other purchases as he came across them. These funds are mostly on deposit in South Africa, although there are some in the Bahamas. These funds are never allowed to fall below a total of a hundred million dollars. As I have said, this money is nearly all on call, so is available as you wish it. And of course there is the production from the mine, which is down considerably from the peak years, but is currently running at a hundred and twenty million dollars a year. Just under half of this comes to Mr Pat. To you, I should say."

David had been writing as he spoke, and Alison had watched the figures slowly forming in front of her. She had supposed she might be a millionairess. Six zeroes. Not ten, even if the original two-point-seven billion were halved. She felt almost sick with the realisation of it . . . and fifty million a year coming in, apart from the worth of the investments.

And yet . . . she had no concept of accounting practice or problems, taxes and company accounts, but she did have a good head for figures and a quick brain. She stared at the sheets of paper, while David waited for a comment.

"David," she said at last. "What is forty-five per cent of two-point-seven billion?"

He had clearly been expecting the question, and replied without hesitation. "One billion, two hundred and fifteen million."

"Then these figures don't add up."

"Yes," he agreed.

"You mean you know that?"

"Yes. As I said, the real estate is at cost, exactly what Mr Pat paid for it. The deposit accounts are as paid in. I suppose Mr Pat lived on about a hundred thousand a year, he paid a hundred and fifty thousand for those airplanes, and he spent three hundred thousand on this place. He also pays the Mexican Government a million dollars a year."

"The Mexican Government? Why?"

"In lieu of tax. He did a deal with them."

"He was paying a million dollars a year for the right to live here in a desert?"

"That was the deal. You must understand that if he'd lived anywhere else he'd be paying ordinary tax, that would have amounted to something like fifty times that."

"Shit!" Alison commented. It was not a word she normally used, but she felt the occasion called for it.

David ignored the expletive. "Let's say he's taken eight million out of the business over the past six years. That is peanuts. So what I have here represents six hundred million in real estate, one hundred million in ready cash, and another eight million spent, say eight hundred million total . . . but his share of the take has been one-point-two *billion*. That means there's something like four hundred million dollars unaccounted for. A third of the total amount."

"Unaccounted for? You're the accountant."

"I've been with Mr Pat for four years, Mrs Pat. He'd already started on his investment programme. Since then, the receipts from the mine have been, as I said, paid into either South Africa or the Bahamas. I've been informed of this by the accountants there. You must remember I only handle Mr Pat's personal accounts, and the real estate holding company, Grange Estates. In other words, I get all my information second or third hand. Once the

193

cash reaches the Bahamian or South African personal accounts, I'm responsible. When Mr Pat wants to buy something, whenever you want to buy something, you just tell me, and I make sure the money is available. But what happens between that gold coming out of the ground and the cash equivalent finding its way into the accounts, I don't know."

"Then who does? Mayne?"

David pulled his nose. "I doubt that, Mrs Pat. Mr Pat and Tony had a lot of good times together, but I think Mr Pat had Tony sized up pretty good."

"You mean he didn't trust him."

"Not with money, anyway."

"How does the gold come out of the mine?"

"I suppose as ingots. I've never seen any of it."

"And then?"

"Well, I suppose it's shipped, after the Brazilian Government has collected its ten per cent, and sold and converted into whichever currency Mr Pat wanted. I don't really know about that end of it."

"Who looks after the shipping?"

"Mr Pat did that personally. I guess that's up to you, now."

Alison just couldn't take that responsibility in, at this moment. She preferred to concentrate on the matter in hand. "But of what's come out so far, only two-thirds ever got to any destination."

"I'm afraid that's so, Mrs Pat."

That sounded like Pat, with his paranoic fear that someone was going to rob him. Like some outsize squirrel, he had cached four hundred million dollars worth of gold ingots . . . or converted it to create a completely separate financial empire . . . which also sounded like Pat. But who had he left that to? Or did that also belong to her, only whoever was running it had no idea as yet that Pat was dead.

And did it matter? Even without it, she was worth seven hundred million. But if it was there . . . she shook her head. What was the matter with her? Was she going to change overnight into another Pat?

"What would you like me to do, Mrs Pat?" David asked anxiously.

"Why, just keep things ticking over for the time being."

"I was thinking of the missing money."

"I don't think there is anything we can do about that, until I have had a chance to go to Brazil. And that has to wait on the trial." She smiled at him. "First things first."

This time his answering smile was sad.

Alison saw Jonny Carter the next day, as Puig had promised. She didn't have a black dress, and she felt one would certainly be appropriate, so she went into the city early and bought one, changed in the shop, and appeared at the Station looking suitably sombre.

She was shown into an interview room, and a moment later Jonny was brought to her; to her annoyance, two policemen remained in the room all the time, and she had to assume they understood English.

She was even more perturbed by Jonny's appearance. He looked perfectly fit, and there were no bruises to be seen, but they had taken away his belt and shoe laces, and somehow he appeared to shamble.

"They don't want me to commit suicide," he explained, as he sat opposite her across the table.

She put out her hand to touch his.

"No touch," snapped one of the guards.

"Oh . . . fuck him, to quote my late husband," Alison said. "These people make me so angry. Jonny . . . you wouldn't commit suicide, would you?"

"Not while you're on my side. Incidentally, I don't know how to thank you for what you're doing. Señor Puig has told me you're financing the entire operation."

"I've virtually offered them a blank cheque. But it

seems they can't be bribed. I always thought Mexicans could be bribed. Pat certainly thought so."

"Alison," he protested. "Whether they can or not, you don't want to go throwing your money away."

"There's some to spare." She told him just what was involved, and he blew a gentle whistle.

"That's a lot of motive."

"But you didn't know about it. Did you?"

"I knew that mine had to be worth quite a lot. But a couple of billion and still producing . . . I think that makes it the richest gold strike in history."

"And he left it all to me. I'm the one with the colossal motive. But they won't go for that at all."

"Well, of course not. Whatever Pat was paying the Mexican Government for the right to live here, they don't want to give it up. If they decided to hang you, they'd lose it."

Alison hadn't thought of that. But surely that strengthened her position, if it became necessary to flex her muscles.

"Señor Puig says you have to stand trial now. He is trying to have the whole business expedited. Can you sit it out, Jonny?"

"Sure I can. Providing I'm acquitted."

"Oh, we'll see to that. Señor Puig tells me their evidence is too circumstantial to stand up in court."

He made no comment, so she hurried on.

"You understand that I'm being called as a prosecution witness."

"That figures."

"But I can't hurt you," she assured him. "Or at any rate, I won't, no matter what they ask me."

"Sure you won't," he agreed.

Alison was disappointed in his reactions, in his mood, but reminded herself that he wouldn't be human if he wasn't upset by his situation . . . especially when he compared it with hers, and the world which had so unexpectedly unrolled itself at her feet.

Everything would be different after the trial, she promised herself. But it was a very long eight weeks.

Puig had recommended, after the refusal of the courts to grant Jonny bail, even when they had virtually been told that the sky was the limit, that she keep a very low profile in case she attracted bad publicity both for herself and for Jonny. But in fact the publicity was pretty horrendous anyway. It would have been, in the simple plastering of her name on the front page of every newspaper in the world as the richest woman in the world, even had Pat died of a heart attack. The fact that they had been fighting over a divorce, that threats had been uttered, and that her lover was on trial, turned her immediately into the most scarlet of women, and if most people accepted the fact that there was no evidence suggesting that she had had any part in the murder, most observers seemed to feel that she had to have been in partnership with Jonny, had to have told him about the tunnel, and seemed unable to understand why she wasn't occupying the cell next to his.

Puig had explained this, but the Mexican Government was also keeping a very low profile, until after the trial. They were each playing a game, Alison supposed, with Pat's millions on the end of it . . . but it was a game of which she did not even yet know the rules.

She did not leave The Keep again until it was necessary to attend the trial; she knew the ordeal that was awaiting her. Indeed, there was sufficient evidence of it every time she looked out of the window. Hordes of people drove out from Mexico City every day, gawking at the *hacienda*, snapping away with their cameras, using binoculars in the hopes of seeing the infamous Mrs Grange. Enterprising reporters even hired aircraft to fly low over The Keep, again with cameras snapping.

197

Alison protested to Guimard, but was told it was a free country, and there was nothing he could do.

"A free country?" she snorted. "Mexico? I am being subjected to harrassment, Captain, and you know it."

But there was nothing she could do about it either.

Actually the people she could see were less distasteful than those she could not, who wrote her letters. She opened the first batches with eager interest, expecting condolences, and discovered that for every letter of sympathy they were ten containing obscenities or hatred or just begging.

"I never knew there were people like that in the world," she told David.

"I'm afraid there are. Would you like me to sort the mail, Mrs Pat?"

"Yes, please. I don't want to see any more of these. Except . . . David, there's been nothing from any member of Mr Pat's family."

David frowned at her. "Mr Pat had a family?"

"Well, of course he did."

"He never mentioned it to me, Mrs Pat."

"Well, I know he quarrelled with them, quite violently. I've never met any of them. But I also know they were there. Are there. And cut right out of his Will. Do you think we could find them, Dave?"

"I guess it's possible to find anyone, Mrs Pat. But . . . are you thinking of making some kind of settlement on them?"

"Well . . . don't you think they've been treated a little badly?"

"However they were treated, it was what Mr Pat wanted to do."

"I know. But I'd still like you to find them for me, Dave."

"Anything you say, Mrs Pat," he agreed. "You're the boss."

*   *   *

She liked to hear him say that, but she was truly grateful for the support given her, not only by David, Clem and Hugo, but by Mayne as well. Between them they handled all the problems, and dealt with anyone who attempted to get in; the first thing Alison did after the funeral was to have the tunnel boarded up.

Yet if Jonny hadn't killed Pat – and of course he hadn't – one of these so faithful retainers could well be the murderer! She didn't want to accept that possibility, wanted to believe that the police were right in their claim that someone had used the secret passage to gain access . . . but wrong in their assumption that it was Jonny.

But even if they were all innocent, she knew she had to accept that their loyalty was entirely financially-based: she was worth protecting because she was their meal ticket. As the Mexican Government obviously felt the same way, she also understood that this was something she was going to have to get used to, for the rest of her life, perhaps. To everyone she was going to meet, she would be simply a large dollar sign. True friendship, much less true love, was going to be impossible.

For the first time she gained some insight into Pat's feelings of loneliness – especially if his mail had been anything like hers – and the reason he had fallen so heavily for her . . . simply because she had been so disinterested in his money. Now she was stuck with having to try to cope with it.

Thus the period of self-imposed imprisonment in The Keep was useful, as it gave her time to come to grips with herself and her new situation.

The children were a great source of comfort. Not that they provided any comfort in themselves; they were too young to have any idea of what was going on, although Alison was beginning to suspect that Ben at least understood his father was not coming back. But they needed to be sheltered and protected, entertained and never to be allowed to suspect for a moment that their mother had anything on her mind, apart from being their mother, and this required concentration took her out of herself.

Yet she knew she was only counting the days, until they all had to go to the city.

Hugo and Clem were very upset. "What are we to say, Mrs Pat?"

"You tell the absolute truth."

"Yeah, but . . . we both heard Carter threatening Mr Pat," Hugo said.

"Sure you did. But as Mr Carter didn't murder Mr Pat, it can't hurt, can it?"

There was a session with Puig before the morning's hearing commenced.

"Yesterday was all the routine stuff," the lawyer explained. "How the body was found, results of the post mortem, evidence of arrest . . . that kind of thing. But now the real calling of witnesses has begun."

"How is Señor Carter?"

"He is in good shape, *señora*."

"But you don't look very happy about the situation."

"Well, *señora*, as you know, the prosecution must by law give the defence a list of all the witnesses they intend to call."

"Yes?"

"Here is the list."

Alison glanced down it. Apart from Captain Guimard, Clem, Hugo, David, Mayne and herself, there were no names she recognised.

"I'm not with you."

"That name: Sanchez. I happen to know that is the name of the man who informed Captain Guimard of the existence of the secret tunnel."

"Well . . . somebody must have done it."

"I have not been allowed to question Señor Sanchez. But there is something else: the police have found the murder weapon."

Alison frowned at him. "Where?"

"Not far from the entrance to the tunnel. In the *arroyo*, half buried."

"Then it is a plant. They searched that *arroyo* immediately after the murder, and found nothing."

"They are saying it was a careless search. The sergeant is being reprimanded. I shall of course make a great deal of this, but . . ."

"Were there fingerprints on the gun?"

"No, *señora*. But one would hardly expect this."

Alison found herself in an extremely agitated state: Puig seemed to have lost a lot of his confidence. But again there was nothing she could do, except be patient. Meanwhile she and Hugo, Clem, Mayne and David all moved into the Grand Hotel in Mexico City, taking a whole floor so that they could be assured of privacy. She wanted to be on hand all of the time, and the drive in and out from The Keep had become a purgatory of staring faces and flashing cameras.

She was bracing herself for an ordeal, but next day, when she was called, it was for a surprisingly brief appearance, and the questions were but a repetition of what Guimard had asked her: how long had she been married, the age difference between Pat and herself, their estrangement – "because I discovered my husband to be a liar and a cheat," she said in a clear voice – their quarrel when she asked for a divorce, Jonny's threat, whether or not she had known about the tunnel, and her relationship with the dogs.

When Puig cross-examined he asked only a couple of questions. "Señora Grange, did you ever discuss the possibility of Señor Grange's death with the accused?"

"Never," Alison said.

"Was Señor Carter your lover before you went to New York to seek a divorce from Señor Grange?"

"No."

"Did you know of the existence of the tunnel beneath the wall at the *hacienda*?"

"No."

He might have been defending her rather than Jonny, she thought. She gave Jonny a hasty smile as she left the witness box, after which, having been escorted through a vast crowd of reporters and flashing cameras by both policemen and Clem and Hugo, she regained the relative privacy of her hotel room.

The case continued for two more days. Alison refused to read what was going on. She only wanted it over and done with, and went into a small nervous breakdown until it was finished. And at last on the third evening Puig telephoned her to tell her that the jury had retired.

"Is it all right?" she asked.

"We must hope so, *señora*," he said enigmatically.

"Call me the moment you have any news," she said. "No matter what time it is."

Dinner was a strained affair, at which she ate almost nothing. Mayne tried to be humorous but was met with black stares from the others. Alison didn't suppose they were the least bit concerned about Jonny's innocence, but they were concerned that "Mrs Pat" shouldn't be upset.

She decided that she liked Mayne, less and less. But that didn't necessarily make him a murderer.

She went up to her room and took sleeping pills which sent her into a heavy dreamless coma, but she was awakened by Lucia just after dawn.

"Señor Puig is here, *señora*."

Alison jumped out of bed, pulled on her dressing gown, and ran into the sitting room of her suite. Puig stood in the centre of the room, twisting his hat in his hands, and she needed only one look at his face to know what had happened.

202

"Señor Carter has been found guilty by the jury, *señora*. It was a unanimous verdict."

She stared at him. "The sentence?"

"Death, *señora*. By hanging."

CHAPTER 8

Bewilderment

Slowly Alison sat down. "You told me that couldn't happen."

"Believe me, Señora Grange," Puig protested. "I did everything I could. But the evidence of the man Sanchez was overwhelming. He testified that he had met Carter in a bar, and told him of the passageway."

"And Carter admitted that?"

"No, he denied it. On the stand. Well, I had to put him on the stand, *señora*, after that. But . . . he did not make a good witness. The Prosecution asked him about his prospecting days with Señor Grange, when he had been abandoned for dead, and he had to admit that he had hated Señor Grange then, and would have killed him had he had the opportunity. Then they took him apart on the law suit. And then . . ." Puig sighed. "They asked him about you, about his relations with you. They asked him, *señora*, if it was not true he had pursued you only to get some revenge on Señor Grange."

"What was his reply?" Alison asked in a low voice.

Puig sighed again. "He denied it, of course. But . . . nobody believed him."

"Just as they did not believe him about Sanchez. Who is this man, Sanchez, anyway? How did he know of the tunnel?"

"The *hacienda* stood derelict for some years before

204

Señor Grange bought it. Sanchez says he lived there for a while, without rent. How do you say in English?"

"He was a squatter."

"Squatter. That is the word. Well, while he was there he explored, and found the tunnel."

"And told no one until Señor Carter? Really, Señor Puig . . ."

"Sanchez says he met Señor Carter in the bar at the pension, and Carter told him of his love for you, but how he could not get to see you . . . so he told him of the tunnel."

"And the police accepted such rubbish?"

"The jury accepted it, *señora*."

"You intend to appeal, of course."

"*Señora*, I have nothing to appeal about. To appeal I must be able to show misconduct by the police, misdirection by the judge, or new evidence."

"Right. I wish to see this man Sanchez."

"*Señora*?"

"Sanchez. I wish an interview with him."

"*Señora*, do you think that is wise?"

"Arrange it," Alison told him. "And also arrange for me to see the President."

Puig gulped. "The President?"

"Arrange it."

Everyone at the hotel was very aware of Alison's feelings, and was as sympathetic as he or she could be.

"You'll get him off, Mrs Pat," Hugo said reassuringly.

"I need all the help I can get," Alison told them. "This man Sanchez is obviously a plant, in the biggest possible way. I want all four of you to sit down and make a list of everyone, every last person, who had any reason to hate Mr Pat."

"You mean, hate Carter," Mayne said.

"No, Tony. I mean hate Mr Pat. Johnny was obviously just a convenient set-up."

"But wait a moment," Hugo argued. "Who knew that Carter was coming down here?"

Alison frowned. "That's right. The murder happened the day after he arrived, and even I didn't know he was coming."

She looked from face to face, not for the first time.

"You can see how the police feel they have a case," Mayne said.

Alison glared at him. "I can see a lot of things, Tony," she snapped, and left the table.

Had he done it? Either way he was the key man in her life at the moment. Because life began again for her at El Dorado. Not only had it been her life's ambition to see the mine, but it was from there that the four hundred million dollars had gone missing, and if Mayne had killed Pat, it was there that she was certain she'd find the necessary motive.

But it needed planning. She summoned David to her room.

"All of these companies I've inherited. What do I have to do about them?"

"Why, nothing, Mrs Pat. Unless you want to start selling."

"I want to visit all the properties."

"Of course. Just name the day. It'll have to be quite a few days, though."

"After I've sorted out Jonny, and after I've been to El Dorado. You do understand I have to begin there. I have to orientate myself. And there are a lot of other things as well."

David nodded. "You're right. May I say, Mrs Pat, that you are being quite tremendous. I mean, a lot of women, well . . . the mere fact of their husband being murdered would flatten them. But even if he hadn't been murdered, the mere idea of inheriting a billion-dollar estate would equally flatten them. But you . . . well . . ." he flushed.

"Say it," she invited.

"Mrs Pat, you don't look like a businesswoman. You're so small, and petite, and chic, and . . . well . . ."

The poor gink was falling in love with her. Or was it with those millions?

"I'm not a businesswoman, Dave. You're going to have to teach me how to be one. But beginning at the mine is something I have to do. The problem is the children. Listen. I want you to try to get in touch with a Charlene Gorman."

David wrote the name down. "Address?"

"I can't remember the exact address, but she lives in New York City. Can you find her for me?"

"I should think so. Not another reluctant beneficiary?"

He had, as he had promised to do, written to the Grange family during the trial; Pat's parents had died during the War, apparently – which would explain why he had made no effort to contact them, Alison supposed – but he had a married sister. She had been rather dismissive at first, until she learned that there could be a great deal of money in it: then she had accepted a "bequest" of a million dollars. But she had not written to Alison either to thank her or to offer condolences: she was very obviously Pat's sister.

At least it was off her conscience, Alison thought thankfully.

"Not in the way you mean," she told David. "Charlene used to work for me. I'd like her here, at The Keep, helping Hannah with the children."

David was frowning. "You mean to live here, Mrs Pat? I thought . . ."

"You thought right. Although I intend to keep the property. I mean, Pat is buried here. But the children have to have somewhere safe to live until I get back from Brazil, and they have to be looked after by people I can trust." She rested her hand on his. "Dave . . . you know Pat and I were through."

"I kind of got that idea," he muttered.

"Okay, so it's possible to say I don't have any right to all of this. But I've got it. You don't expect me to give it away, do you?"

"I never thought you were nuts, Mrs Pat. But . . . you want me to come with you to Brazil?"

"I want you to stay here and hold the fort. I told you, I have to leave behind people I can trust."

"Mrs Pat," he said. "If you think Carter is innocent, then you must have some ideas on who actually killed Mr Pat."

"I do."

"Well . . ." he looked embarrassed. "I reckon it has to be someone who was pretty close to him."

"Yes."

"Well . . ."

She squeezed his fingers. "I hope to come back with the proof."

"Then, Mrs Pat, I think I should go with you. Unless, of course, I'm the guy you have in mind."

"No. I don't have you in mind," she reassured him. "And I can take care of myself, really and truly. I want you here, holding the fort." She smiled at him, "Literally."

He looked doubtful, and perhaps he understood more of the dangers of her situation than she did herself. Jayme Puig arrived at the hotel very early the next morning, looking as if he had seen a ghost.

Well, perhaps he had. "*Señora*," he gasped. "It is terrible."

"What now?" Alison asked.

"The meeting with Sanchez . . . I went to arrange it, and *señora* . . . Sanchez is dead."

"Dead?! How?"

"He fell from his apartment window. Forty feet to the ground, *señora*."

"You mean he was pushed."

"The police do not think so, *señora*. They say he had been drinking."

"Oh . . . they seem to believe just what they feel like believing. It's as plain as a pikestaff why he died: to stop him talking with me. Therefore we know who killed him."

"*Señora?*"

"The murderer, Señor Puig. The real murderer. I'm going to see Guimard. What time was he killed?"

"He fell, *señora*, at some time during the night," Puig said patiently.

"Right. What about the President?"

"Well, *señora*, he is a very busy man . . ."

"When do I see him?"

"This morning at twelve. He can spare you five minutes."

"He can, can he? Right. I'll be with you in a moment." She rang for David. He'd already heard the news.

"Mrs Pat, I think we, you certainly, should get the hell out of Mexico City. If there's a killer running around loose . . ."

"Oh, nonsense. What good would killing me do anyone? I haven't even made a Will yet. And anyway, there's too much to do here. Dave, I want you to find out what Tony Mayne was doing last night."

David frowned. "Tony? You don't think . . ."

"Yes, I do think."

"With respect, Mrs Pat, I think I should report on all of us. Me included."

"Yes. I suppose you're right. Now, I have a lot to do. You look after that for me."

She went first of all to see Guimard, who was his usual urbane if somewhat weary self.

"But isn't it obvious," Alison said, "that Jonny Carter cannot be the killer? You had him locked up when Sanchez was pushed to his death."

Guimard sighed. "Señor Sanchez was not pushed, *señora*. He fell."

"You know that's nonsense."

"I know that you are determined to believe he was killed, because that will suit your theory. *Señora*, a policeman cannot fit facts to his theory; he must fit his theory to the facts. There is absolutely no evidence that Señor Sanchez was pushed, or that he even had a visitor. There *is* evidence that he had been drinking just before he fell from his open window, and this evidence has been confirmed by the autopsy I have had performed. Now, would you like to see Señor Carter?"

"Yes," Alison said. "This afternoon. After I have seen your president."

Alison dressed very carefully for her meeting with General Camacho, wore a new black dress trimmed with gold, and her most expensive rings, which meant she was carrying something like fifteen thousand dollars on her fingers. The General was a dapper little man, with a waxed moustache, who wore a white tunic the breast of which was filled with decorations. He gallantly bowed over her hand, and was clearly impressed by what he saw. But she felt he was quite pleased with the rest of her as well.

"Señora Grange," he said. "I cannot tell you how I, how all Mexico, feels about the death of your husband. If there is anything, anything at all, that I can do for you, you have but to ask."

Alison felt herself warming to him, although he was the sort of man she would normally have instinctively disliked. "You are very kind, your excellency," she said. "All I seek is justice."

"And justice you will have. You will take coffee?"

They sat together on an internal *naya* in the palace, Camacho's aides standing a discreet distance away.

"You are not planning on leaving Mexico, I hope," the General remarked.

"That depends," Alison sparred.

"You must tell me what is this justice you seek."

Alison outlined the case to him, although she had no doubt at all he had been kept fully informed concerning the trial. She also naturally laboured her point about the impossible coincidence of Sanchez's death.

Here too the President had been briefed. "The police assure me that there is no connection between this man's death and the murder of your husband, *señora*."

"And I am sure they are wrong."

He gave a deprecatory smile. "I believe it is the custom in your country always to believe the police are wrong. Here in Mexico we find it simpler always to believe they are right."

"I am English, your excellency, not American. We have the same point of view in England. But even in England, the police do make mistakes."

"My police never make mistakes," Camacho asserted.

Alison finished her coffee and put down the cup with a rattle. "Not even where justice is involved?"

"I am informed that justice has been done, Señora Grange. I must accept that what my advisors tell me is the truth. But I understand that you feel there may be a small amount of doubt regarding the man Carter's guilt, and I should be very reluctant to send an innocent man to execution. You understand I cannot overturn the verdict of the courts. My constitutional rights extend only so far as a prerogative of mercy."

"I understand," Alison said, heart pounding. "That is all I am seeking."

"Good. We were going to discuss your future plans."

"Oh, were we?"

"My dear *señora*, you are Mexico's wealthiest resident. I am sure everyone in this country is anxious to know your intentions. As I have indicated, we should hate to see you leave."

"Ah!" Alison began to get the drift. "As a matter of fact, I do intend to leave."

Camacho raised his eyebrows.

"It is a matter of educating my children, and attending to my various business affairs."

"Your husband, your late husband, managed to conduct his affairs from Mexico."

"Actually, he didn't," Alison pointed out. "He spent no more than a couple of months here every year. And as you probably know, he was contemplating returning to England to live."

Camacho smiled. "But they would not meet his requirements. Here in Mexico we had a very sensible arrangement with Señor Grange. He wished somewhere to live, where he would not be troubled by red tape and foreign exchange regulations and fluctuations in tax rates. We on the other hand needed all the financial resources we could obtain for the building of schools, and hospitals . . . for the modernisation of our country's social services. Señor Grange was very happy to donate these things to us."

Alison nodded. "He donated a million dollars a year, I believe."

"That is correct."

"Well . . . I will be prepared to continue that donation, whether I actually live here or not."

"Why, that is most generous of you, *señora*. However, the fact is, that what with the inflation caused by the War . . . Señor Grange and I were actually in the process of renegotiating our arrangement . . ."

"My husband always spoke of you as an honest man."

"Why, that was very kind of him. I believe I am. Would you like me to produce accounts to prove to you that every cent donated by your husband to Mexico has been properly spent on the social projects I outlined to you? I *am* an honest man, *señora*. Even my enemies concede that. I am also, I hope, a patriot, and even . . ." he gave a faint smile' "a businessman. And we are discussing business, are we not?"

Alison sighed. "How much?"

"The figure we had thought of was one point five million per annum."

"Very well. One point five million, per annum. In return for Señor Carter's release from gaol."

Camacho frowned at her. "I'm afraid that is not possible."

"Not . . . you said we were discussing business?"

"Business which does not, and cannot, have anything to do with the fate of a convicted murderer."

Alison gazed at him.

"However," the President continued. "I am prepared to exercise my prerogative of mercy, and commute the death sentence . . . to life imprisonment."

"To *what*?"

"That is all I can do, *señora*."

"And if I say that isn't good enough, and refuse to pay your blackmail, Jonny dies, is that it?"

"My dear *señora*, you are so very vehement. And so very insulting. Were you not a pretty woman I might easily take offence. I have said, there can be no connection between your business affairs and the life of Señor Carter. I have also said that his life will be spared. When I have said I will do something, I do it. Perhaps you should consider that life imprisonment is not quite as severe as it may sound. There is always the possibility of parole, or even of release were new evidence ever to arise. In any event, it is surely always better to be alive than dead, is it not?"

Alison knew she was beaten, and she had never been one to cry over spilt milk. "Will he be well treated?"

"I give you my word."

As long as my million and a half arrives every year, she thought grimly. She stood up. "Then I must accept your offer, your excellency."

Camacho kissed her hand. "I wish I could do more, *señora*."

* * *

Alison went back to the hotel. She felt she had been through a ringer, stripped off her sweat-wet clothes and gave them to Lucia, then soaked in a hot tub.

She wondered at her lack of emotion. But she had never really thought about Jonny and herself, before. Those couple of days in New York seemed utterly remote, as if they had happened in a previous existence. Then she had thought only of escaping Pat, with the aid of a tower of loving strength like Jonny. Even when he had so unexpectedly appeared in Mexico, once she had got him removed from the possibility of a beating, she had been happy only to know he was there.

But since that day so much had happened, so much, as David Brook had suggested, that would have overwhelmed an "normal" woman. She knew now that Jonny's arrest and her fight to free him had been the principal causes of her apparent calmness. She had allowed it to dominate her mind, to shove into the background the quite overwhelming awareness that she was at once a widow and a billionairess. Well, she had failed to free him, even if she had purchased his life for what might turn out to be a quite astronomical sum of money. A king's ransom . . . for a man she really didn't know very well.

The important point was, did she love him? Her instincts told her that if she had to ask herself that question, then she didn't. But the same thing applied to Pat. Then had she ever loved anyone? And could she, now? The possession of vast wealth was supposed to make some people incapable of such a weakening emotion as love. But had she been like that even before she had inherited Pat's money?

Now, she would never know whether men were after her or her fortune. She didn't even know that about Jonny. Apparently he hadn't been very convincing on the matter in court.

But she had to believe he was innocent of murder.

Lucia knocked. "Señor Brook is here, señora."

"I'll be right out." She got out of the tub, and Lucia, having delivered the message, was back to wrap her in a vast towel and gently dry her. Then she took off her cap and wrapped herself in a housecoat, thrust her toes into her high-heeled mules, and went the bedroom.

David had been standing by the window looking out. When he turned he gave a gulp. "I didn't mean . . ."

"You didn't." Alison sat at the dressing table. "What did you find out?"

"I'm afraid not a thing, Mrs Pat. The fact is that anyone could have left this hotel at any time during the night. The people at the reception desk go home at eight o'clock, and although there is a porter supposed to be on duty all night, he apparently always goes to sleep."

"With the front doors locked, I presume?"

"I'm afraid not, Mrs Pat. The doors were unlocked. I have tried going in and out of them myself, and it is really very simple."

"But surely the restaurant stays open pretty late?"

"It does, Mrs Pat. But there is a separate entrance on to the street, and as you know, hotel guests do not have to return to the lobby to reach their rooms from the dining room. I reckon a hundred people could have passed through that lobby, in and out, last night without anyone noticing."

"Well, then, who have alibis for last night?"

"I'm afraid . . . none of us, Mrs Pat. We all went to bed immediately after dinner, and we all stayed there, so we say. That includes me." He gave a nervous smile. "That includes you as well, I believe."

She glared at him. "Oh . . . get out!" she shouted. "Just get out!"

He hastily left.

"You too," Alison told Lucia.

"Oh, yes, *señora*." Lucia fled.

Alison took off the houserobe and threw herself across the bed. She felt as if she were a fly, caught in the middle of a gigantic web. Someone had killed Pat. Somenone very close to him, who had known everything about him, about the dogs, and about the arrival of Jonny Carter . . .

and had determined to take advantage of that situation. And who had known about the secret tunnel, because that was how he had pinned the crime on Jonny. And it could only be one of the four men with whom she had lived on terms of real intimacy for the past four and a half years. She felt like screaming.

She then raised her head and stared at the wall. If there was a web . . . surely she was the spider. She was at the centre, and she controlled everything. As such, she *might* even be in danger. Whoever had killed Pat, unless it had been a sheer case of revenge for some past injury – which was not impossible – must have been disappointed in the provisions of the Will. But killing her to obtain something from that Will would accomplish nothing, because, as she had reminded David, she had never even made a Will of her own . . . and when she did . . . she had no idea, save that she did not intend to leave a penny to any of Pat's associates. It would all go to her children.

And the murderer would know that.

She called Lucia back, got dressed, summoned Hugo, and went to the prison. Needless to say there were a couple of reporters waiting, knowing that at some time she would wish to see her lover, and they snapped their cameras vigorously and shouted questions at her, but Hugo pushed them away.

Inside she was shown into a small room split into two by a wall of bars, and a moment later Jonny came in, to stand on the other side of the wall. As in front of the wall, on each side, there was a cross bar set in the floor some three feet back, there was no possibility of their getting close enough to touch each other, but in any event two warders remained in the room with them.

"I guess this is goodbye," Jonny said. He looked surprisingly fit after his ordeal, but the good suit he had worn at the trial had been taken away, and he was in prison garb of a shapeless blouse over equally shapeless pants.

"Never goodbye," Alison said.

His face twisted. "I want to thank you for all you've done. I guess you were right the first time . . . I should've stayed away."

"Jonny . . . you aren't going to die."

He frowned at her, and some colour appeared in his cheeks.

"I've seen the President. Your sentence will be commuted." She bit her lip. "To life imprisonment."

He stared at her. "How much did that cost you?"

"Nothing," she lied. "Nothing at all. Jonny . . . I can't stay in Mexico. I have so many things to do. But I intend to employ the best private detectives in the world to prove your innocence. I will do it, Jonny."

Still he stared at her for several seconds. "Yeah," he said at last. "I know you will, Alison." He turned and signalled to the warders that he wanted to leave. He didn't look back.

Alison bit her lip again to stop the tears. Maybe she had been too abrupt about it, too sudden. He had clearly composed himself for death. Now he had to come to terms with the fact that he was going to live. In prison, for the rest of his life . . . unless she could indeed free him. And for all her brave words, she didn't know that she could.

Or what he would be like when she did . . . if it took too long.

Hugo drove her back out to The Keep.

"Hugo?" she asked. "Did you kill Mr Pat?"

The car gave a swerve. Fortunately the road was empty.

"I have to know," Alison said.

The car drew to a halt at the side of the road.

"Because if you did," Alison said, putting her hand into her handbag, "you had better kill me now, or I will send you to the gallows."

Hugo twisted in his seat, his face a mask of concern. "I didn't kill Mr Pat, Mrs Pat. But I would've, if that fellow Carter hadn't come along, if I had had to, to stop him roughing you up."

She looked into his eyes. "I think I believe you."

"Mrs Pat, you're the only person in the world I give a damn for. You're the only person in the world who's ever treated me as a human being."

"Dear Hugo," she said. "You're coming with me to South America."

"Am I, Mrs Pat. Gee, that's gonna be great."

"To protect me. At all times."

"Oh, you bet, Mrs Pat. Nobody's gonna trouble you while I'm around."

"Then let's get home and talk to the others."

"Yeah." But he hesitated. "Mrs Pat . . . if I'm gonna protect you . . . you took one hell of a risk just now, asking me a question like that on this lonely road. If I *had* been the murderer . . ."

Alison took her hand out of her bag, holding the revolver.

"Holy shit!" he commented. "Begging your pardon, Mrs Pat. But . . . you've never fired at a human being in your life. Have you?"

"No," she agreed. "But I'm just in the mood to start."

The others had already returned to The Keep, and were waiting for her, somewhat anxiously.

She went to the children first. They were actually quite relaxed, but Hannah was as nervous as everyone else.

"Now, Hannah," Alison said. "I am going to have to go away for a few weeks. I shall try not to be longer than that. You will remain here, with the children. I am obtaining some extra help for you, and Mr Brook will be here as well. You will defer to his judgement in any matters which may arise."

Hannah swallowed. "Yes, ma'am."

"Are you going to see Pa?" Benjamin asked.

"Hannah says Pa isn't coming home," Shirley explained.

218

Alison looked at the nurse.

"I didn't know what to do, Mrs Pat. You said they weren't to be told what happened, and I've done my best, but they hear other people talking . . ."

"Yes," Alison said. It had probably been a total abdication of responsibility, to have tried keeping the truth from them for so long. "Take the little ones out, will you, Hannah?"

Hannah summoned two of the Mexican nurses, and Pat junior, Stefanie and Harry were removed.

Alison sat on the sofa, a child in each arm. "Hannah was quite right. Pa isn't coming back," she said.

"You mean he's gone to Brazil for good?" Ben asked.

"No. He's gone to heaven for good." Supposing a man like Pat had any hope of that.

She waited for some reaction.

"You mean he's dead," Ben said at last.

"Ah . . . yes."

"Is that why all those policemen were here, and everyone's been upset?"

"Yes."

There were no tears. But then, she supposed they had not seen their father more than a month, in total, for their entire little lives.

"But you'll always be here, Mom?" Shirley asked. "You're not going to die and have to go to heaven?"

"Not for a long time, I hope," Alison said. "But, as I just told Hannah . . . I'm afraid I am going to have to go away for a little while. I have to go to Brazil, to sort out Pa's business there."

"Take me with you, Mom," Ben begged.

"An' me, an' me," Shirley shouted, jumping up and down.

Alison hugged them. "I can't. But after this trip, then we're all going to go away together. That's a promise."

* * *

She joined the men. "Let's talk," she told them, and went into the library. They trailed behind, seated themselves around the big reading table.

"David," she said. "You won't forget to find Charlene Gorman?"

"I'm already working on it, Mrs Pat."

"Good. Now I have another job for you. I want you to hire the best private detective in the United States, and get him down here. His brief is to find evidence that will prove Jonny Carter to be innocent."

"That could turn out to be a tall order," Mayne objected.

Alison ignored him. "You'll be here when this man arrives, Dave. I want you to co-operate with him in every possible way."

David nodded, thoughtfully.

"Clem, I want you also to remain here, and assist David in everything."

"You going someplace, Mrs Pat?"

"Yes." She looked at Mayne. "You and I, Tony, are leaving for Belem just as soon as possible."

Mayne stared at her with his mouth open. "You want to go to Brazil?"

"I'm going to the mine."

"Yeah, but say . . . Mr Pat always said that the jungle is no place for a woman."

"You just have to get things straight, Tony," Alison said. "I'm the one making the decisions now. I want you to arrange the passages, and I want you to make up a list of all the clothes and gear I'll need. Hugo can help you. He'll be coming with us."

Hugo wore a great happy smile.

"Hugo ain't never been in a jungle in his life, Mrs Pat," Clem objected. "I should be the one coming with you."

"Now, say . . ." Hugo bristled.

"I'm sure he'll learn," Alison said. "David, what have I forgotten?"

"Well . . ." David as usual looked slightly embarrassed.

220

"I think you should make a Will, Mrs Pat. I mean . . . going off into the jungle . . ."

"Of course. I was thinking of it. You must get Señor Puig out here tomorrow. But it will be very straightforward. I intend to leave everything to the five children, in equal proportion."

"Ah . . . yes, of course. When would they get the money?"

"Well . . . it would have to be administered, of course, and their schooling paid for; each inheritance would be paid at the age of twenty-one."

"Then you have to have executors, or an executor, Mrs Pat, who would appoint an administrator."

"Ah." How utterly lonely she was, she suddenly realised. If only Mummy and Daddy, or Tom and Harry, had been alive. Aunt Audrey was her sole living relative . . . and Aunt Audrey's letter of condolence on Pat's death had not been particularly warm. She was acutely aware that the four men were all staring at her, perhaps trying to influence her thinking. As if she could possibly trust any of them with such an immense responsibility . . . certainly on his own. Aunt Audrey would just have to do her bit. "Right," she said. "I will name four executors. Señor Puig. Mr George Ruthven of New York City. Miss Audrey Bennett, of London, England. And yourself, David. All decisions to be unanimous."

David had been writing away. Now he raised his head. "Meetings might take some arranging."

"Then they will have to be arranged," Alison told him. "I'll have a word with Puig, but would you get letters off to the other two informing them of my decision."

He nodded. "Right away."

Sometimes she felt the web was choking her. There was so much to be thought about, so many things she had never even considered before.

She was leaving the children, for the first time in their

221

lives. It had been so easy to plan, to determine . . . and so difficult to do. She might never see them again. But that would only happen if she were dead, and she had every intention of staying alive.

She was leaving Jonny Carter, to languish in gaol. But she couldn't help him by remaining in Mexico. She had to rely on the detective, whoever he might be. And be patient.

And, having taken the decision, and actually left The Keep, she could feel her excitement taking over. She had been a prisoner of Pat's will for seven years. Now she was free. Free, free, free. Free to do anything in the world she wished. And thus she was doing what she wanted to do more than anything else.

Just being on the ship ploughing south through the sunlit Caribbean was the epitome of freedom. Hugo was his old self, too, overjoyed to be her sole guard, solicitously trying to anticipate her every wish as she basked on the upper deck in her chair.

But even Mayne was in the best of humours, while Lucia quickly got over her initial consternation at being whisked away from her home. It seemed as if leaving The Keep had lifted a great pall of depression from them all. Alison was only sorry for those who had to stay behind. But they would soon all be on their way to a new home . . . save for poor Jonny.

To start brooding on Jonny now would be self-defeating. She was doing all she could.

And she was carrying at least one problem with her. She found that on board a ship, and away from The Keep, it was impossible to envisage Tony Mayne creeping along the darkened gallery with a gun in his hand and murder in his heart. He was, as she had discovered at The Keep, a most interesting companion, and if now she suspected that his tales of the discomforts and dangers of the bush were somewhat exaggerated, either to frighten her or to make sure she relied on him rather than Hugo when she got there, they were none the less exciting for that.

He could not have been more polite, more sympathetic, and more fulsome in his praise of Pat. Of course, words were cheap . . .

"Did you have anything to do with shipping the gold from the mine?" she asked him one evening after dinner as they sat on deck enjoying the warm breeze, watching the stars which seemed close enough to pluck from the sky.

"No, ma'am. I was strictly the mine manager. Still am, I guess." He gave her a sidelong glance.

"Of course. But you were aware it was being shipped?"

"Oh, sure. But that was Mr Pat's business. My job was to mine and smelt the bullion. It was then accumulated until Mr Pat and Alvarado were both at the mine, and then shipped down to Manaos. Brother, you should have seen the precautions. Mr Pat employs virtually as many trained gunmen as the Brazilian army – and the army was generally involved too."

"I must meet this man Alvarado," Alison said thoughtfully.

"I figured you'd want to do that," he said. "I've sent him a wire. He'll be waiting for you at Belem. Say, Mrs Pat . . . can I ask you a question?"

"Anything you like."

"Well . . . Mr Pat ran this whole outfit, his whole empire, if you like, himself. You aiming to do that?"

"With a little bit of help from my friends."

"You can count on that. But you're gonna need more than a little bit of help. This is a man-size job you've inherited. Mr Pat, well, he'd been fighting, and struggling, and developing, if you like, all of his life before he struck it rich. He had a skin like leather, both physical and mental, and the same determination that had kept him from starving or dying from malaria on a hundred occasions alone in the bush."

"And I've lived all of my life on milk and honey. I know that, Tony. But the events of the past few months are having their effect, I can promise you that."

"I still think . . . well, what you need, Mrs Pat, is a

223

man who knows the ropes standing beside you. And not as a servant. Anyway . . ." he grinned. "A pretty girl like you needs to be married."

"Married," she said. "Ah! Yes, it probably would be a good idea. Who did you have in mind?"

He looked away again. "It's who you might have in mind that counts, Mrs Pat. Or may I call you Alison?"

Alison stood up. "I think I'm for bed. Maybe Mrs Pat would be more appropriate for the time being, Tony."

My God, she thought as she climbed into her bunk.

Pedro Alvarado was indeed waiting for her in Belem. He was short, plump, not unhandsome, and surprisingly young, certainly not more than forty.

"*Señora?*" he said, kissing both her hands. "Pat spoke so much of you, I feel I have known you for years. But how can I express my feelings about what has happened . . ."

"They are much appreciated, *señor*," Alison said. "We have much to discuss, you and I."

"I know this, *señora*. And I am entirely at your disposal."

"Then dine with me," she suggested.

She made Hugo and Mayne sit at a separate table, out of earshot, in the restaurant; she knew there was no way she could dismiss them altogether, as whatever their varying motives, they both so obviously regarded her as their private responsibility, and in Mayne's case at least, his private ambition. But that thought, however horrific, was also reassuring; even if he had murdered Pat, he would hardly have a go at her while wanting to marry her.

Besides, *had* he murdered Pat? The possibility seemed to grow more remote with every day. And was more remote than ever as she found herself sitting with this smooth-talking Brazilian, who appeared anxious to be added to the ranks of her watchdogs, but who had been a friend of Leighton's . . . according to Mayne.

"You know that I have inherited everything?" she asked, studying his face.

"Oh, indeed, *señora*."

"Then you and I are partners. I think you should call me Alison."

"It will be my pleasure . . . Alison."

"Tell me about our other partners."

He raised his eyebrows. "Other partners?"

"You must know that Pat had to obtain financing to work the mine."

"I knew this, Alison. But it was none of my concern. I do not believe Pat took any more partners. He never told me of it."

"Did you not know a man called Leighton?"

"Ah! Jimmy Leighton."

"He was your friend."

"We were acquainted. When Pat told me he needed much money to develop the mine, I thought of Leighton. He had some money, and was looking for an investment."

"So he invested in El Dorado. For a ten per cent return."

"I believe so."

"And then for some reason gave the shares back and got out."

"I think he had lost faith in it. Pat paid him back his original stake."

"And then he went off and committed suicide? There must have been more involved than that."

Alvarado shrugged. "I am sorry, but I do not know about it."

Alison gazed at him. "Have you never heard of a man called Carlo Rubio?"

"Rubio? I have heard of this man, certainly. Sometimes he is in the newspapers." He frowned. "He was connected with Pat? And the mine?" He began to look genuinely alarmed.

"Leave that one with me," Alison said reassuringly. "I'm just happy he had nothing to do with the mine itself. I'm going up there tomorrow. Are you coming?"

"Of course. If you would like me to."

She studied him. He presented a façade of the most utter innocence. Which could well be true, knowing Pat. But no man who over seven years had picked up two hundred and ninety million dollars without ever having lifted a finger could be that innocent.

"Tell me how you and Pat worked," she said.

"Well . . ." he looked embarrassed. "I had very little to do with the operation. It was necessary for Pat, as it will be necessary for you," he added carefully, "to have a Brazilian partner. When Pat first found the mine, he approached me and asked me to be that Brazilian partner. I had known him for some time, and I agreed. Of course, at that time I had no idea how valuable the mine was going to turn out . . ."

Or you would have claimed more than ten per cent, she thought. "But you have done quite well out of it," she remarked.

"Well . . ."

"Nearly three hundred million dollars, and it is still coming."

"This was my worth to Pat as a front," Alvarado said. "But now that I shall be required to take an active part in the running of the mine . . ."

"Why should you do that, Pedro?"

"Well, a young woman like yourself, Alison . . . well, you will need all the help you can get. You have said so."

"Not in running the mine," Alison said. "I am seeking help in other areas."

"You intend to operate the mine yourself?"

"Through my manager, yes."

"Tony Mayne," Alvarado growled, casting a glance at the table where Mayne and Hugo were sitting.

"Do you not like Tony?"

"Since you ask me, Alison, no, I do not like Tony."

"Why not?"

Alvarado shrugged.

"Well, in that case you may well be able to help me. I am searching for two things. The first is the identity of Pat's assassin."

Alvarado frowned. "But there has been a conviction. The man Carter."

"The fact that Jonny Carter was convicted does not mean he was guilty, Pedro."

Hoods descended over Alvarado's eyes as he considered that statement.

"The second matter on which I need information is how the gold was shipped. I understand you took part in this."

"Yes," Alvarado said absently.

"Tell me about it."

"Oh . . ." he concentrated. "It was accumulated at the mine, and twice a year Government assayers came up to inspect it and value it. It was then shipped down to Boa Vista, and from there to Manaos."

"Did Pat always accompany it?"

"Oh, indeed."

"And yourself?"

"Of course. It was a legal requirement."

"What happened in Manaos?"

"Well, now that it is an established system, the Government takes it over in Manaos, and it is shipped by them. We are paid according to its value, less the Government's percentage, of course."

"How are you, we, paid?"

"By cheque."

"In escudos?" She was astonished.

"No, no. In US dollars. This was the agreement. There were some problems in the early days, because of exchange control. But now that the Government knows it can sell the bullion to the Americans, why, everyone is happy."

"I see. So . . . you received a cheque for ten per cent of each shipment, the Government took its ten per cent, and the other eighty went to Pat."

"Yes," Alvarado said, pointedly.

"From which he had to defray the costs of working the mine, and then pay what he owed to his various backers."

"He received a great deal of money."

"Oh, I know that," Alison agreed, realising that she was no further ahead.

But she was getting closer to El Dorado.

They left Belem the next day, taking the ferry steamer upriver to Manaos, and despite herself Alison found herself forgetting about murders and missing millions, and becoming instead utterly fascinated by her surroundings. She had dreamed of these for so long, and now she was here. In an odd sense, she realised, she was actually missing Pat, for the first time since his death, because her dream had always had him standing at her side.

For the first time she wore bush clothes, khaki pants and a bush tunic, a slouch hat, thick canvas boots and equally thick stockings beneath, no matter that her feet were immediately bathed in sweat. Lucia and Hugo were similarly equipped, and if Hugo immediately looked like the great white hunter, and insisted upon wearing both a revolver on his hip and a rifle slung on his shoulder, at all times, just to accentuate his new image, Lucia resembled something stolen from a pantomime.

They had also, on Mayne's orders, been dosed with quinine before leaving Belem. This was quite the most foul-tasting stuff Alison had ever had in her mouth, and she was nearly sick.

"It'll keep malaria away," Mayne told her. "You'll take it every day from now on."

She felt like putting out her tongue at him. He had assumed complete control of the party from the moment they boarded the ferry, even giving orders to Alvarado, who raised no objections.

"He has made this journey many more times than me," the Brazilian told Alison.

"With Pat."

"Oh, yes of course. Pat did it more often than any of us."

Alison was equally quite content to let Mayne have his head, for the time being. There was so much to see and hear, and he was the man to explain it all to her.

The journey, upriver and thus against the current, took four days from Belem to Manaos. The ferry first of all proceeded up the rapidly narrowing Para, and thence north to join the Amazon proper at Itatupa. Here, some seventy-five miles from the sea, the river was still fifty miles wide, although filled with huge islands. From there the way lay generally south-west, with stops at Almeirim, Prainha, Santarem and Itacoatiara, before they reached the fork where the Rio Negro and the Rio Salinas joined to form the Amason proper. Here, some seven hundred miles from the sea, was the city of Manaos.

Each day of the voyage was unchangingly similar, and yet fascinatingly different. It began just before dawn, when the ferry got underway; for all its flat bottom and the experience of its crew, no one was prepared to attempt to navigate the river by night.

The bustle and the rumble of the engine woke everyone up. The cabins were in any event very small, and hot, and stuffy, and there were not very many of them, which meant that Alison and Lucia had to share. But after the first night Alison followed the example of the men and slept in a hammock on deck, taking off only her boots and her hat and smothering every exposed inch of her skin in foul-smelling citronella, which apparently not even the mosquitoes could stomach.

Thus getting out of bed was a very rapid operation,

and Hugo was always there with a steaming mug of black Brazilian coffee, so sweet – the beans were actually ground with sugar – that it needed nothing added, and so thick that if one did place a spoon upright in it, it took about a full second to fall over.

Served with this there was usually somewhat rough bread, toasted on an open fire, and an assortment of jams.

By then the ferry was underway, sometimes pushing through banks of reeds, sometimes skirting sandbanks, occasionally making a good speed over open stretches of river. At some stage in every day she struck, and there was much shouting, while the passengers were required to move from side to side to create a constant change in weight, and the engine was put astern . . . and invariably the ship finally slid off and into deeper water.

Alison could understand why there was no navigation at night.

The mist usually lifted about eight, as the sun rose above the trees, and for about an hour the sky would be clear. Then the clouds began to gather, and by the time the steamer stopped for lunch it was usually raining, to become a downpour within half an hour, heavy, windless and sullen, the almost solid sheets of water shutting out the banks to leave the ferry, and its passengers, isolated in a private world.

By three in the afternoon the rain had stopped, and the sky was again cloudless. For an hour the forest steamed, huge clouds of white vapour rising towards the sky.

By five this had cleared, and it would be the most perfect afternoon, spoiled only by the hordes of insects which came whirring out of the swamps to either side as the sun dropped to the west. The sun disappeared at six, and ten minutes later it was deep night, with the stars out, and, if there was a moon, almost as bright as day. But by then the ferry was again either anchored or tied up to the bank.

In the middle of the night it would rain again, another

downpour so heavy that it precluded normal conversation. By two the rain would have stopped, and around four a cold breeze would come sweeping out of the west, causing a hasty reaching for discarded covers, and bringing up the dawn mist. And so another day began.

Probably because of the noise of the engine, Alison was disappointed at the absence of life on the banks for most of the journey. During the night, when the steamer was stopped, she could hear all of the sounds she had anticipated, the roar of the howler monkeys, the high-pitched chatter of the sakkiwinkies, the rumble of a jaguar on the hunt, and sinister plops and sudden splashes in the river itself, while at dawn she awoke to the shrill cries of the kisskadees, the small yellow and black birds which asked an eternal question – *qu'est-ce-vous-dites?* as the French had named them – and the raucous cry of the toucans.

The river itself was very obviously filled with life. As the steamer chugged its way to the west the sailors would trail lines or even nets to pick up fish for lunch, and these could be lukanani, great thirty-five pounders which could feed everyone on board. Alligators were often to be observed basking on the sandbanks, but to Alison's further disappointment she saw no anacondas.

"You have to wait for the real jungle for creatures like that," Mayne told her.

In fact, the most interesting aspect of the Amazon part of the trip were the Indians at the various stopping points, short-legged and squat, high-cheek-boned and lank black-haired, shapelessly dressed where they were not practically naked, who clustered to the river bank when the ferry came as close as possible and dropped its long, wide gangplank, and engaged in on the spot markets, buying and selling, shouting news and exchanging gossip, having the time of their lives at the

231

sight of this link with the outside world.

Hugo stared at the forest in terrified amazement.

There was no disappointment in Manaos, however. The city had been built half a century earlier as a shipping terminus for the rubber being lapped on the upper Amazon. Before the introduction of the rubber tree to Malaya, at the turn of the century, the headwaters of the Amazon, situated in Bolivia as well as Brazil, had been the centre of the world's rubber production, at a time when civilisation, thanks to developments such as vulcanisation and the pneumatic tyre, had not been able to secure enough of the precious *cahouchec*, again as the French had named the wild balata.

The rubber barons had been the richest men in the world for about a generation. They had used their enormous prosperity in the most flagrant manner, apparently unable to conceive that their boom could ever end. Their houses were reputed to have been palaces, long deserted and reclaimed by the jungle, in which the most elegant furniture and manners had gone hand in hand with the most bestial treatment of their peons, who had been reduced to a slave level of wage-indebtedness.

Hearing about them from Alvarado and Mayne, Alison could not help but suppose that Pat would have fitted perfectly into their society.

Manaos, or as the Portuguese liked to spell it, Manaus, remained the visible monument to their affluence. The last port on the river navigable by ocean-going ships, it had been the despatch point for everything going out, and the dispersal point for everything coming in, and the barons had determined to make it into the capital city of South America. Much of it now also lay in ruins, with weeds sprouting through the streets, and only one or two trams still running, but no decay could diminish the splendour of the Theatre Amazonas, the Opera House, with its huge colonnade facade and its immense central dome, as if Paris had been transported to the jungle . . . as indeed had been the intention.

There were hotels in Manaos, and hot baths, and good food and wine. "Is this our last contact with civilisation?" Alison asked.

Mayne grinned. "Depends what you call civilisation, Mrs Pat. Next stop, Boa Vista."

To get to Caracarai involved another boat trip of four hundred miles, up the Rio Negro to Tupanaoca, and thence north on the Rio Branco. Soon after entering the Rio Branco, although the river itself kept to the valley it had carved out over the preceding three hundred centuries, the land to either side began to rise.

"More than three thousand feet, in places," Mayne told Alison, "with peaks, such as Roraima, getting on for ten plus."

The journey was again made by water, but this was a far cry from the ship which plied between Belem and Manaos, and was hardly more than a large double-ended open boat, operated by a very noisy outboard motor, around which were stacked innumerable spare cans of gasolene, and above which the helmsman smoked endless cigarettes.

"Is this thing safe?" Alison had to ask.

"Most of the time," was the unreassuring answer.

Now there was no question of cabins or stringing hammocks on deck; the hammocks were taken ashore to be hung between trees at each night's stop. This was the real bush at last. On their first nights' stop Alison was so excited she hardly slept a wink, but lay awake listening to the sounds of the forest and the unceasing swish of the river, watching the fire, which was kept blazing all night by whoever happened to be on watch, wishing she could have someone with her with whom she could really share the experience.

"There's a plan to punch the Pan-American Highway through this bush," Mayne told her. "Then Manaos and Boa Vista will be linked by a fast motor road, and we'd be there in twelve hours instead of twelve days."

"I think it'll be a shame, when that day comes," Alison commented.

"You're a romantic," he told her with a grin.

Well, she wasn't going to argue with that.

There was of course a down side to travelling by open boat through the forest, which did not change its habits. In fact, as they actually crossed the Equator the day after leaving Tupanaoca, it got more and more hot and steamy, and the daily downpours became ever heavier. In the boat or on the bank there was no shelter, and ordinary raincoats were useless. Alison and Hugo and Lucia were given ponchos to wear, shapeless squares of waterproof cloth with merely a small hole in the centre through which the head fitted. Beneath these one's clothes could remain reasonably dry, from rainwater, although in the heat Alison quickly found herself swimming in sweat. While not even her bush hat could keep the wet from her hair. She and Lucia had to laugh at the sight of each other's bedraggled appearance.

Other aspects of the journey were less amusing. Disappearing into the forest as was necessary remained a terrifying and humiliating experience; the two women always went together, but were always terribly aware of the masculine eyes watching them coming and going. The habit of washing or even bathing in the river first thing every morning was something else Alison could not get used to. She had brought a bathing suit, but using soap inside a bathing suit when watched by a dozen men, especially as the men were naked, was next to impossible.

"You might as well take it off, Mrs Pat," Hugo suggested.

She wasn't going to do that, even if she realised that she wasn't quite as emancipated as she had supposed.

234

Then there were, as Mayne had promised, bush ticks and chiggers. Every morning Alison and Lucia had to present their bare toes for inspection; the fact that everyone else was doing the same in no way made them feel any less like a pair of errant schoolgirls, especially when the little insects were discovered burrowing beneath their skin, and had to be dug out with a needle.

The ticks were even more embarrassing, as they sought the dark recesses of the human body. How they got there Alison never knew, but every so often she felt an intolerable itching. The first time she attempted to scratch, discreetly, she discovered that again every man in the party had been surreptitiously watching her.

"Don't scratch!" Mayne was on his feet.

"What?"

"If you just pull or knock the tick off, its head will remain in your flesh, and it will fester and cause a serious sore. Far worse than chigger eggs."

Alison looked at Alvarado.

"I'm afraid this is true," the Brazilian agreed.

"So what do I do? Just sit and suffer?"

"It must be burned off," Mayne told her.

"Come again?"

"If you touch the tick's head with a hot match, or a lighted cigarette," he explained, "the shock will make it relax its grip. It will fall off of its own accord, head and all."

Again Alison looked at Alvarado.

"This is also true, Alison."

"Where is it?" Mayne asked.

She gulped. "In my armpit."

"Right. Take off your bush jacket."

"Here?"

"Well, perhaps we should leave the camp."

"You come with me, Lucia," Alison said.

Mayne grinned. "Anyone would think you don't trust me."

"Just let's say right now I'm in need of all the feminine support I can get," Alison told him.

The whole idea was distasteful, even if she was fortunately wearing a bra. But she had not shaved her armpits since Manaos, and he was actually going to have to touch her. Actually, Mayne proved very efficient and surprisingly gentle, and did not appear to be distracted, by anything. He lit a cigarette, sifted through the silky pale brown hairs, and then she felt the sudden heat on her flesh. She gave a little gasp, expecting to be burned, but was not, and a moment later he was holding the tick between thumb and forefinger in front of her.

"Ugh!" she exclaimed. "I never knew they were that big." It was as large as her middle fingernail.

"They aren't, until they're gorged with blood. Your blood." He popped it between his two thumbnails, and she gave another gasp as his hands discoloured. "Your blood," he smiled. "Hold on," as she made to put on her bush jacket again. He produced a tube of ointment and rubbed some into the flesh where the tick had been. "You were lucky, you know. Often they attack far more intimate places. Maybe one of these days I'll get lucky."

Up till that last remark, she had almost been warming to him.

Alison actually did discover a tick between her legs just before they reached Caracarai – but she had no intention of allowing Mayne, or any of the men, even Hugo to do anything about it. She summoned Lucia and the pair of them disappeared into the bush together. She lit the cigarette herself, took a few vigorous puffs – she had never smoked in her life – and then gave it to Lucia. Lucia was terrified, and her hand was shaking, with the result that Alison got a scorch mark on the inside of her thigh, but the tick was disposed of.

"I think from here on we'll look after each other," she told the Mexican girl.

Lucia, who had already had two ticks of her own removed, entirely agreed.

Caracarai was very much a frontier town. When Alison remembered how she and Mummy and Daddy had gawked at the people in Belem ten years before . . . here there was not a western-style suit to be seen. But Boa Vista, a further forty miles upriver, was surprisingly civilised, and even possessed a primitive hotel, in which Alison could have a badly needed hot bath. Here there were people from El Dorado waiting for them, mostly Brazilians but two American engineers as well as the German doctor, Johann Kailer. Alison's initial reaction was that it was too close to the end of the War to be employing Germans, especially in such a vital position, but it appeared that Kailer had lived in Brazil since the early thirties, and had no affinity with the Nazis.

He, and everyone else, was welcome personified to their new employer, mixing sympathy and adulation in treacly proportions. He also wished to examine her, and this she permitted. She needed reassuring that she was surviving this enormous adventure, and was greatly relieved when he pronounced her entirely fit. She reckoned he could not only be a good friend but a source of information, and looked forward to getting to know him better once they reached El Dorado.

Of the two Americans, Bob McCall was apparently an experienced mining engineer. Harry Brum was a very young man, recently hired by Mayne. Both appeared utterly in awe of their rather beautiful new boss. Neither had been on El Dorado more than two years, so neither would have anything to tell her of those early days . . . and both were obviously Mayne's men.

From Boa Vista there was the "road" Pat had carved through the jungle to transport his mining equipment.

It was not much more than a track. and the company apparently had to employ gangs of labourers to work on it constantly to keep it usable at all, but they boarded a fleet of jeeps, left the settlement at dawn, and were at El Dorado by dusk.

The trip, bumpy and dusty and then wet, was rendered the more exhilarating for Alison by the thought that this place of which she had heard so much was momently coming closer. Her only disapointment was that it was dark within half an hour of her arrival, but already she had seen the huge shaft and the towering machinery – "Goes down four hundred feet, now," Mayne told her – as well as the immortal lake. She stood on the bank that night after supper, and tried to envisage it as it might have been when Pat had first seen it. This was difficult, because although it had been allowed to fill up again with water once the last skeleton had been removed, now it was entirely surrounded by houses; El Dorado was a substantial little village.

Yet Pat had stood here, she knew, before going into the water . . . no, someone else had done that, and she had no idea who. No one did. No one had ever had the guts to question Pat's story, even after learning about his phobia.

His hand was everywhere. El Dorado was entirely surrounded by a barbed wire fence several miles long, which was patrolled constantly by armed men supported by dogs; she might have been back at The Keep. Within this there lived and worked close to a hundred men, with their dogs and various other pet animals; not all were miners, for Pat had also installed a farm for chickens, pigs and milch cows to ensure a regular supply of food, while there was additionally an extensive field producing local vegetables, such as okra and eddoe, but principally cassava, which was also used for making a very coarse bread.

There were also a considerable number of half naked and decrepit looking women, and even several children.

238

"Well, men have to have women," Mayne explained.

"You mean those aren't wives."

"Well, some of them may be. I've never asked. As long as there's no fighting . . . Doc here looks after their health."

"You approve of this kind of living?" Alison asked Kailer.

The German shrugged. "There's not a lot we can do about it, Mrs Pat."

"I'm afraid I don't agree with you," Alison told him.

She agreed with them even less the next day, when she was shown the miners' living quarters, over Mayne's objections. By then she had been taken down the mineshaft, had experienced her first ever touch of claustrophobia, and had inspected every square inch of her land, including the extensive cemetery just outside the perimeter fence. Only about half the men interred there had died natural deaths.

That evening she sat with the white employees on the verandah of the mess hall, looking out at the lake, and listening to the mournful strumming of a guitar from the native quarters.

"There's a lot to be done," she remarked.

They waited.

"You tell me the mine is safe and working conditions are good, Tony. I can't argue about that, I don't know."

"It's as Pat set it up and as he wanted it, Mrs Pat."

"I have no doubt of that. I think I may have a look at some other mines some time and see how they are operated. However, I don't want to talk about that now. I want to talk about living conditions. Let's begin with housing."

"Don't you like your bungalow, Mrs Pat? It's the one Mr Pat always used. Designed it himself."

She nodded. "I am very satisfied with my bungalow, as I am sure you all are with yours. I am concerned about the conditions for the workers."

Mayne raised his eyes and glanced at Alvarado.

"That communal barracks is a disgrace," Alison stated. "I'm amazed those people still work for us. For me," she corrected, with deliberate emphasis. "Do I pay them that well?"

"They get their wages. But they can't quit."

"Why not?"

"They owe us too much money."

"I don't understand that."

"Well, Alison," Alvarado came in. "They are given unlimited credit at the Company store as soon as they come to work here. They don't have too much idea about money, so they all buy far more than they can afford. Then, well . . . their wages have to go on repaying the debt.."

"Which you constantly encourage them to increase."

"It's a free world. We keep a well-stocked commisariat, yes."

"Well, that has to stop. The Company will liquidate all outstanding debts to the commisariat, and from then on no man will be allowed to run up an account totalling, at any time, more than two-thirds of his monthly wage."

The men looked at each other.

"They'll quit," Mayne remarked.

"Then we'll hire others. But I'm not sure they will quit, not once working conditions are improved. You'll put building in hand immediately. I wish each man to have his own, separate bungalow. I wish each man to have a proper domestic set-up. I wish a church to be built, and a school for their children. I wish these things done now."

"My dear Alison," Alvarado protested. "The cost . . ."

"Will be peanuts compared to what we are taking out of the ground."

"This is Roraima Province, not New York State," McCall muttered.

"If you don't like working here, Mr McCall, you can

240

always go someplace else," Alison told him. "I want all of that started tomorrow. I'll expect the plans to be available by the evening." She smiled at them and stood up. "Good night, gentlemen."

Next morning, to Alison's surprise, they were all smiles. Clearly they had talked it over last night and decided that the little woman had to be humoured, at least up to a point. But she understood immediately that when Mayne suggested she have a look at the real forest, beyond the fence, he had been deputed – or had determined on his own – to try to talk some sense into her.

The prospect didn't bother her in the slightest. She felt she had their measure now, and more important, they had hers.

"You're not seriously bringing that great lout along, are you?" Mayne asked in dismay as Hugo began putting on his cartridge belts.

"Of course. Hugo accompanies me everywhere." She smiled at him, sweetly. "That's how Mr Pat wanted it."

"It's just that with all that gear he's liable to shoot himself in the foot. Anyway, I kind of hoped for a private chat."

"You shall have one," she promised him. "Hugo will stay out of earshot."

"If you say so, Mrs Pat."

He escorted her out through the northern gate.

"Keep about fifty yards back, Hugo," Alison instructed, and the big man nodded.

Alison followed Mayne into the bush. For the first few hundred yards it was easy going, for in the process of making the mine village much of this land had been cleared, even if never used. But gradually the foliage grew thicker, at the same time as the sun disappeared; Alison could not tell whether it had been obscured by clouds or simply by the huge trees reaching so high above her head.

She looked over her shoulder, but could not see Hugo. On the other hand, she could hear him, clumping through the bush.

"Don't you think we should wait for him?" she asked.

Mayne grinned. "He knows where we are. Have you ever seen anything quite as beautiful as that?"

He was pointing at a huge red and black butterfly.

"It's exquisite," she agreed, pleasantly surprised. She had never suspected Tony Mayne of possessing any aesthetic tastes whatsoever.

"The jungle is full of little gems," he told her. "And I'm not talking about gold, either. Oops, rain."

The first drop came crashing through the leaves like a vertically descending bullet. Mayne had brought both their ponchos, and these they put on, but by now the rain was thudding all around them.

"We'll find some place to shelter," Mayne shouted, and held her hand to drag her forward.

"Hugo!" she protested, but there was nothing they could do about Hugo now. She tripped and staggered, pulled on by Mayne's hand, while trailing branches caught at her pants and poncho, snatched at her hat. Then he stopped so suddenly she bumped into him.

They stood on the edge of quite a large stream, almost a river, its brown water drifting slowly to the north. Mayne led her along the bank until they arrived in the shelter of a huge tree, which bent over the water and provided a useful roof.

They knelt beneath it, panting. "Is this safe?" Alison asked, as she listened to a rumble of thunder.

"Oh, sure," Mayne said.

"I really am worried about Hugo. I mean, suppose he stumbles into that river? I'm sure there are some nasties in there."

"And you're quite right. It's certainly got piranha

fish. But he'll see the water in time," Mayne assured her. "Anyway, if he has any sense he'll be sheltering as well."

Alison had got her breath back and her heart started to settle down. "How long will this last?"

"The usual, about an hour. But we'll be quite snug here."

"You almost make me feel you were coming here deliberately."

"Sure I was."

"You mean you've been here before?"

"I've spent most of the past eight years in this bush, Mrs Pat. I know it pretty well."

"Oh." Suddenly she was uneasy. She wished she knew where Hugo was.

"I said I wanted to have a heart to heart talk with you," Mayne said, his voice as quiet as it could be and still be heard above the pounding of the rain.

"I understand. But I am not going to change my mind, Tony. There is no reason in the world why the mine village should not provide decent living standards. That it hasn't been done before is simply because Pat never thought of it."

"I wasn't going to talk about that," Mayne said. "At least, not in detail." He sat on the sodden ground, and after a moment's hesitation she did likewise; she was soaked through anyway. "But it's all aspects of what's happening to you. You've been dumped right in the deep end, quite unprepared for what's involved. I think we're all agreed that you're handling it magnificently. But it's just too much for a girl like yourself. You need a man around, to look after you, and to look after your businesses. A man who already understands what it's all about, and how to cope."

He paused for breath, and Alison looked at him.

"Maybe, when I find such a man, I'll take your advice."

He grinned. "You got one, Mrs Pat. I'm right here. Now, you know you couldn't do no better. I know

243

everything there is to know about El Dorado. And I was Pat's best friend. I'm just like him."

"Forget it, Tony. I agree that you probably are just like Pat. But I was busy divorcing him, remember?"

"For that madman Carter? You need your head examined. The man's a murderer."

"Because you say so? I have my own ideas on that."

"Yeah? But no matter what you think, Carter ain't gonna be around for a long, long time. If ever. And I'm here." He grinned at her. "Ready, willing and able."

He had made her angry, both by disparaging Jonny and by the very idea that he could be her husband. "I wouldn't marry you if you were the last man on earth, Tony Mayne."

"Yeah?" He cocked his head as the sound of a gunshot echoed through the forest. "Hugo's getting lonely. And he's lost."

"Then we'd better signal him." She reached for the revolver at her own belt, and Mayne plucked it from her fingers and threw it into the bushes.

"What the hell . . .?"

He leaned on her, and she fell over. Instantly he was lying on top of her, his weight pinning her to the wet leaves, while he groped beneath her poncho for her belt.

"You just let me go!" she shouted. "You bastard. You . . ."

"Calm down," he said, attempting to kiss her. "Listen, I love you. I adore you. I always have. You just gotta get that through your head. Your trouble is you're just confused by everything that's happened."

"Will you get off me," Alison panted.

Mayne allowed his body to slip sideways, and she could breathe again.

"And get your hand out of there," she snapped.

His hand slipped down from beneath the poncho, but only as far as her crotch, on which his fingers gently closed.

"Your trouble is you ain't had a man recently."

"You're fired," Alison said. "As of now. Get out! Go!"

He grinned, and bent his head towards her again. "I'm going to marry you," he said.

His lips were attempting to close over hers, his hand was still encircling her groin. Alison bit, as viciously as she could, and his head jerked back as he gave a shout of agony; blood filled her mouth and dribbled down his chin, and she realised that she had half bitten his lip off.

She sat up "Oh, my God! I didn't mean to hurt you like that. But you brought it on yourself."

She watched the pain and anger reach his eyes. "You little bitch," he snarled. "Pat always said you were a bitch. Well, now . . ."

His hand, which had left her crotch, returned, and his other hand tried to throw the poncho up. Alison swung her own hands, left and right, fingers curved. Her nails slashed into his face and he gave another shout of pain and fell away from her. She reached her knees, but he was on his feet before her, towering above her, face now quite distorted with rage and pain as there was blood dribbling from his cheeks as well as his mouth.

Alison realised she was in physical danger, of at least a severe beating as well as rape. She threw herself to one side, kicking as she did so. Mayne turned with her, and the toe of her boot connected immediately behind his left knee. He gave a gasp, and fell to his knees. Alison kicked again, this time connecting with the side of his jaw. Mayne threw up his hands and stumbled backwards, on to the bank of the river, and then as he tried to regain his balance, tripped and fell into the water.

Now his yell was sheer terror. Alison staggered forward and almost overbalanced herself. The current was faster than she had supposed, as the water was deeper than she had thought, and Mayne was already several feet from the bank and several feet downriver as well, beating the surface, blood still dribbling down his face into the water.

"Help me!" he screamed.

Alison ran along the bank. "Can't you swim?" she shouted.

Mayne didn't immediately reply. He had come up against the broken branch of a tree, apparently embedded in the mud at the bottom of the river, its subsidiary branches just breaking the surface, and to these he was holding, his face a picture of terror.

Clearly he was afraid to move. Alison didn't know what to do. She was a strong swimmer herself, but she wasn't sure she had the strength to pull a man like Mayne from the water. On the other hand, she couldn't just let him drown.

She stood on the bank, pulled off her poncho, and then sat down to drag off her boots. She stood up again, dropped her cartridge belt and holster, debated whether to take off her pants for freedom of movement, and heard the most blood-curdling scream.

Her head jerked as she stared at Mayne, his face suffused, his eyes staring, his mouth open and uttering yet another quite unearthly howl of pain and terror. Around him the water was starting to bubble.

CHAPTER 9

Dreams

Alison found herself on her knees, staring at the discoloured water. All movement had ceased, and Mayne had disappeared.

The rain had stopped, and a few minutes later she heard crashing noises in the bush. She turned her head, and saw Hugo coming towards her. At any other time she would have burst out laughing. The big man had lost his hat and his wet hair was plastered to his head, his shirt and pants were torn, and he looked quite distraught, as well as sopping wet.

But his face broke into a great grin as he saw her. "Oh, Mrs Pat! I have been so worried. Where's Mr Mayne?"

Alison tried to stand, and couldn't; her legs wouldn't support her. She couldn't speak, either: her mouth was too filled with saliva. She pointed instead.

Hugo stood beside her. "He fell in?"

She merely looked at him.

"Holy Jesus Christ! You pushed him?"

Alison licked her lips. "We were fighting, and he fell in."

"Fighting? You and Mayne?"

"He was trying to rape me."

Hugo looked as if he was about to blaspheme again, but changed his mind. "So you pushed him in. The bugger deserved it. But . . . he drowned?"

"No," Alison said, "He didn't drown."

Hugo looked at the water again, and gulped. "Shit!" he commented.

Alison got to her feet.

"Maybe . . . maybe we'd better keep this to ourselves," Hugo muttered.

The temptation was enormous. But that would be to put herself in Hugo's power, and Alison had no intention of ever being in anyone's power again.

"We'll tell exactly what happened," she said.

It was easier than she had supposed. If everyone at the camp was shocked, no one seemed inclined to disbelieve her story. Everyone knew that Mayne was a strong swimmer, and he had also been twice her size. Her revolver was found, undischarged, as were Mayne's weapons. Her clothes had been torn, and several of the men remembered Mayne's hints that he intended to bring little Lady Muck down to size. There was no reason for anyone to question what she said.

The police came up from Boa Vista, after a considerable delay, during which Alison went about carrying out the improvements she had determined on. It kept her busy, and she had a couple of brandies every night to help her sleep; Kailer prescribed pills, but she preferred the liquor – she didn't really like liquor, she felt there was less chance of becoming addicted.

Even so, there were times when she lay awake and stared into the darkness, listening to the whirring of the fan and the buzzing of the mosquitoes trying to get through the netting, heart pounding and her entire body bathed in sweat.

It was not merely the recurring memory of Tony Mayne being torn to pieces. He was a loathsome man and when she thought of him touching her she almost wanted to be sick . . . but what a terrible way to die. More than that, however, there was the suspicion that El Dorado, for all the fabulous wealth that it had delivered – or perhaps because of it – was an evil place, which spawned sudden death. Jonny Carter should have died, Geoff Waller had died, as had Mark Leighton. Pat himself had been murdered, as had the man Sanchez, she was certain, and now Tony Mayne . . . his death was officially regarded as an accident, but she knew in her heart that had he attempted to come at her again and she been able to secure her gun she would have shot him.

And those five did not include the untold others who had died and of whom she knew nothing. The cemetery was the proof of that.

More terrifying was the understanding that Mayne might after all have been right. She had been pitchforked into a situation of which she knew nothing, and which frightened her more and more with every day. She had refused to accept that until Mayne's death, but she had known that she was caught up in something so immense she had been afraid to analyse it. In Mexico City she had thought of herself as a spider in the middle of a gigantic web. But spiders controlled events, within their webs. Was she not more like an inexperienced juggler who was attempting to keep several balls in the air at the same time, without a clue as to what to do when they started to hit the floor?

Worst of all, however, was the thought that if Mayne had killed Pat – and how desperately did she hate to believe that, now – with him had died that last hope of obtaining the evidence to free Jonny.

"What are you going to do?" Alvarado asked, after the inquest, held in Boa Vista, had confirmed the verdict of accidental death.

"I am going to return to Mexico, in the first instance," Alison replied. Her nerves had begun to settle down.

"Of course. But I was speaking of El Dorado. It must have a manager."

"Oh! Yes, of course." It had seemed to run quite smoothly during the few weeks since Mayne's death. There had even appeared to her to be a sense of relief amongst the workforce that Mayne was gone. But there was no telling how long that would last.

"Would you like me to find the man for you?" Alvarado asked. "Or would you prefer to advertise the job?"

Alison studied him. How much do I trust you? she thought, where it seems I cannot trust anyone else? How had Pat trusted people? The answer was that Pat had *not* trusted people. He had bound them to him by the power of his money. Then she would have to do the same. And become like him? She was determined never to do that. Yet she might have to *appear* to be like him.

"He will have to be someone absolutely trustworthy," Alvarado explained. "And equally someone who knows how to deal with the workers, and who knows about gold mining."

"Yes," Alison agreed, and sent for Bob McCall.

McCall sat, uneasily, twisting his hat between his fingers, clearly expecting immediate dismissal.

"You and Brum were hired by Tony Mayne," Alison said. "What are your plans?"

"Well, ma'am . . ." there was some more hat twisting. "I reckon there's still a job to be done here."

"Right. How long have you been in gold mining?"

"Seven years. I was in South Africa before coming here."

"Right. How would you like to take over as Mine Manager?"

"Ma'am?" He was utterly astonished.

"On certain conditions."

"You name them, ma'am."

"I intend to. Firstly production. Last year El Dorado produced one hundred and twenty million dollars worth

250

of gold. The year before it was one hundred and forty-five million. So there is some decline."

"All gold mines get played out eventually, Mrs Pat."

"I understand that. As my husband was alive and in charge of production last year and the year before, I have no doubt that those figures are correct. Now, I have neither the knowledge nor the desire to keep as close a watch on events here in Brazil as did my late husband, but I do not intend to be cheated."

"Why, ma'am . . ."

"Just listen," Alison told him. "I will accept a ten per cent fall in production per annum, but it must be accompanied by the relevant figures. If I hear the slightest suggestion of fraud you will not only be fired but you will be blacked from every gold mine in the world. Understood?"

McCall licked his lips. "I understand, Mrs Pat."

"Good. Now the second point is labour. I want all of my programme carried through, and I want the labour force treated as human beings, not animals. Understood? Your job here depends upon it."

"You got it, Mrs Pat."

"All right. What about Brum?"

"He's okay. He'll do what I tell him."

She nodded. "All right, Bob. As of this moment, you're in charge."

"Heck!" McCall's eyes glowed. "I sure am grateful to you, Mrs Pat."

"I want you to prove that."

"Oh, I will. And if there's anything, anything, I can maybe do for you . . ."

"There is something I want you to remember, Bob. Don't ever, ever, try to treat me like a little woman. Or a woman at all. Got me?"

McCall swallowed. "Yes, ma'am, Mrs Pat."

She said goodbye to them all, shaking hands with each peon and every woman and child, boarded the boat for

Manaos, and then home. She looked at the brown water flowing past. "Are there piranha fish in this river?" she asked Alvarado, who was accompanying her.

"Yes. There are piranha fish in most South American rivers."

Alison shuddered.

"I've never seen a human being taken by piranha," Alvarado said casually.

"It's something to avoid."

"I'm sure you're right. Will you be coming back to Brazil?"

"Of course I will."

He rested his hand on hers. "I shall look forward to that."

Oh. Lord, she thought. Another one. "So shall I," she agreed. "On my next visit, I would hope to meet your wife."

"Ah . . . yes, of course. In the meantime, if there is anything, anything at all I can do for you . . . after all, we are partners, are we not?"

"Yes," she agreed. "I would like to ask you a question."

"Anything."

"As I am sure you know, Pat took something like one-point-two billion dollars out of El Dorado, up to the time of his death."

Alvarado nodded. "I would say that is reasonably accurate."

"All in US dollar cheques, you say."

"Yes."

"One cheque every year?"

"Twice a year. We shipped twice a year. But I think it was several cheques for him. He had to meet so many payments, you understand. I mean, the money had to be paid in to several different accounts, apart from his own."

"Quite. Nevertheless, of his personal share, only eight hundred million dollars is accounted for."

Alvarado frowned at her.

"I don't want you to think I'm crying poor," Alison said. "I'd just like to know what Pat did with the money. Do you have any idea?"

"Me? I know nothing of Pat's business affairs."

"Ah! That's a pity."

"But we can discuss it further when we are in Manaos." he smiled. "I will take you out to dinner."

"Why, that's awfully sweet of you." Alison said. "But I should warn you that I always sleep with my door locked."

She appreciated The Keep for the first time, properly, when she got back. And she appreciated David Brook even more. Everything was as she had left it, save for one vital difference: Charlene was there to help Hannah with the children.

She and Alison hugged and kissed each other, and then there were hugs and kisses for all of the children, who seemed to have grown enormously in her absence, even baby Harry.

There was an even more enthusiastic welcome from the dogs.

Then there was a hot bath in her own tub, and the pleasure of wearing silk again . . . and a long session with David.

He listened to the tale of what had happened in Brazil with a serious face. "Mayne," he said, when she had finished. "You don't suppose he killed Mr Pat?"

"I don't want to believe it, Dave, because that would leave Jonny up the creek without a paddle, right?"

"Then you may be interested in what Harry Preston had to say."

"Harry Preston?"

"You told me to hire the best detective in the States, Mrs Pat."

"And you did? Oh, David, I could kiss you."

He could tell she didn't really mean it, and after a momentary hesitation continued.

"He came up with some interesting facts."

"Tell me."

"Well . . . seems there was someone else in the village the afternoon before Pat died."

"Who?"

"No name. He drove down from Mexico City, then disappeared. He didn't check in at the pension, and there is no record of his staying anywhere in the city, either."

"But he was here."

"That's right. And we have a description. The attendant at the pump remembered him, when he stopped for gas."

"Yes?"

"Below medium height, lean build, and face, lank dark hair."

"But . . . that's . . ."

"The same description as Geoff Waller's brother. Or at any rate, the guy who attempted to break in here."

"That's tremendous news. Wait till Guimard hears this."

"Well, Mrs Pat . . . he's already heard it. I took it to him right away."

"And?"

"He wasn't impressed. I think he feels we've manufactured this character."

"Isn't the pump attendant willing to identify him?"

"Well, you see, Mrs Pat, these people reckon it's possible to buy anyone, with your kind of money."

"Oh, for God's sake . . . is there no other corroboration that this man was here? They tracked him down pretty successfully the last time."

"They don't seem able to have done so this time."

"Then your man Preston simply has to find this Waller. That's his next assignment."

David nodded. "I've already put him on to that. But

. . . it may take some time. Waller, if it was Waller, flew to Mexico City from Miami, and then flew back again, and disappeared. Like he did the first time."

"So it'll take time. He must be found."

"We'll find him, Mrs Pat." David was, as ever, totally reassuring. "But . . . there's nothing else you can do right now."

"You think so?" Alison growled. "I'm just going to make that Guimard listen."

But she got nowhere. She talked with Guimard, she talked with Jayme Puig, and she talked with General Camacho. None of them felt the introduction of a shadowy figure from the past, who might or might not have been in the *pueblo* the night Pat had been killed, proved anything more than that she would go to the limits of her power, and her financial resources, to free her lover.

Alison felt so frustrated she wanted to scream. Instead she drove out to the state prison, against the advice of both David and Puig, to see Jonny. Accompanied by both Hugo and Clem, she felt well protected, but it was a horrifying experience. The prison itself, walls rising craggily from a desert far more depressing than that surrounding The Keep, left her feeling she was entering a world created by Dante. The interior was even more depressing, a place of clanging iron-barred doors, screaming or wailing inmates, and iron-jawed guards who looked at the little blonde woman as if they would have liked to eat her for breakfast, all surrounded by and shrouded in heat and stench and a general miasma of despair.

Coming face to face with Jonny Carter was most unpleasant of all.

She was shown into a small, windowless room, where there was a total absence of furniture save for the inevitable iron bars, behind which Jonny eventually appeared. He looked fairly fit, although he was thinner than she remembered. It was his face which had changed; there was a harshness about his mouth she did not remember, and a remoteness about his eyes.

"How was Brazil?" he asked.

"I'd better bring you up to date." She told him as rapidly as she could what had happened there.

"Some girl," he commented when she had finished. "Tell me something: you didn't actually shoot Pat, did you?"

She made herself believe he was joking, although there had been no humour in his voice.

"Do you still think Mayne did it?" Jonny asked, when she didn't reply.

"Up to that moment. But since coming back . . ." she told him about Waller, or Waller's look alike.

"But nobody wants to know," he commented. "Why should they go through all the hassle of re-opening the case, when as far as they're concerned, it's closed?"

"I'm not going to stop trying, Jonny."

"Then you're a fool. Look, you're the richest woman in the world, save maybe for a queen or two. You have the looks to match your wealth. You have a horde of lovely kids and a horde of doting servants, now you've got rid of Mayne. Why the hell don't you get out of here and enjoy all of those things?"

Alison bit her lip. But she was resolved not to be upset.

"Are they treating you all right?"

"Oh, for God's sake," he shouted. "They feed me shit and they work me until I drop. Then they flog me and kick me about. Then I'm locked in a cell with three other guys who just want to bugger me. I'm alive. They're treating me great."

"Jonny . . ."

The guards had moved forward.

"Get out of here," Jonny shouted. "Go to fucking hell, and leave me alone, you stupid little bitch. I don't want to see you again."

The guards dragged him through the doorway.

*　　*　　*

Alison was still trembling when she got back to the car.

"Rough, eh?" Clem inquired.

"Oh . . . drop dead," she snapped.

By the time she got back to The Keep her nerves had settled, at least externally; she did not suppose she was going to recover from the psychological effect of Jonny's outburst for some time. But for the moment, at least, she was angry. She summoned David.

"Did you set up the administrators of my estate?" she asked.

"I wrote to them all. Puig is all right, of course, and so is Ruthven. I haven't had a reply from the Bennett woman. But it doesn't matter now, does it? You're back safe and sound."

"Yes," Alison said. "Right. Now tell me, can I go to New York? London?"

"What's to stop you?"

"What about this tax thing?"

"Ah! Were you talking of visiting, or settling?"

"I certainly don't want to stay here."

"Well, the important thing is that you don't stay more than a few months, I would say three is the limit, in any other place. You have an apartment in New York. I would buy a flat in London, if I were you, and then two more in other pleasant parts of the world. You'll buy them in company names, of course, and I'll set things up so that they can't be related back to you."

"And then I keep moving."

"It's how most of the very rich do live."

"And you think that's any life for children?"

"Well, Mrs Pat, I think moving about might be fun for children, certainly at this age, as long as their mother moves with them. As they grow older, of course, you're going to have to settle them in schools . . . but you could use governesses until they're old enough to handle that."

"You make everything seem so easy, Dave."

"Everything *is* easy, Mrs Pat, so long as you're determined to make it so, and . . ." he grinned, "have the money to do it."

Yes, she thought. Unless you happen to be a born loser like Jonny Carter.

"Anyway," he went on. "There are all those properties you wanted to visit."

"Um," she said. "What about the dogs?"

"Well, it's only the British Isles and Scandinavia that go in for this quarantine business. I shouldn't think New York City is the ideal situation for a pair of big dogs, but someplace like the south of France, where if you had a house you could settle them in and be sure they were well looked after, and would always be there when you came home . . ."

Alison gave a little shiver. "There is so much to be organised. I mean, as you've just said, all of these homes will have to be staffed, and . . ."

"Just choose your spot and say the word, Mrs Pat, and I'll attend to it."

"Why?"

He raised his eyebrows.

"You're devoting your entire life to me. Why?"

David looked embarrassed. "Those were the terms, Mrs Pat."

"Terms?"

"I thought Mr Pat would have told you. When he took me on, he said, 'Dave, I am going to pay you fifty thousand dollars a year. In return, you forget everything, but everything, save me and my welfare.'"

"And you agreed to that?"

"Mrs Pat, fifty thousand dollars a year is about three times more than a guy like me could earn anyplace else."

"But . . . don't you have family? A girl?"

"No family, Mrs Pat. As for girls, there'll be time for them, I reckon."

"Join the club," she said savagely. "In reverse, if you follow me. Right. As of now your salary is sixty. Just don't ever walk out on me."

"There's no chance of that, Mrs Pat."

They gazed at each other. Another one hoping to muscle in, she wondered? But he'd never shown the least interest in her, as a woman. As he had confessed, he had been bought, body and soul, and he was happy to stay bought. He was the coldest of fish. But that was what she needed, right now, to protect her against her own impulses.

Had it not been for the underlying layer of misery about Jonny which made getting out of bed every morning a painful chore, life would suddenly have become deliciously exciting. But money meant she could even buy off her own conscience. She went into Mexico City and arranged with a department store there to send Jonny Carter a large hamper of food and English-language books every month, then went to see General Comacho and told him that if the parcel did not reach Jonny she would abandon Mexico altogether, and his million and a half a year.

The general smiled indulgently, and promised to take care of it.

Alison then packed up The Keep, although she left it as a going concern – it remained the ultimate refuge – and removed herself and her family, including the dogs, to the New York apartment.

They drove up, so that she could stop and see what had happened to her filling station in Texas. But that was derelict, Joe long disappeared with whatever profits there had been. She still owned the land and the station, however, and it had escalated in value.

It seemed that everything Pat had touched turned to gold. Her gold.

* * *

Maria had also disappeared. She had apparently done that some time ago, and Charlene, until she had been summoned to Mexico, had been coping with the apartment on her own. For the past few months, therefore, it had been shut up. But it was soon fresh and clean again, even if terribly overcrowded, so much so that Alison had immediately to take another apartment for Clem and the Mexican nurses, who came in every day. Hugo moved back into his old room: he was more than a bodyguard now – if David looked after everything in the public world, Hugo did the same for Alison's private world.

David had of course also accompanied them, but he preferred to live in an hotel and also turn up at the apartment every day. Alison gathered he was glad to be back in town, even if his private life remained as nebulous as ever.

There was a lot to be done. The news of Pat's murder had of course made headlines all over the world. Now the arrival of his widow was no less exciting to the media, it appeared, and Alison was subjected to endless interviews, and speculative articles. Questions varied from "Tell us the truth about your husband's murder, Mrs Grange," through "What does it feel like to be a billionairess?" to "When are you going to marry again, Mrs Grange?"

These she could handle. When however they asked her if it was true she and the convicted murderer had had an affair she usually threw the interviewer out, which did not make her very popular. But then, as Pat Grange's widow, she had never supposed she was going to be very popular with the media.

The news that Alison Grange was back in town had social New York buzzing. The Ruthvens were the first callers.

"Oh, my dear," Edith said, kissing her several times and holding her hands. "The things you have been *through*.

260

And such lovely children." The dogs she eyed with distaste.

George of course wanted to discuss plans, and listened gravely. "You'll want to settle down, one day," he remarked.

"One day."

"How about, well . . . personal plans?"

"I don't have any. There's too much to do."

The Ruthvens set about putting that right, by throwing a huge party in Alison's honour. After that, invitations came thick and fast, and she fell back into the old habit of having intimate dinner parties in return. But all suggestions of flirtations were firmly rejected, especially from Al Boskis.

There was simply too much on her mind. First and foremost, there was Tom and Harry. So much had been going on for the past six months that she had not had the time to chase them up as she had intended. Now that she did, she discovered they had both died in a Japanese prison camp. Aunt Audrey seemed somehow to hold her responsible for this, in that she had gallivanted off to become rich while they had been fighting for their country.

Now I have no family, Alison thought. Then what of friends? She wished she could tell how many were just interested in her because of her money.

For varying reasons, Pat had left so much behind him.

David kept reminding her that she must not overstay her welcome, but despite her feeling of insecurity as regards human relationships she was so enjoying her return to civilisation she was reluctant to pack up once again. Quite apart from the pleasure of being once again the lion of the social season after so long, and of being able to enjoy Edith's company – Edith was one of the very few people in the world, and the only woman, with whom she felt she could totally relax – she could again play bridge and tennis. There was the delight of being able to take Ben and Shirley to the Empire State Building and the Zoo, to the Statue of Liberty and indeed, just riding on the Staten Island Ferry, or skating in Central Park, while with Hugo's help she introduced Ben to the pleasures of watching baseball at the tail end of the season – it was not a game she knew a great deal about.

Her excuse for lingering until the last possible moment was that she was still awaiting news from Harry Preston, who was still seeking the elusive Bert Waller. If he existed. Sometimes she doubted it herself.

But if he didn't, then Jonny was doomed to spend a very long time in gaol.

She wished she could be sure about her feelings there, at least; she knew it would go a long way towards solving her mental confusion. As Jonny had said, she had every reason to be the happiest woman in the world, and she was the most miserable. She desperately wanted to love Jonny . . . but how much of that was to salve her own conscience? She didn't want to admit to herself that she had just allowed him to pick her up simply because she had been in the mood.

Equally she desperately wanted to believe in his innocence. It was of course easy to tell herself that Mayne could have, must have, killed Pat and then Sanchez. But where was the motive, unless he was even then hoping to make a play for her? But that was too Hollywood-scriptwriterish to be acceptable.

Jonny *could* have been guilty. That was the most damning thought of all. He could have met Sanchez, and learned about the secret passage . . . and Sanchez's death could have been the accident the police claimed it was.

That was something she simply could not accept, but

nothing could alter the fact that Jonny had been viciously rude to her. That even if he was innocent, he was being changed, and brutalised, by his imprisonment. She was not sure she could love this new Jonny Carter. And if she could not love him now, what were the chances of loving him in ten or fifteen years time?

But if that were the case, had she ever loved him? Love, as she understood the word, did not fly out of the window at the first sign of trouble. It had taken six years for her to stop loving Pat.

That took her back to square one, and another sleepless night.

"All right," she finally told David. "Let's get out of here. Where are we going first?"

"We have to establish you, first, Mrs Pat," he said. "I take it you don't want to spend three months of every year in The Keep?"

"No way," she said vehemently.

"Right. Then we have to find three more homes for you. I would suppose London would be a good starter for number two – considering this apartment as number one, that is."

"London?" she asked uneasily.

"Well, somewhere in England. I mean, that's your real home, isn't it?"

"Um."

"And I had assumed you would wish your children to be educated there."

"I do."

"Well, then, having a home there in which you can spend three months of every year would seem essential."

"It means putting the dogs in quarantine again. You said something about the South of France."

"I think that would make a good third home, yes."

"And there's no quarantine, taking the dogs into France?"

"Not so far as I know."

"Well, then, let's go there first, settle the dogs, and then pick our spot in England."

"You're the boss," he agreed.

The decision made, Alison felt much happier, even if the Ruthvens and their friends gave a howl of dismay.

"But I'll be back," she told them.

Once again packing. They were going to cross to Cherbourg on the *Queen Mary*. It was the day before she was due to leave that Hugo came in, bearing a card.

"There's this guy to see you," he explained.

Alison looked at the card: Walter Bernard, attorney-at-law.

"To see me?" Alison went into the sitting room where a somewhat small, very precise looking man who wore a *pince-nez* awaited her. "Mr . . ." she looked at the card again. "Bernard?"

"Mrs Grange." He shook her hand, and she almost thought he was going to kiss it, but he didn't.

"Do sit down, Mr Bernard," she invited. "And tell me what I can do for you."

"I'm here on behalf of Mr Rubio," Bernard said.

"Ah" Alison said.

"You know of Mr Rubio?"

"I have heard of him. I have never met the gentleman."

"I wish you to know that Mr Rubio was heartbroken when he learned of the assassination of your husband, Mrs Grange."

"I understand entirely," Alison said. "Please tell him how much I appreciate his sentiments."

"I will certainly do so. It is because of his appreciation of your feelings that he has hesitated to make contact with you before now. But, now that very nearly a year has elapsed since Mr Grange's death, and you have made no effort to contact *him* . . ."

Alison raised her eyebrows. "Was I supposed to?"

"Mr Rubio had assumed that you would wish to resolve all of Mr Grange's outstanding accounts."

"Mr Rubio has an outstanding account with my husband?"

"Oh, come now, Mrs Grange. Surely you are aware that Mr Rubio financed the development of the El Dorado mine?"

"I knew he put up some money . . ."

"Four hundred thousand dollars, Mrs Grange."

"I see. And Mr Rubio says my husband never paid this debt?"

"That is correct, ma'am."

"I see," Alison said again. "My husband was of the opinion that he did."

"One hates to speak ill of the dead, Mrs Grange, but Mr Grange, well . . . he had kind of selfish ideas about money."

Alison couldn't argue with that point of view. Nor did she want to be engaged in a lawsuit over what was, to her, a somewhat insignificant sum of money. "Very well, Mr Bernard. Let me have a copy of the agreement between my husband and Mr Rubio, and I will let you have a cheque."

"Heavens, Mrs Grange, there wasn't any written agreement. Mr Rubio doesn't work that way. His word is his bond. And he supposes that everyone else's word is their bond, as well. In many ways, Mr Rubio is like a child in business matters," Bernard added, somewhat unrealistically.

"I see. So I have only your word for it that my husband borrowed four hundred thousand dollars from your client."

"You calling me a liar?"

"I wouldn't dream of it." Alison went to her desk. "Very well, Mr Bernard, I will accept your figure, and write you a cheque for the amount. However, your client may not like to write things down, but I do. I wish a receipt in full for the amount, stating quite clearly that any indebtedness of my husband to Mr Rubio has been liquidated in full."

"Oh, I can arrange that, Mrs Grange. And let me say that it is a pleasure to do business with a lady who knows what is what. I'll just give you the amount."

"You said four hundred thousand dollars," Alison said, taking out her cheque book.

"That was the original sum, Mr Grange. There was interest involved."

"So?"

"The interest was to be at one hundred per cent per annum, compound."

Alison turned her head.

"So," Bernard said, blandly. "As nothing has been paid on capital, the interest has been accumulating since March of 1938. The outstanding debt now totals one billion and twenty-four million dollars."

"Would you mind repeating that?" Alison asked. She could feel a tingling throughout her entire body, the sort of feeling she had had when Mayne had been assaulting her.

"One billion, and twenty-four million dollars," Bernard said again.

Alison turned her chair, got up, and went to the door. She opened it. Predictably both Hugo and Clem, were standing there.

"Come inside," she invited.

Bernard gulped as he saw the two very large men. "Now look here, Mrs Grange . . ."

"I think you're the one who needs to look here, Mr Bernard," Alison said, speaking very quietly. "You come to me with some totally unsubstantiated story of my husband never having repaid what he borrowed from Mr Rubio. I was prepared to go along with that. But now you try to pull some astronomical figure out of the hat . . . is this because you reckon I'm a helpless little woman?"

"I'm quoting the figure given me by Mr Rubio," Bernard protested.

"Then I suggest you go home to Mr Rubio and tell him, the lady says, nuts. I'm prepared to pay him his four hundred thousand dollars, with compound interest at ten per cent." She returned to her desk, sat down, and made some quick calculations. "I make that seven hundred and seventy-nine thousand dollars. Let's call it eight hundred thousand in round figures. So your client has doubled his money in eight years. That's not bad going." She wrote the cheque. "There you go."

Bernard took it, gingerly. "Mr Rubio ain't going to like this, Mrs Grange."

"So tell him to sue me."

Bernard swallowed. "Mr Rubio don't believe in courts."

"Is that a fact? Are you threatening me, Mr Bernard?"

"Mrs Grange . . ."

"Because if you are, on behalf of your boss, tell him I recommend he think very carefully about that. If he has me assassinated, he loses the lot. My money is tied up until he'll be too old even to add two and two, by the time he gets out of gaol. If he wants any rough stuff, he's welcome to it. My boys here adore rough stuff. If he has any sense, he'll settle for my very fair offer. Off you go, Mr Bernard."

Bernard left.

But Alison knew she wasn't in any state to take on an outfit like Carlo Rubio's, not with five small children – unless she intended to hire a private army. She called David immediately, and he came right up.

He whistled when he heard her account of the conversation.

"What do you know of that debt?" Alison asked.

"As I told you, Mrs Pat, I don't know anything about that side of the business. Mr Pat never said a word to me about any outstanding debts."

"Which makes me think he probably settled them all," Alison mused. "I mean, with his kind of income, there was no reason not to. Maybe that's where that four hundred million went."

"With respect, Mrs Pat, the amounts don't altogether tie in. Four hundred million over eight years is fifty million a year. If Mr Pat had taken out fifty million to settle Rubio's four hundred thousand, he could have done so with ease the first year, or the second or third. It's only in the last couple of years that amount would have become astronomical."

"Um," Alison commented.

"You don't suppose there's any chance that it was Rubio had Mr Pat killed?" David suggested.

"Why?"

"Well, he may have dunned Mr Pat, and Mr Pat may just have told him to get lost. They were both pretty tough men. Rubio may have reckoned he was screwing Mr Pat for his shirt with that hundred per cent interest clause, but Mr Pat may have reckoned that as it was a verbal agreement, he'd screw Rubio when the time came to pay up."

"Which would explain why he had The Keep made into a fortress," Alison said. "But how would killing Pat help Rubio get his money?"

"Simply that he must've figured, or perhaps he knew, that Mr Pat would leave everything to you, and that it would be a much easier business to put the screw on you, as he has just done."

"So what's he going to do now? Go for the children?" She began to tremble at the thought.

"I'm not sure he'd risk that. Kidnapping is a very serious business," David said reassuringly. "Rubio has got where he is, and stays where he is, by graft and corruption here in New York City. Kidnapping is a Federal offence, and it'd mean the chair for those proven responsible. There's no way he's going to corrupt a Federal judge or jury. No, his best bet would be to threaten to *kill* one of the children if you didn't pay up."

"Oh, cheer me up. You mean murder is regarded as less important than kidnapping in this country?"

"You could say that. Murder isn't a Federal offence. Kidnapping, or at a least, taking someone across a state line, is. So, maybe we'd better make ourselves scarce for a while. The *Queen Mary* sails tomorrow. Until then, I suggest you keep the children indoors, and don't admit anyone you don't know to the apartment."

"And won't Rubio be able to find out we're sailing?"

"He will, eventually, obviously. But for the moment we're booked in false names."

"David, you are a genius. But . . . there's no hope we can escape publicity when we get to France."

"Maybe not. But Rubio cuts no ice in France, Mrs Pat. He'll be easier to cope with over there."

He had thought it all out, as usual. And Alison was happy to let him do it. Once again, excitement. Had it not been for her fears regarding the children, she would have enjoyed it thoroughly. Of course she was recognised when she boarded the ship and the cameras clicked, but by the time the prints reached the papers she was on the high seas, relaxing completely for the first time in months.

Was she scared? Again, but for the children, she did not think she was. If she had to choose a word for her mental state, she would have opted for "overburdened". Once again she thought of the analagy to a rather inexperienced juggler trying to keep too many balls in the air at the same time . . . the children's safety, Rubio, the missing money, what exactly she intended to do with her life . . . and of course, Jonny Carter.

Which brought her back to the very personal question of her love life. She had never considered herself a very sexual person. She enjoyed the physical act, but she enjoyed the romantic aspects of sex more, the letters and the notes, the smiles across a crowded room, the surreptitious touch of the hand. The amazing thing was that while she had been on the end of all of those from her various admirers in New York, none of them had been the least attractive as possible bed partners, and the two men with whom she had slept had never indulged in such irrelevant foibles since Pat's worldwind courtship of her eight years ago.

And now, somehow, that entire aspect of life had just passed her by.

She felt it most acutely at sea, which was in any event a romantic place to be. Naturally she was the most popular woman on board, sat at the Captain's right hand throughout the voyage, danced every dance every night, and could not venture on deck for a promenade with the dogs without immediately being surrounded by half a dozen men all anxious to be the one at her elbow.

What the dogs thought of it was difficult to say. What Hugo and Clem thought of it was easy to decide from their lowering glances and muttered asides – but then, what her escorts thought of Hugo and Clem, who had access to her suite as and when they chose, did not bear consideration. She did not suppose the passengers and crew of the *Queen Mary* had ever had such a fruitful source of gossip.

But where did that leave her, she wondered? The voyage lasted only four days, but there was all of her life ahead of her. She was not yet twenty-seven, and every man in the world, eligible or not, wished to get his hands on her. Or her money. How she wanted to accomodate one of them, to feel the warmth of a man's love and protection. For that she thought she might even willingly give over control of her empire.

But to choose the wrong man . . .

From Cherbourg they drove down to the Riviera, in time for Christmas and the winter season. David had hired a villa for her, at an astronomical rent, and here she was established, with the dogs and her bodyguards, her own private beach, and all the peace and sunshine she could desire.

"Until Rubio catches up with me," she said.

"We'll handle him," Hugo promised. The villa was surrounded with a fence which David had had electrified, and he hired a couple of extra men to patrol the perimeters, while whenever any member of the family went out he or she or they were accompanied by either Hugo or Clem – both if it was a family outing. Alison's arrival at the villa had not attracted a great deal of attention, but her way of life did, and soon there were newspaper articles, and photographers perched on the surrounding hills equipped with telescopic lenses hoping to catch a glimpse of her.

She realised that, quite without knowing how it had happened, she was living an even more secluded and guarded life than Pat. What a way for the richest woman in the world to exist! Of course in the South of France there was a great deal of social activity, and entertaining the famous Mrs Grange became the cachet of the season. Alison could not help but enjoy the adulation, even if she knew much of it was based on her wealth rather than her looks or her personality, and she accepted the necessity of being escorted by Hugo and Clem, both armed; they always waited discreetly in the car until she was ready to leave, and if their presence effectively discouraged any of the many gigolos who haunted the Riviera from attempting to make a play for her, that was a good thing. But she really blew her top when she decided to have a large dinner party herself, and her bodyguards wanted to search each guest as he or she arrived. "You can just forget that!" she snapped, but the two big men were there all the time, staring, and putting a distinct damper on the evening.

At least Rubio also obviously knew what was happening, because Alison did not hear from him again. She reckoned he was waiting for her to go back to the States, and she didn't mean to do that. But then David put her mind entirely at rest, in that direction, by announcing one morning, "You won't believe this, Mrs Pat, but Rubio has negotiated your cheque."

"What exactly does that mean?"

"Well, he's paid it in to one of his accounts. Because it's gone through your New York account. It's here on your latest bank statement, duly endorsed."

He was looking very pleased.

"Is that good?" she asked.

"Well, of course it is, Mrs Pat. It's an acknowledgement that he's accepted your offer."

"You mean he's not going to come back for the rest, as he sees it?"

"Well, legally, he can't. You made an offer and wrote him a cheque in the amount, and he has now accepted that."

"And what about illegally? Isn't that how he usually operates?"

"When he reckons he can get away with it, sure. But I think maybe he's got the message, that you're not going to be scared, and that getting any more out of you is going to be a tough business."

"If you are right, Dave, that is the best news I have had in a long time."

After that, Alison felt she could allow herself to appreciate the relative warmth and the relaxed attitude of most of the people on the Riviera, although for all the entertainment offered, she was happiest in the grounds of her home, preferring to lounge around the pool with the children and the dogs, and feel the well-being slowly creeping over her. She enjoyed the south of France, so much so that at the end of the season she made an offer for the villa, which was accepted.

But in the spring it was necessary to get going again, and she felt she should, in the first instance, do this on her own. There was a great deal to be organised, not least her domestic arrangements. Ben was soon going to be seven, and Shirley six, so she engaged a live-in governess, Miss Holdsworth, an English lady who seemed to combine the right mixture of academic learning and gentility fallen upon hard times. Then she felt she could leave the younger children under the care of Hannah and Charlene, and the protection of both Hugo and Clem, while she went with David to England. Hugo as usual was upset at being left behind, but she convinced him that the children were more important that herself, and that in any event, if Rubio was no longer going to be difficult, none of them was really in any danger.

Travelling without her "*entourage*" it was possible to slip into England with the minimum of fuss. David had investigated the tax position, and she bought herself a London flat as well as a large house in a quiet Sussex village. They were both in the name of a company he had already set up, and which was not affiliated, so far as anyone could tell without a very detailed examination of her affairs, to either of the two companies Pat had already created in England to deal with his investment property purchases.

Being in England enabled her to visit Aunt Audrey, but there was no longer any rapport between them. Aunt Audrey clearly felt that in some unfathomable way Pat's death had to be Alison's fault, and she had not enjoyed the publicity given to her niece's affair with the convicted murderer.

The English scene established, Alison actually had the four homes David had recommended, save that one of them was The Keep, and she was in no hurry to return there. She had written to Jonny twice since leaving Mexico but there had been no replies. Preston was still hunting for Waller, so far as she knew – his bills came in regularly enough – but he was having no success. She was not calling him off though; if he was nothing else he provided a sop for her conscience, which from time to time reminded her that if she truly loved Jonny she would have remained in Mexico.

It was a fading reflection.

*   *   *

The fact was, she was slowly coming to understand the immense pleasure that could be obtained from being rich enough to do, or buy, anything she chose. That she could walk into a London real estate agent's office and request to be shown half a dozen properties, and then simply decide which one she would have, that she could do the same at any furriers or couturiers in the world, that she could decide to do anything, go anywhere, on the spur of the moment, and have it all immediately and expertly arranged for her by David, left her permanently elevated it seemed several feet off the ground . . . and unlike most dreams, she did not see how she could ever be required again to set foot on that ground.

Wherever she went she was wined and dined. Men of every description, famous and infamous, wealthy and desperately trying to appear wealthy, sought her out. She enjoyed their company, their admiration . . . and gently turned aside their proposals, whether of marriage or less; not one ever got past her bedroom door. The trauma of Pat and Jonny, Jonny and Pat, and then Mayne, left her unwilling to share any of her secrets, mental or physical, with anyone.

More and more she delegated, principally to David. She had no real desire to return to Brazil; he went in her stead and brought back the necessary accountings and the necessary cheques. Jim McCall was doing a very good job, the work force seemed happy, and the output, if continuing to dwindle, was actually doing so at less than the ten per cent she had stipulated as the minimum acceptable.

David also attended to the investing of these new funds, and as he rapidly realised that Alison was not interested in accumulating properties, began to use the various stockmarkets.

Presumably there was a chance that she was being cheated, but from the various returns he produced it did not appear so – as he had prophesied, the value of her six million dollars worth of property holdings began to escalate rapidly as the world settled down to peace and rebuilding – and in fact, she would not really have cared all that much; young as he was – not yet thirty – David had become as essential a part of her life as Hugo, who represented the unfailing loyalty of the others. He and Clem were her devoted watchdogs, and the presence of Charlene brought out the best in Hannah, while Miss Holdsworth fitted smoothly into the household.

The staffs of the various establishments were all hired by and answered to David, but they never left her in any doubt that they knew the source of his power.

Alison and David had only one cause of friction, and it was a recurring one: her desire to give away large sums of money each year to charity.

"Conscience money," he grumbled.

"Why, yes, I suppose it is."

"Do you realise, Mrs Pat, that of every hundred pounds you give to charity, as a rule only about five actually reaches the people you're trying to help? The rest goes on admin."

"So we'll just have to give more," she said.

She fell into the peripatetic way of life he had recommended without the slightest difficulty, in a limited fashion. All idea of going to visit every piece of property she had inherited was quickly abandoned. She spent September to December in New York, flew to Nice to spend Christmas in her villa, and remained there until March, moved to England until June, and after all returned to Mexico for the summer. This seemed backwards to most people, as these were the hottest months of the year in the desert, but she enjoyed the heat. The first time she returned it was a real act of abnegation, but the welcome she received from the peons was so enthusiastic as to be irresistible. Indeed, she was welcomed by everyone. Captain Guimard came out to make sure she was all right, and she was even invited to take coffee with the new President, Señor Aleman. Señor Aleman was the first civilian ever to be President of Mexico, and he was anxious to establish the difference between himself and his predecessors.

"I have set up a board of investigation to review the facts of your husband's death," he said. "I do not know what will come of it . . . but it is our business to establish the truth."

She went out to the prison with the good news, but Jonny Carter refused to see her. She felt that even if, and hopefully that, Aleman's board of inquiry found Jonny innocent, their relationship was ended.

Sadly, she paid off Harry Preston.

Once Alison's routine was established, the children and the dogs accompanied her everywhere, except that on her visits to England the dogs remained in France. Ben's name was down for an exclusive British prep. school when he was ten from whence he would go on, she intended, to Welton College. She meant to follow the same pattern with Shirley, and then the others, each attending different public schools, and reflected that it was still seven years before the last, Harry, would have to go. Because they were now her entire life.

Her staff were happy enough, especially those close to her. David was the only one who perceived that she was turning more and more inward, but his solution was a typically masculine one.

"I think you should interest yourself more in the business, Mrs Pat," he said, when they returned to the Riviera house for the following winter.

"There's nothing wrong, is there?"

"Oh, no, no. But . . . well . . . you're not using your mind. And . . . well . . ."

"I'm going to too many parties, drinking too much champagne, and generally turning into a layabout," she agreed.

276

He chose to ignore that. "I'm not suggesting you get bogged down in the day to day running of affairs, as long as you're happy with what I'm doing . . ."

"I am perfectly happy with what you're doing, Dave."

"Thank you, Mrs Pat. But I was wondering what you intend to do about that missing four hundred million."

"Frankly, I haven't a clue," Alison confessed. "The gold was paid for by cheque. Several cheques. Pat had them made out to the El Dorado Company, and to himself, and to Alvarado, and whomever or whatever else he wanted. Obviously he had a separate cheque for the four hundred million. Separate cheques, I suppose, every year. But what he did with the money, God alone knows. I don't see how we can find out."

"It's a tricky one. But don't you think it's worth looking for? Four hundred million dollars is a lot of dough."

"It'll turn up," Alison promised him. "We just have to keep our eyes open."

Edith Ruthven took a much more positive view.

"Your trouble is you just aren't meeting the right men," she announced. She had her own ideas on that, and when Alison was next in New York, in the autumn of 1948, threw an enormous party for her. It was one of the events of the season, and she had clearly planned it very carefully. Alison had barely got through the door, wearing a shot silk taffeta gown in navy and green, with puffed sleeves and a pronounced décolletage, when she was introduced to a tall, dark, and extraordinarily handsome man, whose name was Paul Schleyer.

CHAPTER 10

Dreams

Alison could not help but be impressed. Paul Schleyer was as tall as Pat had been, and had the same broad shoulders. But there the resemblance ended. He wore a gray suit as if he had been poured into it, where Pat had always looked as if he had fallen into his clothes; he had a quiet voice with an almost caressing quality; his hands were dry, his shake firm without the slightest effort to indicate strength, although the strength was most certainly there.

His face was handsome, in a chiselled, aquiline fashion, his teeth large and white, his eyes gray and smiling. There were traces of gray at his temples, but for the rest his black hair was brushed straight back from his forehead.

"This is a great pleasure, Mrs Grange," he said. "I have been hearing so much about you."

"How very boring for you."

"On the contrary. It was all very interesting."

She gazed at him, and he raised one eyebrow. She couldn't be sure whether or not he was poking fun at her.

They were separated, but a few minutes later Edith got her aside.

"What do you think of him?" Edith was plainly very excited.

"Of who?"

"Oh, Alison! Paul, of course."

"Oh, you mean Mr Schleyer. He seems very nice. A little too good to be true, wouldn't you say?"

"He was so anxious to meet you."

So is everybody, Alison thought, but she didn't say it. "Well, now he has," she pointed out.

"I think you should invite him to your next soirée."

"Someone I've only just met?"

"You will like him, I know."

"Edith," Alison said severely. "You are matchmaking. Just what do you know about this character, anyway? How come I've never met him before?"

"It's a long story," Edith said. "Come to tea tomorrow, and I'll tell it to you."

Alison went to tea, because by then she had received a dozen red roses, with a card which read, "I enjoyed meeting you last night, and would like to call. Shall we say, tomorrow? Yours, Paul."

It was totally unexpected and unusual. They had encountered each other once or twice again during the party, and engaged in small talk. If he had looked at her in a meaningful fashion, most men did that. When she had decided to leave, there had been no immediate leaping forward to offer her a lift – which she would in any event have declined, as Hugo was waiting downstairs with the car.

And then the wording of the note. No mush. No suggestion of subservience. And a very definite suggestion of decision. She could not help but be intrigued.

"The reason you have not met him before is that he was not here," Edith explained over tea. "But you two have a lot in common."

Alison raised her eyebrows.

"South America," Edith said importantly. "Paul has just returned from cattle-ranching in Argentina."

"And that's common ground? That's like saying a Swede has necessarily to have a lot in common with a Spaniard, simply because they both happen to be Europeans."

"You know what I mean." Edith refused to be put off. "When he was demobilised – he has both the Silver Star and the Purple Heart, you know – he took this job in South America, with this cattle baron, and did so well that he became general manager of the ranch."

"I thought ranches had foremen."

Edith refused to have her leg pulled. "Not ranches this big. So here he is in New York on holiday."

"A ranch foreman," Alison pointed out.

"A general manager," Edith insisted.

"He's coming to call, tomorrow," Alison said. "Supposing I'm at home."

"Oh, but you must be at home," Edith cried. "Alison, he is the right man for you. I just know it."

"You have got to be joking," Alison said. "What about Jonny?"

"Oh, really, Alison, you can't be serious. You tell me this Carter person refuses to see you. He's obviously a criminal, for all you know he could have murdered Pat . . ."

"Leave it," Alison suggested. "Just let's say, I'm not in a marrying mood."

But it was still a pleasure to be courted, in such a charmingly forceful fashion by such a charming man. Alison's initial hostility soon faded as Paul sent her more flowers, took her dining and dancing, to the theatre and the opera, always revealing the most impeccable manners, and never even attempting to hold her hand where the situation did not demand it.

Within a few weeks she was actually waiting for his telephone call. Here again, there was no suggestion of proprietorial "next time". They said goodnight very formally, and then a couple of days later there would come an equally formal call, inviting her out again. It was a way of courtship she had never experienced. It made her feel very young, and almost virginal. Well, she supposed she was, almost virginal, as it was now three years since that night with Jonny in New York.

But Jonny! If only she could make up her mind what to do. Supposing Paul ever suggested she do anything.

As Paul only took Alison out in the evenings, the children were not really aware of what was going on. That their mother seemed a happier person than usual clearly pleased them, especially the older pair, Ben and Shirley. The staff, however was naturally not happy with the situation. Hugo and Clem glowered, Charlene looked pensive, and even David seemed more concerned than he usually was about her private life.

"I wonder if I may have a word with you, Mrs Pat," he requested one morning.

"Well, of course, David. You don't have to ask."

"It's a somewhat personal matter. And a delicate one."

Alison frowned at him. "You're not quitting?"

"Oh, good lord, no, Mrs Pat."

"Then you want to get married. I think that's just great. Do I get to meet the bride?"

"There is no bride, Mrs Pat. I wish to talk about Mr Schleyer."

"Oh, yes?"

"I'm afraid I have to admit that I have had Mr Schleyer investigated."

"Who told you to do that, Dave?"

"It was something that had to be done. You hire me to look after your finances, Mrs Pat."

"And you think Mr Schleyer poses a threat to them?"

"I think he may well do so."

"How?"

281

"Well . . ." David looked embarrassed. "If you were to fall in love with him . . ."

"If I were to fall in love with Mr Schleyer, Dave, that would necessarily mean that I would trust him, absolutely."

"That's the point, Mrs Pat. Mr Schleyer, well . . . he's not what he appears."

"Tell me." Bang goes another dream, she thought.

"Well, first, there is no record of a Paul Schleyer receiving either the Silver Star or the Purple Heart. In fact, I can find no record of war service at all."

"You didn't serve, did you, Dave?"

"Well, no, Mrs Pat. I was working for Mr Pat in Mexico."

"Does that make you a scoundrel?"

"I hope not, Mrs Pat. But then, I never claimed to be anything I wasn't."

"I suppose there's more."

"I'm afraid so. I have been in touch with someone I know in Argentina, and there is no record of any Paul Schleyer managing any vast ranch for anyone."

"He must have done something. He's not short of money."

"That is the most disturbing thing of all, Mrs Pat. I can find no record of any employment for him, any business, any organisation. He certainly has no credit rating."

Alison remembered that Paul had never paid for anything either by cheque or credit card, always by cash – although there had always been a thick wad of cash.

"What are you trying to tell me, Dave?"

"Well, Mrs Pat, when a good-looking, smooth-talking guy with no visible means of support suddenly latches on to one of the world's wealthiest women, it's difficult to draw more than one conclusion."

"He could be a professional gambler, I suppose," Alison mused.

"That would hardly improve his standing, Mrs Pat. But I thought of that one, too. I can find no one who

282

recognises Mr Schleyer as a regular at Vegas or Atlantic City, or anywhere else, for that matter. Including the race tracks."

Alison went to see George Ruthven.

"Schleyer had a letter of introduction from our correspondent in Buenos Aires," Ruthven explained.

"Which you never followed up."

"Well . . . I didn't have any reason to. He seemed perfectly genuine. It wasn't as if he tried to borrow money from the bank. He didn't even open an account. It was, and is, a purely social contact. And then . . ." he gave an embarrassed grin. "Edith kind of went for him."

"That I know."

"But you think he's a fraud."

"According to David Brook, he is," Alison said. "But I don't know if it matters," she added, truthfully.

In an odd fashion, David's revelation had enabled her to relax. Before there had been the recurring question of "should she marry?" – supposing Paul was going to ask her – and foist a stepfather on the children as well as limiting her own life, or at least, giving it another direction. Setting this against the other question of would she ever find anyone more attractive, more meaningful, than Paul, then, where that would leave Jonny Carter, and was she utterly cold-hearted . . . if David was right – and she never doubted him for a moment – and Paul was a gold-digger out for what he could get, well then, why shouldn't she take whatever she wanted from him, with absolutely no strings attached, and therefore no conscience? Jonny could hardly blame her for having an affair.

Did she want an affair? Deep down inside her private mind she knew that she did. She had been living on a starvation diet as far as human relations went, surrounded entirely by servants and sycophants, for too long. And sexual relations? There too.

Besides, she could not stop herself from sometimes thinking, "Here I am one of the richest women in the world, who could snap her fingers and have almost any man in the world . . . and I am so hidebound by my petty bourgeois background I have never done it."

The trouble was, Pat had started to think like that too, after finding El Dorado. Yet she knew she was going to do it.

As to what that would leave her, afterwards . . . but she was Alison Grange. She could do anything she liked. And so far she had done nothing. To let herself go, just the once, with the most attractive man she had ever met . . . oddly, the thought that he might be a scoundrel made him more rather than less attractive, especially as she was invulnerable.

Yet she was quite nervous the next time they went out to dinner.

"I guess this has to be goodbye for a while," she remarked.

He raised an eyebrow.

"I leave New York next week."

"Why?"

"To avoid becoming liable for US tax."

"Ah! You have it all worked out."

"Well, let's say my accountant has."

"The famous David Brook."

"Famous?"

"Anyone who has the handling of the Grange millions has to be at least well known, Alison. But I guess you know what you're doing."

"Yes," she said.

"It'll be a wrench, when you go. I don't ever recall having enjoyed anyone's company more."

They gazed at each other, and Alison allowed the tip of her tongue to show between her lips.

"Where are you off to?" he asked.

"The south of France. I have a villa there." She drew a long breath. "Want to come and visit?"

They stared at each other.

"Suppose I said yes, I would very much like to come and visit?"

"Then you're invited."

"Is it a big party?"

"There is no party. Only my children and my staff."

"And you. And me? People will talk."

"People have been talking about me since the day I married Pat Grange. I guess I'm used to it."

Again a long stare, and now his hand moved, to close gently on top of hers. "I would like to give them something to talk about, Alison. I have dreamed of that from the moment I first saw you."

"Yes."

He frowned, and his fingers tightened on hers. "You know this?"

"Yes."

"And you have still invited me to visit with you?"

"Yes," she said.

He held her hand, lightly, on the drive back to the apartment. Yet he had still not kissed her. She became aware of a growing excitement. Perhaps his forebearance had been deliberately intended to awake her appetite. In which case he had most magnificently succeeded.

"You'd better come up," she said, when the taxi stopped.

He paid the driver and got out.

"You may find me a little gauche," Alison warned, as they entered the elevator. "I've not done this before."

He took her in his arms and kissed her. As usual with this man, she was surprised: she had expected some kind of mushy condolence on her loneliness or concern at her self-imposed chastity. But Paul was a man of deeds, rather than words.

Hugo opened the door for them, and gave the intruder a very dirty look.

"That will be all, thank you, Hugo," Alison said. "You can go to bed now."

Hugo hesitated.

"Bed," Alison said, firmly.

Hugo left the room reluctantly.

"You simply have to think of him as a large, very faithful, watchdog," Alison explained.

"Just so long as he doesn't sleep at the foot of your bed."

"Drink?" She stood by the bar.

"No thanks."

She turned, and watched him coming towards her. He kissed her with absolute assurance, apparently certain not only that she wanted his kiss but that she would enjoy it. Yet there was no possession, at this stage; his hands rested lightly on her shoulders.

Possession came soon enough, but by then she wanted it, desperately. His confidence combined with his gentleness to make her feel like a woman, for the first time since . . . perhaps for the first time ever, she realised. Pat had been slow to take physical possession, but from the moment of that lunch at the Savoy Grill he had sought mental dominance. Jonny had been a glorious accident – neither had willed what had happened. Paul was in total control, but always with the clear assumption that he was doing what she wanted, which left her with the comforting feeling that were she to raise a finger in protest, he would stop and apologise.

Not that she considered that for a moment, even if his lovemaking was unlike anything she had ever dreamed about, much less heard or read of. The realisation that his hands were underneath her skirt, that her panties were being deftly removed, that she was lying down beneath him and that his own pants had somehow disappeared or dissolved only reached her moments after he was already inside her, slowly and carefully, but so definitely.

I have never been so filled, she thought. And fulfilled.

To her astonishment, even after climaxing, he wanted to continue making love, stripped off her clothes to kiss and caress her, and was able to enter her, while she sat on his lap, an hour after that. Even then the night had only just begun, as he took her to bed. They did not fall asleep until nearly dawn. By then she had performed fellatio, for the first time in her life, had indeed encountered sex in its every form, without the slightest feeling that it was not the most natural thing in the world. She had never encountered a man so virile. Perhaps Jonny Carter might have been, but on the one occasion they had got together she had been too hungover to notice.

Two hours later she stared at him across the breakfast table, having been served by a pot-faced Hugo. Had she really done all of that, with this man? To this man? And had it done back to her?

What had she been missing all of her life?

"I love you," he said.

Alison opened her mouth and then closed it again. She didn't want to say it. She couldn't love a man because he had just given her the best night of her life: she had thought that about Jonny Carter. Again the haunting thought came back to her, that she had never loved at all. She sought sexual gratification, when she sought it, with her entire being, as a kind of justification for what she was doing, and then thought herself in love . . . until someone else came along who did it better. What a terrible indictment!

But she had invited this man into her life deliberately, to enjoy him but not to love him.

"We're going to have a lot of fun, together," she promised.

*　　*　　*

287

How much fun she hadn't realised. It wasn't merely that every time they had sex the experience was more consuming that before, so much so that by the end of their first month on the Riviera if she was not having at least one climax a day she was feeling bereft. But Paul had also developed the art of living to the nth degree. He was interested in everything, he did everything well.

He revealed a great knowledge of gardening, and virtually redesigned the villa grounds, employing a small army of workmen to carry out his concept. It cost a fortune, but Alison pointed out to David that it was enhancing the value of the property.

One of the improvements Paul made was to install a tennis court, for he played a very strong game. Alison had never been anything more than a moderate player, and most of their neighbours were far better, but with Paul as her doubles partner she got on quite well, and he was never critical, even after the most terrible mistake. He did attempt to coach her, but five minutes alone on the court, especially with him against her showing her how to hold or swing the racket, had them heading for bed.

I am absolutely besotted, she thought – happily.

Paul adored throwing parties. Well, so did Alison, especially when they were hosted by such a handsome man. Invitations to Alison Grange's villa had always been sought when she was in residence; now people were virtually begging for them. There were dinner parties and fancy-dress parties, cocktail parties and breakfast parties, and of course, pool parties, at which, led by Paul, the guests all stripped off and skinny-dipped. Alison was scandalised the first time this happened, but was soon encouraged in, and after the first time she never wore a swimsuit, whether they were having a party or not. Although she didn't specifically make any rules for the staff, they discreetly kept out of the way when the boss lady was cavorting in the water with her "man".

The children joined them in this fun. "Prudery is bad for the mind," Paul told her, and she agreed with him entirely. She would have anyhow, as she was relishing her new found mental freedom. It really made her happy to see how Paul took an interest in all the kids, especially Ben and Shirley, who, at eight and seven respectively, were at the age to learn rapidly and well. He taught them to swim and play tennis, sat with them and walked with them and rode with them . . . they had of course been taught to ride at the Keep almost as soon as they could walk. Alison was delighted to see how they adored him back. For the first time in their lives they had a father.

He is the perfect man for you, Edith had said. Well, of course he was, but could she ever be sure he wasn't after her money. She was funding everything they did, but everything they did was for her enjoyment or the betterment of her possessions – he had never once asked for anything for himself, and she remained sufficiently old-fashioned not to buy him things, except on his birthday.

But the greatest impact Paul had on Alison's life was when he introduced her to the delights of sailing.

They were invited out on a friend's yacht. The fact that Paul was apparently Alison's permanent houseguest, although they were not married or even engaged, upset few people on the Riviera, whatever it might have done in London or New York, and Alison enjoyed herself enormously. She explored the boat – a forty-foot sloop – from stem to stern. "I think it's just splendid," she said. "The idea of being able to get away from it all . . . can it sail out of sight of land?"

"This little ship has crossed the Atlantic," the owner said proudly.

"Oh, that sounds just tremendous!"

"Did you mean it?" Paul asked that night at dinner.

"Oh, I did. You know I have some stressful situations to cope with."

"I do know."

"Well, just to be able to get on a boat like that and sail away whenever the going got rough . . ."

"Why don't you?"

"Simply because I wouldn't know what to do first."

"The sort of yacht you would own would have a crew."

"You reckon? But I'd still kind of like to know what was going on."

"I'll teach you all about it, if you like."

"You?"

"I've been sailing all my life," he told her.

Another revelation. But it appeared to be true. He chartered a small, thirty-foot, yacht, and the two of them spent a fortnight at sea together. They began by cruising up and down the Riviera, but after a week, when they happened to be in Monaco, he suggested they cross to Corsica. It was the first time Alison had been out of sight of land, except in a large ship, but Paul was so confidently expert in everything he did there was no time for apprehension, while being able to take off all her clothes and just bask was quite heavenly.

They cruised right round Corsica. The yacht itself was primitive. There was no bathroom, just a shower in the "head", as Paul called the toilet compartment. The galley consisted of a parrafin stove and there was no fridge. The bunks were mattresses on top of boards, and were not wide enough for them to sleep together – although there was room enough for love-making, providing they were proceeding vertically.

For the first time in a very long time Alison found herself sweeping and scrubbing, and doing her own laundry over the side. That and the constant sail changing wrecked her nails and brought up callouses on her hands. Yet she loved every moment of it, the actual sailing, putting into little coves for the night, knowing that they were completely cut off from the teeming thousands on the shore only a few hundred yards away. They could do what they liked, say what they liked, think what they liked, just sit facing each other in the cockpit, naked, knowing that whenever next they felt like it they would be nestling in each other's arms without the slightest risk of disturbance by either callers or telephones.

"I love you," he said.

"I think I love you too," Alison replied, and bit her lip. She hadn't intended to allow herself to feel that, much less say it.

She became both an expert foredeck hand as well as a good helmswoman. She regarded her chapped fingers and disintegrating nail varnish – no matter how carefully it was applied at breakfast it was destroyed by lunchtime – with a mixture of alarm and delight. She felt that for the first time in her life she was actually alive.

"Can we take the children with us the next time? Well, Ben and Shirley."

She had expected some resistance to the idea of an encroachment on their privacy, but Paul was all for it. "The younger they learn, the better," he said.

Charlene and Hannah were horrified, but Ben and Shirley were naturals on the water. Soon the entire family would go off sailing, the children carefully ensconced in lifejackets and secured to various strong points on the boat by harnesses. It was the happiest time of Alison's life, but it was obvious that the chartered yacht was too small.

Then it was David's turn to be horrified, when Alison decided she wanted to buy a real yacht, as recommended by Paul.

"Fifty-two feet? Do you have any idea how much those things cost, Mrs Pat?"

"The one I want is priced at seventy-five thousand pounds."

"The one you want, or Schleyer wants?"

Since his warning chat in New York, he had kept quiet, up till now.

"It's the one I want, Dave," Alison said quietly.

"Then there's the crew . . ."

"Two."

"Plus the insurance, and the mooring . . ."

"Are you trying to tell me I can't afford it?"

"Of course you can afford it, Mrs Pat. It's just that . . ." he changed his mind about what he would have said. "You're the boss. May I ask a question?"

"You can ask any question you like, Dave."

"Well . . . we were wondering if Mr Schleyer was coming to England with us, next month."

"We?"

"Well . . . Hugo, and Clem, and Charlene . . . all of us, I guess."

"I see. Actually, I haven't asked him, yet."

"But you mean to?"

"Yes."

"And then I guess he'll be coming on to Mexico."

"Probably. Is it really any business of yours, Dave? You're hired to look after my money, not my morals or my love life."

"I was just wondering if I should put Schleyer on the payroll, Mrs Pat."

He flushed as her eyes flashed steel.

"Don't you ever, ever, say something like that to me again," Alison told him. And was immediately contrite as he looked so like a frightened little boy. She squeezed his hand. "Dave, I know you have only my best interests at heart. But give me credit for some common sense. In a couple of months I'm going to be thirty."

He prudently made no reply to that. "Would you like to go through the books with me?" he asked.

She frowned. "Why, is there something wrong?"

"No, ma'am, there's nothing wrong. Things couldn't be better. But . . . well, with the kind of cashflow you have, you'd think you'd be interested in what was happening to it. You haven't looked at the books, or asked a question, for months. Not since that . . ."

"Don't say it. I'll look at the books when I'm good and ready. Don't worry about it, Dave. I trust you. Absolutely."

He had no reply to make to that either.

But she could understand his feelings. So what *was* she going to do? She was having the time of her life. In fact, she often wondered if she had ever lived before, at all. Her entire existence was centred around Paul. He filled her in every possible way, and it was quite impossible to contemplate life without him.

But she had sworn to herself that she would not marry him. Why? Because he was a sham? Or because of Jonny Carter? But Jonny was now a senseless aberration from her past. As Edith had said, she didn't even know for certain that he was innocent. He had never actually stood up, except as a matter of form in court, and declared himself to be not guilty.

So, then, what about the sham who had taken over her life? Except that, if he had been a sham about his claims to be a war hero or an Argentinian gaucho, he was most certainly not a sham on a tennis court, or at a party, or on a yacht. And most of all, not in bed.

"We're off in a couple of weeks," she said at breakfast the next morning, watching the children disporting themselves in the pool.

"Again?"

"Well, it's this tax thing, see?"

"All worked out by David Brook."

"Okay, so you don't like him. I don't think he likes you all that much, either." She glanced at him. "He regards you as a gold-digger."

"I suppose to many people I am." He ate his eggs.

"But are you?"

He raised his head.

"We're going to England for the next three months," she said.

He frowned. "What about the boat? And the dogs?"

"The boat'll stay on its mooring until I come back. The dogs'll stay here, for three months. Then they'll fly straight across to Mexico City, and I'll pick them up when I get down there in June."

"And after that?"

"Well, New York in September, here in January . . ."

"God Almighty! Brook's idea?"

"Do you think you could figure out a better one?"

"Well . . . with your kind of money, Alison, couldn't you just settle on paying tax somewhere?"

"Do you know, I probably could. Actually I do, in Mexico."

"Mexico? Why, on earth?"

"I have a deal with them. I travel on a Mexican passport. So do my children. That lets us, and more especially the boys, out of any nasties like conscription, no matter where they happen to be living."

"Mexico has conscription."

"But my sons are exempt. That's part of the deal."

"You sure have things worked out."

"I try to. Or David does. On the other hand, I couldn't bear to spend all the year in Mexico."

"You lived this kind of life with your husband?"

"Oh, no. Pat divided his time between Brazil and Mexico. But that's how he liked it."

"You like to move around more."

"I don't really like either Mexico or Brazil. But I'm stuck with them, so . . . are you coming to London?"

"Do you want me to?"

"Of course I do, or I wouldn't have invited you."

He got up from the table, stood on the edge of the pool, watching eight-year-old Shirley expertly diving into the deep end. "I've never been a kept man, before. I don't know for how long I can sustain the role."

"Then abandon it." She was amazed at the calmness of her voice, when her heart was pounding so hard she felt he had to be able to hear it.

He turned towards her. "You mean, go out and get a job? I'm afraid I have no money of my own."

"Did you ever?" Alison asked.

His face twisted. "You have the ability, as well as the power, to hurt people."

"I didn't mean to. Come and sit down." She waited for him to do so. "What I meant was, I knew from the beginning you had no money. And no medals. And no Argentinian background."

He had regained his composure. "Is this my dismissal?"

"I hope not. I knew all of those things, because . . . well, a woman in my position needs to know them when a strange guy comes into her life."

"So you decided to enjoy yourself at my expense." His voice was more sad than angry.

"As a matter of fact, yes, I did. You were, are, handsome, attractive, charming, sophisticated . . . and you turned me on like mad. And owing to circumstances, even while married to Pat, I guess I had lived a somewhat sheltered life. I wanted to flap my wings, and you have helped me to do that."

"And now you're ready to fly away."

"Yes. With you."

He had been staring into his coffee. Now he raised his head. "Warts and all?"

"I've been very frank with you, Paul. I'd like it very much if you'd be perfectly frank with me in exchange. But yes, warts and all."

"No matter how big the warts?"

She swallowed. "Don't tell me, you're an escaped convict."

He grinned. "Nothing quite as big as that. But I am a fraud."

"Why? You should have everything going for you . . . looks, talent . . ."

He shrugged. "Maybe you've put your finger on the problem. It's all been too easy. All my life, I mean. So . . . I suppose I found it simpler to con people than to go out and work."

"Well . . . I asked for frankness." She glanced at him. "And you set out to con me?"

"No. No way. Please believe that."

"Then what did you set out to do?"

"I . . ." he sighed. "I managed to get myself some money, a small deal I put through in the midwest, and so I thought I'd have a season in New York, see how the other half lived."

"With a forged letter of recommendation."

"Well, you should know . . . or maybe you don't, as you've always been on top of the dunghill that calls itself society. But the fact is, Alison, you're not allowed to play in that yard unless you have a vast amount of proven money, or an entrée from some direction or other. I didn't have enough money, so I chose an entrée from someplace which seemed sufficiently remote." He gave a twisted grin. "When I chose South America, I had no idea you were going to pop up. Or that the Ruthven dame was going to get the idea that I was the man you'd been looking for since your husband's death."

"She told you that?"

"She made it pretty clear."

"So . . .?"

"So I thought I'd play a little . . . and I was the that one got hooked."

"Really and truly?"

"If you don't believe that by now, Alison, well . . . I guess I *had* better leave."

She laid her hand on his. "You can't blame me for being cautious about my relations with people. Especially men. Paul, I need you. I love you. I want you to come with me to London. And then Mexico. And then New York."

He toyed with his spoon. "Alison . . . I can't be some kind of lapdog. And you'd kill your reputation. The Riviera is one thing. London and New York are something else again."

Alison drew a very long breath. "Then marry me, and leave them all with nothing to gossip about." They stared at each other, and she attempted a smile. "I'm sorry. I know it's not a leap year, but I figured you weren't going to ask me."

He held her hands. "Alison, how can I marry you?"

"Do you know, I asked my first husband that same question, when he proposed. For the same reason, I guess."

"I can't touch your money. It would make me a . . . well . . ."

"I don't expect you to touch my money. But listen, I'll settle an income on you."

He frowned at her.

"It'll be yours. And Paul, it'll be yours for life. We'll write it into the marriage contract. You can walk out on me the day after the wedding, and you'll still get it. Two hundred and fifty thousand dollars a year, tax free."

He stared at her. "You have got to be nuts. You're going to give me a quarter of a million a year, with no strings attached? That's the craziest thing I've ever heard."

"Maybe it'll sound that way to a lot of people. So we won't tell them. No one will know except David. But don't you see, Paul, I don't want you to be a kept man. I want you to be your own man, to be free to do anything you like. You've made me happier than I ever supposed I could be, or had the right to be. I want that happiness to continue. But it only can on the same basis as now, that you're you and I'm me."

He licked his lips. "The money would still come from you."

"From Grange Estates. That's a company. I'm offering you a non-voting directorship."

They stared at each other for several minutes. Then he asked, "What am I supposed to say to that?"

"Yes," she suggested.

Predictably, there were no cheers from the staff, but when Alison ordered a couple of cases of Bollinger to be opened that lunchtime, they all dutifully drank the health of the happy couple.

At least Ben and Shirley were delighted, as were the dogs, with whom Paul had become a firm favourite. Pat, Stephanie and Harry were just happy there was a party.

That afternoon, following a siesta and a swim to clear her head, Alison summoned David to her office.

He gulped when he heard her proposal.

"Well," she pointed out. "You suggested I put Paul on the payroll."

He gulped again. "Two hundred and fifty . . ."

"That's the deal."

"It's one hell of a price to pay for . . ."

"Don't say it. One of these days you are actually going to make me angry, Dave. I've told you what I want done."

"You're the boss, Mrs Pat. When does this deal start?"

"As of now. You'll open an account for Paul in New York tomorrow morning and pay into it twenty thousand eight hundred and thirty-three dollars and thirty-three cents, and then on the first of every month after that."

He nodded, and wrote the instructions down. "And that's it."

"What do you mean?"

"Schleyer has nothing to do with Grange Estates."

"He will be paid as a director. I've just said so."

"But he will have no executive authority?"

"No."

"Even after he is your husband?"

"No, David. No."

"I'm sorry, Mrs Pat, but I have to know where I stand."

"You stand where you have always stood. You are employed by me, you take your instructions from me and nobody else, and you act always in my best interests. Now, and always. Okay?"

"Yes, ma'am. Ah . . . what happens in the event of your death?"

"Nothing is changing, David. My Will isn't changing. Paul knows this. He wouldn't have it any other way. Every penny goes to my children in proportion as they reach the age of twenty-one. Until then, my estate will be handled by my four trustees."

"Mr Schleyer has no say in that?"

"Mr Schleyer wishes no say in that. But . . ." she pointed. "He continues to receives his two hundred and fifty thousand a year from Grange Estates for life. I want that understood."

"I do understand that, Mrs Pat. That's all I wanted to hear. However . . . may I make a request?"

She glared at him. "What now?"

"Will you promise me that you will never, under any circumstances, sign any document without allowing me to read it first."

"Just who the hell do you think you are?"

"Your employee, Mrs Pat, who is endeavouring to act in your best interests."

She continued to glare at him for several seconds, then grinned. "You should have been a politician, Dave, not an accountant. Okay. I'll promise that, if you'll make me a promise in return."

"Anything, Mrs Pat."

"I want you to promise me that you'll be fair to Paul, in your judgements, and that when you realise you've made a mistake about him all this time, you'll admit it."

"I promise that willingly, Mrs Pat. Should the day come."

"It will. I promise you, Dave. It will."

Alison had always dreamed of marrying in a church, with an elaborate ceremony and hundreds of guests – when she married again. But she knew that was impossible unless she was prepared to submit to the kind of publicity she loathed. So again she settled for a very small and very private ceremony, in the drawing room at the villa. This she achieved, with only the children, the staff and the village priest present. But the priest spread the news, and soon the villa was anyway invaded by newspapermen and cameramen.

Alison left David in charge, and she and Paul departed early for London to honeymoon at the Savoy; she preferred this to the flat as she wanted to be waited on hand and foot. Besides, at the Savoy she felt more able to keep the press at bay than at either the flat or down in Sussex, unless she was prepared to use Hugo and Clem as heavies, and she didn't want to do that. Of course the press got to hear of her arrival with her husband soon enough, and if the hotel switchboard obeyed Alison's instructions to put no calls through unless they came from David, she was faced with headlines such as: WORLD'S WEALTHIEST WOMAN MARRIES MAN OF MYSTERY.

"Does that bother you?" she asked.

"Not if it doesn't bother you," he replied.

Paul was as thoughtful and kind and loving as a husband as he had ever been as a lover, and gradually the truth of his background seeped through. He was reluctant to talk of it, because he was ashamed, but Alison persuaded him not only that she had a right to know but that there was nothing to be ashamed about.

His parents had both died when he had been quite

300

small, and he had spent his adolescence in an orphanage. From then on life had been a struggle, and he admitted that he had been foul of the law once or twice. But he had certainly lived, even if, until her, there had been no pot of gold at the end of his rainbow. He had served as a deckhand on a yacht, which had given him his knowledge of the sea and sailing, and had briefly been a tennis pro. He had wandered the world. "Looking for you, without knowing it," he would smile.

She loved the thought of that, that somehow their getting together had been karma, just as she loved every moment she spent in his company. But inevitably there were areas which now needed adjusting.

"I'm not sure how long I can take it," he confessed soon after they had been joined at her English country home by the rest of the "gang", as she called them.

"Stand what?"

"Being glowered at all the time by your two heavies."

"I know," Alison said sympathetically. "I'll speak to them."

"I don't think that will do a lot of good. Why are you employing them at all?"

"Well . . . to protect me, I suppose."

"From what?"

"Well . . . kidnapping, or something. Then there's the children."

"I've never seen them paying much attention to the children. Only you. But tell me this, has anyone ever attempted to kidnap you, or harm the children?"

"Well . . . no. But . . ."

"From what you've told me, the only person who ever needed protection was Grange himself. Even that chap Waller was obviously looking for Grange when he broke into the Mexican house."

"Well . . ."

"If you need protecting, darling," Paul went on, "surely that is now my business?"

"Yours?" She smiled. "You'll be telling me next you're a crack shot and a Black Belt."

"I am, a crack shot and a Black Belt. Would you like me to demonstrate?"

"Of course not." She had no doubt at all that he was what he claimed, in those areas, and it turned out that he had served in the US Marines. "It's just that they've been with me for so long. Ten years!"

"Give them a golden handshake. They'll be perfectly happy."

They weren't at all happy, even though Alison gave them each fifty thousand dollars.

"You mean I'm just to go?" Hugo seemed unable to believe his ears.

"You don't want to spend the rest of your life looking after me, Hugo," Alison said.

"That's I want to do, Mrs Pat. That's what I've always done. Let me stay, Mrs Pat. I won't get in the way."

To her consternation, she saw there were tears in his eyes. But if it had to be done . . . "I'm sorry, Hugo. Terribly sorry. But I just don't need you any more. Go and do something with you life, for God's sake."

His shoulders were hunched. "That's final?"

"Yes," she said. "That's final."

He turned and left the room.

Clem, predictably, was merely angry. He looked at the cheque she had just handed to him.

"A kiss-off," he commented. "After ten years. Just like that."

Alison stuck with the same line. "I'm sure you can think of something better to do with your life than hanging around me, Clem."

"Oh, sure, Mrs Pat. I'll think of something. Providing this cheque don't bounce."

"My cheques don't bounce, Clem."

"Yeah. You got it all. But one day maybe your luck will change. I'll look forward to that."

Almost he made it sound like a threat.

"I feel like the biggest heel on earth," Alison confessed to David. "At least about Hugo. But Paul was quite right; they had become totally redundant."

"Oh, quite," David agreed. "I imagine I'll be redundant next, when Mr Schleyer turns out to be a qualified accountant."

"He is not and you will never be," Alison assured him. "I want you right there, in charge, always. Promise me you'll always be there, Dave."

"It's where I want to be, Mrs Pat," he assured her in turn.

In fact, Paul had more sense than to suggest replacing David, but he did encourage Alison to regain her interest in her affairs. Together they returned up the Amazon, making the journey this time by plane, for McCall had laid down an airstrip at El Dorado. The trip became a pleasant jaunt instead of a hard slog . . . yet Alison knew she would not have missed that earlier safari for anything, although it had ended in tragedy.

The mine was still producing an enormous amount, even if it was down to less than a hundred million a year. What pleased Alison much more, however, was the way in which a proper township had grown up around the shaft, and the happy smiles on the faces of the workforce and their families. She visited the school, and addressed the children, and they sang her a song and presented her with a bouquet of flowers, while Paul smiled proudly.

They went down to Rio and were entertained by President Vargas, as well as Alvarado and his wife. "Did you ever find that missing money?" Alvarado asked.

"I haven't been looking very hard," Alison confessed.

"What missing money?" Paul asked.

"Some funds Pat stashed away someplace nobody knows," Alison told him. "In many ways he was very like a magpie. But it's nothing to worry about."

Much as she adored Paul, she knew that the thought of four hundred million dollars being "misplaced" would occupy his mind to the exclusion of everything else.

When they returned to Mexico, for the first time she made no attempt to visit the prison and see Johnny. A meeting with Jayme Puig elicited the information that Jonny was well and apparently being a model prisoner, and that he was receiving his food parcels every month.

"But now you are married, *señora* . . . do you wish to discontinue your parcels?" Puig asked.

"I wish the parcels to continue," Alison told him.

The next four years Alison thought were the happiest she had ever known. To her usual perambulation Paul wanted to add visits to just about every country in the world, and this she thoroughly enjoyed, often combining pleasure with business as she visited various apartment blocks or building sites which Pat had purchased, almost like a universal magpie. Paul wondered why she did not continue the system, but she was content that David should invest half of her income and play the exchanges with the other. If she still refused to delve too deeply into her affairs, she still knew that her wealth was escalating every year: her invested capital had in fact doubled since 1946, as David had prophesied it would, and was worth one point four billion dollars, while her income from the mine was still some thirty million a year.

By the summer of 1954, Ben was fourteen, and had left his prep. school to attend Welton College. Thirteen-year-old Shirley was at Broadhurst Ladies College. Eleven-year-old Pat was at another prep. school – Alison was sending them all to different schools to avoid any sibling rivalries – while ten-year-old Stephanie and eight-year-old

Harry continued to be taught by Miss Holding, who travelled around the world with the family.

Keeping up with school speechdays and open days and half terms took some organising, but here again Paul was the perfect father. He was always happy to drop whatever they were doing and fly off to England to sit down with her and a form master or mistress and chat about progress, or lack of it, to squirm on uncomfortable seats while prizes were handed out – seldom to anyone named Grange – or to sing carols with her at the Christmas services. Alison did not suppose any children could have had a better and more caring father.

Hugo and Clem had disappeared, and had ceased to trouble Alison's conscience.

Her greatest pleasure, however, remained sailing, and she and Paul spent a lot of time at sea in the Mediterranean each summer. The ketch was named *Roundabout*. Alison didn't like the name, but it had been the choice of the previous owner and Paul said it was unlucky to change a ship's name, so she was stuck with it.

Name apart, she loved everything about the yacht. It had a spacious master cabin aft, with a comfortable heads; a large central wheelhouse which contained an efficient and labour-saving galley, two double cabins forward with a shared heads, and best of all, in addition to over a thousand feet of sail, two sixty-five horsepower diesels in the engine space beneath the saloon, which enabled her to motor as comfortably as she sailed.

They had begun by having a crew, a man and a girl, for deckwork and cooking, but as Alison got more proficient and the children started to get bigger and stronger, she did away with any help except that provided by family, and watched with pride as Ben and Shirley became experts. She invited David to come with them on more than one occasion, but he was always seasick and she could tell he was miserable.

Actually, this relieved her, because she felt that on the yacht Paul really came into his own. Whatever any of them knew, they had learned from him, and there was never any argument, at sea, as to who was in command. David's presence would always be a reminder to Paul that his authority ceased the moment they stepped ashore.

But at sea he was happy, and she loved to see him enjoying himself. She was therefore enormously pleased when, as the season was getting underway, Paul said he wished to set up his own business; yacht brokerage.

"After all, I must have something to do," he explained. "As you will not let me help you in Grange Estates."

"Does that rankle so much?"

"It is your decision, my dearest girl. And I am happy to accept that. But you will not begrudge me an attempt to make something of myself." He grinned at her. "I will make you a director."

She blew him a kiss. "Then I accept. How much money do you need?"

"Not a penny. I have my own, remember?"

Schleyer and Company was launched a month later with a big party at the premises Paul had rented near the harbour in Cannes. It turned out that he had done a great deal of spadework before ever mentioning the subject to Alison, and had an impressive list of clients already on his books.

"Who's a smart businessman, then?" she asked.

"This is going to be the biggest and best yacht agency in the world," he promised her.

She was even more impressed when she inspected the offices the next day, and watched the secretaries at work, listened to the telephones jangling and the telex machine clattering . . . "Now surely even you must admit you had Paul all wrong," she suggested to David, who was also invited to see the set-up.

"Looks good," he said. "We'll have to see how it turns out."

Alison stuck out her tongue at him. It seemed the two

men were never going to be friends, and she couldn't blame Paul when he employed his own accountant, a Frenchman.

"Local talent," he explained.

Gerard was certainly extremely pleasant, and like everyone else, totally deferential to her.

"Now we must have our first board meeting," Paul said.

"Who are your other directors?"

"You."

"And?"

"That's it."

"Just you and me?"

"And Gerard."

"So what do I do?"

"Well, believe it or not, we've already made three sales."

"Have we? I mean, you? Good heavens."

"So now we need to transfer ownership. That means we have to sign them over to the new owners, if you follow me. I'm afraid there's rather a lot of fine print. Do you wish to read it?"

"Well, I suppose I should . . ."

"I think you should too."

He gave her the first Agreement, which was indeed a lengthy document, all about tonnes and Thames measurement, what additional work would be required to obtain an up-to-date AI rating from Lloyds, what needed doing to the machinery . . .

Paul and Gerard waited patiently while she read it through.

"Now you sign it," Paul said.

"Me?"

"Well, all three of us sign it. But I've put your name at the top."

As he had. She signed her name, and the Agreement was passed back to Paul, who also signed, and then to Gerard, who signed last.

"Don't the new owners have to sign as well?" Alison asked.

"You bet. But they won't unless we have first. I'm going to see them this afternoon. Now here's the next one."

"Oh, lord, not another. Do I have to read it?"

"Not if you're happy. It's exactly the same as the first one, except for the name and the figures, of course."

Alison signed.

"One more."

He flicked open the third Agreement, and again she signed. Gerard was busily signing the second one, and now Paul gave him the third as well.

"There," he said. "Those three are putting ten thousand in the account."

"I do like being married to a successful man," Alison said. "Let's go for a sail."

"Sorry, darling I can't. I'm a working man now, you know. I have to get these agreements countersigned."

"Oh," she said humbly. It was so long since she had had the slightest constraint put upon what she felt like doing at the moment she wanted to do it that she had forgotten that not everyone enjoyed her privileges. "Well . . . see you at the villa."

She drove home, had a swim, and romped with the dogs. There was a new butler, Lucien, and he duly appeared with a cocktail, before she went upstairs to dress. Paul arrived at six, and David joined them for a drink, as he invariably did, before retiring to his apartment, again as was his usual practice. Alison sat with Pat and Stephanie and Harry while they had dinner, chatted with Charlene and Mrs Holding, and then rejoined Paul for coffee.

"You're looking tired," she remarked. "Don't tell me . . . one of your clients reneged."

"*Our* clients, darling," he corrected. "This is our firm, remember?"

Presumably it was his way of reproaching her for

refusing to give him any executive power in Grange Estates, but she continued to smile. "Our company, then. What happened?"

"Not a thing. Everything is going swimmingly. I am tired though. Maybe I'm coming down with something."

"Oh, no! Well, an early night."

"I won't say no to that."

Their bedroom was on the first floor, looking out down the hillside at the sea from a wide, deep, balcony. It was a typical June Mediterranean night, distinctly warm. The bedroom was air-conditioned but Alison hated the combination of humming machinery and stale air, and only used it when the mosquitoes were very bad. This night there were certainly some bugs about, and she closed up and switched on. But to her distress, Paul seemed to find breathing very difficult.

"You think I should call a doctor?" she asked.

"For God's sake, I'm not dying. It's just a touch of hay fever. Listen, do you think you could stand the bugs and give me some fresh air?"

"I guess so, if you can stand the stink of citronella."

She got up, went to the bathroom, and coated herself with the evil-smelling scent, then switched off the air-conditioning and threw open the windows.

She slept heavily, as she always did, but awoke when the dogs barked. What memories that evoked. But they often barked here on the Riviera, alerted by a distant sound. Nonetheless, she stretched out her hand to touch Paul, and discovered he wasn't there.

She sat up. "Paul?"

He came in from the balcony. "Sorry. Did I disturb you?"

"I think it was the dogs disturbed me."

"Yes. They disturbed me, too." He sat beside her, took her in his arms. "Did I ever tell you how much I loved you?"

"I don't think you ever did," she said, and kissed him.

"Mmmm," he murmured, and fell on to his back, dragging her on top of him. "Oh, you gorgeous creature," he said. "Come up a bit."

He put his hands into her armpits, and raised her, at the same moment holding her away from him. As he did so, Alison felt an enormous slap in the middle of her back.

PART THREE

Woman of Gold

CHAPTER 11

Recovery

Noises drifted through Alison's consciousness from a very great distance, muted and dull, fuzzy, uncertain. From time to time she was aware of people touching her, and sometimes there was pain, but that too seemed far away. Until at last she found herself staring at a white ceiling, and a white-clad woman as well, who wore an enormous convoluted headdress, and was smiling at her, a trifle anxiously.

Alison licked her lips; her throat was too dry to enable her to speak.

There was a muttered conversation before two people raised her head and a glass of water was held to her lips. It tasted better than anything she had ever drunk before. But the effort of swallowing left her exhausted. She gazed at the smiling faces of the sisters, who were soon joined by a doctor, tall and angular, with a small moustache.

"*Madame*," he said. "It is good to see you awake. Your husband will be very pleased."

"My husband," Alison whispered. "Is he all right?" Because she knew something was wrong, even if she could not recollect what.

"Oh, yes, *madame*. I have telephoned him. He will soon be here." He gave her a somewhat uncertain smile. "The police are also anxious to speak with you, when you are strong enough."

"The police?"

"You were shot, *madame*. Do you not remember?"

Alison stared at him in disbelief.

"You do not remember," the doctor said.

"Shot?" Alison whispered.

"You were very nearly killed, *madame*. Indeed, it is a miracle that you were not."

"But . . ." she remembered the sudden feeling of being hit very hard in the back. "Who . . ."

"That is what the police would like to know, *madame*. When you are strong enough. Now you must rest. I will see that you are not disturbed until you are ready. No reporters, eh?"

"Reporters?"

"Well, the hospital was surrounded by them, *madame*, when you first came in and the news broke. Over the past couple of weeks they have found other things to do . . . well, you know what reporters are like. But there are still a couple hanging about. Now I will leave you . . ."

"Wait," Alison said. "Did you say, over the past couple of *weeks*? How long have I been here?"

"Just under four weeks, *madame*. You have been in a coma. Your life was despaired of more than once. But now . . . just rest, *madame*. Just rest, and you will soon be well."

Rest, Alison thought. How could she rest when apparently an entire month had been ripped out of her life! The children! The dogs! Everything!

And she had been shot, just like Pat! By the same person? How could that be? But suppose the murderer hadn't been Mayne, but had been Hugo or Clem? And he had come back . . . the dogs had barked. But they had gone on barking this time. They had not known the assassin.

And Paul! He had been in the bedroom with her. He had actually been holding her in his arms! Paul!

314

She became very agitated, as the sisters could see, and they became very fussy, insisting she rest, holding up her matchstick-like hand so she could see how weak she was.

But at least next day they brought Paul to see her. He sat beside the bed, staring at her, his expression utterly anguished.

"Oh, my darling girl," he said. "My darling, darling girl. I have been so worried."

That she could tell; there were deep shadows under his eyes and he had lost weight.

"What happened?" she asked.

"Some marauder shot at you, from the balcony."

"But . . . how? Why?"

"Nobody knows. It is inexplicable. The man got away. He actually fired again, but that bullet missed, and by then I was rushing him."

"Oh, Paul! You could've been killed."

"I thought you *had* been killed, darling. I think I went berserk. But I couldn't catch the fellow. He jumped down from the balcony and escaped. I suppose I was too anxious to get back to you. Oh, my darling . . ." his fingers were tight on hers.

"He didn't make it," she said, and squeezed back as best she could. "I want to see the children."

"And they want to see you. So does David, as you can imagine."

David! she thought. He also had been there when Pat had been shot. But David . . . her most faithful retainer? What could he possibly hope to gain?

Anyway, the dogs would not have barked, for David.

"But first, I'm afraid the police wish to ask you some questions."

"Yes," she said.

"Would you like me to be present?"

"Yes."

*　*　*

315

The police were allowed to see her the following day. By then Alison had had a square meal, and was feeling much stronger, which was just as well. Inspector Brillot was not very pleased to have Paul in the room, but Alison insisted, so he sat beside her bed while a sergeant wrote in a notebook.

"You will understand, *madame*, that we carried out a very thorough investigation at the time of the murder attempt, but I am afraid it has led us nowhere," the Inspector said. "However, it is our opinion that the assassin was either a member of your staff, or someone who knew the grounds of your villa, and the layout of the villa itself, very well. He knew exactly how to get in, and what is more important, he knew exactly where the dogs were locked up and that they *were* locked up, and he knew how to get out again, even though your husband claims to have been in hot pursuit."

"Claims?"

"Well . . ." Brillot looked embarrassed. "No one actually saw all of this happening, you see."

"Whatever my husband says happened, happened," Alison said severely.

"Of course, *madame*. Of course. The point is, the way the crime was carried out rules out the possibility of burglary, or of some itinerant: the man who fired at you went to your villa with that express purpose in mind. Now, *madame*, we know so little about you. We know you are very rich, very beautiful, very, it seems, happy in your marriage and your family . . ." he paused to give Paul another quick glance. "Yet someone tried to kill you. So I must ask you to tell me who this person might be? Do you think the attempt is linked to the murder of your first husband?"

"I don't see why it should be."

"Because that murderer is locked up. But he might have had an accomplice . . ."

"Because there were people who might have had a reason for killing my first husband," Alison said evenly.

"I do not believe Mr Carter to be guilty. But I can think of no one with a reason to kill *me*. There is no one who can possibly benefit from my death."

"Oh, come now, *madame*, you are a rich woman . . ."

"All of my money goes in trust to my children, Inspector. The eldest is just coming up to thirteen years old. Are you suggesting *he* hired someone to kill me?"

"Oh, *madame*, of course not. But . . ."

"And even if he did, it would do him no good. The money is held in trust until he is twenty-one."

"I am sure there must be other beneficiaries," the Inspector said stubbornly. "Your husband . . ."

Alison glared at him.

"I am sorry, *madame*, but I must ask these questions."

"Well, it may interest you to know that my husband receives nothing in my Will at all."

"Nothing, *madame*?"

"Not a franc. He has his director' fee from Grange Estates, and that is contractually payable to him for life, whether I am alive or dead." She smiled at Paul.

Brillot scratched his temple with his pen. "Then it is all very strange. *Someone* tried to kill you, *madame*. He must have had a reason. Let me ask you this: have you recently dismissed anyone from your service, who might harbour a resentment, and who would know the lay-out of the villa?"

"Well . . ." again Alison glanced at Paul.

"I think you have to tell them, darling," he said.

"Well . . . I used to have two bodyguards. I kind of inherited them from my husband, my first husband. When I married again, I felt I no longer needed them, and let them go."

"Were they resentful of this?"

"Well . . . yes, I suppose they were. But it wasn't recently. It was four years ago."

"Nevertheless, I should be obliged if you will give me their names."

Alison did so.

Brillot nodded, and closed his notebook. "We will find them."

"But you don't know they're guilty."

"We will decide that when we find them, *madame*."

"I feel such a heel," she confessed to Paul, after the police had left.

"It had to be done, darling. As the man said, someone did try to kill you."

She knew he was right, and her conscience was soon submerged in the joy of seeing the children, who were accumulated from their various schools, as it was necessary for her to spend another month in hospital. She was quite horrified when she was shown in a mirror the deep brown scar on her back.

"You were a very lucky lady," Dr Fouquet told her. "The bullet managed to miss lung, liver and kidney before lodging in one of your front ribs."

"Ugh," Alison commented.

"It was the phenomenal loss of blood which all but killed you," the doctor explained.

But she was regaining her strength every day, and sent for David. He looked even more distressed than Paul had done, and she thought she knew why.

"Don't tell me: we should've been out of France a week ago."

"Well, yes, Mrs Pat, there is going to be a tax problem. But the French don't take these things quite as seriously as the Brits or the Yanks. I'm sure we will be able to sort something out. But the whole thing . . . someone trying to kill you . . . Maybe we should've kept Hugo and Clem on."

"So they wouldn't have a reason for killing me?"

"I don't think it was them, Mrs Pat. Neither of those lads are killers. And they would've protected you. Let's face it, Mr Schleyer didn't do a very good job."

"David, watch it. Paul has said some very nice things about you. And yet for some reason you're still suspicious about him. What on earth more could he do than chase the man away?"

"Nothing, Mrs Pat, if that is what happened."

"You've been talking to that beastly Brillot."

"I haven't talked with anyone about that night, Mrs Pat."

"Then you're adopting a very strange attitude."

"It was a very strange night, Mrs Pat. I thought you usually slept with the windows shut and the air-conditioning on?"

"Well, the bugs weren't too bad, and Paul was feeling stuffy . . ." she gazed at David with her mouth open.

"Right. Now, Mr Schleyer says the assassin fired twice. Well, this is absolutely true. One bullet was found in you, and the other in the wall."

"Well?"

"Mrs Pat, those bullets came from a Colt automatic pistol, fitted with a silencer. Those guns carry a nine-shot magazine. It just isn't logical for a guy to set out to commit murder without making sure his magazine is full. So he enters the grounds, of which he has been given at least a plan, knows exactly how to get to your balcony, and also that your windows are going to be open, most unusually, and shoots. As far as he knows he's killed you. I can tell you we all thought you were dying when we came to the room. But he shoots again, either at you, or at Mr Schleyer, when Mr Schleyer goes at him. He misses, and then runs off. Well, he might just have done that, lost his nerve, maybe, although that doesn't sound like a hired hit man to me. But then, with seven bullets left, and knowing that only Mr Schleyer could stop him escaping – no alarm was given until after he had left the grounds and none of us knew what was happening until then – he doesn't shoot again when Mr Schleyer goes in pursuit. Or if he does, he misses. You know, that sounds like a poor movie script, the kind of thing where every time the hero fires he hits somebody, and the bad guys blaze away for half the film and the good guy never even gets nicked."

Alison, propped up on her pillows, stared at him. "Just what are you trying to say, Dave?"

"I've said it, Mrs Pat."

"You think the murderer was a hired gunman."

"I think so, yes."

"Hired by someone who wants me dead. Okay, I'll buy that, although I can't think of anyone who could possibly benefit by it. I told the police so. But you also think Paul isn't telling the truth about pursuing the fellow and chasing him off."

"I'm sorry, Mrs Pat, it doesn't ring true."

"Therefore," Alison said slowly. "You are suggesting that Paul had something to do with the attempt on my life, that he made an issue about opening the windows just so the gunman could get at me."

David hung his head, as he had a habit of doing, looking like a schoolboy caught with his hand in the cookie jar.

"Okay, David," Alison said. "I am not going to get angry with you. I have a notion the police are unhappy about that too. But as I know the opposite, you and I are going to set about making sure everyone else knows it too. Right?"

"You *know* the opposite, Mrs Pat?"

"Oh, for God's sake, Paul is my husband! We love each other."

"Yes, ma'am."

"Oh . . . you make me so mad. All right. Give me a motive. A single, solitary motive. I deliberately set up our marriage so Paul would be his own man, so his wealth didn't relate to mine at all. He wanted that. In fact, he didn't even want the quarter of a million. I insisted on that, so something like this could never arise. And he has always known the terms of my Will. Yet you're not satisfied."

David sighed. "You have to admit that you met Mr Schleyer in very unusual circumstances, that you

320

know nothing about him save what he has chosen to tell you . . ."

"Christ, here we go again. Do you guys never let up? What are Paul and I supposed to do to prove that we love each other and that there is no possible *reason* for him to wish to harm me in any way?"

One of the sisters came in. "*Madame*, we can hear you shouting. You must not excite yourself. It is very bad."

"Okay, okay. I'll stop shouting. And then, in addition to all of that, I did everything you wanted me to, never signed a single document . . . not that Paul ever asked me to. Dave . . . please have the guts to admit you're wrong."

David sighed. "Mrs Pat, I hope to God I am." But he was frowning. "You're a director of Mr Schleyer's company."

"Yes. Why?"

"You never signed anything in that capacity?"

"Well, of course I did. The very day I was shot I signed . . ." for the second time she stopped in mid-sentence.

"What did you sign, Mrs Pat?"

"They were transfers of ownership of yachts."

"And you had to sign? Why?"

"Well, because I'm a director, I suppose."

"You are director of a yacht agency. To transfer the ownership of a yacht it is usually only necessary to obtain the signature of the previous owner, and the new owner if there is some payment negotiation. Your signing a transfer of ownership would have no legal validity whatsoever. It would be totally unnecessary."

Alison stared at him. It can't be true, she thought. It just can't.

"But you read the documents before signing then?" David asked.

"Well . . . only the top two. Paul said they were all the same. Oh, Dave! But . . . what can he possibly have been trying to do?" She felt sick.

321

"Most likely you signed a revised Will, cancelling the original and giving him control of your money."

"I can't believe that. I just can't. Anyway, that has to be ridiculous. Paul saved my life when he chased off the gunman. But you're suggesting he hired the man in the first place. Dave, that makes no kind of sense at all."

"I agree," David said. "But I still feel it's too much of a coincidence that on the day you signed a document, which you must have found out very soon it wasn't necessary or even appropriate for you to have signed at all, someone tries to kill you. Mrs Pat, I hope you understand how sorry I am that this has happened at all, much less that I have to be the one to raise the point . . ."

"I know, Dave. I once said I don't know what I'd do without you. I still don't know. Listen . . . leave it with me."

David hesitated. "If someone had your murder in mind once, Mrs Pat, and didn't make it . . ."

"He'll try again, you reckon? Do the police still have a guard on my door?"

"They do. But what happens when you leave here?"

She smiled. "Maybe you'd better find Hugo before the police do, and re-employ him."

"I wouldn't describe the situation as amusing, Mrs Pat."

"Neither would I. But figure this, Dave: if you're right and Paul did hire a hit man to kill me, he must've changed his mind, right?"

"Or he thought you were dying, Mrs Pat. The rest of us did."

Alison felt like screaming until her heart broke. Or was her heart already broken?

She loved. She had loved. She still loved.

But she had thought she loved before. She had allowed herself to fall in love with Pat, when all the time she had been being purchased, lock, stock and barrel. She had wanted so desperately to fall in love with Jonny. Now she still didn't know whether or not he was a murderer. She had thought to bury that emotion in her love for Paul. She still wanted to do that, more than ever. Even when, as she now recognised, all the motivation seemed to point in his direction. She knew as well as David that Hugo would never try to kill her; he loved her too much. That left no one in the whole world with a motive . . . save for someone who might hope to gain by her death. She had arranged things so that there was no one who could do that . . . she had supposed.

But if signing those "transfers of ownership" had been unnecessary . . .

It was not in Alison's nature to be devious.

"Sold any more boats while I've been laid up?" she asked Paul when he came in that afternoon.

"A couple. Business has actually been quite good."

"Who signed the transfers?"

A very quick frown passed across his face. "Why, I did, and Gerard. Our clients knew all about your being ill."

"Paul, what exactly was I signing that afternoon?"

The frown was back, but this was artificial. "Transfers, darling. You read them."

"I read the first. You said the others were all the same."

"Well, they were."

She gazed at him. David is right, she thought, and you are lying to me. Therefore you have lied to me from the moment we met. For God's sake, I *knew* that, and still wanted to love you.

"Paul," she said. "I have discovered that it was not only unnecessary for me to sign those papers, but, if they were transfers it was probably illegal."

"My darling girl . . ."

"Please don't say things like that any more. Paul, I wish you to leave this hospital, go to the agency, and bring me here every paper I signed, including the new

323

Will, or Codicil, or letter of instruction or authority, or whatever it was."

He stared at her with his mouth open. But she knew he was acting.

"You think . . . my darling . . ."

"Shut up!" she snapped. "If those documents, all of them, are not here in one hour, I will tell the police exactly what happened, and let them decide what to do next."

"But . . . Alison . . . I'm your husband. I love you. I saved your life."

"Why?"

He gulped. "I . . ." he licked his lips. "I love you."

"But you hired someone to kill me, after having me sign away control of my companies in the event of my death. Isn't that the truth?"

Another quick lick of the lips. "You don't understand."

"Then make me understand, Paul. Now."

"The documents . . ."

"You can fetch them after. Make me understand."

He sighed, his whole body seeming to curl up. "I work for Carlo Rubio," he muttered.

"*What* did you say?" She couldn't believe her ears.

"Rubio," he said. "He's a New York gang boss."

"I know who and what Rubio is," Alison said, feeling sicker than ever. "And you . . . work for him?"

"Mr Rubio feels that your late husband owed him quite a sum of money," Paul explained. "Which you have refused to pay . . ." he paused.

"I owe that thug nothing," Alison said.

"He's a hard man to cross, Mr Rubio," Paul said. "But he felt to try to strong-arm a pretty little lady like you would be counter-productive, so . . ." he sighed.

"So he sent you, to romance me until I fell in love with you, and then to have me sign a new Will without knowing it, so that you could have me killed and inherit everything, which you would then turn over to him. God, what a fool I am!"

"Listen," Paul said.

"You listen," Alison told him. "You are the lowest crawling thing I have ever not stepped on. But by God, I'm going to step on you now."

"Listen," he begged again. "Okay, so I'm all kinds of a heel. I was employed to do a job of work. But Alison, you have to believe me, I fell in love with you."

"You!" she said contemptuously.

"Look, it was all set-up. The moment you signed that paper you were going to be killed. But I couldn't go through with it, Alison. I love you. I did everything I was supposed to do, like opening the windows, but when I saw the guy there . . . I couldn't do it."

"For God's sake, he shot me, didn't he? Everyone thought I was going to die."

"I couldn't stop the first shot. But I prevented the second, or at least, his hitting you. Then I chased him off."

"Chased him?"

"Well . . . I told him to get out while he could."

"Which explains why he didn't shoot you too," Alison said. "He was your buddy."

"I had never seen him before in my life. Alison . . ." he tried to take her hand, but she drew it away from him. "Because I couldn't go through with it, because of my love for you, I have broken every rule in the book. I changed a Company plan. And I've left Mr Rubio without the money he wants. Alison, there'll be a contract out on me by now. The only reason I haven't been done yet is that I told the hit man you were already dead. Rubio's only waiting to see if that is true. Everyone knows you've been pretty close to it this last month. Once the news gets out that you've recovered . . ."

"What am I supposed to say? We'll die together?"

"I just wanted you to understand."

"Oh, I understand," Alison said. "I understand that I have been made the biggest fool in history. Okay, so I asked for it. I'm not asking for it any more. You go get that document and bring it here. Now."

Paul got up, hesitated. "Alison . . . I need your help. I'm in real trouble. Alison, I'm your husband."

"Just get the papers."

"Alison . . . say you forgive me."

"Get those goddamed papers, you lousy bastard!" she shouted.

No sooner had he gone than she began to feel sorry for him. Of course he was a lousy bastard . . . but he had given her the happiest four years of her life. So it had all been a sham, it had none the less been real while it had been happening.

Now he swore he loved her. *Had* he saved her life? According to David he might just have easily have been sure she was dead. Goddamed David, with his analytical brain, always putting his finger on the weak point in any argument.

David, who had argued against Paul from the very beginning, and had been proven right. Oh, God*damed* David!

So what was she going to do now? The first thing was to settle with Carlo Rubio . . . and she was determined not to do that by paying over any vast sum of money. If he wanted a fight, he was going to get one: she had never been so angry in her life.

She telephoned David, asked him to come right down.

But where did that leave Paul? No matter how true his protestations of love, she couldn't remain married to him. She didn't *want* to remain married to him. The very thought of his touching her, as he must have touched her for four years always with murder in his heart, made her skin crawl.

But she couldn't just throw him out, either, to become a marked man for Rubio's thugs.

His safety would have to be made part of the settlement deal with Rubio.

* * *

David arrived in half an hour.

"I've been thinking of what we were talking about," Alison said. "I've had a word with Paul."

"And?"

"He's admitted everything." She told him what Paul had said.

"Oh, shit, Mrs Pat. I really am sorry," David said when she had finished.

"Why? You were right, as you are always right. I need a keeper. Thank God I've got one. But I've had enough of this Carlo Rubio. I intend to fix him."

David began to look uneasy. "Mrs Pat . . ."

"I'll have all the evidence I need, in Paul's testimony."

"You reckon he'll go through with it?"

"He doesn't have any choice: only I can protect him, now. However, I know I'm playing a dangerous game, so what I want you to do is, get hold of Clem, and Hugo – we knew they're innocent as you always said they were – and then the three of you recruit me a little army. We have time, because Rubio can't do anything once I've destroyed that false Will. He'll have to think about something else."

"Heck, Mrs Pat, what you're thinking of doing . . ."

"Is what Pat would have done, right?"

"Well, yes, I guess so. But he was a man . . ."

"One day you are really going to make me mad. Just do as I ask."

"Yes, Mrs Pat. And where does Schleyer fit into all this?"

"Wherever I choose. You'd better stay here until he comes back with those papers. He's due in five minutes."

David looked relieved.

They talked about what she was planning to do. To confront Rubio with evidence that he had planned her murder was indeed a highly dangerous game, and not only for her. Plans had to be made for the protection of the children, and for a whole host of other eventualities. Alison could tell that David was extremely unhappy with the whole situation, and felt she was biting off more than she could chew: his solution was Pat's – surround herself with bodyguards and ignore Rubio . . . someone was bound to get him eventually. But she would not be swayed. She could not contemplate living the rest of her life looking over her shoulder, or her children's shoulders. She wanted a confrontation, now, and an end to the matter.

As usual, she had no doubt at all she was going to win, with Paul in her pocket.

And then she realised that Paul had been gone well over the hour.

She called the Agency, and to her surprise got Gerard. She would have expected Gerard to have done a bunk once Paul told him what had happened. But he sounded perfectly normal.

"Is Paul there?" Alison asked.

"Why, no, Mrs Schleyer. He's gone sailing."

"What?"

"He came here, about forty-five minutes ago, then left again. He said he was going for an afternoon sail in the *Dragon*."

"But . . . did he take anything with him?"

"Ah . . . he wrote a letter, before leaving. A personal letter, I'd say, because he wrote it in longhand."

"Is the letter there?"

"No, *madame*. Mr Schleyer said he would mail it at the marina."

"Thank you." Alison hung up, looked at David. "Get down to the Club, as fast as you can. I don't know what Paul is up to, but . . ."

There were feet in the corridor, and a heated discussion.

"What on earth . . . Paul?" Alison shouted. "Is that you?"

David got up and hurried through the door, to return

a moment later with one of the sisters.

"It's Robert, from the Yacht Club. He says something terrible has happened. Do you wish to see him?"

"Yes," Alison said, her heart seeming to slow.

"*Madame*," the sister protested. "You must not excite yourself."

"Send him in," Alison insisted. "Or I'll go out to him."

The sister hesitated, but David was already opening the door again, to admit the yacht club steward.

"Oh, Madame Schleyer?"

"What is it? What has happened?"

"Oh, *madame* . . . Monsieur Schleyer, he came to the club half an hour ago, and took out his small boat, the *Dragon*, for a sail, as he often does . . ."

"Yes," Alison said. "Yes." She was fighting an urgent desire to scream. "What happened?"

"Oh, *madame*, Monsieur Schleyer . . . he sailed out beyond the harbour entrance. Conditions are good, a light on-shore breeze. But suddenly . . . he fell overboard."

"Fell?"

"That is what the people who were nearest said. He was sitting at the tiller, and he suddenly stood up . . . and just went over the side."

"Is he all right?"

"Oh, *madame* . . ."

"You said there were other people there."

"Some distance away, *madame*. And there was not much wind. Also, they expected him to climb back on board. When they realised he was not going to, they sailed across, but by then he had disappeared. *Madame*, the police are out there now. But your husband's body has not been recovered."

CHAPTER 12

Boss Lady

It took French Navy divers several hours to recover Paul Schleyer's body. He had apparently tied the anchor to his waist and held it against himself when he had "fallen" overboard.

"Because I wouldn't say I'd forgiven him," Alison muttered. "I killed him, Dave."

"Now that's nonsense, Mrs Pat," David protested. "He was rotten, through and through. And scared stiff. He knew Rubio's people were going to get him."

Alison had to make herself believe that was true. As it probably was. But she could not help but wonder what difference it might have made had she told him she could still love him.

But that would have been a lie.

Next morning Paul's letter arrived. It was a full and complete confession, of what Rubio had employed him to do, and of what he had done. It ended with a statement of his love for her, and a hope that she would be able to use the letter to bring Rubio down, or at least safeguard her own future and that of her children.

The children! They had looked on Paul as a father, and Ben and Shirley and Pat, at the least, were old enough to need to know the truth.

Alison wept when she read the letter, but she soon

dried her tears, and sent for David. He whistled as he in turn read it.

"Can I bring Rubio down with that?"

"Long odds, Mrs Pat."

"Will it stand up in court?"

"Yes, I think it probably would. We can produce hand-writing experts to prove it was written by Schleyer, and in the circumstances, it's virtually a deathbed confession. Equally I'm sure Preston or any competent detective can find the proof that Schleyer was connected with Rubio, which would be a pretty hefty piece of circumstantial evidence, given that everybody knows about Rubio's activities."

"So what's the catch?"

"Simply that Rubio's lawyers will make a meal out of it. They always have, and they always will. They'll string the case along for years, and even if there was a conviction, they'll string it along for years more on appeal, with him out on bail. While for the rest of your life you'll be in the hot seat."

"You wouldn't say I'm in the hot seat now?"

"Well . . . I guess you are. But I've already started hiring people . . ."

"Dave, is it ever possible, absolutely, to protect oneself against assassination, or kidnapping?"

"Well, no, Mrs Pat, not in this day and age. Not assassination, anyway, where a guy with a high-powered rifle can kill at maybe a mile. All you can do is make it too difficult to be worthwhile trying."

"When we're talking about a billion dollars it won't ever be too difficult."

He looked anxious, as he so often did.

"So we'll have to go for what is attainable," Alison said thoughtfully. "The bastard tried to kill me, but I don't suppose there were any personal hard feelings. It's just a way of life with him. Okay, Dave. Tell Fouquet I want to see him, and Brillot. Any reporters about?"

"They're flying in by the planeload."

"What do the local papers say?"

"Well . . . you know what they're like."

"Show me."

He took an example from his briefcase.

"PAUL SCHLEYER COMMITS SUICIDE.
ALISON GRANGE'S HUSBAND DROWNS HIM-
SELF.
HUSBAND OF WORLD'S WEALTHIEST WOMAN
OPTS OUT."

"Bastards," she muttered.

"Don't worry. Not one of them will get near you."

"But I want them to, Paul. Just as soon as I've seen Fouquet and Brillot, we'll have a press conference."

"Yes, ma'am," he said doubtfully.

"Meanwhile, will you book us out on the *Queen Mary* next week, for New York."

"Yes, ma'am. Ah . . . what do you mean to do about Schleyer's accountant, Gerard? I don't think he was involved in the murder. But he was certainly in on the attempted fraud. You want to prefer charges? Schleyer's letter will certainly convict him."

"I don't want to get involved in any minor lawsuit here," Alison said. "Fire him, Dave. And close down the Agency. Today."

"I understand this tragedy has been a terrible shock, *madame*," Dr Fouquet said. "But to leave hospital so soon . . . I do not think it is wise."

"I have things to do," Alison told him. "I'll be careful, I promise."

She wondered just what he would say if he had the least idea just what she *meant* to do.

*　　*　　*

Brillot studied the letter.

"In the circumstances, I wish you to consider the case closed," Alison told him.

"I cannot do this without revealing to the Press the reasons for my decision, *madame*."

"Be my guest," Alison said. "I intend to reveal it to them tomorrow."

Brillot stroked his chin. "You mean to tell the world that this man Rubio tried to have you killed?"

"Yes."

Brillot stroked his chin some more. "Then I must ask you to wait until I have spoken with the Prefect."

"Why?"

"Well, *madame*, I will need additional men to protect your villa."

"That will not be necessary," Alison told him. "I shall be leaving for America, the day after tomorrow."

Brillot scratched his head.

Although the hospital sisters had been making her take exercise up and down the ward ever since she had regained consciousness, Alison was still far too weak to stand for more than a few moments at a time. So, having been driven home, she received the press, seated in her own drawing room, flanked by David and Charlene, who had assumed the domestic nursing duties.

There were a surprising number of people present, not less than thirty, and several of them were women, while film and T.V cameras had also been installed.

"Ladies and gentlemen," Alison said. "As I believe you know, just over a month ago someone tried to kill me. And two days ago, my husband committed suicide. These two events are linked." She waited for the gasp and watched the pencils moving back and forth. Then she raised Paul's letter. "I have here a confession, written by my husband shortly before his death, in which he admits he was employed by a New York hoodlum to seduce me, marry me, and obtain control of my fortune, for the benefit of that hoodlum. My husband decided not to go through with the plan, but it was too late."

She smiled at the television camera.

"Are you prepared to tell us the name of the hoodlum, Mrs Schleyer?" someone asked.

"Of course," Alison said. "His name is Carlo Rubio." There was another gasp.

"Do you intend to bring a charge of attempted murder against Mr Rubio?" someone asked.

"Unfortunately, Mr Rubio is an American citizen, or at least, an American resident, and is not subject to French law," Alison said. "Unless, of course, he comes to France."

"But he's not going to do that, Mrs Schleyer. So what are you going to do?"

Alison smiled at the camera again.

"I intend to go to America," she said. "And have a talk with Mr Rubio."

Then she sat down with the children. They were not habitual newspaper readers, and they accepted that both their mother and their stepfather lived unusual and often apparently disorganised lives. That Uncle Paul, as they called him, had not returned for two nights was not especially odd. But they could sense that something was happening, however pleased they were to have their mother home again.

"Darlings," Alison said, having thought long and carefully and realised there was no way but the truth. "Uncle Paul is dead."

They stared at her with enormous eyes.

"He committed suicide," Alison said carefully, "by falling overboard from his boat with an anchor tied to his stomach."

Another pregnant silence. Then Ben asked, "Why did he do that, Mom?"

334

Alison sighed, conscious that she was acting. "Because . . . because he was a bad man, I'm afraid." She told them what had actually happened. She wasn't sure Stephanie and Harry could take it all in. But the others certainly did. When she was finished, Shirley leapt up and threw both arms round her neck.

"Oh, Mom," she said. "Oh, Mom."

"The rotter," Patrick commented. "Boy, if he was here now . . ."

"He's dead," Alison reminded him, gently.

Ben got up and walked to the window to look out at the swimming pool. "I liked him," he said, and turned back to look at them, defiantly. "He was a real father to us."

"But he was horrid, really," Shirley argued.

Ben looked at Alison. "What are we going to do?"

"Well . . . go on living, I guess. So I made a mistake. It wasn't the first one."

"I meant, are you going to marry again?"

His face was drawn with anxiety.

"Come here," Alison said. He sat beside her, and she hugged him. "No," she said. "I am not going to marry again. Ever. That's a promise."

"But what are you going to do about this guy Rubio?" Pat wanted to know.

"I am going to squash him like the creepy-crawlie he is," Alison said. "That's a promise too, gang."

"Telephone call, Mrs Pat," David said. "From New York."

"On cue." Alison took the receiver.

"Mrs Schleyer? This is Walter Bernard. Remember me?"

"How could I forget you?" Alison asked. "But it is good of you to call."

"Now, look here, Mrs Schleyer, just what are you trying to pull?"

"Let's get one thing straight, Bernard," Alison said. "I am no longer Mrs Schleyer. As of this moment I am reverting to my original married name: Alison Grange. Have you got that?"

"Oh, ah . . . okay, Mrs . . . ah, Grange. Now look here, I want to tell you that on behalf of Mr Rubio I am instituting a slander suit against you tomorrow morning."

"Oh, good," Alison said.

There was a brief silence.

"Good?" Bernard asked. "We are going to take your ass."

"No, no," Alison said. "You have it all wrong, Bernard. Ever heard of a chap called Oscar Wilde?"

Another brief silence. "There was a boxer named Wilde, once, but his first name was Jimmy."

"I'm talking about a poet, Bernard. He didn't like what was being said about him, so he sued for libel. And you know what? He got sent to gaol. The person he sued, you see, had proof. You tell Rubio to look up the Wilde case."

"Now, look here . . ."

"So I'll see you in court," Alison said. "I'm on my way to New York, so there's no need to serve a writ over here. I'm travelling on the *Queen Mary* and we dock next Friday week. See you then." She hung up.

"Jees," David muttered. "I'd better round up the guys."

"I don't need any guys," Alison told him. "Don't you see, David? I am now the best protected person on the face of the earth. If anyone, anyone at all, takes a pot at me, Carlo Rubio is going to be blamed. He's going to do all the protecting I need."

"And you seriously mean to go and see him? Who's going to protect you then?"

"Why, he is, of course. But even better when I've finished with him. Dave, I want you to do some shopping for me."

He listened to what she wanted, his expression slowly changing into an incredulous grin.

"Goddam, Mrs Pat, if it comes off . . . but if he catches you out . . ."

"He's bound to," she said. "But on my terms."

She sent the older children back to school, left the two younger ones at the villa with Miss Holding and Hannah, and some of David's bodyguards; he had not as yet been able to locate either Hugo or Clem, which was a disappointment, but in addition to her own people she asked for and got police protection for the villa from Inspector Brillot. In any event, she was certain she was protecting her family far more effectively by carrying the fight to Rubio than by cowering behind police protection for the rest of her life.

She would have preferred to leave David in France as well, for fear he would get in the way, but he insisted on coming.

"Look," she said. "You're my conscience, my keeper, my watchdog, my warder . . . don't you think I can do *anything* on my own?"

"The things you want to do on your own are what frighten me, Mrs Pat. Anyway . . ." he flushed. "If anything were to happen to you . . ."

They gazed at each other, and his flush deepened.

"Oh, hell," she said. "When something is in your own back yard, too often you don't realise it's there."

"I didn't mean to offend you."

"How in the name of God could anyone be offended by something like that?" She leaned across and squeezed his hand. "Dave . . . I have to settle with Rubio, before I can even think about anything else."

"I know," he said. "But forgive me for wanting to be there when you do start thinking again."

*　　*　　*

337

Your own backyard, she thought. She had always felt that David was the one man in the world unaffected by either her femininity or her wealth: he knew too much about both. For her part, she had always thought of him more as a younger brother than as an employee. Certainly she had never thought of him as a man.

Yet he was a man, and an attractive one, in every way. Not least in his total devotion to her.

But hadn't she been bitten too often? Anyway, there would be something almost incestuous about becoming involved with David. Becoming involved! She didn't want to think any more concretely than that.

Quite apart from her promise to her children, only Rubio mattered now.

Alison had deliberately opted to travel by ship to give herself more chance to regain her full strength. At the same time she was very conscious that part of her present strength was the picture she presented of a frail, battered woman setting out to take on one of the most formidable men in America. To the absolute delight of the press photographers, she had ended the conference in France by changing into a two-piece bathing suit and allowing them to take shots of the scar on her back – that picture had adorned the front page of every newspaper in the world.

The great thing was that she was not the least afraid. Not only was she sure she held all the high cards, but she really didn't give a damn. Even more than immediately after Pat's death, she was fed-up with being kicked around. And every time she remembered how she had been taken in by Paul her blood seemed to boil.

The other passengers had read their newspapers and listened to their radios, and clearly could not make up their minds whether to get as close to her as possible or hastily to remove themselves to the other side of the ship whenever they saw her approaching. However, as she knew the captain and most of the officers, and was seated at the captain's table throughout the voyage, she did not lack for company, although the officers strictly avoided any reference to the looming confrontation.

There was no such reluctance on the part of the American press, however, when the ship docked. The reporters came on board in a huge rush, to surround her and besiege her with questions.

"What are your plans, Mrs Schleyer?"

"When are you meeting Mr Rubio, Mrs Schleyer?"

"Where are you staying, Mrs Schleyer?"

Alison smiled at them all. "My name is Grange," she said. "I want you all to remember that. I am staying at my apartment. As for meeting Mr Rubio, I expect him to contact me."

"Are you scared, Mrs Schleyer?"

Alison turned her gaze on the young woman who had asked the question.

"I meant, Mrs Grange," the woman said.

"What have I got to be scared about?" Alison asked.

Nevertheless, David insisted on going on ahead to check out the apartment for any booby-traps, but could find nothing.

"Not even a writ, waiting for you," he said, when Alison arrived.

"I didn't think there would be."

She hadn't even unpacked, however, when the street bell rang.

"A Captain McCormick, NYPD," David said.

"Invite him up."

The Captain was a very hard-looking man. "It's Mrs Grange nowadays, is it?"

"It always was, Captain," Alison told him. "Save for a four-year aberration."

"Yeah. That was tough. Now, lady, what do you want from us"

"Want?"

"In the way of protection."

"I don't want any protection. I don't need any protection."

"Lady, this ain't no schoolboy you're playing with."

"I hope not."

"Well, then . . ."

"Captain, as of this moment, if I walk down 5th Avenue and someone takes a shot at me, or even if someone tries to run me over in a car . . . where are you going to start looking first?"

"Well . . . Rubio, I guess."

"Don't you think he knows that?"

McCormick scratched his nose. "I guess he does. But . . . Carlo Rubio has been around one hell of a lot longer than you have, Mrs Grange. He's been in this business all his life. If he means to get you, he will get you, at a time and place where we can't pin anything on him. It may be tomorrow, it may be next week, it may be next year. He can wait a long time. He's like that."

"And you would like to give me police protection for the rest of my life?"

"Well, when you're in New York, I guess you're our baby."

"I'm not going to be here very long," Alison promised him. "I think I can manage. But I may need a little bit of help, Captain. May I call you?"

The Captain had barely left when the street bell rang again.

David looked embarrassed. "It's Hugo."

"Hugo? I thought you hadn't been able to get in touch with him?"

"I haven't. But now he's here. I guess the fact that

340

you're in New York is pretty well known. You want me to send him away?"

Alison hesitated. But she knew she should never have let him go. "No, show him up. But . . . maybe you should be present, Dave."

"Oh, I will be," David said.

Hugo stood in the doorway, twisting his hat in his hands.

"Hi, Mrs Pat."

"Hi, Hugo. You're looking well."

"Thanks. I got myself a little eatery with the dough you gave me."

"Great. I'll come down and see you some time."

"I'd like that. But say, Mrs Pat, this set-to you're aiming to have with Rubio . . . you're gonna need a hand. Take me back, Mrs Pat. That's all I ever wanted to be, your bodyguard."

Alison considered. But she had certainly missed the big man, even if she didn't feel he could have protected her from the assassin, given Paul's involvement . . . and she didn't think he was going to be any use to her on this occasion either: any bodyguard would entirely negate the picture she was endeavouring to create.

But afterwards . . .

"All right, Hugo," she said. "You can have your job back, if you wish. But after I've seen Rubio."

"Now, say, Mrs Pat . . ."

"That's it, Hugo."

He was the picture of desolation.

Bernard telephoned that afternoon. "Mr Rubio wants a word," he said.

"Put him on."

"Mr Rubio don't like telephones. He likes to talk, face to face."

"That suits me," Alison said.

"He'll be at the Midnight Club, tonight."

"I'll be at the Midnight Club, tomorrow morning, for lunch. Tell Mr Rubio I don't like going out at night."

"Lady, the Midnight Club is what it says it is, a niteclub. It don't open during the day."

"Who does it belong to?"

"Why, Mr Rubio, of course."

"Then he can open it for lunch tomorrow."

"Lady, you're making life kinda difficult. He's gonna be annoyed."

"I'll be there at twelve. Oh, and tell him I'll have a fillet steak for lunch, medium rare. He can choose the starters. With the main course we'll have Chateau-Lafitte 1946. I also want quiet piped music in the background. Glenn Miller. You tell him to do all of that, and that if he's not there to give me my steak, the whole world is going to know he's a big, fat, frightened chicken. Goodbye, Bernard."

She dialled the NYPD. "Captain McCormick? I thought you'd like to know that I'm lunching with Mr Rubio tomorrow. At the Midnight Club."

"You can't lunch at the Midnight Club, Mrs Grange. It's a niteclub."

"Captain, over the years I have got into the habit of doing what I like when I like. I am lunching at the Midnight Club tomorrow."

"So you want protection."

"Well, no, not exactly. But as you offered, I'll tell you what I want."

When she had finished with the Captain, she called a press conference. She thought, looking down from his cloud, or much more likely, up from his furnace, Pat would be proud of her.

Punctually at eleven forty-five the next morning, as Alison had arranged with Captain McCormick, eight police outriders arrived at the apartment building. By then the hired limousine was also waiting, as well as several carloads of reporters and cameramen.

Even Hugo was reassured, and David was all smiles. "Rubio is going to flip his lid," he said.

"That's what I had in mind," Alison agreed. "See you later."

"Take care, Mrs Pat."

She hesitated in the doorway, then turned and came back to him. She was so exhilarated that she knew she was going to do something stupid. She held his face between her hands and kissed him on the mouth. "I'm coming back," she told him.

Behind a wail of sirens the motorcade rolled towards the Midnight Club. There was quite a crowd outside the building, and amongst then were several very obvious bodyguards, but they scurried off when they saw the police.

"You want us to wait, Mrs Grange?" asked the sergeant.

"I don't think that will be necessary."

"But say, the Captain said . . ."

"But I'd like you to come back at three o'clock sharp," Alison told him.

"Three o'clock? Well, if that's what you want . . ."

Alison waited for the reporters and cameramen to disgorge from their vehicles. "Now, you guys are going to behave yourselves," she said.

"Oh, sure, Mrs Grange."

She nodded, straightened the smart beige suit she was wearing with a matching hat, wrapped her fingers around the strap of the fashionably large handbag – no one but her knew how heavy it was – went up to the door, and found it was open.

"The boss is expecting you," the beetle-browed man said.

"Thank you." She stepped past him.

343

"Not so fast," the bouncer said to the reporters. "Hey, stop that shoving. You guys ain't coming in here."

Alison, standing beside a curtain which had already been drawn for her, looked back. "Where I go, they go," she said. "I promised them an exclusive."

"All of them?" a man asked from the interior of the room.

Alison smiled at him. "I like company," she explained, and went down the steps into the well of the niteclub. Here the tables had all been pushed back against the walls, save for one, a very large one, which occupied the entire centre of the floor. This was surrounded by six waiters, while at the head of it there sat Carlo Rubio, the man who had asked the question.

He was younger than Alison had expected, in his middle-forties, she estimated, not very tall, and distinctly overweight. He was bald, save for a fringe of black hair, but was not at all bad looking, save for his mouth, which was like a steel trap. But when he smiled, as he was now doing, he was quite handsome. His clothes were impeccable; he might have been poured into his three-piece suit, which had been freshly pressed.

"But I have only ordered lunch for two, Mrs Grange," he protested.

"They just want some photographs," she told him, and went down the steps to stand next to the table. "Okay, boys." Rubio hastily got up and stood behind her. The flashlights glared, and he put his arm round her shoulders.

"Now you all come back when I suggested, and I'll tell you what we agreed," Alison said.

"We'll be there, Mrs Pat," they chorussed as she had requested, and trooped out.

"You always travel with half the New York press draped round your neck?" Rubio asked.

"Most of the time," she assured him.

"So you're a famous dame." He himself held her chair for her, opposite him. "Cocquil St Jacques," he explained.

"They're a speciality of the chef. And I thought a glass of Bollinger . . ."

"I like Bollinger." She raised her glass to him. "Where's the music?"

He signalled one of his people, and *Chattanooga Choochoo* began to play softly in the background, effectively shutting out all other sound. "When do you want to talk?" he asked.

"When I've finished my meal. And you've got rid of your goons."

"For you, anything," he smiled.

They ate, and made small talk. Then when the coffee was served and they had been poured their Hine Antique, Rubio waved the waiters away; they gathered in a respectful group at the far end of the room in front of the bar.

Then he grinned at her. "Now I guess you want the bill. It runs into ten figures by my reckoning"

Alison allowed her fingers to drift down to her handbag, releasing the clasp, which in turn did more than that. "Are we eating Dutch?"

"Lady," he said. "You have fooled around with me long enough."

Alison sipped her brandy, and placed her elbows on the table. "Rubio, I haven't started to fool around with you yet. No, shut up and listen," she told him as he would have interrupted her.

He stared at her with his mouth open.

"You have managed to make me angry," she said. "You have messed me about, made a fool of me as regards Paul Schleyer, tried to have me murdered . . ."

"You can't prove that."

"You don't think so? I have a signed confession, made just before Paul killed himself."

"It'll never stand up in court. And it happened in France."

"Sure. And you're not stupid enough to have a go at me while I'm in New York. But you're never going to have a go at me again, no matter where I am, and I'll tell you why. There are going to be no more Paul Schleyers. I may be a slow learner, but I do learn. Marriage is out, as of this minute, unless it's to someone I know very, very well. Second, all of my money is so locked up you could never get it no matter what happened. Third, I have placed a statement of my own along with Paul's confession in my safe deposit box. This states that if anything happens to me, or to any of my children, and that includes kidnapping or harassment, you and you alone are responsible, and I have proof of it."

"What kind of proof. You ain't got nothing on me."

Alison smiled at him. "Maybe I don't. But you are the one who is going to have to prove that if my statement is released to the press, who, you may have gathered, are rather keen on me. And if you did happen to be involved, you might find life a little difficult. Fourthly, I am not without resources of my own, and if anyone I don't like the look of gets too close to me my boys are going to flush him straight down the wastepipe. I hope you have got all of that."

Rubio continued to stare at her.

"However," Alison went on. "I am willing to concede that my late first husband did obtain financial backing from you, and that in his own way he was just as big a thug as you are. Thus I am prepared to settle his debt. But not at your astronomical rates of interest. Two years ago I worked out that Pat Grange's estate might owe you eight hundred thousand dollars. I'm prepared to round it out at a million."

"Big deal."

"In exchange for which I would require a receipt stating that you have no further claim on Grange Estates, and a written undertaking that you will never again trouble me in any way. This undertaking will include a confession that Paul Schleyer worked for you, and was intended to get his hands on my money for your benefit."

346

"You think I'm crazy?"

"Don't you ever tell the truth? Paul did work for you, and everyone knows it."

"I'm not signing anything that says he did."

"You can at least tell me, seeing that I'm the person he was sent to have killed."

Rubio stared at her. "Lady, you have got the gall of . . . hell, I can't think of a word." Then he grinned. "You know something, I'm glad Paul and that lunatic Artiglio messed it up between them. But if you think I'm gonna get myself involved . . ."

Alison looked at her watch, and smiled back. "But you just did, Rubio. You just made a full confession."

His smile changed into a frown. "Just what do you mean?"

"I think I have enough. You can turn off the music now."

Frowning, Rubio signalled his men, and the music died; Instantly the gentle whirr of the tape became audible. Alison smiled at him, reached into her handbag and switched it off.

"What the hell . . ."

Alison closed her bag. "You must keep up with modern science, Rubio." She stood up. "I'll see myself out."

Rubio stood up as well, waving his hand. The men against the wall stepped forward.

"You think I'm gonna let you walk out of here with that in your bag?" Rubio asked. "Hand it over, baby."

"What, do you mean to assault me?"

She was entirely surrounded.

"I am gonna bust your ass," Rubio told her.

"My husband once said that to me," Alison remembered thoughtfully. "Just before he was shot. I think your doorman wishes to speak with you."

She did not even have to turn her head; it was three o'clock.

"Say, Mr Rubio," said the doorman. "There's a whole gaggle of reporters out here, saying Mrs Grange told them to come back at three o'clock. And those cops are back as well."

Rubio looked at Alison, who waggled her eyebrows. "Well, they knew I was here."

Rubio continued to stare at her for several seconds, then suddenly he gave a bellow of laughter. "Show them in, Billy."

The press came bustling down the steps, flashguns at the ready.

"So what's the word, Mrs Pat?" someone shouted. "You and Mr Rubio settled your differences?"

"You'll have to ask Mr Rubio that."

"Sure we have," Rubio said. "And Mrs Grange . . . or is it, Mrs Pat? I like that better. Anyway, like I was saying, Alison and I are having dinner together, tonight." He pointed at them. "And no cameras."

There was champagne waiting for her at the apartment, then Charlene drew her a hot bath.

"You're not really going out *tête-a-tête* with him?" David asked.

"Sure I am."

"But . . ."

"He's going to give me that receipt, tonight," she told him.

"And after?"

"We're due in England, aren't we? You put that tape in my deposit box with George Ruthven's bank?"

"That's all done, Mrs Pat. I don't know what to say. You are just something else again."

"Am I, Dave?"

They looked at each other, and then he picked up her glass to refill it.

Alison took his instead, and drank from it.

He put her glass down, still uncertain.

"I'm riding a high, Dave," she told him. "If you don't take advantage of it . . ."

He put down the bottle as well, licked his lips, glanced at the open door.

Alison picked up the bottle and her glass, walked past him and through the door, along the corridor to her bedroom. She did not look back. Placing the bottle and glass on her bedside table, she stepped out of her shoes, and for the first time realised that she was dripping with perspiration.

She took off her jacket and blouse, then her bra, held her skirt up to her waist, and stood in front of the air-conditioning unit to allow the cool air to shroud her body.

Behind her, the door closed, very softly.

She unfastened her skirt, let it slide past her hips to the floor, as she turned. He stood in front of the closed door, looking more nervous than ever.

He had never turned her on. But was that because she had never allowed herself to be turned on?

"Do I frighten you?" she asked.

"I think you do."

"You're bigger than me," she pointed out. "Just."

"Size doesn't come into it, Mrs Pat."

"I think you should try Alison."

He didn't reply, and she let her knickers follow her skirt, then unclipped her suspender belt and sat down to roll off her stockings.

She had never seduced a man before, and she had no idea what came next.

"You have either got to do something, now," she told him, "or we had better call it a day. Either way, I need to lie down."

She heard him move, but didn't look up until he was standing in front of her.

"I think I fell in love with you the first time I ever saw you," he said.

Then she did raise her head. "You're a great actor."

"Well . . . the boss's wife? And then the boss herself. I . . . I've never been much with girls."

349

Alison lay down, her head on the pillow. "Be my guest."

He sat beside her. "You sure, Mrs . . . Alison? Certain sure?"

She sat up. "Listen. I'm a woman. I think a lot of the time I'm a pretty confused woman. I guess life just took me over before I was ready for it, and like a salmon or whatever, I went with the stream. I've made some pretty horrendous mistakes." She smiled at him. "Most of which you told me were mistakes before I made them, but I went ahead anyhow. I'm surprised you stuck with me, really and truly."

"I had nowhere else to go," he confessed.

She frowned at him. "You know, that's always puzzled me. Don't you really have a family?"

"My parents both died."

"When you were a child?"

"No, I was lucky there, I guess. I was at college."

"You call that lucky?"

"I think I was more able to cope."

"And then you went for the top," she said. "I'm glad you did that."

"The top," he muttered, and took her in his arms.

He was hesitant, and very very gentle. But that was what she wanted, after Pat and after Paul.

He was also surprisingly hard-muscled, as well as being not very much larger than herself. The only men she had ever had sex with before had been over six feet tall.

"I'm sorry I'm so scrawny," she said. "I'll fill out."

He traced round the aureole of her right nipple with a light forefinger. "I think you are just beautiful, anyway."

"You're not too bad yourself," she said, thinking of the number of times she had watched him swimming, both at The Keep and in France, and never really taken him in.

350

They played with each other for a long time, and she suspected he was afraid actually to do it. Because suddenly she was afraid too. Two mental virgins, lying naked against each other, wanting to touch, to have and to hold . . . and afraid of what came after.

Because what could come after? But was it so impossible, for Alison Grange to marry her own accountant? It would give the world something new to scream about. But the world would always find something to scream about, where Alison Grange was concerned.

The problem was, she didn't want to marry anyone, right this minute, and yet some deep subconscious seam of morality insisted that she only have sex with marriage in mind.

She put her hand down to hold him, but it was too late; he had gone soft. Not through ejaculation, though. He'd be back.

"I guess I'm a bit of a disaster," he said.

"I'm a patient woman," she reminded him, and held him close to kiss him some more, and feel him come back. When he was ready, so was she, and it was much better than if he had pushed his way in immediately.

"You still mean to have dinner with Rubio?" David asked.

Their heads lay together on her pillow. "You aiming to be possessive?"

"Heaven forbid. But you can't blame me for worrying."

"I told you, there's nothing to worry about. I'll run us a bath." She sat up and swung her legs off the bed.

"Us?"

"Why not?" She grinned at him. "I'll bet you've never bathed with a woman before."

"I haven't."

"David, I'm going to teach you how to *live*."

"Are you, Mrs Pat?"

She looked down at him. "*Don't* you think you should start calling me Alison? At least in private. Would you like that?"

"More than anything else in the world, in private."

"And you're going to teach me a thing or two as well. Right?"

"Is there anything?"

"All those companies, all those properties, I should've inspected six years ago and didn't."

"You know, I've never seen most of them, myself."

"We'll explore," she promised. "And . . . I'll take you up the Amazon, as well."

"And we'll find that missing money. I've been doing some investigating of that . . ."

"Later," she told him.

She had never felt so happy. Because at last she was entirely her own mistress. She had felt that, briefly, when Pat had died. But then she had been bedevilled by Jonny. Now Jonny was just a painful memory, but she had still felt lonely, in need of a man, a man who would lead. She had thought she had found him in Paul, and come close to catastrophe.

Now she no longer felt that need. She knew she could compete with the best, and win. And she knew too that she could be happy with David. As to their exact relationship, she did not know. The important thing was that she felt no urgency to solve the problem, because it wasn't a problem. They would live together, as they had lived together, virtually, for ten years. They had experienced together and they had calculated together and they had fought together, and most important of all, they had been friends together.

Now they had discovered that they could make good sex together. There really was nothing else needed resolving.

*   *   *

352

"Little lady," Carlo Rubio said over dinner. "You are really something. How the hell did a louse like Pat Grange get hold of you in the first place?"

"If you call Pat a louse again I will empty this glass over you," Alison told him.

"So pardon me. I didn't know you still had anything going for him."

"He was my husband, and he is the father of my children. Have you got the receipt?"

"Yeah." He took the envelope from his pocket. "Have you got the cheque?"

She took it from her handbag, and they exchanged. Alison read the receipt very quickly; it was exactly as she wished.

"Hey, wait a minute," Rubio said. "This is for only two hundred thousand dollars."

"That's right."

"You agreed on a million. You just give me that receipt back."

"Rubio, I paid you eight hundred thousand dollars five years ago, and you negotiated the cheque. I have it, with an endorsement showing it was paid into one of your accounts."

"For Jesus' sake . . . why don't you run for president or something?"

"I can't. I wasn't born in the States."

He grinned. "You wouldn't care to work for me?"

"Thank you, no."

"Then how about marrying me?"

She raised her eyebrows. "Don't you have a wife?"

"Oh, sure. But she's been around awhile. I could do something about it."

"I'm sure. Forget it. I'm not in a marrying mood, right this minute."

"Okay. Be my mistress."

"Don't you have some of those as well?"

"They'll all go. I give you my word."

"Not my scene, Rubio."

"Jesus, you're a hard women. Okay, just tonight. Your place or mine?"

"I think you should go to your place, and I'll go to mine."

"I don't do nothing for you, right?"

"That's life."

"But you want to be my friend?"

"Sure I do."

"Listen, I want you to know how sorry I am about that shooting business. If I'd gotten to know you before . . . hell I needed my head examined."

"It's forgotten. Just try to keep out of my hair in the future."

"Keep out of your hair? Alison, I'm gonna look after you, whether you want me to or not. As of this moment, no one, but no one, gets up your nose without answering to Carlo Rubio." He grinned. "And that goes for your ass, too, until I've been there first."

"Rubio," she said. "You can worry about my nose, if you choose. But no one is running my life for me, in or out of bed. Got it?"

He gave another of his disarming grins. "You're the boss, little lady."

It occurred to Alison that he could be absolutely right, and she enjoyed the sensation. She was thirty-two years old, and she had no more worlds to conquer.

She could even justify her existence, and instead of merely enjoying the utter luxury with which she was surrounded, she started to work as hard as she had ever done in her life. The lazy pattern of four three-monthly residences was ended. No doubt it had been necessary while she had been getting to grips with her situation. Now it was irrelevant.

She travelled constantly. She flew to Rio at least once a year, then up to Manaos, and then up to El Dorado. Production was well down now, but there was still an awful lot of gold coming out of the ground, and besides, Alison wasn't sure she ever wanted to close the mine down, even when it began to run at a loss: she loved going there and seeing her very contented workforce, attending church with them, inspecting the school and being presented with bouquets by the scrubbed and polished children.

She still loved the jungle, and would take a safari into the bush north of the mine, often with just Hugo for company.

In Rio she was always a guest of the Alvarados, with whom she was becoming good friends.

She bought herself an executive jet for getting around Europe and America, so that she could be in England for every half-term holiday or birthday, and she spent the school holidays with the children, usually in the south of France, and more often than not on the boat. All of them were growing up to be keen on yachting, and the whole family would sail down to Cabrera to anchor in the great, empty lagoon and feel at peace with the world, or even to the Greek islands.

During term, she travelled to the various property holdings, sometimes selling, sometimes buying, always inspecting, giving instructions for renovation and upkeep. She did a lot of renting and enjoyed meeting her tenants.

David usually accompanied her on these trips, both to explain financial situations and because she wanted him to be there. They slept together quite regularly, and she felt as much married to him as she ever had to anyone, but they never discussed the actual business of getting married. He could tell she liked things the way they were, and she didn't see how he had too much to complain about – he seemed happy enough. She was paying him a hundred thousand dollars a year to be her general manager, and he was worth every penny of it.

When David wasn't with her, Hugo was always at her shoulder, a large, obedient shadow. Hugo was almost as intimate with her as David – as he had been long before she had known David existed – but he never once overstepped the bounds of propriety of servant/mistress relationship. With him she always felt secure.

There were changes in the staff. Lucia fell madly in love with a Frenchman and got married, and was replaced by a French girl called Aimée. As even Baby Harry became old enough to go to school the nurses gradually became redundant, and Hannah quit. She was not the marrying kind and went off to work in a prep. school herself. Charlene remained, more as a kind of live-in companion than anything else.

Life was very busy, very exciting . . . and yet, totally empty. As Alison had thought after her dinner date with Rubio, she had no more worlds to conquer, no more peaks to climb . . . and absolutely nothing to be afraid of. There were no emotional upsets, because what Mrs Pat wanted, Mrs Pat got. Rubio regularly sent her flowers and presents, and invitations to his bed, and she laughed at him . . . but she often dined with him when she was in New York. She sailed energetically regardless of the weather and loved having her children around her, together with a new set of dogs. But there was no challenge.

Even the missing four hundred million dollars no longer bugged her. In any event, it seemed to have gone forever, as not even David's best efforts could find it.

He had, as he had mentioned, done his best to track it down, and had made some progress. Pat, having received his large cheques from the Brazilian Government, passed them through US dollar accounts in George Ruthven's bank. From here the money was redistributed as Pat wished, and all that preliminary part of the business was done by Pat personally, without ever setting foot in the States – he wrote his instructions to George.

George was totally co-operative, but not very helpful. There were always large block amounts, which were simply transferred to the Bahamas or South Africa or Mexico, or any other tax-friendly countries where Pat was sure he would not be troubled. Then there were relatively smaller amounts, relative only in the sense that they might be fifty thousand dollars a time rather than a quarter of a million or more. There were several of these every year, cheques drawn by Pat personally, and made payable to Mr Smith or Mr Jones or Mr Brown. The cheques arrived back all duly endorsed by the various payees, and cleared from some very odd places indeed. David had worked out that these miscellaneous cheques when totalled represented the bulk of the missing four hundred million, and he had done his best to follow them up, but with no success. Foreign bank managers were not all as co-operative as George. A good deal of the money was traced as far as Switzerland, but there it disappeared into numbered accounts. The fact that Pat had left his entire fortune to his wife made no difference here – by the time the money had arrived in Zurich there was absolutely nothing to connect it with Pat Grange.

"It's the damndest thing I ever came across," David confessed. "Obviously he was building up some other financial empire someplace, but where? Four hundred million dollars? You'd think we'd have had a smell of it by now."

"Probably not, if he kept it split up into small parcels," Alison said.

"But the thought of it, just accumulating interest . . . heck, Alison, it would have doubled by now."

"Um," she commented. She really wasn't interested in the money, as money; she had more than enough. It was the thought that Pat might have set up a kind of second life, complete with wife and children, as Jones or Smith or Brown, disturbed her.

But it was not something she intended to let disrupt her life. She had not supposed anything could do that, until the day David came into her office in the French villa, looking as if the end of the world was nigh.

Perhaps it was.

"Mrs Pat," he said. "Jonathan Carter has been released from gaol."

CHAPTER 13

Children

Alison put down her pen. "How do you know?"

"Simply that our last parcel was returned, unopened. I was not immediately told about this, of course; the food store informed the bank to cancel the standing order, because Señor Carter is no longer in prison. I'm afraid the bank did not think it important enough to inform me, and I didn't pick it up until going through our last batch of statements, when I discovered the standing order had been cancelled. I then immediately contacted Señor Puig, who told me that Carter had been released as part of a general amnesty."

His efficiency, as always, was almost frightening. She could only wish everyone else she dealt with was as good.

"When was he released?"

"Ah . . . March 17th."

"But that's three months ago."

"Yes. Señor Puig seemed surprised that we had not heard from him. Having been released, Carter was promptly deported."

"Where to?"

"The nearest British territory: Jamaica."

"Three months ago," Alison muttered. "And not a word." She raised her head. "We'll have to find him, Dave."

David swallowed. "May I ask why?"

"Well . . ."

"Are you still in love with him?"

Alison felt her cheeks burn. "Well, no. But . . ."

"Do you feel you owe him something?"

"For God's sake, an innocent man was locked up in that living hell for . . . ten years!"

"With respect, Alison, but you don't *know* he's innocent. You never did. I know the evidence was all circumstantial, but the fact is, no one else quite fits the bill. He had a motive, he had the means of access, he had the weapon . . ."

"That's not true," Alison snapped. "It was never proven that the murder weapon belonged to Jonny. In my opinion the whole police case fell apart on that one issue. They were simply determined to obtain a conviction"

"The gun must have belonged to someone."

"Oh . . . I've never been able to understand why the ownership couldn't be traced, or why your man Preston couldn't trace it."

"These things aren't always easy to do . . ." He was looking his usual defensive self.

"I'm not blaming you, Dave. You know that."

"But you still want to find Carter. Alison, this guy has been locked up as a murderer, with a lot of other murderers and strong-arm men and thugs of every description, for ten years. He may have been innocent when he went in, but I am damned sure he isn't innocent now. He's been out for three months, and he hasn't made any attempt to contact you, although he must know where you are – you don't make any secret of it. I have got to say that I regard that as a bonus. To go looking for him . . ."

Alison got up and went to the window to look down at the swimming pool. "And you don't want to take any risk of him muscling in on us," she said softly.

"Would I be human if I didn't worry about that?"

"No." She turned. "No, I guess you wouldn't. Okay, Dave, we close the chapter on Jonny Carter."

360

It was something she knew she would have to live with for the rest of her life.

But of course that was much easier to say than to do. Jonny had been released. After ten years, as David had reminded her. He would be nearly forty. A man whom life had treated with the utmost harshness. And who still loved? Or had learned to hate. Undoubtedly David was right there again, and it would be the latter.

In any event, he would be a total stranger.
He simply had to be forgotten.

Early July brought the usual clutch of speechdays, and for Benjamin it would be the last; he was eighteen and bound for Cambridge, where he would read Law and Business Studies. He did not seem to have any clear idea what he was going to do after that, but Alison was determined he was going to do *something*, although as he was going to come in to more than half a billion dollars in three years time it was difficult to be dogmatic about it. But although he had passed both his Junior- and Senior-levels without difficulty, and seemed certain to get good results in his Higher, he had spent a fairly lifeless school career, playing only those games which were compulsory, and never becoming a prefect – quite unlike Shirley, who was already Captain of Lacrosse and due to become Head Girl during the coming year.

Alison worried about the situation, because she felt it could be disastrous, especially as she and Benjamin had seemed to drift apart over the past couple of years. He had become increasingly withdrawn and introverted. Alison presumed that he still brooded on the death of Paul, which he had seemed to feel more than any of the others, just as he was certainly aware of her relationship with David, and perhaps resented it. Equally, as he grew older, he was no doubt undergoing a slow mental coming to grips with his situation. There was the enormous wealth he would control when she died, although that was surely a long way into the future. She certainly wanted him to appreciate what lay ahead of him, but she didn't want him to get too concerned about it, or guilty at being better off than almost everyone else in the world. Neither did she want him mentally criticising her, or looking over his shoulder at what might have been. Thus she planned to spend the whole summer sailing with him, and using the opportunity to have a series of heart-to-heart talks.

As had become her new practice, she moved from France to her English house in mid-June, to the usual press interest, although nowadays this was merely a recording in the various newspaper "diaries" that Mrs Grange was back home.

From Sussex she could go up to London for the big end of term cricket match. Ben was no cricketer, but he was able to sit with her, and she had obtained permission for Shirley to be with them as well. She would stay at the flat and they would join her there for dinner and the night before returning to their respective schools the following day.

First there was Harry's speechday, however, and she drove down to Kent to watch him receive a prize for literature. It was a sunny and thoroughly enjoyable day, and Harry was his usual bubbling, energetic self. He had no doubts about what he wanted to do – become an astronaut. When Alison pointed out that that would require taking out US citizenship – unlike Ben and Shirley Harry had of course been born in Mexico – and then joining the United States Air Force, with all the amount of study and work that would have to go into that kind of career, he merely grinned, "But that's what's life's all about, Ma. And space is the future."

Alison believed it was still the distant future, even if Gagarin and Glenn had proved that it could be done. But she wasn't going to discourage him too much; she only wished some of his mental energy would rub off on Ben.

She arrived home with Hugo and Charlene, who had accompanied her as they always did, tired but happy, to find David waiting for her with another of his long faces.

"There have been some phone calls for you, Mrs Pat."

Alison took off her hat and stripped off her gloves, giving them to Charlene, and heading for the library-cum-study. "Important?"

"Well, I don't know for sure. One was from Ben's housemaster. And the other was from Ben himself."

Alison turned her head, sharply. "What's happened?"

"Well . . . Ben's disappeared."

"Disappeared?" she shouted.

The possible kidnapping of one of the children was a recurring nightmare.

"I think of his own accord, Mrs Pat."

"How can an eighteen-year-old boy disappear of his own accord?"

"It does happen. There's a woman involved."

"A what?" Her voice rose another octave.

"I think you had better sit down. Hugo . . ."

Hugo hurried forward with a brandy and ginger.

"Mr. Brightwell telephoned just after lunch," David explained. "Apparently Ben had a pass for last night to attend a play. He wasn't alone; nearly the entire sixth form went, and they were accompanied by a master. Well, you know how it is in these big public schools. A sixth-former is regarded as an adult and treated like one. They're not shepherded. The play over, they drove back by bus to the school, and went to bed. It was only this morning that Ben was discovered to be missing. Even then there was no great flap for a while. As I say, he is regarded as a responsible adult. But when it was clear that he had absconded or been kidnapped, the housemaster took action. His first reaction was apparently that Ben had somehow joined you for an occasion of which the school had not been informed. They are all somewhat overaware that Ben is on the verge of his inheritance, you see."

"Yes," Alison said grimly. "So what did you do?"

"I immediately telephoned Tunleigh. But you had just left for the drive back here. I then thought of the police, although I wasn't sure how you would react to that . . ."

"I want him found," Alison said.

David nodded. "I was going to raise the alarm, but before I could do so the phone rang again, and it was Ben?"

"Ransom?"

"No, no, nothing like that. He said you weren't to worry, but he had decided to finish school, forget university, and get married."

Alison stared at him.

"That's what he said," David repeated.

"Married? How can an eighteen-year-old boy get married? Who's he going to marry?"

"Well, he didn't say, but . . ."

"It's some kind of trick."

"He didn't sound the least scared, or under any kind of restraint. He just sounded, well . . . excited."

"I want him found, Dave. I don't care what you have to do, I want him found."

"Do you want to go down to Welton?"

"No. Not unless you think it'll help."

"Well, if he has run off with a woman or a girl or something, maybe some of his school pals would have an idea who she is."

"Yes. You do it." She had never felt so angry, but at the same time so humiliated, in her life.

"And the police?"

"Let's see if we can leave them out of it for the time being. If you're absolutely sure there is no hanky-panky going on. And tell Brightwell that we don't want any publicity either.'"

*　　*　　*

Alison had a hot bath and went to bed with a couple of aspirins. She was trying to keep absolutely calm, to rationalise. There was no *need* to call in the police and make a worldwide scandal out of it. There was no need to tell the other children. Still waters run deep. Ben, who of all her children she would have supposed was the most introverted, the least likely to do something like this . . . it was the knowledge of the money, of course. Oh, God damn the money.

She slept eventually, heavily, and by the time she awoke David had already left for Welton. She had no doubt at all David would sort everything out. He always did. But her hands were shaking as she opened the newspaper. Not a word. Brightwell had succeeded so far, at least. She wondered how much longer he could.

She spent the morning pottering about the garden. Charlene was as always a tower of strength, chattered about irrelevancies and kept smiling. The following day they were due at Stefanie's school for her speechday. A whole twenty-four hours, waiting for something to happen . . .

David telephoned just before lunch.

"Yes?" Alison was breathless.

"I'm afraid there seems no doubt at all that Benjamin has eloped," he said.

"Eloped? Eloped!!! Who with?"

"Well . . . I'm sorry, Alison, but all the evidence points to a Mrs Joanne Wallburn."

"What did you say?" Alison had taken the phone standing up at her desk. Now she slowly sat down.

"Mrs Joanne Wallburn."

"Mrs? Did you say Mrs?"

"Yes."

"How in the name of God . . ."

"It seems that Ben has been going to see this woman whenever he has obtained a pass into the village, and on other occasions as well. As I said, sixth formers at Welton are not very closely supervised, but the boys I have spoken

365

to seem to think the relationship has been going on for over a year. That is, when he was in the Fifth."

"Relationship?"

"There doesn't seem any doubt that they were sleeping together, Mrs Pat."

"My son, and some . . . who is this woman, anyway?"

"A barmaid."

"A *what*?"

"That's why he's been able to get away with it for so long. Seems that last year he joined the Birdwatching Society, and this society gets afternoons off to ramble through the woods close to Welton. Whenever they went on one of these rambles, Ben simply sneaked away from the party, which spread itself over a fairly wide area. His friends covered for him, of course, and he was never gone more than an hour. But you see, it was when the pubs were closed, and Mrs Wallburn was at home."

"And you say this has been going on for a year?"

"At least."

Which would explain so much about his recent odd behaviour, she thought bitterly. "What did this woman's husband think about it?"

"She's divorced."

"How old is she?"

"There's some difference of opinion about that. Probably around twenty-five."

"Twenty-five! Shouldn't I be able to sue the school, or something? Lack of adequate supervision? Allowing a seventeen-year-old boy to become entangled with a woman nearly ten years older than himself . . . but listen, they can't get married, can they?"

"Not legally."

"Then surely they can be traced?"

"Well, it's not that simple. This Mrs Wallburn had a car, and it seems they simply got into it and drove away."

"With no money, no clothes?"

"Well, *she* probably had clothes. As for money, she

probably had some of that too, and regards whatever she spends as a good investment."

"Well, she is going to have another think coming," Alison said. "I assume you have the car number?"

"Yes, and a description."

"So?"

"Well . . . how do you want it handled? What I mean is, if I inform the police, we will probably catch up with them in twenty-four hours. If I don't, it could be some time. And I should warn you that Ben had his passport with him."

"Oh, shit!" Alison growled. "Well, I suppose you will have to inform the police."

"And what will be the grounds?"

"For God's sake, how do I know? Kidnapping?"

"I don't think that will stand up in view of Ben's call."

"Then what do we do?"

"You'll have to have Ben made a ward of court."

"A . . . oh, my God! The publicity!"

"I'm afraid we're stuck with that. But . . . there's one other way of handling it."

"Tell me."

"By ignoring it. Officially, at any rate. I'll get someone on to tracing them, quietly. As I said, it'll take time. But for the rest, you just play it dead cool. Tell Brightwell that Ben has your blessing. He's taken his Higher examination, and he's past the legal age for compulsory schooling anyway. Obviously his masters are going to complain, but if you tell them you have taken him out of school there's nothing legal they can do about it."

"And all the while he'll be sleeping with this . . . this prostitute."

"Well . . . if he's been doing that already for over a year . . . a few more weeks isn't going to make that much difference, surely."

"How do we know it's only going to be a few more weeks?"

"I don't think this Mrs Wallburn can have *that* much

367

money, Alison. There's going to have to be an appeal some time."

"Oh . . . all right, Dave. Get things moving and come on home."

Alison thought that if Ben were to walk in the door at that moment she'd shoot him. Yet who was she to blame for the debacle but herself? She had known, ever since Pat's death over ten years ago, that Ben, all of the children, were going to inherit a fortune on their twenty-first birthdays. She had, in fact, done her best, and successfully, to make that fortune grow. She had supposed that, by being a good and caring mother, she would automatically make them into good and caring children.

She hadn't reckoned on them all watching what was happening to her, how she was ordering, or misordering, her life. Of course they all knew everything about Jonny Carter, as they all knew about Schleyer, and her meeting with Carlo Rubio . . . and undoubtedly they all also knew about her relationship with David.

And there were four more growing up. Thank God for Shirley.

But Shirley had to be told, of course. In all the circumstances Alison had no desire to watch a lot of schoolboys playing cricket, and so she telephoned Broadhurst and told Shirley to go straight up to London. They met for lunch at the Savoy, and Alison explained the situation.

Shirley stared at her in disbelief. "Ben did that?"

"Yes," Alison said grimly.

She watched Shirley's face break up as she started to laugh.

"Big joke," she commented.

"Oh, really, Ma . . . well, I mean, who'd have thought Ben had it in him?"

Alison glared at her. At seventeen Shirley was the

absolute living image of herself at that age – even twenty years on they were almost twins in their colouring, their features, their curling yellow hair, the only difference being that Shirley still wore hers long.

Twenty years ago, Alison remembered, she had already met Pat Grange.

"So when are *you* planning to elope?" she asked.

Shirley made a move. "Chance would be a fine thing. They don't allow us out on our own at Broadhurst, I can tell you that. Tell me, what are you going to do when Ben comes home, with his Mrs Wallburn in tow?"

Alison opened her mouth and then closed it again.

"This is 1958, Ma," Shirley explained. "You can't be too old-fashioned."

"You're not going to pretend there's the slightest chance Ben is in love with her?"

"I think there's every chance."

"And she with him?"

"Ah, now, that's a different matter."

"So you would agree that I'd be within my rights to stand her at the top of the steps and give her a good hard kick in the pants."

"Oh, undoubtedly. As to whether that would do your relationship with Ben any good, I wouldn't care to say."

"Do not ever use that word 'relationship' to me again," Alison told her. "I do not have a 'relationship' with my son."

She still had no idea how to handle the situation, and she did not suppose she was going to get much different advice from her younger children. The fact was that she was out of touch with modern youth, she supposed. She saw as much as possible of her children, and she thoroughly enjoyed their parties . . . . but to this moment they had always been – children. That they had been changing had not occurred to her, and of course on their holidays with her she had always been totally in command.

Now she was quite out of her depth.

David had as usual worked wonders.

"Mrs Wallburn's car has been found parked in Dover," he said that evening. "So it seems obvious that they took the ferry to Calais. I suspected that was what they had in mind the moment I heard that Ben had taken his passport. But I don't see how they can stay there very long, as the travel allowance is only twenty-five pounds."

"Um," she said.

"He'll come back," David said.

"I know he will, David. That's not the point. I seem to have made the most colossal foul-up of being a mother."

"I wouldn't say you're that different to any other mother. Maybe . . ." he hesitated.

"Well?"

"Maybe it's not having a father."

She looked at him.

"And maybe you're suffering from not having a husband," he went on.

"Are you asking me to marry you?"

"Yes. Yes, I am."

Alison got up and poured herself a drink. "There are times I wish I smoked."

"There are cigarettes downstairs. Would you like me to get you one?"

"No, I wasn't serious." She sat in a chair, her hands clasped in her lap, facing him.

"You're not keen on the idea," he muttered.

Alison sighed.

"I don't satisfy you, is that it?"

"Oh, don't be stupid."

"Well, then?"

"Do you really suppose that if we're good in bed together we are guaranteed a happy marriage?"

"Well, no . . . but in every other way . . . for God's sake, we've lived together for sixteen years."

"And you've never put a foot wrong," Alison conceded.

"As a servant."

He'd said it.

"And you don't think I could make the transition," he went on as she didn't comment.

"I'm not sure either of us could do that," Alison said. "Anyway, I promised the children I wouldn't marry again."

"Oh, really, Alison . . . do you expect me to believe that?"

"It happens to be the truth." She could not stop a chill from entering her voice.

"You may have made the promise, but do you seriously think they expect you to keep it? Why not *tell* the truth: you enjoy being the boss lady too much."

It was the first time she had ever heard him sound bitter.

"Look," she said. "I'm stuck with it, Dave, and you know that as well as anyone. In fact you're the person who's always hammered that home to me. You wouldn't dream of suggesting that if we got married I should make everything over to you, would you?"

To her surprise, and dismay, he hesitated before replying. "Would it really make that much difference?" he asked. "I've handled all of your money for the past ten years anyway."

"Meaning you could have helped yourself to whatever you fancied whenever you fancied."

"Well, I could."

"But you didn't, I hope."

"You can have the books audited, if you like."

"For God's sake! Are we having a quarrel, simply because I don't want to get married?"

"You don't want to marry *me*."

"I don't want to marry anyone, Dave."

"And when Carter walks in the door?"

"Carter? I thought we'd written him off."

"Oh, he'll be here," David said. "When he's ready."

"Well, I intend to cross that bridge when I come to it."

371

"Then you haven't *quite* written him off, have you?"

Alison found herself getting angry. He seemed to be in a most peculiar mood, a most un-David like mood. And at what a time, when she needed all the support she could get.

"Oh, bugger off," she growled, and went to bed.

Next morning what she had feared happened. She opened the newspaper and soon found the item: SCHOOLBOY HEIR TO GRANGE MILLIONS DISAPPEARS. BENJAMIN GRANGE, ELDEST SON AND HEIR OF THE LATE PATRICK GRANGE, THE GOLD MILLIONAIRE, HAS DISAPPEARED FROM HIS PUBLIC SCHOOL, WELTON. STAFF AT THE EXCLUSIVE SCHOOL – FEES TWO THOUSAND POUNDS A YEAR – WERE RELUCTANT TO BE INTERVIEWED ON THE MATTER, BUT IT IS NOT BEING TREATED AS A KIDNAPPING. "THE YOUNG MAN LEFT RATHER SUDDENLY" HIS HOUSEMASTER TOLD OUR REPORTER. "BUT WE UNDERSTAND IT IS WITH THE CONSENT OF HIS MOTHER". SOME OF BENJAMIN'S FELLOW PUPILS, HOWEVER, HAVE TOLD US THAT THERE IS A WOMAN INVOLVED, AND THAT MRS GRANGE ONLY BECAME AWARE OF THE SITUATION AFTER HER SON HAD ALREADY LEFT WELTON.

There was then the inevitable potted biography of Pat, to which was tacked on one of her, with full coverage of the attempt on her life, and of her "confrontation" with the notorious New York gangboss, Carlo Rubio.

In disgust she hurled the newspapers at the foot of the bed and glared at Charlene.

"There's people waiting to see you," Charlene said. "And the phone's been ringing."

"Tell David to handle them. He knows as much about it all as I do."

"David isn't here."

"Oh, my God! He hasn't quit?"

"Well, I don't think so, Mrs Pat. His clothes are in his room. But he went off early this morning. Said he had things to do."

He was in a huff, of course. But . . . things to do? He could well be looking for another job. Not that there was the slightest chance of him finding one which would pay as well as this one, she reminded herself.

"Oh shit!" she commented.

"What am I to do about these reporters? Hugo wants to throw them out, but I don't reckon that'd be a good thing."

"No," Alison said. "It wouldn't. All right, I'll speak with them. But they'll have to wait until I've had a bath."

"I think they'll do that," Charlene said.

The reporters did wait, to hurl questions at her while their photographers were snapping away. Alison met them all with a smile and a considered response.

"Boys will be boys," she told them. "Ben is eighteen years old. He's old enough to be conscripted into the army. That means he's old enough to fall in love."

"Have you met the young lady, Mrs Grange?"

"I have not yet had the pleasure. But I am looking forward to doing so." She was telling the absolute truth.

"When will the wedding take place?"

Alison gazed at the questioner. "There has been no talk of marriage as yet. I think eighteen is rather young for marriage."

"Then what you are saying . . ."

"I am saying that at this moment there is no talk of marriage."

"What do the parents of the girl think of that, Mrs Grange?"

"I haven't asked them."

"Can you tell us where your son and the young lady are now?"

"I am not going to tell you that," Alison said, leaving them to suppose she preferred not to have her son hounded than that she didn't know. "Now, I am sure you people have a lot of better things to do." She stood up. "I know I have."

She telephoned each of the other children to put them in the picture. With the exception of Pat junior, who was probably the most serious-minded of them all, they seemed to be both amused and approving.

Meanwhile the telephone was ringing whenever she wasn't on it, and David had still not come back to help her out. Mostly the calls were from other newspapers, and Charlene did most of the coping, while Hugo stalked around with a face as black as thunder.

David returned that afternoon, utterly contrite.

"Where on earth have you *been*?" Alison shouted.

"Mooching around, thinking."

"About what?"

"Us, I guess."

"And what conclusion did you come to?"

"That you're the boss, I guess. You always have been, and you always will be."

She had prepared herself to be very angry with him, but then realised she couldn't be: he looked so woebegone.

"Oh, Dave." She squeezed his hand. "Anyone who'd want to marry me needs his head examined."

"Yeah," he said, unconvincingly.

"Anyway, welcome home," she told him.

"Thanks," he said, again unconvincingly.

Alison told cook to prepare a special dinner, and Hugo to open a couple of bottles of good wine. She just felt like sitting down and getting drunk, and with her most

374

faithful employee. She went upstairs to shower, and was just drying herself when Charlene knocked and came in.

"There's the phone."

"Tell whoever it is I've answered all the questions I'm going to, today."

"This isn't a reporter."

Alison turned, sharply.

"It's a guy called Jonny Carter," Charlene said.

Alison sat on the bed.

"You want me to put him off?" Charlene asked.

"Maybe . . ."

Charlene went to the bedside phone. "I switched it up here," she said.

"No," Alison said. "Wait. I'll take it."

"Okay." Charlene left the room, carefully closing the door behind her.

Alison moved round the bed to sit beside the phone, found herself taking deep breaths. Then she lifted the receiver. "Hello? Jonny?"

"Alison? My God, it's good to hear your voice."

It certainly sounded like Jonny. The old Jonny. She hadn't ever wanted to forget the old Jonny – only the man who had snarled at her in the prison.

"Alison?"

"I'm here. It's good to hear your voice, too."

"I've been reading about you."

"Yes. Well, when you have a lot of children these things are bound to happen, I guess. I . . . I had thought I'd hear from you before now."

"There were things to be done. Alison, I've love to see you."

Alison licked her lips. "Where are you calling from?"

"I'm in London."

"Ah. Well . . ." he couldn't come down; David would absolutely go berserk, after her promise. But she did want to see him again, too. "We could lunch together."

"Tomorrow?"

"Yes. Somewhere very private."

"Where?"

She couldn't risk the flat, because she simply didn't want David to find out about it. She'd had sufficient traumas over the past couple of days. But in any ordinary restaurant she stood the risk of being recognised by someone . . . "The Savoy."

He did a little gulp. "Yes. All right."

Alison smiled into the receiver. "It'll be on me, silly. Meet me there at half past twelve."

"The Grill?"

"No. The hotel lobby. Half-past twelve. I won't actually be there, but if you go to the desk and ask for me, they'll show you where to go."

"I'll be there. Alison . . ."

"Yes?" She was breathless.

"I've waited a long time for tomorrow."

"So have I, Jonny. Half-past twelve."

She hung up, waited a moment, then called the Savoy and told them what she wanted. Then she got dressed. Her hands were shaking, and she scratched her ear with one of her earrings, and had to dab at the little spurt of blood with a paper handkerchief. But nothing was going to spoil her mood of excitement. It was nearly over ten years since she had last seen him. And before then . . . she could just about count the occasions on the fingers of her hand. Yet she felt she had known him all of her life.

And what of her understanding that he would not, could not, be the man with whom she had spent those tumultuous two days in New York?

That would have to take care of itself, tomorrow. He had sounded the same. For the time being that would have to be enough.

"Who was the call?" David asked. "A laggard reporter?"

"Ah . . . yes," she said.

"What did you tell him?"

"Same as I told everyone else."

"Makes sense. I'm hoping to hear from one of our people in France tomorrow."

"So soon?"

"Oh, yes. We know they went Dover-Calais. Their trail should be pretty easy to pick up. You'll be here all day tomorrow?"

She glanced at him. "As a matter of fact, no."

He raised his eyebrows.

"I'm going up to London."

"Business?"

Of course it couldn't be business: he knew all of her business.

"There's a little shopping I want to do."

"Oh, right. You'll be lunching at the flat, so I'll call you there if anything comes through."

"Ah . . . yes," she said. "You can call me there. If anything comes through." She didn't expect it would.

The dinner was quite spoiled. Could he possibly suspect, or know?

"Dave," she said. "I'm feeling a little tired, and, well, upset, I suppose. So if you don't mind . . ."

"And you haven't quite forgiven me yet, for yesterday," he suggested.

"Oh, don't be silly," she said. And that was the truth. It wasn't a case of not forgiving David, it was a case of him not forgiving her if he knew what was going on. And then she thought, but what the hell? I'm the Boss Lady. It's what I say matters.

But she still didn't feel she could stand another scene. She sent for Charlene.

"You didn't tell anyone about that phone call from Mr Carter, did you, Charlene?"

"No, ma'am. I thought you'd kind of like to keep that private."

"Yes," Alison said. "I would. Thank you, Charlene. Let's keep it that way."

* * *

Surprisingly, she slept soundly, but she was aware of a growing excitement when she got up next morning.

"They tell me you're going into town today, Mrs Pat," Hugo said as he served breakfast.

"That's correct, Hugo."

"Shall I get the car out?"

"Yes, please. But I just want you to drive me as far as the station."

"The station?"

"I rather thought I'd take the train today, Hugo."

"The train? You never use the train, Mrs Pat."

"For God's sake, Hugo, can't I just for once do something I *feel* like doing?"

"It ain't safe."

"Why on earth isn't it safe?"

"Well . . . you could be attacked."

"Who is going to attack me? Nobody is going to know I'm on the train until the moment it pulls out of the station. Really, you are being quite absurd."

She went off to have her bath and dress. When she came downstairs David was waiting for her.

"Hugo says you're going up to town by train."

"Yes," she said. "Yes, I am."

"You've never done that before."

Alison exploded. "What the hell is going on?" she shouted. "Look, I am thirty-eight years old. I am in full possession of my faculties, and I am also, you tell me, the richest woman in the world. I am damned well going to do what I feel like doing, this morning, now. Right now. And the next person who questions my right to do it is out on the street the moment after. Is that understood?"

She glared from face to face, because in addition to David and Hugo and Charlene, several of the resident staff had gathered in the hall.

"Right," she said. "I'll see you this afternoon. Hugo?"

Hugo held her mink for her, opened the car door, and got behind the wheel himself.

"You spending the night in town, Mrs Pat?" he asked.

378

"Probably not."

"The rush hour is from about half-past four to half-past six," he remarked, apparently to himself.

"I shall almost certainly be on the train home before half-past four."

"You want me to be at the station, Mrs Pat?"

"I can see no point in your hanging around the station, Hugo. I'll call you from Waterloo, and tell you what train I'm on."

"Yes, ma'am," he said unhappily.

He bought her ticket, fussed over her, and settled her into a first-class non-smoker, bought her a newspaper and a magazine, and stood on the platform to watch her out of sight. She blew him a kiss, and then settled back with an enormous sigh, at once excitement and relief.

It was incredible, that she, Alison Grange, should feel like a schoolgirl let out of class for a day. Or more accurately, playing truant. She might almost still be married to Pat!

Then she frowned. Because the fact was, she *was* still married to Pat. She was married to the world he had created, and there was no way she was ever going to escape that world. She had sought to do so, with Paul, and it had been a catastrophe.

And presumably, whether she had been aware of it or not, that was the real reason she simply could not contemplate marrying David – he was too much a relic of Pat.

Then what of Jonny Carter? But she wasn't contemplating marriage to Jonny. She wasn't going to contemplate anything today. She was going to have the time of her life. A truant schoolgirl. Only she was calling the shots.

Her excitement grew.

She reached the hotel at twelve.

"Your suite is ready for you, Mrs Grange," the Manager said, himself greeting her. "But . . . do I understand you are not staying the night?"

379

"Oh, I wish I could," she said truthfully. "But I simply can't. All I want is a lunch in complete privacy."

"Of course."

"I'll go up now. There's a Mr Carter coming at twelve-thirty. Will you send him right up."

"Of course, Mrs Grange."

Alison went up in the lift. She stripped off her gloves and coat, threw them on the bed, and returned to the sitting room to pour herself a drink from the minibar. She nearly jumped out of her skin when there was a tap on the door: it was only twelve-fifteen.

It was the floor waiter, armed with various menus.

"I wondered if you would like to order now, madam," he said.

"Why not?" She only needed a glance at the list. "Maltese oranges, salmon steaks, and a bottle of the good Pouilly Fumé."

"Very good, madam. A sauce with the steaks?"

"A white sauce, on the side."

"Vegetables?"

"Ah . . ." Jonny would probably have a good appetite. "New potatoes and . . . courgettes."

The waiter bowed, and withdrew. Alison opened the fridge, made sure there was a bottle of Bollinger, then poured herself a gin and tonic. She needed a stiff one, and giggled at the *double entendre* in the thought.

When, twenty minutes later, there was another tap on the door, she was ready.

"Come in," she called.

The door swung in, and Jonny stepped through.

And Alison had to suppress a gasp.

She had deliberately refused to allow herself to contemplate what he might now look like, had concentrated on remembering what he had looked like that day in New York.

But that was eleven years in the past, and for Jonny

they had been the longest eleven years imaginable. He remained tall, and thin, perhaps thinner than she remembered him. There was much to remember in his face, too, although she might have been looking at the older brother of the man she remembered – or even the father. The handsome lines had become ridges which suggested a great deal of strength, but also a great deal of suffering, while one cheek was split by a scar which she suspected had never been stitched; it made him look lop-sided. The eyes were never still, but sought the remote corners of the room even when apparently in repose.

The hair was dead white, and thinning.

She drew a long breath. "Jonny?" she whispered.

He closed the door behind him. "When you decide to have privacy, you have privacy," he remarked.

She waited, staring at him.

"But I suppose that goes for everything, where Alison Grange is concerned."

"Maybe you'd better go out and come in again," she suggested. "If you really want to."

He hesitated, and she watched his hands opening and shutting. While his shoulders sagged. She seemed to have this effect on all men, she thought sadly.

"I'm sorry. I guess I'm out of touch with polite company."

"Jonny." She held out her hands, and a moment later was in his arms. But his kiss was hesitant, almost wondering . . . perhaps when I am going to bite him, she thought.

"What took you so long?" she asked.

"A lot of things."

She released him, opened the bar. "How long is it since you've opened a bottle of champagne?"

"Too long. But I don't think I've forgotten."

She gave him the bottle, set out the glasses. He did it well and quietly. But then, she supposed, opening bottles of champagne is like riding a bicycle – you never quite forget.

He poured. "What are we celebrating?"

"You. Us. Everything."

They sipped, staring at each other.

"Does that mean what I hope it means?" he asked.

She made a moue. "Just let's be together, Jonny. I think we need to get to know each other, all over again."

"Yeah."

She gestured at the sofa. "Tell me about it. If you want to."

They sat together, and she traced the line of the scar.

"A fight," he said.

"Tell me about the other guy."

"He broke his arm. When I was getting the knife away from him." A dreadful look crossed his face. "They gave me thirty days solitary for that."

"Thirty days . . . what do you do?"

He glanced at her. "Do you really want to know?"

"Maybe I shouldn't."

Then she realised he was going to tell her anyway. "The odd thing is, when you're first given solitary, all you feel is relief. You're away from all the others, from the fights and the farts, the homos and the hysterics. You're on your own. You feel you can breathe. That lasts, maybe for forty-eight hours. Because they take away all your clothes, and there's no slopping out in solitary. At least, not where I was. What with one thing and another . . ." he paused to look at her, see if she understood. She understood, but she didn't know how to convey it. So he went on. "By the end of forty-eight hours you're beginning to hate yourself. Then you have to think very straight not to go nuts."

"Yes," she said.

He gave her another glance, looked down at his empty glass.

Hastily she drank hers. "Fill us up. Tell me what you did after leaving prison."

He poured. "Tried to get straight."

"Did you have any money?"

"Oh, sure. I had a fair sum on deposit in a bank in

382

England, and it just accumulated interest during my eleven years. From a normal point of view, I'm quite a wealthy man. Of course, I had to work at anything I could find to raise the money to get back at my money, if you follow me."

Alison nodded. "I only learned you were out a couple of weeks ago."

"The Mexicans didn't tell you?"

"I reckon they're afraid I'll stop my contribution to their social security, as they call it."

"God, when I think . . . you've spent eighteen million dollars . . ."

"It wasn't all on you. Having Mexican citizenship has been very useful. And for the kids."

Lunch arrived, and they chatted about irrelevancies as it was served. They finished the meal just after two. Hugo had told her to be on a train by four-thirty if she wanted to avoid the rush hour. That gave her at least an hour and a half, she reckoned. And then remembered that if she wished to, she could easily telephone home and inform them that she wasn't coming back tonight.

She simply had to keep reminding herself of that. She wasn't their prisoner; they were her employees.

But did she want to spend a night, or even the next hour, with this man? He looked at her too hungrily for comfort. Of course that was a compliment, but she had no desire to be savaged. And anyway, what was the point? She had no desire to go to bed with Jonny Carter, or anyone, just for the sake of going to bed with him. She was a healthy, vigorous woman, and she needed sex – but that was taken care of by David, without any hang-ups or leftovers to be sorted out.

Or at least, it always had been until a couple of days ago. Now it seemed that anything she did would leave left-overs to be coped with.

She had hoped for so much from this meeting. Far too much. She had, in fact, been incredibly stupid, believed what she wanted to believe, that Jonny would somehow, miraculously, revert to the man who had swept her off her feet in New York, and thus become the man to share her life, from a position of equality. Now she did not see how that could happen.

And it was time for a decision.

"Mind if I use the bathroom?" Jonny asked.

"It's through there."

He went into the bedroom, and she remained sitting on the sofa, drinking the last of her coffee.

He stood in the doorway. "You staying here?"

"No. I just hired the room for lunch."

"Can you do that?"

I can do anything, she thought. "Well, you have to take it for the night, of course. But there's no law that says you have to sleep in it. So . . . I'll be going home, instead."

"Sussex."

"Yes."

He continued to gaze at her, waiting for the invitation. It was now, or . . . never? She did not feel his brittle personality could stand a total brush-off.

She patted the sofa. "Come and sit down."

He hesitated, and looked beyond the door, at the bed, she knew.

"I think we need to talk," she said.

He sat beside her.

"What do you plan to do?" she asked.

"Now?"

"With your life."

"My life," he said contemptuously.

"Jonny, how old are you?"

"Forty-three when last I counted."

"So you have a lot of living to do." She watched the look cross his face, and hurried on. "So you had a horrendous deal. But you're free now. That's all that matters."

"You reckon? They don't train you for anything save breaking rocks in a Mexican gaol."

"But before you went in . . ."

"I was a pilot. I'm a bit old for that now."

"You were in war surplus."

"There's not a lot of that lying around either, now. Look, I'll get a job. You don't have to worry. I have enough money to tide me over for a while."

"I have to worry, Jonny."

"Because you're the reason for me going in?"

She hadn't anticipated it being put as bluntly as that. But as it had . . . "Yes. I feel responsible. Would . . . would you like to work for me?"

"Work for you? What as?"

"Well, tell me what you feel you'd be good at."

"Your husband."

Again, the bluntness took her off guard, even if she knew that had to come up.

"I thought you'd agreed with me," she said quietly. "That we need to get to know each other all over again. I don't know how much you've changed in the past eleven years, but I know I'm a completely different person. If we were able to see a lot of each other, for a while, maybe things would just drop into place."

"Look . . ." he held her hands. "I kept sane by dreaming about you. In my book you haven't changed a bit. I still want you more than anything else in life. All we have to do is establish we can still make love. Be honest, Alison, that's why we're here, in this room, with a bed next door. You want that as much as I."

She could not stop herself allowing a fatal hesitation, because that *was* what she had had in mind, in her dream world, with her dream man. "We're here because I wanted privacy," she said. "I've been having more than the usual amount of publicity recently. That's how you knew where to find me, right? I hired a suite because I didn't think you'd want to eat in a bedroom."

"You really expect me to believe that?"

As with David, he could make her so angry. She got up. "You'd better, because it's the truth." She went into the bedroom, put on her mink, picked up her gloves, turned. He stood in the doorway. "You can have any kind of job you like. Think about it, and give me a ring."

"But I can't have the job I really want."

"Not right now, no."

"What you mean is, you came here today prepared to bed me, prepared to take up where we left off, and then you took one look at this white-haired wreck of a man and you said to yourself, you win some, you lose some, I'd better look elsewhere. Isn't that the truth?"

Again that damned hesitation. Because it was so close to the truth.

"I said, give me a ring when you've thought it over." She walked towards him where he blocked the doorway, gazing at his face. The idiot was working himself up to be macho, because he thought, like Tony Mayne, that that might clinch it. But she was determined to make him force the issue. "It's been great seeing you again, and I really do hope you'll come and work for me, Jonny. Then . . . who knows." She stood on tiptoe to kiss his cheek. "I'll be home all day tomorrow."

His hands closed on her arms, and she felt herself being carried backwards.

"Don't be a fool, Jonny," she said softly. "If you assault me I'll have you back in gaol so fast you won't believe you ever left."

For a moment longer he held her, then his hands fell away.

"Call me," she said, and stepped through the door. She didn't look back at him.

She telephoned from Waterloo as promised, and as she was on the train by just after three, she had a very comfortable ride down. She bought herself some magazines and read vigorously. She didn't want to think. But the ball was firmly in his court.

"Found what you wanted, Mrs Pat?" Hugo asked.

"No," she said.

"Always the way," he commented.

Charlene drew her a hot tub. By the time she was out of it, David was waiting to see her. She received him in her sitting room, wrapped in a huge white bathrobe, while Charlene did her toenails.

"I called you at the flat," he accused. "But you weren't there."

"I had a bite in town," she explained. "Any news from Ben?"

"Well, not from him, exactly. From Lasalle at the Banque Nationale de Paris. In Paris."

Alison raised her eyebrows. "Not overdrawn, are we?"

David was not apparently in the mood to be amused. "Ben's been to see him, asked for an advance on his inheritance."

"Good thinking, if it works. What did Lasalle do?"

"Called here, to find out what you want him to do. But you weren't here."

Again the accusatory tone, and she wasn't in the mood for it. "Well, I'm here now. Call him back and tell him to arrange a ticket back for Ben and his lady friend, and make sure that he and she use it. Today. If it can't be done today, he can put them up at an hotel for the night. But no cash."

David nodded, hesitated. "I wonder if I might speak with you alone, Mrs Pat."

"I'm just finished," Charlene said.

Alison inspected her toes. "Thank you, Charlene."

Charlene closed the door behind her.

"How was Carter?" David asked.

Alison gazed at him.

"Did you really think you could get away with it?" David asked. "When you weren't at the flat, and in view of your mysterious telephone call of yesterday, which Charlene refused to tell me about, I put two and two together. You're a creature of habit, Alison."

She continued to gaze at him.

"So, I called the Savoy. When I told them who I was,

and that I had something urgent to discuss with you, they were most co-operative. But you had just left to catch a train. However, Mr Carter was still there if I would like to speak with him."

"Did you?" Alison asked, quietly.

"No, I did not. Just what the hell do you think you are playing at?"

"David," Alison said. "I'm a little confused. I want you to put me right. Do I work for you, or do you work for me?"

He gulped, but he was clearly very angry. "You promised . . ."

"And I changed my mind. It's a woman's prerogative."

"So what happens now?"

He was desperately seeking reassurance, and it would have been so easy to give it to him. But now she was angry as well.

"What happens now, David, is that if you ever, ever, again attempt to interfere in my private life, you are fired on the spot."

"In other words, you're planning on taking up with Carter again."

"All right," she said. "That's it. I will not be spoken to like that, and it's obvious that you can't change your attitude. I'm sorry, Dave. You have been my right hand man for a long time, and more than that recently. But the fact that I allow you into my bedroom doesn't give you any rights over me. You'd better pack up and go. I shall send a telex message to all our accounts cancelling your signing powers." She stood up and held out her hand. "I want to thank you for all you've done. You'll have a golden handshake – half a million."

He looked down at her hand, and then up at her face. His expression was a mixture of amazement and anger, and for a moment she thought she had another physical crisis on her hands. But David wasn't the physical type. He didn't say a word, merely turned and left the room.

* * *

Alison sat down again with a bump. She really was in a destructive situation, she thought. But hadn't she seen this one coming, for a long time? The fault was hers, as usual, for allowing it to develop in the first place. She kept reminding herself that she could do anything she liked – and then she did everything wrong.

She had no idea how she was going to survive without David. But she was certainly not going to allow him to rule her life, as he obviously wished.

There was too much to be done to allow time for moping. She got dressed, then telephoned her bank manager in London, at his home, and explained the situation. He issued immediate cancellations of all of David's powers of attorney, to take effect from the next morning, and would handle South Africa as well. George Ruthven was still at his office, and he promised to take care of the American side of the matter, including Mexico and the Bahamas. Lasalle was also at home, but the French side would also be looked after; he told her that Ben would be returning to see him the next morning, and that he would take care of that matter too.

She sent a wire to El Dorado, and another to Alvarado, and then felt she had done all she could. By then it was quite late and she was exhausted . . . and if Ben and his Mrs Wallburn were coming home tomorrow she was going to need to be on the ball.

"Has Mr Brook left?" she asked Hugo at dinner.

"Yes, ma'am, he left over an hour ago. Ma'am, he was one unhappy man."

"Yes. But I had to do it, Hugo."

"I know you did, ma'am," Hugo said faithfully.

Alison took a couple of aspirins and slept heavily. Next morning she was up early. She felt on top of the world. David had definitely been becoming oppressive. Of course she wished him every success in whatever he did next, but

389

from here on she intended to manage her own affairs. In every way.

She spent her morning in the study, going through the various accounts which were to hand, making telephone calls to all her banks to obtain more information and issue more instructions. Now for the first time she really was the spider, at the centre of her vast web. But she only used one phone; the other was left strictly for the call from Paris, which came just after ten, English time.

"I'm afraid Mr Grange was not responsive, *Madame*," Lasalle said.

"What did he say?"

"Well, *madame* . . ."

"Tell me."

"Well, *madame*, he said, tell . . . oh *madame*!"

"I would like his exact words, please."

"He said, tell the old cow to get stuffed, *madame*."

Alison gazed at the receiver.

"*Madame*? I am sorry, *madame*, but . . ."

"You didn't give him any money, I hope?"

"Oh, no, *madame*. No money, as you said."

"And I assume he didn't take the ticket?"

"No, no, *madame*."

"All right, Mr Lasalle. You did exactly what I told you to. Thank you very much."

She hung up. There was someone else who was going to have to get a sharp come-uppance. She needed advice. The law about one-quarter of everything going to the children was a Mexican one. She had no intention now of ever going back to Mexico, or of paying them another cent. Therefore . . . in any event, she was in the mood to change her Will, for sure.

But that could wait until Ben got home. He wasn't going to be staying away too long, with no money.

But how long was too long? The next few days dragged by. There was a lot to be done, and a constant stream of telephone calls from all over the world. She had never realised how busy David was kept . . . nor just how much power he had held in her name, how many decisions he had obviously made without ever referring to her. Well, that was how she had wanted it.

But she did not think she would ever want it to be like that again.

Yet, busy as she was, her days seemed to be empty. There was no intellectual stimulus without David. Hugo and Charlene were concerned only with domestic matters. And she worried for David. To have thrown up virtually a life's work because of jealousy . . . but then, she worried about Jonny Carter as well, on the one hand willing him to call her and accept her offer, on the other knowing that if he did, in David's absence, she was liable to do something stupid.

As for Ben . . .

How she wished the children would come home. It was only a few more days now, to end of term. Then they would all leave this place and go back to France, get on the yacht, and sail away. She wanted to do that quite desperately.

She lunched, the following day, served by a silent Hugo, who could tell that his mistress had a lot on her mind. It was just as he was pouring coffee that Charlene came in, carrying the telephone.

"It's Broadhurst, Mrs Pat. Mrs Pat . . ."

"What's the matter?" Alison looked at the stricken woman's face, then grabbed the telephone. "Yes? This is Mrs Grange."

"Oh, Mrs Grange . . . Miss Parton here. Oh, Mrs Grange, something terrible has happened."

"To Shirley? What is it? Has she been taken ill?"

"Oh, Mrs Grange! Shirley . . . she's been kidnapped."

CHAPTER 14

Catastrophe

For a moment Alison's mind went blank. Yet some part of it was still functioning, for she heard her own voice speaking, as if from a great distance. "How do you know she's been kidnapped?"

"Shirley went riding this morning, Mrs Grange. The senior girls normally do the last day before we break up. There were six girls and a mistress, riding on the downs. They . . . they saw a car on a nearby road behaving strangely, and when it stopped, a woman got out and waved at them. They didn't suspect anything, Mrs Grange. It seemed obvious that something was wrong with someone in the car, so they cantered across, and sure enough, the woman appeared in a desperate state, because her husband had had a heart attack, and had only just stopped the car before it went off the road. My girls naturally wanted to help; several of them are trained in first-aid. They dismounted, and went to see what they could do . . . and then, the man sat up and produced a gun, Mrs Grange. Pointing at my girls. The woman also had a gun. It was terrible."

"Go on," Alison said. Her brain was slowly unfreezing itself.

"Well, they forced Shirley to get into the car with them. She had no choice, Mrs Grange, it was at gunpoint. Then they drove off."

"Where?"

"Well, in the direction of Paffley. That's where the road leads."

"But your girls, and your mistress, obviously can describe these people?"

"Oh, yes, the woman . . ."

"They can also describe the car, and can remember the registration number."

"Oh, yes."

"What did they do about that?"

"Well, they came back to school, as quickly as they could. One of them fell off during the gallop. She is quite badly bruised."

"Isn't there a police station in Paffley? Wouldn't it have been quicker to go there?"

"Well, they panicked, I suppose, Mrs Grange. They were very frightened. I mean, they're only schoolgirls and a junior mistress. The man had said if they attempted to follow him he would stop and shoot them. They were very frightened."

"Yes," Alison said. "So what have you done?"

"Well, I called the police first, of course. And then I called you."

"How long after the kidnapping were the police called?"

"About forty-five minutes. The girls had to get back here, Mrs Grange."

"And that was?"

"Ten minutes ago, Mrs Grange."

"But then you gave them all the descriptions."

"Oh, yes."

"Thank you, Miss Parton. I'm sure you'll keep in touch."

"Will you be coming down, Mrs Grange?"

"Probably."

Alison replaced the receiver, looked from Hugo to Charlene.

"I can't believe it," Charlene said.

All manner of thoughts were chasing themselves through

393

Alison's mind, competing with an urgent desire to break something. She sat absolutely still for several minutes, while her two faithful retainers waited.

Then she picked up the phone again and called New York.

"I'm sorry, madam, but Mr Rubio is in conference."

"You tell him Alison Grange wants a word."

A moment later she was through.

"Alison, little lady. Don't tell me, you wanna come and visit."

"I thought you and I were friends, Carlo."

"Little lady, you keep using that word. You know what I want us to be."

"Carlo, listen very carefully. I want my daughter back, within twenty-four hours, and quite unharmed, or I am going to send you to prison for the rest of your life, if it costs me every penny I possess to do it."

"Eh? What the . . . you telling me someone snatched your daughter?"

"That is what I am telling you, Carlo."

"And you think I did it? Hell, little lady, I wouldn't do a thing like that. Not to you."

He sounded so genuinely injured she knew he was telling the truth.

"But whoever did it is gonna answer to me," he went on. "Listen, I'm on the next plane. Where you calling from?"

"England."

"I'll be there tonight. You hold on there, little lady. Carlo is on his way. I love you, little lady."

Alison replaced the phone. She felt a surge of warmth. If Carlo Rubio was on her side, whoever had done it would have to start looking over his shoulder.

But if Carlo Rubio hadn't done it, then who? Her brain was tumbling again.

And what about Pat and Stephanie, and Harry? What about Ben?

* * *

Laughton, the butler, appeared in the breakfastroom doorway. "There are some police officers to see you, madam."

"Show them in."

"I guess I have things to do," Charlene said.

"Stay here," Alison told her. "And you, Hugo. Just wait over there."

The two policemen looked their part; they even wore slightly decrepit raincoats, but had given their slouch hats to Laughton.

"Mrs Grange. Detective Inspector Broughton. This is Sergeant Lucas."

Alison shook hands.

"I can't tell you how horrified we are by this event, Mrs Grange," Broughton said. "I mean, we don't normally encounter this sort of thing in England."

"I'm very glad to hear it," Alison said. "You have come to tell me you have caught the kidnappers."

"Ah, no. Not yet."

"But you have a description of the people, and the car, and even a licence number."

"Yes, we do."

"And you know where it was going. Paffley Village."

"Yes. But it never got there."

"What do you mean?"

"Simply that they changed cars before reaching the village. We've found the abandoned car."

"And you don't have a description of the other car?"

"Nothing definite. It could be a blunt-nosed Morris; one was seen parked near where the first car was abandoned. But Paffley is fairly busy in the middle of the morning, and it is difficult to establish a strange car, definitely."

"But you have a description of the people," Alison insisted, fighting back the growing panic which was threatening to engulf her mind.

"Ah . . ." Broughton took a notebook from his pocket. "I'm afraid these weren't of great value. The woman was described as very blonde, dressed in a green pants suit, and wearing dark glasses. The man as being large, that is, both tall and heavy, with a thick moustache, wearing a sports coat over gray pants. He also wore dark glasses."

"Well? That seems fairly striking to me."

"Unfortunately Mrs Grange, everything I've told you, except for the size of the man, is meaningless. In the car we found a blonde wig, a false moustache, and two pairs of dark glasses. We also found a green pants suit and a man's sports jacket. This was a carefully planned exercise, Mrs Grange. They knew exactly what they meant to do, and how much time they would have to do it in."

"So the woman is probably black-haired and the man is clean-shaven."

"I'm afraid that is only too true. We will of course be able to trace the car we found, but it was probably stolen. We will also be able to trace the clothes, but I imagine they were picked off the peg in some crowded store."

"But while all this was going on, they had Shirley with them. How were they going to to disguise her? Surely any report of a man, a woman, and a girl in riding gear . . ."

Broughton sighed. "I'm sorry, Mrs Grange, but we also found a hypodermic needle in the car."

"A what?"

"It is undergoing forensic tests now, and we will know what it contained in a couple of hours. But obviously your daughter was injected with some sedative drug, and was concealed either in the back seat or the boot of the second car when they drove away."

"But . . . my God, she could have suffocated."

"I don't think they would have wished to kill her." He hesitated, and Alison understood that he had nearly said, yet.

"What you are telling me is that they have got clear away," she said. "My daughter has been kidnapped, in broad daylight and in front of her friends, and you have no idea who did it or where she is, or even if she is still alive."

Broughton sighed again. "I have said that we are sure

your daughter is still alive, Mrs Grange. And believe me, we will do everything we can to get her back just as quickly as possible. The point is that some time very soon you will receive a ransom demand . . ."

"Yes," Alison said.

"Now, what I would like to do, with your permission, of course, is put a tap on your telephone lines, so that we may overhear any conversations."

"You can do that if you wish, Inspector, but if it comes to a question of money against my daughter's life, I intend to pay the ransom."

"Of course," he said soothingly. "We just wish to be fully informed of what is going on."

She nodded.

"There is another way in which you can help us regain your daughter," Broughton went on.

"Tell me?"

"You are of course a very wealthy woman, and therefore it is possible that this kidnapping is simply a matter of money. However, we have to consider every possibility. Do you have any enemies who might wish to hit at you by kidnapping your daughter?"

Alison stared at him. She hadn't allowed herself to think of that possibility. Did she have any enemies? Off hand she would have said none. But when she thought about it . . . the kidnapper had been a big man. Jonny Carter was a big man, and as far as he was concerned she had just slapped his face.

But would Jonny descend to kidnapping? Why not? He had spent the past eleven years locked up with criminals. But to accuse him, and have him arrested all over again, when he might not have done it . . . and he *could* not have done it, if the Inspector was right and this thing had been carefully planned. She had only seen him the previous week. There had just not been sufficient time for such a carefully timed operation to be put together.

Unless he had already put it all together, and had just

397

waited until he had learned her reaction to him to set it in motion.

Broughton had been studying her face. "Any information you may give us, of course, Mrs Grange, will be treated in the utmost confidence, and any inquiries we may make will be most discreet."

Alison drew a deep breath. "I'll have to think about that one, Inspector."

"Very good, madam. It is, of course, a matter of considerable urgency. Every minute that your daughter spends in the hands of those people . . ."

"I know that. I will be in touch. Now I wish to ask you about my other children."

Broughton raised his eyebrows.

"I have four other children, Inspector, all of whom I must now presume to be in danger."

"Well, ma'am, as to that, they're probably safer at this moment than at any previous time in their lives."

"That may be your opinion. But as you say, there is a possibility that Shirley was taken, not for money, but for some kind of revenge. I wish my other children adequately protected."

Broughton exchanged glances with his sergeant. "Protecting children at school . . . I take it they are all still at school?"

The wretch, she thought; undoubtedly he read the newspapers. "The three younger ones are at school, Inspector. My eldest son is enjoying a brief vacation in France."

"I see. Well, ma'am, as I was saying, mounting a security operation at a public school is a difficult business. Term is nearly over anyway. I would suggest you bring them all home. We can certainly protect them here."

"I can protect them here myself," Alison pointed out. "But I will take your advice."

"And I would get hold of your eldest boy and tell him to come back, just as quickly as he can."

Alison gazed at him, wondering just how much he

398

actually knew about Ben's escapade. "I will do that, Inspector."

He nodded. "My people will install the phone tap now. Whoever does telephone, it would be a great help if you could keep them speaking for as long as possible."

"Yes. I will try to do that."

"Then I'll take my leave." He stood up and gave her what was presumably meant to be an encouraging smile.

"What are we going to do, Mrs Pat?" Hugo asked.

He certainly looked as if he wanted to do *something*; his big fists were opening and shutting.

Do? she wanted to shout. How do I know what we do? She had never felt so lonely in her life. If only David were here, to turn to. David would know exactly what to do. He always did.

"We have to wait," Alison said. "We can't do anything until the kidnappers make a move. But we can get the others home."

She was trying to rationalise, trying to be calm. Presumably she had been monumentally over-confident in not maintaining bodyguards for all the children. She had been so anxious for them all to live as normal lives as possible. And as the Inspector had said, kidnapping was not a common crime in England; the island was too small and too crowded, and too difficult to get off in a hurry.

Although Ben had done it. But that was because he had wanted to go. How she wished he'd come back.

She telephoned the remaining three schools. It was necessary in each case to speak with the headmaster or headmistress, and explain the situation, in the strictest confidence. By the time she had contacted them, Hugo and Charlene were already on their way by car to the various establishments. She received a totally sympathetic response, and also to her request for absolute secrecy.

Hugo was of course unhappy at the thought of leaving her alone, as he put it. She pointed out that, including the gardeners, there were seven other servants in the house, as well as four policemen in the cellar with their bugging device. He merely growled, "They're not us."

And in fact when they had departed she did feel an increased sense of loneliness, a growing tension. These people were too civilised. She couldn't imagine what Laughton the butler would say if she gave him a gun and told him to shoot anyone who entered the grounds.

But then, had she, or any of them, truly been safe at The Keep, or in the French villa?

To her dismay, there was a report on the lunchtime news. It had to be one of the schools which had let her down there. Now she could only brace herself for what was coming.

Reporters descended on the house in a swarm an hour later. By then Alison, having had a glass of milk and a biscuit for lunch, had received another telephone call from Rubio, to the effect that he couldn't get a flight until that evening, but that he would be with her early tomorrow morning. He remained full of fire, and told her to tell anyone who rang up with a ransom demand that they were going to have to reckon with him as well as the police.

Was he going over the top, deliberately? She felt absolutely hemmed in. But as the situation had been blown, she wanted to meet the press, and received them in her drawing room, and told them exactly what had happened, in so far as she knew what had happened.

"You had no doubts about calling the police?"

"My daughter's school did that before contacting me," Alison pointed out.

"Do you regret that?"

"No, I would have done the same thing."

"And what are the police doing about it?"

"You will have to ask them that."

"Have you had a ransom demand as yet, Mrs Grange?"

"No, I have not."

"When you do, are you going to tell the police?"

400

"That depends what the demand calls for," Alison said carefully, understanding that everything she said was going to be read by the kidnappers in fairly short order.

"Mrs Grange, have you any idea who might have committed this crime?"

"No," Alison said shortly.

"How are your other children taking it?"

"I haven't seen them yet."

"Aren't you concerned for their safety, Mrs Grange?"

"Yes," Alison replied. "I have that much in mind."

No doubt it was an unsatisfactory press conference, from their point of view, as Alison neither broke down nor made any pleas to the kidnappers, despite being invited to do so. So they took their photographs and trooped out into the hall. Alison went with them, looked past them at the car drawing up before the front steps, and watched David Brook getting out.

He checked at the sight of her, then came forward. The reporters closed around him, as they all knew who he was.

"Is there any news, Mr Brook?"

"Where have you been, Mr Brook?"

"Have you been in negotiation with the kidnappers, Mr Brook?"

David looked at Alison, who had come out on to the terrace.

"You'll have to ask Mrs Grange for the answers to those questions."

Heads turned.

"Mr Brook has been carrying out his duties as my business manager," Alison announced. "I have told you, neither of us can do anything about the kidnappers until we receive their ransom demand. Good day to you."

She turned and went back inside. Laughton was hovering, uncertain what to do next, his expression registering stark horror as he saw the tears which were suddenly cascading down his mistress's cheeks.

It was as if the sight of David had released some spring in Alison's mind, and triggered all the emotion which had been pent up all morning.

She listened to his feet behind her. "I had to come, Mrs Pat. But . . . I'll go again if you want me to."

"I want you to stay," she muttered, and ran for the stairs, waving her hand in a summoning gesture. She hurried into her bedroom, dabbing at her eyes with her handkerchief. She left the door open, and he stood there. She turned round and was in his arms.

"Oh, David!" she said. "Thank God you came back."

"Did you think I could stay away?" He kissed her, held her close. "I need my head examined for behaving as I did."

"But you're back. Just promise me you won't ever run off again."

"I promise." He half carried her to the bed, and she lay down with a sigh. He sat beside her and held her hands. "Bring me up to date."

She did so. "David, what are we going to do?"

"You're quite sure about all of these times?"

"Yes. I think so."

"So what you are saying is that Shirley was taken something like six hours ago."

"Yes."

"And there's been no ransom demand?"

"No. Oh, God, Dave . . . you don't think . . ."

"Don't think," he told her. "I'm here to do that."

"David . . ." she clung to him. "She's dead."

"I said, don't think, Alison."

"But you know there should have been a demand by now."

"There'll be a demand."

It was almost reassuring.

*   *   *

402

The three younger children all arrived by four o'clock. They had gathered something was wrong from Hugo and Charlene, but had been given no details. Now they listened in grim-faced silence to what Alison and David had to tell them – they had of course no idea that Alison and David had quarrelled and were now reconciled; from their point of view, David was a permanent fixture in the Grange household.

"We'll get her back, Mom," Pat said.

Alison hugged him.

Soon there was another telephone call from Carlo, waiting at Idlewild for his flight. He wanted an up-date, and made the usual threatening noises when he discovered there was nothing to up-date him about. Alison just wanted to get him off the phone, to leave it free for the kidnappers, if and when they decided to call.

The afternoon dragged into evening, and she sat down for a serious chat with David.

"We have to accept that it's not a ransom job," she said. "So it's revenge, for something or other. I'm sure it's not Carlo. So that leaves . . .?"

"A large man who hates your guts." David tapped his chin. "Clem?"

"Why should Clem hate me enough to do something like this? All I did was fire him. And that was years ago."

"You're assuming Clem is a rational, thinking human being. I don't know that he is. But if it's not him . . ."

They stared at each other.

"What actually happened at the Savoy last week?" he asked.

"Nothing. Not a damned thing. Jonny wanted something to happen, and I refused."

"Was he happy about that?"

"No, he was not happy. Don't you think I've been brooding on that? But all I did was suggest we needed to get to know each other better . . ."

"And then walk away from him."

"That's a motive?"

"Well, again, we don't know too much about Carter's mental processes. Eleven years in a Mexican gaol . . ."

"I know." He was putting into words what she had earlier thought. "But to point the police at him, all over again, if he *didn't* do it . . ."

"We're talking about Shirley, Alison."

She hunched her shoulders in despairing indecision.

"I think I'd better ask the police to come back for another chat," David said quietly.

Alison sighed, and nodded.

She had a bath and dressed for the evening. Pat and Harry were knocking up on the tennis court, watched by Stephanie. The three younger children were really much closer to each other than they were to her, which she supposed was not at all unnatural, in all the circumstances. Now they had closed ranks together in the face of catastrophe, which she supposed was a good thing.

But Ben and Shirley had equally been very close. Now they were both gone, both in a sense kidnapped. But Ben . . .

She gazed at Charlene, who was actually smiling. She hadn't smiled all day.

"Shirley?" Alison didn't dare believe it.

"No, Mrs Pat. I'm sorry. But . . . Mr Ben is calling."

"Ben!" Alison grabbed the telephone. "Where are you?"

"Paris. Listen, Mom . . . I'm on my way. I only heard the news this afternoon."

"You're coming home, Ben? Home?"

"You bet. Listen, Mom, have they found Shirl yet?"

"No," Alison said. "Oh, Ben, take care. Have you got money?"

"I got my tickets from the bank. Mr Lasalle organised it for me. I'm calling from his office."

"You thank him for me," Alison said. "When will you be in?"

"There's a late crossing from Calais. I'm taking the train up there in half an hour, and I'll be in Dover at ten."

"Right, I'll have someone there to meet you. Is . . . is Mrs Wallburn with you?"

"Yes, Mom. Well, I couldn't leave her behind. Anyway . . . you're going to love her."

"Um," Alison commented. But she wasn't in the mood to quarrel with any of her children at that moment. "Just get home, Ben. I love you."

She hung up, called Hugo, sent him off to Dover to meet the ferry. She felt almost happy. But how could she feel happy? Half an hour later Inspector Broughton was back.

"You haven't met my business manager, Mr Brook," Alison said.

The two men shook hands; Alison did not think they cared for each other.

"I gather there's been no demand," Broughton said.

"No."

"Well, Mrs Grange, in the circumstances, I think you are just going to have to be more co-operative."

Alison began to get the feeling that he didn't much care for her either.

But he was right, of course. "Yes," she said. "You'd better sit down, Inspector."

He did so, and she told him about Jonny Carter, from the beginning to their meeting the previous week. The sergeant made notes.

"Hm," the Inspector commented. "We've agreed that the kidnapping of your daughter was a very carefully planned operation. Did Mr Carter give you any indication, during your meeting, that he might have arranged something like this if you wouldn't co-operate? What I mean is, was there any suggestion of a threat in his demeanour? Think very carefully."

"I can't remember anything which might suggest that.

Jonny was always a little abrasive, and eleven years in a Mexican gaol hadn't improved that . . ."

"And probably did some other things to his personality as well. Very good, Mrs Grange. I wish you'd told us about this man this morning. Do you have any idea where he is staying?"

"I'm afraid not, Inspector."

"He could've left the country by now, sir," Sergeant Lucas put in.

"Not with Miss Grange in tow. There's been a total closure of all ports and airports since twelve o'clock this morning. We'll find him, Mrs Grange, if we have to put every man in the force on to it. And . . ." he looked up as Laughton entered the room behind a discreet knock.

"Forgive me for interrupting, madam, but there is a gentlemen here to see you."

"I've seen the press," Alison said.

"He said it was a personal matter."

Alison stood up, and the policemen and David stood with her. Heart pounding, she took a step towards the doorway, and gazed at Jonny Carter.

"Alison," he said. "I just heard the news. I came straight down. Alison . . . I'm so terribly sorry."

Alison licked her lips, and looked at Broughton.

He stepped forward. "Detective Inspector Broughton, sir, leading this investigation. You are . . ."

"Jonathan Carter," Jonny said, and looked back at Alison. "Just what is going on?"

"We would like to ask you some questions, Mr Carter," Broughton told him.

Jonny continued to gaze at Alison. "You mean you think I . . . you think that, Alison?"

"I . . . there's been no ransom demand," she explained. "No word at all. So . . . we think it had to be a revenge kidnapping more than a ransom one."

"And you think I did that?"

"I don't know what to think!" Alison cried.

Jonny looked at Brook.

"David Brook, Mr Carter," David said. "We did see each other before. At your trial for the murder of Mr Grange."

"Why, you little runt!" Jonny took a step forward, and the sergeant quickly stepped between him and David.

"With respect, sir," Broughton said. "I'm sure you will appreciate that we have to explore every avenue of investigation open to us. All you have to do is provide us with an account of your movements over the last twenty-four hours. I'm sure Mrs Grange will have no objection if we sit down and discuss the situation in a civilised manner?"

"Oh, please," Alison said, waving her hand at the room they had just left. "Do you want me . . ."

"No, I think it would be a good idea if you stayed, Mrs Grange." The Inspector glanced at David, but he had got the message that David, even if he had been absent from the morning interview, was actually an integral part of this household, and he made no objection when he came in as well.

Alison summoned Laughton and ordered tea. She did want this to be as civilised as possible. Besides, she had abandoned any idea that Jonny could be guilty. He looked far more angry than guilty, and in any event, she had never heard of a kidnapper turning up to offer sympathy to his victim's mother.

"Now, Mr Carter," Broughton said. "I understand you lunched at the Savoy Hotel with Mrs Grange, last Thursday."

"That's correct."

"May I ask what you have been doing since?"

"Thinking."

"You have spent an entire week thinking?"

Jonny gave a twisted grin. "I had a lot to think about."

"Would you care to explain that remark, sir?"

"It is simply that Mrs Grange offered me a job, and I was trying to make up my mind whether or not to accept it."

"I see. May I ask where you have been living during this time?"

"At my hotel."

"Which is?"

"Well, it's a boarding house, really. Just off Northumberland Avenue, behind Trafalgar Square. Okay, it's not the Savoy, but then, my name isn't Grange."

Broughton wrote down the name of the hotel. "Very good. Now can you tell us what you did yesterday, and more specifically, today?"

"I did the same as I do every day, just about, Inspector. Wandered around London."

"I see. Did you go out last night?"

"I go out most nights."

"I see. What time did you leave your, ah, hotel, sir?"

"About half past six. I went to a pub, had a few drinks, a bite of dinner, a few more drinks, and when the pub closed went back to the hotel to bed."

"Presumably the people in the pub will identify you?"

"I very much doubt it. It was pretty crowded."

Broughton sighed. "Very good, Mr Carter. Now, today. What have you done today?"

"I got up about seven, had what they laughingly call breakfast, went to the bank as soon as it opened, to get some money, and then, well . . . I just mooched around. As usual."

"Can you give me a list of places you went to?"

"Oh, for God's sake. I just wandered about. I know I took in the National Portrait Gallery. I spent some time in Foyle's, too."

"Ah, did you buy anything?"

"No."

"Pity. Where did you lunch?"

"Some little delicattessen in Charing Cross Road."

"Don't tell me, it was pretty full."

"That's right."

408

"When did you hear about the kidnapping?"

"When I went back to the hotel this afternoon. I switched on my radio and heard it then. I was horrified."

"So you came straight down here."

"Yes."

"But in the meantime, you cannot really account for your movements between four 'clock yesterday afternoon and eleven o'clock last night, and between nine o'clock this morning and arriving here half an hour ago."

Jonny stared at him. "No, I can't."

Broughton turned to his sergeant. "How long does it take to get from say Waterloo to Paffley?"

"Forty-five minutes, sir."

"So, Mr Carter, you could have been in Paffley by ten yesterday morning. The kidnappers were certainly there then. Miss Grange was taken at ten forty-five. We know they were clear of Paffley again by eleven-thirty. But that would have given ample time for one of them to have got on a train back to London."

"Leaving my daughter alone with the woman, Inspector?" Alison asked.

"Well, as you know, ma'am, it's our opinion that Miss Grange was probably heavily sedated. But in any event, we don't know there were only two people involved. Only two people took part in the actual kidnapping, but there may well have been others standing by to play their part."

Jonny looked at Alison. "Do you honestly think I did it, Alison?"

Alison hesitated, and looked at the Inspector, apologetically. "No. I don't. I'm sorry, Inspector. I know I . . ." she looked back at Johnny. "I had to give them every name I could think of. But now . . . no, I don't."

"You're entitled to your opinion, madam," Broughton said. He stood up, and the sergeant closed his notebook. "I am bound to say that I am very disturbed at the absence of any attempt to contact you by the kidnappers. Mr Carter, would you like a lift back to town?"

Jonny continued to gaze at Alison. "I hired a car and drove down," he said. "I can find my own way back."

"Would you like tò stay to dinner?" she asked.

Both Broughton and David grunted together.

"That would be very kind of you," Jonny said.

Broughton grunted again. "You'll be staying then, Mr Carter."

"Yes, I will."

"Very good, sir. I wonder if you would do something for me?"

"Of course." He grinned. "If it's legal."

Broughton did not share his sense of humour. "I would like you to telephone Scotland Yard just before you leave here to return to London. And when you get back to your hotel, I would like you to call again. Will you do that?"

"Of course."

"I should add that when you call the second time, Mr Carter, you will be requested to hang up and wait, in your hotel, to receive a return call. You do understand this?"

"Of course I do. Now, Inspector, may I ask you a question?"

"Of course, sir."

"Am I under suspicion for the kidnapping of Miss Grange?"

"Yes, sir, I'm afraid you are under suspicion of being connected with it."

"Then why don't you charge me?"

"I shall do that if and when suspicion becomes certainty, Mr Carter. Do not forget to telephone. Good evening to you, Mrs Grange."

He marched out in front of his sergeant, who gave Alison an apologetic smile.

"Laughton, will you tell cook there will be an extra cover for dinner, please," Alison said.

David and Jonny were gazing at each other.

"Listen," Alison told them both. "I have had all the trauma I can stand, for one day. You two are going to

410

sit down and have dinner like civilised human beings. David, it is past six o'clock. I think we could all have a drink. Champagne cocktails."

"May I just ask one question first, Mrs Pat?"

"Shoot."

David looked at Jonny. "Did you have anything to do with the kidnapping of Shirley?"

"No I did not," Jonny replied.

They continued to stare at each other for several seconds, then David turned and went to the bar.

"Well," Alison said. And then added, "Well."

There didn't seem much else to say.

There were seven for dinner. Alison, David, Charlene, the three children, and Jonny.

It was a sombre occasion. Shirley had now been gone nine hours, and there had not been a word. Alison realised that Jonny's presence wasn't exactly a help, mainly because David, despite her lecture, was so silent, resentful. But she was more than ever convinced of Jonny's innocence. Not that she was any further ahead in deciding what had happened. Or in fighting back the waves of panic which were threatening to overwhelm her.

It was fourteen-year-old Stephanie who finally asked the vital question.

"What are we going to do, Mom?"

Alison looked at David, instinctively.

"She's disappeared without trace, according to the police. It's all been very slick."

"Do you think she's dead?" Harry asked.

"Harry!" Charlene snapped.

"It's a legitimate question," Alison said. "Do you think she's dead, David?"

David looked at Jonny, as if to say, why don't you ask him? Then he looked back at Alison. "I don't know, Mrs Pat."

"Mrs Pat," Charlene said. "Look, these people seem to

want to make you sweat. You gonna sit here and sweat, or are we gonna carry the fight to them?"

"How do you propose to do that?" But her blood was tingling. She certainly wanted to fight someone.

"Well . . . I know of a guy who may be able to help us."

"Tell me of him."

"Well . . ." Charlene looked distinctly embarrassed. "He's a clairvoyant."

Six pairs of eyes stared at her.

"Okay," she admitted. "It sounds crazy, I know. But these things sometimes work. This guy has found people, and things, before. Well . . ." she looked from face to face. "I don't honestly think we have anything to lose."

Alison felt a sense of disappointment. Charlene was normally so practical, and so logical, and above all, so simple, in her approach to life. That she should be clutching at surrealistic straws revealed their total helplessness, in the absence of a ransom demand.

David obviously felt the same way. "I've never heard anything so ridiculous in my life," he declared.

"Look, you got any better idea, wiseguy, why don't you speak up," Charlene snapped.

Another indication of the general tension; Charlene had never spoken to David like that before – and David looked quite nonplussed.

It was time to step in, quickly, or they were just going to disintegrate.

"All right," Alison said. "I'm prepared to try anything. What's this man's name?"

"Linton. Harold Linton."

"How soon can you contact him?"

"I can try him now. It's only nine o'clock."

"Then would you do that?" She smiled around the table, with a confidence she did not feel. "We have to do something, gang. Maybe this is it."

*   *   *

412

Charlene went to telephone, and the rest got up from the table, leaving Jonny and Alison alone.

"I suppose I'd better say goodnight," Jonny Carter said, and his face twisted into a grin. "If you'll let me use your phone, when she's finished."

"Jonny . . ." Alison rested her hand on his arm. "I had to do it. When there was no ransom demand . . ."

"I quite understand. I'm only sorry about last week. I suppose I had built it up so high in my mind . . ."

"I know," she said. "It had been built up in mine as well."

"Oh, Alison," he said, and then she was in his arms, holding him close, feeling the tremendous strength of his prison-hardened muscles closing around her.

"Come back to me, Jonny," she whispered.

"As . . ."

"Just come back to me. You must give me time to think. And I can't think now. But come back to me."

He pulled his head back. "Like when?"

"Right now."

"What will Brook say?"

"I'm not going to sleep with you, Jonny. I'm not going to sleep with anyone until this business is over. But there are several guest rooms. Just stay." She smiled at him. "You can use one of my disposable razors, and there are spare toothbrushes. We'll get your clothes tomorrow."

"Well . . . at least Broughton will be sure where I am."

"Call from the study," she said.

He nodded, and she showed him in.

Charlene was sitting at the desk, still speaking. She looked up, raised her eyebrows, and finished her conversation. "Can't you make it sooner than that? Oh, very well. Tomorrow morning." She replaced the receiver. "That was the damned man's secretary. She says he's asleep and cannot be disturbed, but he'll be down here tomorrow morning first thing. I suppose we must be satisfied with that."

413

"Down here? Isn't he going to the school? Or where Shirley was taken?"

"That's not the way he works. This isn't deduction. It's mental telepathy, or whatever. He'll want to see Shirley's room, look at her books, sniff her clothes . . ."

"Do *what*?"

"That's the way it works. Then he'll go into some kind of a trance, and just see where she is."

"Charlene . . ."

"I know it sounds far-fetched, Mrs Pat, but that's how it works. And it has worked." She glanced at Jonny, who was using the phone.

"Scotland Yard? Jonathan Carter here. I was told to phone in. Yes, well actually I'm not returning to my hotel tonight. I'll be staying with Mrs Grange."

Charlene gazed at Alison from behind arched eyebrows.

"Would you like to speak with her?" Jonny's eyebrows were also in evidence, but he was waggling his.

Alison took the phone. "Alison Grange."

"Is Mr Carter spending the night with you, Mrs Grange?"

"He is spending the night in my house," Alison corrected.

"Ah! Right. Would you mind hanging up, madam, and we will call you back."

"As you wish." Alison replaced the receiver. "They're very cautious."

"Well, I suppose they have to be."

"Charlene," Alison said. "Will you show Mr Carter to one of the spare rooms, and find him a toothbrush?"

Charlene nodded, and went to the door.

Jonathan hesitated.

"I think it should be an early night, for all of us," Alison said.

He followed Charlene up the stairs.

The telephone jangled, and Alison picked it up. "Yes," she said. "This is Alison Grange. Yes, I spoke to you just now. Yes, Mr Carter is spending the night here. Yes, I will call you the moment he leaves."

"Look at it this way," Alison said to David. "This way we know where he is, all night."

"That's one way of looking at it, all right."

She held his arm. "David . . . I'm just about ready to go round the bend. I need all the support I can get."

He kissed her on the cheek. "You have it, from me at least. I'm sorry about Carter, but I just get goosepimples whenever he's too close."

"You think he did kill Pat, don't you?"

"Well, Alison, we sure haven't turned up any other candidate. I mean to say, coincidence is just too much. Carter comes into your life, and Mr Pat is killed. Carter comes back into your life, and Shirley is kidnapped. Well, maybe tomorrow will solve it all."

"But you're sceptical?"

"I'm no believer in mumbo-jumbo. But I'm willing to be proved wrong. You coming to bed?"

"No. I'm waiting up for Ben and Hugo. And Mrs Wallburn."

They arrived just after midnight. Alison had been bracing herself for the kind of experience she could do without, gazed in amazement at the tall dark woman, quietly dressed, not especially pretty but certainly voluptuous and with a generally good figure, Alison decided. More important, there was a lot of strength in her face.

"Joanne, this is my mother," Ben said proudly.

Joanne Wallburn's grip was dry. "I am so terribly sorry, Mrs Grange."

"Thank you," Alison said, trying to imagine Ben in bed with this woman . . . and succeeding all too well. "Ben . . ." she held him close. "Have you eaten?"

"We had a bite on the way."

"Well . . ." she looked from face to face.

Charlene had appeared. "If you'll come with me, Mrs Wallburn . . ."

"She comes with me," Ben said.

Charlene looked at Alison, who raised her eyebrows. "Just let's get to bed."

"There's been nothing . . ." Ben looked at her.

"Nothing. Maybe something will develop tomorrow. I mean, today."

He nodded. "I'm sorry to have caused you all this hassle, at such a time."

"You got in first," Alison pointed out.

He nodded again, lifted the small suitcase which was all the pair of them had, took Joanne Wallburn's arm, and followed Charlene.

"You okay, Mrs Pat?" Hugo asked anxiously.

"Of course I'm all right," Alison said, and went upstairs.

All right, she thought. She wanted to scream and scream and scream. And then get hold of a gun and start shooting people. That's what Pat would have done. And however horrendous his methods, no one had ever succeeded in laying a finger on her or hers while he had been alive.

Oh, Pat!

Charlene came in. "You going to sleep?"

"I doubt it."

"But you have to, Mrs Pat. Listen, why don't you take a couple of pills?"

"Because I have to be on the ball tomorrow. Just leave me be."

Charlene looked doubtful. "Well," she said. "You know where I am." She paused in the doorway. "That girl don't look too bad."

"If she were a girl," Alison said. "I would probably agree with you. But she's a woman, and Ben's a boy. Good night, Charlene."

Amazingly, Alison did sleep, very heavily; she had not realised how exhausted she was. But she had a nightmare

416

and was awake by dawn. She had a bath, dressed herself, and went downstairs; it was only five o'clock, although fully light.

She went outside and sat on the terrace, because the day was already warming up and giving every indication of being a scorcher. She sat on one of the benches, and thought about Shirley. She hadn't allowed herself to do that, yesterday. She had only thought about Shirley being kidnapped, of the why and the how and the when of getting her back.

Now she thought about Shirley herself. Laughing, iconoclastic Shirley . . . being jabbed with a hypodermic needle to make her unconscious, being at the mercy of people who probably had no humanity in them . . . her shoulders hunched as she felt the burning feeling behind her eyes. Then she straightened at the sound of footsteps.

"Hi." It was Ben.

"Hi." She resumed staring at the trees.

He sat beside her. "I know now's not the time."

"No."

"I just wanted you to know that we do love each other, and we would like to get married, if you'll agree."

She turned her head. "We just agreed, now is not the time."

He hesitated, then nodded and got up. "Right."

He went back into the house. How could anyone be so foolish? Well, anyone, she supposed, at that age, virtually a grown man and locked up with a lot of schoolboys and offered something as tasty as that. But not only tasty, there was the rub. Had Joanne Wallburn been some footloose peroxide blonde she would have been relatively simple to deal with: a fat cheque would have settled the matter. This woman looked a shade too intelligent for that . . . although she was going to be offered a cheque anyway.

Because after all, now *was* the time.

People drifted downstairs.

"Did you sleep well?" Alison asked Jonny.

"Actually I did. When does this seer arrive?"

"Any moment now."

Harold Linton actually arrived half an hour later, in the middle of breakfast. He was disturbingly young, but Alison was discovering this about so many people nowadays. She put him at about thirty, with a little moustache and horn-rimmed spectacles. He wore an ordinary, if well-cut, suit, and the only suggestion that he might be someone out of the ordinary lay in his car, which was a Rolls, and the fact that he was accompanied by four people, two men and two women, none of them older than himself, and all fussing about him as if he were royalty.

In many ways he reminded her of her early days with Pat.

"Show me the girl's room," he commanded, having hardly wasted the time to greet anyone, even Charlene. "It is second on the left upstairs, is it not?"

Which was an impressive beginning.

Alison herself took him up. His various minders trooped behind, but she signalled her own people to stay downstairs. She also kept the minders out of the room, stood in the doorway while Linton went inside. They did not object and neither did he, but it made Alison feel distinctly odd to watch him hunt through Shirley's drawers, sift amongst her underclothes, look at her books . . . it was somehow obscene. And ridiculous. But if he could pull off some miracle . . . and he had known where the room was.

Linton spent about forty-five minutes with Shirley's things; when he was finished the room looked as if it had been ransacked. Well, Alison thought, it *has* been ransacked.

"That will do," Linton said.

"Can I tell the maids to tidy up?"

"Yes," he said. "I shall not need it further. Now I wish to see the rest of your household."

She took him downstairs again, to the breakfast room,

where everyone was gathered somewhat anxiously.

"Do you wish them lined up?" she asked.

"That will not be necessary. But I would like them to be silent."

Alison looked from face to face. Pat was only just sub-duing a laugh. Stephanie looked angry, Harry bewildered. Hugo also looked angry, Ben and Jonny disinterested. Joanne Wallburn was totally bemused. David looked utterly contemptuous. And Charlene looked anxious, as well she might, as it was she who had recommended the man.

Linton walked slowly round the room, pausing before each person, some longer than others. He had not asked to be introduced to anyone, and although perhaps he could tell which were Alison's children, he could have no idea of the place of the others in the household. Yet he stopped for longer than usual in front of Jonny, and Alison's felt her muscles tensing. Then he also stopped for several seconds in front of Hugo. Joanne Wallburn he ignored completely, but David also was subjected to a searching stare.

"Now I would like to be alone," he announced.

"Here?"

"No, I will go back upstairs to the girl's room."

"Very well. Do you know the way?"

"Of course, Mrs Grange. I knew the way before I ever entered your house."

Which she had to admit he had.

He left the room, and there was an audible sigh of relief.

"He'd better produce the goods, after all of that," Ben remarked.

"How long does he usually take?" Alison asked the minders.

"It is impossible to say how long he will take, madam," said one of the woman.

"Well, then, I suggest we all get on with living our lives, as best we can," Alison decided. "Mrs Wallburn, perhaps

419

you'd come and sit with me on the terrace."

"Oh. Ah . . ." Joanne Wallburn looked at Ben in alarm.

"Alone," Alison told her.

"Now, Mom . . ."

"I think we have things to talk about." Alison went to the door, and after a moment's hesitation, Joanne joined her.

So did David. "Do you think we should let the police know what we are doing, Mrs Pat?" he muttered.

"No way. That fellow Broughton will assume we're mad as March Hares, and I'm not sure he won't be right. We'll wait and see what our friend comes up with."

He wandered off, looking more disturbed than ever.

Jonny was also waiting to speak with her. "Would you like me to push off?"

"Do you wish to?"

"Well, no."

"Then stay. This business should be finished soon."

"And you're expecting the finger to point at me."

"Jonny," Alison said. "Relax, for God's sake." She went out on to the terrace, Joanne Wallburn following her.

"I really am most terribly sorry to have caused all this commotion at such a time," Joanne ventured.

"I'm not sure it would have made any difference whenever it happened," Alison pointed out. "We'll sit over there."

She sat on the farthest bench from the door, and after another brief hesitation, Joanne sat beside her.

"Now tell me," Alison said. "What you want."

"Want, Mrs Grange? I'm in love with your son."

Alison gazed at her. "May I ask how old you are, Mrs Wallburn?"

Joanne flushed. "I'm twenty-four."

"I presume you can prove that?"

"I have a passport."

"And I presume you have seen Ben's passport."

420

"I'm six years older. That doesn't mean I can't love him."

"Oh, quite. Just put a figure on it, will you?"

Joanne stared at her. "I don't want any *money*."

"But you know that, married to him, you are going to come in to an awful lot. Look, at present prices, Ben is due approximately seven hundred thousand dollars on his twenty-first birthday. That is still three years away, and three years is a long time in the life of an eighteen-year-old. Now, if you are determined to keep your hooks in him, you may get away with it. I can do nothing about his inheritance, from his father's estate. So you're home and dry, with seven hundred thousand. Unless in the three years, three years in which I promise you I will bring every possible pressure to bear on him, he happens to find someone more his own age, and perhaps, more attractive than you. Are you still with me?"

"Mrs Grange," Joanne said. "You are a shit."

Now, where had she heard such a comment before?

"The question is, therefore, which is your cut-off point. I should think a million dollars would be about right. I will write you a cheque for a million dollars, here and now, if you will simply leave this house and promise me never to attempt to get in touch with my son again, and to resist any attempts of Ben to get in touch with you. A million dollars, Joanne. Six zeroes, with a one on the left hand end. Think about it. Do you realise that if you never even invested that kind of money, but left it in a mattress under the bed, you could still spend twenty-five thousand a year for forty years before going broke? And," she went on, "just in case you are thinking, screw the old bag, she's worth a hundred times that, with a fifth at least coming to Ben, let me tell you that if you don't accept my offer my Will gets altered tomorrow, to leave Ben not a red cent more than that seven hundred thousand."

"And if I take the money, make all the promises, and then still see Ben?"

"Oh, when you take the money, Joanne, you are going to do it very publicly, and Ben will know just why you are taking it."

Joanne Wallburn stood up. "Like I said, Mrs Grange, you are out of touch. Okay, so everyone knows you're the richest woman in the world, save the Queen and the Queen of Holland. And I guess you'll put the same point to Ben. You may win. I don't know how strong he is. I don't know how important having a lot of money is to him. I also know I'm on a hiding to nothing, going for a guy six years younger than myself. But that's up to Ben. I'm going to leave here now. Ben will know where to find me." She got up. "I'm sorry about your daughter, Mrs Grange. Ben has told me what a sweet kid she is. I'll pray she comes back to you safe and sound."

Alison stared at her. "You mean you don't want any money?"

"No," Joanne said, and went towards the house.

Alison stood up in turn, undecided whether to throw something at her or run after her, and watched David coming out of the breakfast room.

"Mrs Pat!" he shouted. "Linton has something!"

Alison ran past Joanne to reach the house. Linton had come downstairs, and was sitting in the breakfast room, his head in his hands.

The family had gathered around him, but they made way for their mother.

"What is it?" Alison demanded.

Linton gave a kind of groan. "I see a . . . a house," he said.

"What kind of house?"

"I see animals . . . a cow. No, several cows."

"A farmhouse!" Charlene shouted.

"Where?" Hugo demanded.

Linton shook his head. "There are mountains . . ."

"Scotland," Stephanie suggested.

"Or the Lake District," Pat objected.

"What about Wales?" Ben had gone to the doorway to be with Joanne.

"Several peaks, two very high," Linton said.

"Snowdon, and Glyder Fawr. Has to be," Ben shouted. "The school mountaineering group went there last summer. Where do the peaks lie, in relation to the farmhouse?"

Linton stared at the floor. "There is a castle," he said. "A very large castle. The farmhouse is between the mountains and the castle."

"Caernarvon," Ben said. "The farmhouse is on the north side of the mountains. Can the farmhouse see the castle?"

"I do not think so," Linton said. "I cannot see them together."

"Right."

"Can you find this place?" David asked Ben.

"Sure I can. I know where it is, within a few miles. So we have to knock up every farmhouse in the area. We can do it."

David looked at Alison. "The police?" he asked again.

Alison hesitated. She still couldn't believe it. "You say you see these places, Mr Linton. Can you see my daughter?"

"I can see a girl, Mrs Grange. Well, a woman, really. With long yellow hair, curling . . ."

"Is she alive?" Alison shouted. "Unhurt?"

Linton closed his eyes for several seconds. "Yes," he said at last. "She is alive, and I believe she is unhurt."

"Yippee! The hell with the police," Ben cried. "We'll go out there on our own. Heck, Mom, Harry and I, Hugo and David can take care of any kidnappers."

"And me," Stephanie declared.

"Count me in," Jonny said quietly.

"I think we can manage it, Mr Carter," David said.

Jonny looked at Alison.

"For God's sake," Alison said. "Will you two stop this fighting? We are all going."

423

"Without telling the police?" Charlene said doubtfully.

"That's right. We can call them when we find something."

"These people have guns. You all got guns?"

"There are a couple of shotguns in the gunroom," David said. "We'll take those."

Charlene sighed. "So I'd better come along as well, to pick up the pieces."

"You don't have to," Alison told her.

"You think I'm gonna let you go up into those mountains by yourself, Mrs Pat?"

"May I come too?" Joanne asked.

"Well . . ." Alison shrugged. "Why not. Mr Linton, what do I owe you."

"One thousand pounds, Mrs Grange. And another thousand when you find your daughter."

"But you're not sure we're going to," Pat pointed out. "Or you'd claim the two thousand now."

Linton gave the boy a tired and utterly contemptuous look, then turned back to Alison. "That's my fee, Mrs Grange."

Alison sat at her desk and wrote out two cheques, the second postdated to the next day. "There you are. And thank you."

Linton looked surprised. "If you don't find her . . ."

"I will stop payment on the second cheque. Now, if you'll excuse me, Mr Linton, we have things to do."

She decided they would need both cars, the Rolls and the estate. They were just getting themselves organised, when there was a hooting of horns, and a taxi drove into the yard. Out of it stepped Carlo Rubio and two henchmen.

"Carlo!" Alison screamed, and was folded in his arms, while the others looked on in scandalised amazement.

"Little lady, I came as soon as I could," Carlo said. "Where are you off to?"

Alison explained as briefly as she could.

"Right," Carlo said. "We're with you."

"I must warn you, it could be dangerous," Alison said.

"Shucks, little lady, that's all right with us." He showed her his automatic pistol. "The boys have one each as well. If anyone gets in our way, we're gonna waste them right away."

"Carlo," Alison said. "How did you get those things into the country?"

Carlo grinned. "We got ways. Now, let's go."

"Ah, excuse me, Mr Rubio," David ventured. "But there's not a lot of room."

"So what? I have a car. You . . ." he told the taxi driver, "are hired for the day."

"To go where?"

Carlo looked at Alison.

"Snowdonia."

"Right. You know where that is, bud?"

The taxi-driver gulped. "That's a long way, guv."

"Like I said, the day."

"What I mean is, it can't be metered, see? Like the drive down here couldn't be metered. It has to be negotiable."

"Everything in life's negotiable," Carlo said. "A hundred pounds. Two hundred if it's an overnight trip."

"You're on," said the driver. "I'll just have to make a phone call."

"When we stop for lunch," Carlo told him. "Let's go."

Linton and his people had come on to the terrace to watch them embark.

"Don't you think we should take him with us, Mom?" Ben asked. "When we're close to the place, maybe he can pinpoint it for us."

Alison looked at Charlene.

"I don't think it makes too much difference how close he is to the spot, Mrs Pat," Charlene said.

"Then let's go."

David drove the Rolls, with Alison, Jonny, and the three younger children. Ben and Joanne and Charlene followed in the estate car, with Hugo driving. Rubio and his henchmen in the taxi. By now the policemen in the cellar had discovered that something was going on and two of them had emerged on to the terrace. Alison merely waved at them as she drove away. She did not doubt the telephone wires would be humming, but they would have to be very quick.

Alison opted to drive across country, via Haslemere, Alton, Basingstoke and Newbury, where she could pick up the A34 for Birmingham. They bought sandwiches in Newbury, when Alison called home to discover if there had been any telephone calls, especially, of course, a ransom demand. But there had been nothing.

"Kind of makes you think Linton knew what he was talking about," Jonny suggested.

"So let's go. But say, when is this country gonna get decent roads?" Carlo complained.

"They keep talking about them," Alison explained.

Out of Birmingham they picked up the A5, but it was past five that afternoon before they reached Betws-y-Coed, with the North Wales countryside rolling desolately to either side, dotted with grazing sheep, and Snowden rising stark and high on their front left, glowing in the afternoon sunlight, for it was a perfect day.

They found a real estate agency still open.

"We're thinking of buying up here," David told the one remaining clerk, who was in the middle of locking up.

"I'll just get you out a list."

"We're actually looking for a farmhouse. Someplace rather private, with immediate vacant possession."

The young man grinned. "Shame we don't have more of them!"

"Whaddya mean?" Carlo asked. With Alison he had accompanied David into the office. "Someone else been looking for one?"

"That's right," the clerk said. "And bought it, too."

"When?" Alison shouted.

"Just a week back. It was derelict. I'm afraid we don't have any more with that immediate possession."

Alison looked at David.

"Now that's a shame," David remarked. "A week, you say. The new owner moved in yet?"

"Not so far as I know."

"You don't suppose he might like a quick resale?"

"Well, I don't know about that, sir."

"But he might. Tell us where it is, so we can have a look at it."

"Well, it's not far. You follow the road to Bangor, but turn off at Capel Curis. That takes you through the Pass of Llanberis, between Snowdon and Glyudr Fawr. Just through the pass, but before you reach Llanberis itself, there's a lane down to your fight, to Llyn Padarn. The farm is on the shores of the lake. It was an estate sale, you know, and this man snapped it up."

"Can you tell us anything about him?" Alison asked. "The new owner?"

"Not really, ma'am. The sale was handled by a lawyer's office, and was in the name of a company."

"You mean you don't even know what the owner looks like?"

"I'm afraid not."

"Well, we'll just take a look," David said. "Presumably there's a caretaker?"

The clerk shook his head. "The place is just locked up. Odd, really. It wasn't all that cheap."

"Thanks anyway," David said, and led them outside.

"Think that's our man?" Carlo demanded.

"It's the best bet we have," David said. "Everything looks right." He grinned. "That's how Mrs Pat and I handle all of our property transactions, when we don't want anyone to know who actually owns the place."

"Do we?" Alison asked.

They followed the road as directed through increasingly wild and rugged scenery, traversed the pass, and came to a lane leading to the right.

"Think this is it?" Alison asked.

"Has to be," David said.

Rubio's taxi came bumping up abeam, Rubio waving. The cars stopped, and they all got out.

"You reckon this is the place?" Rubio asked.

David nodded. "We're about a quarter of a mile from the lake."

"Then we don't really want to drive up like some circus," Rubio pointed out.

"That's right," Jonny said. "This is a business for the men, Alison."

"You can forget that. I'm going in."

"Attagirl," Rubio said. "You reckon there's another road out of here?"

"I shouldn't think so," David said.

"Okay, here's how we're gonna play it. Park that wagon right across the road."

Hugo obliged.

"Right. Jimmy lad, you're gonna stay here, and we need another man, with a shotgun. You'll do, fella."

"Me?" Hugo demanded.

"You're our backstop, see. If anyone comes haring down this lane, it's up to you to stop 'em. Let 'em hit the wagon if they like, but stop 'em and hold 'em."

Hugo looked at Alison.

"Mr Rubio is in charge, Hugo," she said. She reckoned Carlo had done this sort of thing before.

"Right," Rubio said. "Now you . . . what's your name, anyway?"

"Jonathan Carter," Jonny said.

Rubio raised his eyebrows. "Right. You work round to the right, with the other shotgun. Take the two boys with you. Now your business is just to stop anyone escaping on the lake. You're not to get involved in any shoot-out, right?"

Jonny nodded.

"I'll go with them," Joanne Wallburn said, as Ben and Pat and Harry moved beside Jonny.

"Sure, honey," Rubio said. "Just keep your head down. Now, then, the rest of us are going to walk up to the house. But you three . . ." he looked from Alison to Charlene to a breathless Stephanie, "are going to lag well behind. It don't make no sense, little lady, for us to get your daughter back at the same time as you're on your way to hospital with a hole in the head. Right?"

Alison knew he was right. "But you're risking a hole in the head."

He grinned. "I've been risking that since I was a kid, and nobody's put one there, yet." He looked at David. "You wanna stay and look after the girls?"

"If you don't mind, Mr Rubio, I'd like to come with you."

Carlo looked at Alison. Make him stay, she wanted to say. But he'd never forgive her.

"Just take care of him," she said.

"Sure. You be ready to hit the deck. Check the hardware, boys."

The two bodyguards examined their automatics, and Carlo did the same.

"Okay," he said.

Alison felt quite unreal. She looked at Hugo, who was out of the parked estate car and standing by the front, his shotgun resting on the bonnet. Carlo's henchman, Jimmy, stood at the back of the car.

Jonny and the boys and Joanne had already disappeared into the trees.

And Carlo, with his other bodyguard and David, was walking down the track to the lake. Her people, she thought. Rallying round. She felt an enormous glow of pride. And confidence.

"I'm scared stiff," Charlene confessed. "You scared, Mrs Pat?"

"I think we're all scared," Alison agreed, and held Stephanie's hand as they followed the men behind the trees.

Five minutes later they saw the glint of the water, and

429

saw too that the three men had stopped, still in the shade of the trees, and were inspecting the house, which now came into sight for them as well.

It was a rather ramshackle place, and certainly wore an air of abandonment. It must have been some time since it had been used as a farm, Alison decided. The doors to the various pens and barns were open, creaking in the gentle breeze. Yet it was in a delightful spot, looking out at the lake, and surrounded by trees. Alison could understand the agent's disappointment that nothing had been done with it.

"It might upset whoever's in there if three guys were to walk up to it," Carlo decided. "So we need a front. Charlie."

The bodyguard nodded, but David interrupted. "I'll do it."

"Those guys may be trigger happy."

"I'll be careful."

"But there isn't anybody there," Alison said. "No cars, no nothing."

"Don't mean a thing, little lady," Carlo told her. "Okay, Dave, let's move. Don't forget to hit the dirt at the first sign of trouble. We're covering you."

David was clearly nervous. He was sweating as he stood up, and cleaned his glasses before stepping out of the trees. But he was also determined to prove himself to her, Alison knew. She only hoped he didn't get hurt.

They knelt amidst the ferns and watched him walk along the track, and then turn up to the sagging gate. This was closed, but he pushed it open and went up the path to the porch of the house itself. He knocked on the door, and waited, looking right and left, and up at the shuttered windows as well, seeking any sign of movement.

He was terribly exposed, standing there.

He knocked again, and again, then turned and looked back at the trees.

"Shit!" Carlo commented. "Looks like a dud. But we'd better have a look. You girls stay well back."

430

He and Charlie led the way, pistols in hand. The three women followed some fifty yards behind.

David came down the slope towards them. "There's no reply to my knock. But come over here."

He led them into the yard, pointed at the fresh wheeltracks.

"*Someone* has been here pretty recently."

"Could just have been the owner's agent," Carlo pointed out. "What do you reckon, little lady?"

Alison stared at the tracks. "There'd be no hope of following these?"

"Not once he hits the surfaced road, no."

"I think we should have a look inside," David said.

"The door open?" Carlo asked.

"It's locked. But I'm pretty sure it can be forced."

"Then we're on a burglary charge."

David looked at the gun in the mobster's hand. "That bother you?"

Carlo looked at Alison.

"We should've brought that man Linton," Stephanie said. "He'd know."

Alison looked at David.

"We're looking for your daughter, Mrs Pat, and we have reason to believe she could be, or have been, in this building. If necessary we'll produce Linton in court. Nobody is going to lean too heavily on you for wishing to make sure."

"Right," Alison agreed. "Let's go in, Carlo."

"Charlie?"

Charlie inspected the lock. "One bullet," he recommended.

"Then you'll be in trouble for carrying guns," David pointed out. "I think a jemmy would be easier."

He and Charlie hunted in the sheds, and came back with a chisel, a hammer, and a screwdriver. It took only a couple of blows to smash the lock.

The door swung inwards, and they looked at a hallway, with stairs leading up, and doors to either side leading to

431

reception rooms. The floor was dirty and dusty, as was the decrepit furniture. A rat peered at them from the kitchen at the back of the hallway, and then scuttled away.

"Grim," Carlo remarked. "Spread out."

"I'll check upstairs," David said.

"You go with him, Charlie," Carlo commanded. "I'll take a look out back."

Alison turned aside into the front room. She felt so painfully apprehensive she almost wanted to vomit. To imagine Shirley being brought to a dump like this! Only she hadn't, surely. Yet there were the tracks outside, and inside the dust had in many places been scraped away, not deliberately, but by someone, or several people, moving through it.

And Linton had seen it!

She heard a sound, and turned, sharply. Charlie stood there, the most terrible expression on his face.

"Mrs Grange . . ."

Alison dashed past him and up the stairs, while Carlo ran in from the back. Alison reached the top of the stairs, and nearly fell over David, who was kneeling there, bent double. For a ghastly moment she thought he had somehow been shot, then she realised he was vomiting.

She made to step past him, and he caught her leg.

"Don't!" he gasped. "Don't go in there."

Alison jerked her leg free, almost fell into the doorway, and gazed at her daughter. Shirley had been dead for very nearly twenty-four hours.

And there were rats.

CHAPTER 15

Judgement Day

Rubio burst past Alison, sending her crashing against the wall. He bent over the naked body on the bed, then turned back.

"Get her out of here," he snapped at Charlie, who had followed him up the stairs.

"My daughter!" Alison shrieked.

"You can't help her now, Mrs Grange," Charlie said, virtually carrying her back down the stairs, past the still stricken David.

Charlene stood at the foot, gazing up. "She's not . . . oh, Jesus!" she cried.

She was as stricken as David.

Stephanie was just staring, with huge round eyes.

Charlie carried Alison into the front room and sat her in a dusty chair. He took a packet of cigarettes from his pocket and offered her one, and she shook her head, and tried to get up again. Gently he pushed her back into the chair.

"My daughter . . ."

She gazed at Carlo, who stood in the doorway.

"We'll have to get the cops," Carlo said.

"How . . ."

"I don't know for sure. I guess she was roughed

up a bit, but . . . look, little lady, you gotta handle this."

Alison's shoulders hunched.

Charlie summoned the others. There was no telephone at the farm, so Jimmy drove into Llanberis to find a policemen. Everyone save Rubio and his men seemed too shattered to understand what had happened.

David had stopped being sick, but he still looked as if someone had dropped a very heavy weight on his head. So did Charlene.

Hugo was even worse, openly crying.

Jonny just looked utterly helpless.

The children took it better. Ben sat with his arm round his mother; Joanne Walburn discreetly kept in the background. Stephanie sat on her other side. Pat and Harry stood together, staring at her.

Carlo took complete control, in the circumstances. He and Charlie covered Shirley's body up, but without actually touching her.

"The cops will want to look at her exactly as she is, little lady," Carlo told Alison. "I'm sorry, but there it is."

Memory galloped back to the day Pat had died. So many people had died. For what? A few hundred million dollars?

Thoughts chased themselves through her mind, but she was in no shape properly to evaluate them.

How *had* Linton known where Shirley was to be found? But Linton had been equally positive she had been alive . . . when she must have been already dead!

The shock of everyone around her . . . some more than others.

The massive control of Carlo Rubio, who had once ordered her to be murdered.

The feeling of closeness to her remaining family.

But above all, the futility of it all. Only vengeance mattered now.

The police arrived, and an ambulance. And reporters. There were interviews, firstly with the police, who were almost frighteningly understanding and sympathetic. The press was more probing, but they too were prepared to respect Alison's grief.

Detective Inspector Broughton was less pleased with the situation, when at last Alison and the family had been returned to Kittering; Shirley's body remained in Wales for a post mortem.

"Rushing off like that," he said. "On your own, with a bunch of American gunmen . . ."

"Look, they're friends of mine," she snapped.

"You keep some strange company. Do you know who this fellow Rubio is?"

"Yes, Inspector, I do. He tried to kill me once."

"But now he's your friend. Has it occurred to you that he may well have organised the kidnapping?"

"That is absolute nonsense."

"Because he's your friend? Who happened to know where to go to find Miss Grange?"

"Because Carlo would have done it for the money, and there was no ransom demand. Whoever kidnapped Shirley was out for revenge."

"Revenge for what?"

"I don't know. Yet."

"An enemy of yours? Or your first husband's?"

"I would have said my first husband. Except . . ."

"What?"

"Well, there's not a lot of mileage to be gained by avenging yourself on a dead man."

"Absolutely. If it was revenge, and I agree with you, because according to our autopsy report whoever did it murdered your daughter fairly soon after the kidnapping . . ."

435

"How?"

"How?"

"Inspector, no one has as yet told me how my daughter died."

"Oh. Ah . . . actually, it was a heart attack. I received the report this morning."

"Oh."

"Brought on by an excessive administration of a sedative drug. She was injected soon after she was kidnapped, and then again at regular intervals, and . . . I'm afraid she just succumbed."

There was almost a sense of relief. "Then she wasn't . . . but she was naked when we found her."

Broughton coughed with embarrassment.

"While she was *drugged*?" Alison screamed.

"Well . . . she must have had some lucid moments. I mean, there was food in her stomach, so shortly before her death she had eaten a meal . . . my God, Mrs Grange, we are dealing with an animal. Probably several animals."

"Several animals," Alison said quietly. "Intelligent animals, Inspector, who could plan such a kidnapping down to the last detail, but who never intended to ask a ransom, just to murder my daughter."

"I don't think that's absolutely right, Mrs Grange. I think Shirley's death was an accident."

"An accident?"

"One doesn't normally kill someone by use of a sedative drug. What I mean is, if the kidnappers had intended to kill your daughter from the beginning, well, why not just shoot her on the spot, or certainly when they got her alone. My estimate of the situation is that they mishandled the drug."

"And the sexual abuse? Is this normal?"

"Well, no. Not in a kidnapping for ransom. I never did think it was that kind of kidnapping, though, Mrs Grange. I am merely saying that I think your daughter may have died accidentally. At least before the kidnapper intended that she should."

436

"You are being enormously reassuring, Inspector," Alison commented, with savage sarcasm. "Whatever you *think*, my daughter is dead. And you do not appear to be any closer to making an arrest."

"Which is what you want more than anything?" he said angrily.

Alison stared at him. "At this moment, Inspector, yes. I would have paid any sum of money to get Shirley back. I was never given that opportunity. Now I want the people who did it, and I want them to hang. So . . . when are they going to do that?"

He gave a little gulp at the vehemence in her tone. "You will have to help us there."

"Tell me."

"Mrs Grange, either this was purely and simply a kidnapping for money which went dreadfully wrong, in which case we have a very long and possibly fruitless investigation ahead of us, or it was a kidnapping for revenge, which was always intended to end in your daughter's death . . . even if that was premature. If the latter is the case, as I have always held . . . the key to an early arrest must lie with you."

"What am I supposed to do?" Alison shouted.

"Mr Carter accompanied you to Wales."

"That's right. And he was as shocked as everyone by what we found."

"Everyone was shocked. Including Mr Rubio?"

"I shouldn't think Mr Rubio was shocked."

"Is that why he took control of the situation?"

"Yes. He took control of the situation. Why haven't you questioned the man Linton? He knew where she was."

"I haven't questioned the man Linton, Mrs Grange, because the man Linton has disappeared."

Alison frowned at him. "But . . . he's an international figure."

"No one, apart from you, has ever heard of him, Mrs Grange."

Alison stared at him in total consternation.

"So perhaps that is a lead. Who put you on to him?"

Alison opened her mouth, and then closed it again.

"It was a member of your staff, was it not?" Broughton pressed.

Alison licked her lips. She just could not believe that Charlene would wish to harm her. Or Shirley. Besides, what was the point? The idea that Charlene would be a party to Shirley's murder just to get at her . . . they were friends. They had always been friends.

And Charlene had been as upset as anyone at what had happened. More upset than anyone, save perhaps for David.

"I would like the name, Mrs Grange," Broughton pressed. "I can easily find it out, you know."

"It . . . it was my companion."

"Companion?"

"She used to be my children's nurse. Now she . . . well, she's my maid. But she's much more than a maid."

"You mean the black woman."

Alison glared at him. "Yes, I mean the black woman."

"And she recommended Linton," Broughton said thoughtfully.

"Yes. Yes, she did. But I wish to speak with her before you do."

"I'm not sure that's wise, Mrs Grange."

"It's what I want," Alison said positively.

"Oh, Mrs Pat," Charlene said. "When I think . . . I loved that girl, really I did."

"I know you did," Alison said. If she had not had sufficient proof of it over the years, she could remember Charlene's grief when Shirley had been discovered dead. "Did you know Linton was a fraud?"

"A fraud?"

Alison studied her face with a sinking heart; Charlene looked frightened. "He has disappeared."

"That means he's a fraud? Maybe he don't want any publicity."

"Maybe. Charlene . . ." she held her friend's hands. "How did you hear of him?"

"Some people I met . . . they were speaking of him."

"What people?"

"I met them in the pub."

"Did you know their names?"

"No, Mrs Pat. We didn't really get around to introducing each other. You know what the English are like. But they offered to buy me a drink, and then we got talking, and the subject of clairvoyance came up."

"They brought it up?"

"Well, yes, Mrs Pat. But I've always been interested in that kind of thing."

"These people, were they men or women?"

Charlene looked embarrassed. "Well, they were two men, Mrs Pat."

"Would you know them again?"

"Oh, sure."

"And was this before, or after, Shirley was kidnapped?"

"Well, before, Mrs Pat. Maybe a week ago."

What a carefully laid plan, she thought. But why? That was what haunted her. She just could not believe that anyone would take the life of an innocent young girl to strike at her mother, even if she could believe that there was anyone in the world who could possibly hate her enough to contemplate something like that. Therefore Broughton had to be right, and Shirley's death an accident.

But her kidnapping hadn't been an accident. And there had been no ransom demand.

And Charlene? But she knew her old friend needed to clear herself completely, for them ever to regain their old rapport.

"You must tell the inspector exactly what you have told me," she said.

* * *

"Will Charlene's evidence be helpful?" Alison asked Broughton.

"I doubt it."

"Two men, with descriptions . . ."

"I don't think they exist, Mrs Grange."

Alison frowned at him. "What do you mean?"

"I think your . . . friend, made them up. I think she is in partnership with Linton."

Alison still refused to accept what her heart and her mind told her had to be the truth. "That's the most absurd thing I have ever heard. Do you know how long Charlene and I have been friends? For God's sake, nearly twenty years. Since before Shirley was born!"

"You've been together all of that time?"

"Yes. Well . . . we were separated for six years during the War and just after. But that was my husband's decision. My first husband. As soon as I could I called Charlene back again."

"Six years," Broughton mused. "Do you have any idea what Miss Gorman was doing in that time?"

"Well, I don't. But I can find out."

"I would appreciate that, as she's unlikely to tell me."

"Are you proposing to arrest her?"

"I have no evidence against her, Mrs Grange. No evidence that would stand up in court. Just a gut feeling. But . . . may I put one or two points to you?"

"I imagine you are going to."

"Well, Mrs Grange, as you may imagine, I did some looking into your background over the past couple of days. You're one of the richest women in the world, and your first husband before you was the richest man in the world. Am I right?"

"Yes."

"Like most very rich people, you have surrounded yourself with apparently faithful employees. Right?"

He might have been Inspector Brillot, in the hospital outside Nice.

440

"Just what are you driving at?"

"Your first husband was shot, Mrs Grange. Mr Carter was convicted of that crime. But you always maintained he was innocent. If he was innocent, someone else had to have done it. Someone close to Mr Grange."

"That's history, Inspector."

"Then you got involved with one of Rubio's hatchetmen. Am I right? And nearly got yourself killed."

"I don't see what this has to do with Shirley, Inspector."

"I'm just trying to make the point that it seems to me all of your troubles, and some of them are big ones, originate close to home. You want to think about that, Mrs Grange." He stood up. "I'd be grateful for any information you may be able to let me have about Miss Gorman."

But Alison's mind still rejected the obvious, simply because, if it were true, there were so many other rocks on which she had built her life which had to be reassessed.

"Look, Inspector, Charlene was just about the most upset person there when we found Shirley."

"Which fits my theory that your daughter wasn't intended to die. Right then."

"And you think she master-minded the whole thing, all on her own? That she created Linton?"

"Of course I do not think that, Mrs Grange. She was here with you when your daughter was taken. So there are at least two other people involved. A woman . . . well we have no leads there. And a big man. You know, you could do worse than check up if Miss Gorman and Mr Carter ever had any relations during the War. You might find that very interesting."

"You probably haven't noticed that Mr Carter has white hair, Inspector."

"He could've worn a wig."

"But you didn't find a male wig amongst the props discarded in the car."

"That doesn't necessarily mean a thing," Broughton told her, and left.

After he had gone Alison sat for several minutes staring at the wall. What he had said was so terrifyingly possible. All of her troubles had indeed started in her own backyard, just as they had started in Pat's own back yard.

Charlene and Jonny? Impossible. But . . . she had only Jonny's word for it that he had served in the RAF. Jonny . . . she raised her head, because there he was, standing in the doorway.

He looked embarrassed. "Alison . . ."

Alison drew a long breath. "Come in, Jonny. And close the door, please."

He frowned as he obeyed her.

"What did you want to see me about?"

"Well . . ." he sat opposite her, every movement anxious. Guilty? "I feel such a fifth wheel. I mean, everyone else has something to do around here, even if it's just to mourn. I'm not family . . ."

"And you don't mourn," she said softly.

His head jerked. "What do you mean?"

"I don't suppose you ever laid eyes on Shirley in your life," Alison pointed out, gazing at him.

"Well . . . I suppose not. That doesn't mean I can't feel dreadfully sorry about what happened; she's your daughter."

"She *was* my daughter," Alison said absently. "How well do you know Charlene, Jonny?"

"Charlene? Oh you mean the black woman."

"Yes, I mean the black woman."

"Know her?"

"Did you know that the police have discovered that Linton is a fraud?"

"Well, I never thought he was up to much."

"But he knew where Shirley was."

442

Jonny snapped his fingers. "And Charlene recommended him. I see what you're driving at."

"But Charlene was here with me when Shirley was kidnapped," Alison pointed out.

"Yes, but she could still have known where Shirley was going to be taken."

"Agreed. However, that still leaves us no closer to the actual kidnappers. Or to why? The Inspector thinks that Shirley died by accident. If that is so, why did the kidnappers wish to lead me to her? Linton was set up long before she could have died. And he was positive she was still alive. The kidnappers wanted me to find her, alive, forty-eight hours after she had been taken. Why?"

"I have no idea."

"Haven't you, Jonny?"

He stared at her. "You think I . . . good God!"

"For God's sake!" she screamed at him. "I don't know what to think! Shirley was taken by a big man. You're a big man. Pat was shot by someone who knew how to get into The Keep. You could have known that. You could have had an accomplice, who killed Sanchez afterwards. Oh, God, to know the truth. Jonny . . . did you kill Pat?"

He stared at her. "You've never actually asked me that before."

"I'm asking you now."

"Is my answer going to make any difference?" His face was dark with anger.

"I'd like to hear it."

"You can go to hell!" He got up.

"Jonny," she said. "If you did kill Pat, or even more, if you were responsible for Shirley's kidnapping and death, I am going to see that you hang."

He was already at the door. Now he looked back at her. "I'm sure that you will. But I suggest you look closer to home. No, Alison, I did not kill Pat. If I'd meant to do that, I'd have walked up to him and looked him in the eye while I squeezed the trigger, not crept up on him in the middle of the night. And just for the record, I did not kidnap Shirley either. If I was going to rape any member of your family it would be you, because I'm stupid enough to be in love with you."

She got up herself. "Jonny . . ."

But the door had slammed behind him.

Alison hurled herself full length on to the sofa, and lay there, her brain tumbling, her eyes stinging. She felt sick. Once she had thought that everything Pat had touched had turned to gold. But it hadn't, really. It had actually turned into a kind of poisonous miasma which affected the lives of everyone even remotely connected with it.

Now . . .

She raised her head at the gentle tap. "Who is it?"

"David."

"Come in, David." She swung her legs to the floor, straightened her skirt.

He looked at once embarrassed and apprehensive, as always.

"Shirley's body is here."

"Oh, God!" Alison sat up. "Must I . . ."

"No. Not unless to wish to."

Alison drew a long breath. "I wish to. Is she . . . does she . . ."

"She looks asleep, Alison. Just asleep."

Alison stood up.

"The vicar rang, about the cremation . . ."

"Tomorrow."

"Yes. That's what I told him. I told him it would be a very small affair. I asked him not to release news of it to anyone. Of course, the way those bastards are hanging around the house, we won't be able to avoid them altogether . . ." his voice tailed away as he could see she was only half listening. "I saw Carter get into that hired car of his and drive off. He wasn't looking very happy."

"No," Alison agreed.

"Trouble?"

Alison told him of her conversations with Broughton and Jonny, although she omitted Jonny's parting remarks. He listened with his usual quiet attention. When she was finished, he asked, "You believe that is what happened?"

"I wish I could believe something, David. Shirley is dead. Somebody killed her. Maybe he or she didn't intend to do it, but in my book somebody murdered my daughter."

"Jonny Carter," he mused. "I did say so all along."

Alison could make no reply to that, because it was true. Her common sense had been bedevilled by her emotions.

"And Charlene," he said, even more thoughtfully. "Have you put this to her?"

"No, I haven't. I don't know how. What am I going to do, Dave?"

"You'd better leave it with me."

"Oh, Dave! I don't know what I'd do without you. What will you do?"

"Well . . . it seems to me the best thing would be for me to scare her a little. Kind of suggest what the police have in mind, and what you have in mind too. That way, she might just react, do something stupid, give us the proof we want."

"It sounds so . . . so cold-blooded."

"If she's guilty, Alison, we're dealing with a cold-blooded person."

Alison sighed, but she knew he was right. Just as she knew that if Charlene's guilt was proved, she would want her old friend to hang. But how she hoped and prayed it would not be proved.

And Jonny? Once again he had disappeared from her life, vowing his love for her. But this time it had to be forever; simply because she did not suppose she would ever *know*, for all his protestations.

She went with David to Shirley's room, where the body lay, concealed beneath a sheet save for the face. It was, as David had promised, a peaceful face, the eyes closed, as was the mouth. Whatever her tormentors, and then the doctor who had performed the autopsy, had done to her, her body was invisible.

Alison stared at her daughter for several moments, then turned away, and encountered Carlo.

"Little lady," he said, and held her in his arms. "I gotta go."

"Where?"

He shrugged. "Back to the States."

"When?"

"Tonight."

"But . . . the funeral . . ."

"Yeah. I'm pretty sore. The fact is, me and Jimmy and Charlie have been deported. Undesirable aliens. All the way from your Home Office."

"Oh, hell," Alison said. "The idiots."

"Well, maybe I am an undesirable alien. I just wish I could stay until tomorrow. Little lady, when next are you gonna be in New York?"

"I don't know, Carlo. I don't know anything right now."

He stared at her for several seconds, then leaned forward and kissed her on the forehead. "I'm always there."

Alison spent the rest of the day alone. She did not even wish to be with her children. There were so many things roaming through her brain.

So many things about Shirley. Shirley, the babe in her womb when she had first met Jonny Carter; she wondered if Jonny had realised that. Shirley, looking at her with those enormous eyes when she had told her and Ben that Pat wasn't ever going to come back. Shirley, laughing and screaming her delight as Paul had taught her how to dive. Shirley, hauling on sheets on board *Roundabout* as if her life depended on it. Shirley, standing to attention and looking so solemn at Broadhurst speech day. And Shirley laughing when she had heard about Ben running away.

Shirley had never had the opportunity to run away. Shirley had never even been kissed . . . except by the man who had taken both her virginity and her life.

Charlene came to see her that afternoon, as she usually did, but she sent her away; least of all did she wish to be with Charlene.

David himself brought her a light supper, sat with her while she ate it. Only David mattered, because only with David could she say whatever came into her mind.

"Have you spoken with Charlene yet?" she asked.

He assumed one of his embarrassed looks. "Actually, no. I kind of thought I'd wait until after the funeral. I haven't even been near her. I mean . . . we don't know what her reaction is going to be."

"Yes," she said. "I'm sure you're right. God, to be able to snap my fingers and put a few things straight. Do you know, I was getting to the stage where I honestly thought I could do that. Do you reckon God is punishing me for such arrogance, Dave?"

"God has nothing to punish you for, Alison."

But she did not feel as reassured as she usually did, when he spoke like that.

Charlene made no effort to come near Alison the following morning, and Aimée helped her mistress to dress. The family was already assembled when she came down, all wearing black dresses or black ties. Pat and Stephanie and Harry were very solemn, standing beside Ben and Joanne Wallburn; Ben was obviously in command. Hugo and David looked as if they were about to burst into tears, while the Funeral Director and his men waited discreetly by the door.

Shirley had already been sealed in her coffin, and now she was taken out to the hearse.

"We'll use both cars," Alison decided. "The four children will drive with me in the Rolls, with Mrs Wallburn. David, will you and Hugo and Aimée and Charlene follow in the estate car?"

"Of course, Mrs Pat. Ah . . ." he looked left and right.

As did Alison. Charlene was not present.

"Maybe she don't want to come," Hugo muttered.

"Well, she is coming," Alison snapped. "Aimée, you go up and tell her I want her down here, right this minute."

"Yes, *madame*." Aimée scuttled up the stairs.

Alison went outside, followed by the children. The cars had already been brought from the garage and were parked behind the hearse, waiting for the signal.

Aimée came back down the stairs. "*Madame*, Charlene's door is locked, and she does not reply when I knock."

Alison looked at David. "You don't think she's run off?"

"Well . . . she could have. But that would be an admission of guilt."

"So is hiding in her room, while Shirley is being cremated," Alison snapped. "Hugo, open that door. Break it down if you have to."

The children shuffled their feet uneasily. They had never seen this side of their mother before, as she had kept her feelings about Paul's betrayal and death secret from them.

But Alison had no intention of letting Charlene off the hook. She waited, walking up and down, while Hugo went upstairs. The thump of the big man's shoulder crashing against the door echoed through the morning.

Then Hugo came down the stairs again, his face ashen. "Mrs Pat . . ."

Alison and David ran up the stairs together. Hugo followed. The children regathered in the hall, looking up.

Alison stood in the doorway of Charlene's room, and gazed at the body lying on the bed, its features stiff in death.

"An admission of guilt," Detective-Inspector Broughton said thoughtfully. "How do you feel, Mrs Grange?"

"How am I supposed to feel, Inspector?" Alison still wore her black dress, soaked in sweat. "I have just buried my daughter, while trying to come to terms with the fact that I have caused one of my most faithful servants to commit suicide. What exactly did she take?"

"It's being analysed now. But we must assume it was the contents of that bottle by her bed. Didn't you know she was using sedatives to sleep?"

"No," Alison said. "She never said anything about that to me."

"Odd. However, there seems no reason for her to commit suicide, unless she was guilty. And if she was guilty, I do not think you have any reason to be upset. She merely anticipated the hangman. We must now see if we can find Carter."

"Does Charlene's death prove anything?"

"Only her own guilt. But the news of it may cause Carter to give us a lead. If he is the person involved, of course. I'll be in touch, Mrs Grange."

"Yes," Alison said. "Do that."

The house was quiet, almost silent. None of the children felt like playing tennis, this afternoon. Alison had no idea what Ben and his Joanne were doing, and she didn't much care. There was just too much roaming around her brain.

"Like a drink?" David hovered in the doorway.

"Not really."

He came in, closed the door. "You mustn't sit here, all by yourself, in the dark."

449

"It's not really dark."

"It soon will be." He switched on the light. "Broughton wasn't particularly helpful."

"No," she agreed. "He wasn't."

David went to the bar, opened a bottle of champagne.

"Don't be vile," she said.

"Medicinal," he pointed out. "You need a lift."

"I need something. And I think I know what it is."

He gave her the glass. "What?"

"Dave, I want out."

He frowned. "Eh?"

"I want to get rid of everything, and just settle down some place, with enough money to live on and nothing more. I want to pay my taxes, and cultivate a little garden, and drive a little car."

"You *are* feeling low." He sat beside her.

"Don't attempt to tease. Or to change my mind."

"I wouldn't dream of it. There's just one point, though: the kids might not like the idea."

"I'm not going to rob my kids. Although God knows, after what I've been through I can't help but feel they'd be better off without a fortune apiece. What I want you to do is set up trusts for them, until they're twenty-five. Everything is to be divided up equally. Leave me just enough, as I said, to live off the invested income."

"Live where?"

"Here. I'm going to sell The Keep, and the New York apartment, and the villa, and the yacht, and this house, and just keep the flat in London."

"Unearned income attracts the top rate of tax in this country. You'd still need a pretty hefty portfolio."

"I understand that. You work it out."

David drank some champagne. "Am I allowed to say something?"

"Sure."

"Promise you're not going to start screaming and fire me again?"

"Oh, David, I'm not likely to be that stupid again . . .

you may not want to go on working for me if I don't have any money."

"I'll always want to work for you, Mrs Pat. What I was going to say was, you're very tired, and very depressed, and that is the last possible time to attempt to make a decision which is going to affect your whole future. You're thirty-eight. You have one hell of a long time to live."

"Watching my children being kidnapped and murdered."

"Your opting out is not going to make any difference to that risk, Alison. But in any event, that's never going to happen again."

"How can you say that?"

"Simply that we are going to make sure it never happens again. Alison . . ." he held her hand. "Don't do it. Please don't do it. You can be happy. You *will* be happy."

She smiled through her tears. "You're going to make sure of that, too?"

"I'm going to make it my life's work. If you'll let me."

He was all she had left.

The children were delighted. Clearly they had put their heads together and decided that what Mom needed more than anything else was a husband. Obviously there could be no question of marriage for several months, but David would in any event have been their first choice as a surrogate father. They had known him all their lives.

And his presence, in his new capacity, made an immediate difference. He sat down with Ben and Joanne, and talked some sense into them.

"I know you're both hot on each other," he told them. "Fair enough. But you're both old enough to understand that there are problems. Now, what I propose is this. Ben has a place waiting for him at Cambridge. It is the wish of both his mother and I that he take up that place, and get his degree. It's a three-year course. During that time you can, if you wish, be engaged. But no marriage until after graduation."

"And during that time you'll be working on him to drop me," Joanne said.

"We won't. You're welcome to visit with us as often as you please. As a matter of fact, you're welcome to move in with us as a member of the family, and come on our travels with us, if that's what you wish."

"Mom agreed to that?" Ben asked in wonderment.

"I have persuaded her to, yes."

"Well, for heaven's sake. Darling . . ."

Joanne still looked doubtful, but she couldn't argue with Ben's enthusiasm.

"Of course she knows she's on a hiding to nothing," David pointed out to Alison. "She's going to be twenty-seven when Ben graduates and comes into his money, and even if she's living here, he's going to be seeing lots of other girls when he's up at Cambridge. And she knows that. While the more he sees her in his own environment, the more he is going to realise she isn't the woman he wants to live the rest of his life with."

"I hope you're right," Alison said.

But she was sure he was going to be. He always was.

There was an enormous amount to be done as letters of condolence poured in from all over the world; most of them were from people Alison had never heard of. She answered them all herself, grateful to know that there were so many people who could attempt to share her grief.

She was opening the mail one morning when she came across a somewhat official looking envelope, carrying a Swiss stamp, and bearing the crest of The Golden Trust it was marked, Most Private and Confidential. David, who as usual was with her, raised his eyebrows as she held it up. "Looks like a charity," he commented. "Probably a begging letter. These people have no sense of propriety."

Alison slit the envelope and took out the sheet of paper inside. It was from a Monsieur Dudevant, who, it appeared, was president of the Trust. She read what he had to say with a slowly slipping jaw.

"Of course you are aware of the terms under which your husband set up this trust, *madame*, and it was in obeying those instructions, never in any way to contact him or you, or to allow the existence of the trust to be known to anyone except us, that I have not written you before, no matter how much I wished to, following the death of Mr Grange, and your own second bereavement.

"However, this latest tragedy, which I know must be the gravest and most heavy burden you have ever had to bear, compels me, for the first and last time, to disobey your husband's ruling and convey to you the deepest sympathy of myself and all my staff. Were the many thousands of handicapped children who have benefitted from your husband's extreme and unique generosity to be aware of where their salvation has come from, I know they too would wish to associate themselves with my sentiments.

"I can only say that your courage has been an inspiration to us all, and to ask you to believe that our thoughts are with you, day and night."

David was frowning at her. "What on earth is it?"

She handed him the letter.

"Good God!" he commented.

Patrick Grange, she thought. The man who wouldn't pay a penny in taxes where he could avoid it, who wouldn't lift a finger to help a soul, who had swindled his first partner and heaven knew how many other people . . . the man everyone had loved to hate, and the man she had wound up hating herself . . . the man who had given four hundred million dollars to charity.

"What are you going to do?" David asked.

"Do?"

"Well . . . this is your money."

453

"No, it's not. We are going to do nothing, Dave. Save utter a little prayer of apology to Pat."

He looked as if he would have argued, then shrugged. "It's your money."

"I'm not going to answer any more of these right now." She got up.

"Where are you off to?" He was anxious.

"Just my room. I'm going to lie down for a while. And have a little cry, I think."

The question of transferring her money into trust funds was tacitly shelved. Alison was suddenly proud of her wealth, for the first time. It was as if Pat had reached out from the grave to comfort her, reassure her. She was almost happy.

She still wanted to leave England, however, and as she had used up her three months for the year in France, and had no desire to go sailing or to enter into any socialising whatsoever, she was left with The Keep. But to her own surprise, regaining the fortress gave her an immense feeling of relief and security. She thought she might even spend the rest of the year here – as there were no tax problems in Mexico – and forego the New York season. She knew she was still suffering from shock, and she just wanted to try to relax.

The children understood this. They all accompanied her to the desert, and went out of their way to please her. Joanne Wallburn was the most attentive of all. Hugo, needless to say, waited on her hand and foot.

While David was the most loving of lovers.

No word was heard from or about Jonny Carter, who had disappeared. Alison did hear from Broughton, but he had been quite unable to find any link between Jonny and the kidnapping of Shirley, or indeed between Jonny and Charlene: there was absolutely no evidence that they had ever even met. Yet it was difficult to suppose that they were not jointly guilty. As David had said, every time

Jonny Carter turned up, the Grange family was faced with catastrophe. Every time he disappeared, life returned to normal.

The thought that he might never be found, as Bert Waller had never been found, that Shirley might remain unavenged, was continually disturbing. If only she could be sure of his guilt, could forget those last words of his.

"If only I could figure out what he could have intended?" Alison told David. "Just to take Shirley, and murder her . . . could any man be that horrible?"

"I think maybe the police were right," David said. "I think Shirley's death was an accident. I think Carter meant to leave you sweating for awhile, before putting in the ransom demand, but something went wrong. After that, well . . . it was a case of getting away with as little damage as possible."

"If that's true . . . we're going to get him, Dave? Aren't we? Somehow?"

"Sure we are," David said. "But there's no point in losing sleep over it, my darling. He'll crop up again, eventually."

With that she supposed she had to be content, and as the summer wore on, the pain gradually dwindled.

"When would you like to get married?" David asked.

"Before the children have to go back to school again. The first Saturday in September."

"Right."

"We don't have to go to a church, do we?"

"Marriage is a civil ceremony in Mexico. We'll have a magistrate come out here, and do it right there in the garden. Would you like that?"

"I think that would be tremendous."

"Then, as soon as the kids have gone, we'll leave on a long honeymoon. Places we've never been before. I'll make all the arrangements."

As usual, she thought. But it was such a comforting feeling. David had taken over her entire life. It was what he enjoyed doing, and she was happy for it. She gave him his head in every way. In fact, almost nothing had changed. He had always had full authority to do whatever he liked with her money, in her name. Now she willingly authorised him to do what he liked, in his own name.

The day before her wedding she sat at the poolside watching the kids swimming, and sipping a rum cocktail. She had bought herself a new outfit, and the flowers were ordered. David was in Mexico City somewhere, making the final arrangements, and she was served by Hugo.

"The big day, creeping up on you, Mrs Pat," Hugo remarked.

"Does that upset you, Hugo?"

"Not this time, Mrs Pat. That Schleyer now, well, we all knew he was a crook. But David, well, he's one of us."

"You can say that again."

"You know what, I reckon that when you're married to him, Mrs Pat, you really will be able to put the past behind you, and live for the future. That's the only way to live, you know."

"You are so right, Hugo. And how I hope you're right."

"You bet I am, Mrs Pat. And for David as well."

"What's he got to put behind him?"

"Well, I guess he must feel pretty guilty about Charlene's suicide."

"Why should David feel guilty about it?"

"Well, you remember, Mrs Pat, you and he talked about it, and he was going to frighten her . . . I'm sorry, but I was mixing drinks and I couldn't help but overhear. I know what he did has been on his mind."

Alison was aware of a sensation she had never known before. A kind of prickling all over her body.

"What did he do, Hugo?"

456

"Well, you know, talking with her, like you agreed. I guess he must've been the last person to see her alive. He couldn't possibly have known she was gonna kill herself."

Now the prickling was like a series of electric shocks, surging outwards from her brain.

"He's never mentioned it to me," she said, her voice seeming to come from very far away. "But of course, he spoke with her the evening she died, didn't he?"

"That's right, Mrs Pat. And you know what, Mrs Pat? I have never seen a man looking so upset as David did when he left her room."

"You saw him?"

"That's right, Mrs Pat."

"You saw him leave Charlene's room. Did he see you?"

"Well, no, Mrs Pat. I was at the far end of the corridor, and like I said, I could see he was upset. I didn't want to intrude."

"Yes, of course," she said. "I can see that it would have upset him."

She left the poolside and went up to her tower room. She was amazed that she could move, so calmly and easily. She knew she should sit down and think, because there was so much to be thought about, so many half-forgotten and quickly dismissed incidents and events, which were dropping into place with thuds which were shaking her whole system. But she didn't want to think. Not until David came home.

In her room she closed all the windows and switched on the air-conditioning; the hum entirely sealed off the room from the rest of the house. Then she did one or two other things before she took off her bathrobe and lay down on the bed. The prickling sensation had not gone away. Rather had it intensified, and although she was naked, lying on a cool bed in a rapidly cooling room, she was sweating.

She lay absolutely still, on her back, her eyes closed, until she heard the door gently open and shut again.

457

"That you, Dave?" she asked.

"That's me."

She opened her eyes, watched him go to the bathroom. She felt no emotion, only an ice-cold intensity, heightened by the prickling sensation.

Perhaps it would go away, when he had answered her questions. The disturbing thing was, she didn't know whether she wanted it to go away or not.

"All fixed?" she asked, when he re-emerged.

"All fixed. It's going to be a great day."

"I'm sure of it. Tell me about Charlene."

He turned, frowning. "You're not still brooding on that. It wasn't your fault. She was guilty as hell."

"I know she was. That was why you killed her, right?"

He came towards the bed, and she slipped her hand beneath the cover to hold the revolver she had earlier placed there.

He stood above her. "Are you out of your mind?"

"No. I'm back in it, Dave. After having been out of it for twelve years."

"Alison . . ."

"Hugo saw you leaving her room, Dave, the evening before the funeral. But you told me you hadn't gone near her, and weren't going to, until *after* the funeral. Why did you lie to me? Because you made her take an overdose."

"Alison . . ." she could almost see his brain working, behind his eyes.

"I'd like to know the truth, Dave. Do you know, I always counted you as the one person who had never lied to me. But now I know you have been lying to me from the beginning. You shot Pat, didn't you?"

"Now, Alison . . ."

"You just waited for your opportunity, and Jonny's arrival in Mexico gave it to you. You knew all about that secret passage, because you had been in charge of rebuilding The Keep. So you saw your opportunity to kill Pat and pin the murder on Jonny. And then, once Sanchez had given his evidence, you killed him. Just as you killed Charlene when she had served her purpose. I suppose you have already killed the other two kidnappers. What about Linton, is he dead too?"

He was standing absolutely still, staring at her.

"But why did you have to kill Pat, David? Did you rob him?"

His nostrils flared. "I never robbed either Pat or you of a red cent. But Pat robbed my father."

He gave a little gasp, realising what he had just said. While Alison stared at him, penny after penny dropping in her brain.

"Your father was Leighton!"

David hesitated a last time, then shrugged, went to the door, and locked it. "That's right. He lent Pat all his savings; twenty thousand dollars. Pat gave him shares in the mine, told him they'd be worth ten times the investment within five years. But Dad didn't know anything about shares, or mines, come to think of it. He just felt that he was on to a good thing. If only he'd shown them to me. Instead, he sent me to college, and began a business of his own. It was to be paid for by the profits from the mine. But no money ever came. When he queried this, Pat said things weren't happening as fast as he'd hoped, and offered to buy the shares back. By this time Dad was being sued all over the place, so he didn't have any choice. He sold them back, and the following month Pat announced profits of a million dollars. The twenty thousand didn't even clear Dad's debts, and I guess the realisation that he'd been rooked proved too much for him."

"So he killed himself," Alison said slowly. "And you went to work for Pat. To avenge your Dad?"

"Maybe I had only that idea in the beginning. But then I began to see I could do more than that. Much more. Pat trusted me absolutely. But you trusted me more. Hell, once Pat was dead I had control of all of his money. You just didn't want to know. did you?"

"No," Alison said thoughtfully.

"The beauty of it was, it was all legal," David told her. "I had the spending of it, but I was doing it legally, in your name."

"And all the while you were suborning my people."

"Well, that wasn't difficult. Save for Hugo. I mean, I got Charlene on my team before you ever returned from that first trip to Brazil; she never forgave you for just abandoning her in New York. And Clem – he was so sore at being left behind when you took Hugo to the mine instead of him; and after you fired him he'd have committed murder for me." His face twisted. "I guess he did, the bastard."

"And Hugo?" Alison asked, feeling sick.

"Hugo, no . . . I never even tried for Hugo. I reckoned he was just too far gone on you. But he's so stupid he never got in the way."

She gave a sigh of relief. "I'm glad of that. But you must have been concerned when I married Paul Schleyer."

"Well, I tried to talk you out of that. But I wasn't too worried. Schleyer was so obviously a crook I knew it wasn't going to last. If it had, well, I'd have had to do something about it. But I was right, wasn't I? Mind you, when you were all but killed . . . I was upset about that."

"I suppose I must be thankful for small mercies," Alison said. "What would you have done if I *had* been killed?"

"Well . . . it would have been tough. But I would still have been one of your trustees, and I reckon the others would have left affairs largely in my hands."

"You couldn't lose, thanks to my trust in you," Alison murmured. "But Jonny Carter was a different proposition."

"I reckon you always had something pretty big going for him."

"Yes," Alison said. "I did. I'd have had more if I'd been certain of his innocence. And to get rid of him, you reckoned you had the right to murder my daughter."

460

"Shirley's death was an accident, and you know it. I regret that as much as anyone. I was horrified when I realised what had happened. I loved that girl, Alison, almost as my own daughter."

"That didn't stop you kidnapping her and raping her."

"There wasn't going to be any rape. It wasn't until that bastard Carter came back and you tried to keep your meetings with him secret that I realised I was in danger of losing you. Then I knew I had to make you understand that I was the only person in the world on whom you could rely absolutely. I had to make you want to marry me, and I felt you were only going to do that if you were sure Carter was as rotten as everyone else. The plan was that Clem and his friend should snatch Shirley and dump her in the farmhouse, and the crisis would make you realise just how much you depended on me. Just as you would start to wonder if Carter might not be the kidnapper. That moron Clem messed it up, just as he couldn't keep his hands off the girl. I should've known better than to trust him. But I've always been able to make the best of a bad job. The finger still pointed at Carter. The point was, it didn't matter whether or not the police ever pinned anything on him; I knew you were never going to be able to trust him again."

"And once Charlene was dead you felt you were in the clear. What about Clem?"

"Clem is dead, Alison. I always knew I would have to get rid of him. After I saw what he had done to Shirley, it was a pleasure. The odd thing is, I never intended to get rid of Charlene. I was sure I could trust her, and I thought I might need her again in the future. But when we found Shirley dead she just started to fall apart at the seams."

"Yes," Alison said. "And Linton?"

David grinned. "Linton is my brother, Alison. He's been working for me, on your payroll, for years. And you never even knew he existed."

"Well," Alison said. "Just to wind it up, tell me about Waller. Was he in your pay, too?"

461

"Waller was genuine. And he had a genuine grudge against Pat too, in my opinion. I think Waller felt that Pat had murdered his brother. And it could well be true. Giving all that money to charity was his way of buying the hereafter."

"But you never really intended Preston to find him, did you?"

"Preston worked for me."

"Then Waller's so-called return to Mexico at the time of Pat's death was a fake, just as the police thought it was."

"I'm afraid so. But even if you'd worked that out at the time, you'd only have felt I was going overboard trying to help you prove Carter's innocence."

"I probably would. And then Sanchez?"

"Sanchez was easy. He was expecting me, with the final pay-off. He'd been drinking to celebrate, before I ever got there. And in that heat, his window was open. Now you tell me something: you were okay when I left here this morning. When did you work all this out?"

"Just now. After Hugo told me he saw you leaving Charlene's room, that night."

"Yes. That was careless of me. And knowing your little ways, I suppose you've taped our conversation?"

"Yes, I have."

"Well, darling, it looks as if we have come to the end of the road."

"Won't that rather be cutting off your nose to spite your face? All of those millions?"

He grinned. "Darling Alison, you signed away your wealth to me, long ago."

"I see. And you reckon you can kill me and get away with that, too? Just how did you get Charlene to drink that stuff, anyway?"

"I told her it was all up. The police knew the whole thing. It was a suicide pact. She didn't want to hang. So we toasted each other, and said goodbye. We were quite fond of each other."

"Only you mixed the drinks," Alison said. "Do you think I am going to be that gullible?"

"No. But I think I can manage it without leaving too many bruises on your body. I think you should hang yourself, Alison, from that beam over there. Everyone knows you've been pretty upset. When I leave here I'll tell the kids and Hugo that you didn't feel like coming down to dinner, and tomorrow morning someone can find you. Aimée would be best."

"You suppose I am going to get up and walk across there and hang myself, because you have told me to?"

"I reckon. I may have to carry you. But with the air-conditioning on no one is going to hear you even if you yelp." He went to the door, pulled the cord from around the waist of the bathrobe that was hanging there. "I reckon this is good and strong enough." He looked at her. "It would be best if you didn't make a scene. I'd hate to hurt you in any way. I really am very fond of you."

"But you still mean to kill me?"

"I'm afraid I must. But I always knew I would have to, one day."

"Am I that repulsive?" Alison asked. "First Pat . . . although he only wanted to beat me up, and then Mayne, ditto, and then Paul, and now you . . ."

"You're not repulsive at all, Alison. You are a quite lovely woman, in almost every way. But . . . you're too rich. Nobody should be that rich. And you're too strong. Nobody should be both rich and strong. I guess you just have too much going for you. Listen . . ." he came towards the bed. "I'll look after the kids. You have my word. Heck, I regard them as almost my own."

"You have got to be stark, raving mad," Alison said. "Or I am."

He grinned. "Maybe we both are. You getting up?"

"No," Alison said, and took her hand from beneath the covers.

He stared at the gun.

"No speeches," Alison said, and squeezed the trigger.

463

The bullet slammed into his groin, and he gasped and doubled up. Alison sat up and fired again, and then again and again and again, at the squirming mass on the floor. Before she had squeezed the trigger a sixth and last time, David was lying still, his blood soaking into the carpet.

Alison stooped over David and took the bathrobe cord from his hand. She threaded it through the loops on the robe, and put the robe on. By then Hugo was knocking on the door.

She opened it.

"Mrs Pat? I heard a funny noise. Almost like shots . . ." he looked past her at David, and his jaw dropped.

"Yes," Alison said. "There were shots. I would like you to telephone Captain Guimard . . . no, he's Colonel Guimard now, isn't he? Telephone Colonel Guimard, and then Señor Puig, and ask them to come down here immediately."

Hugo gulped. "Yes, ma'am. But . . . what are you going to do?"

"Wait for them," Alison said. "Did the children hear anything?"

"I don't think so."

"Well, don't say anything to them. I'll explain it later."

Hugo looked at David again.

"He kidnapped Shirley, Hugo. He murdered Mr Pat. He did an awful lot of things."

Hugo swallowed. "Mrs Pat, if we was just to leave him here, and pack up and go . . ."

Alison squeezed his shoulder. "I know you'd risk all that for me, Hugo. But it really is all right. Believe me. You go and telephone Colonel Guimard."

She did not send for Aimée, but dressed herself, carefully stepping round David as she did so. She knew she was existing in a kind of limbo, that the true understanding of what she had done, of the nightmare that she had been living with for the past dozen years, would later come later. But she did not think she was going to feel any remorse for killing him – because he was the nightmare.

When she was dressed, she took the tape recorder – a new and much more efficient recorder, this, than the one she had used with Carlo – and went downstairs to the library, where she plugged it in.

Hugo came in. "I made those calls, Mrs Pat. I told them it really was urgent, so they're coming right away."

"Thank you, Hugo."

"You want a drink, Mrs Pat?"

She did, desperately, but she had to remain absolutely in control of herself and the situation. "Perhaps later."

The children had by now finished swimming and were changing. Ben and Joanne were first out. "Cocktail, Mom?" Ben asked cheerily.

"No thank you, Ben. I have some people coming out to see me, see us. I think we'll leave any drinking until after they have been."

Ben raised his eyebrows, but made no comment.

Joanne frowned.

The others appeared, and Alison said the same to them. They gathered on the patio, muttering at each other.

Hugo grew more and more uneasy.

Alison, to her own surprise, slowly found herself relaxing.

Puig arrived first. "*Señora*," he said, kissing both her hands. "Something has happened."

"Indeed. But we'll wait for the police."

Three police cars drove into the yard a few minutes later, stared at by the curious peons.

"*Señora*, dear *señora*," Guimard said, while his men arranged themselves watchfully. "There is no trouble, I hope? I have brought the surgeons and the photographers, but . . ." he looked around himself.

"I'm afraid there is trouble," Alison told him. "If you will just sit down, all of you . . ." she looked at the children. "I have a recording I wish to play to you."

They came into the room, and sat uneasily around the table.

"Whatever you hear," Alison said, "I would be grateful if no one makes any comment, or leaves the room, until the tape is finished."

"Shouldn't David be here?" Pat asked.

"David is here," Alison assured him. "Thank you, Hugo."

Hugo started the tape recorder, which Alison had first switched on before she lay down, and thus several minutes before David had entered. The group sat in silence, staring at one another, as the air-conditioning units gently whirred in the loudspeaker, until the door opened.

With the first words a slow tension crept into the room, and well before the shots were heard Ben and Joanne, and Stephanie and Pat, were holding hands. As the cracks of the revolver echoed from the tape everyone stiffened, and when the last one had been fired, everyone stared at Alison, as they listened to her opening the door for Hugo and telling him what to do.

Then Stephanie shouted, "Oh, Mom!" got up from her seat, and threw both arms round Alison's neck.

The others clustered round as well.

Guimard waited patiently for several minutes. Then he said, "Where is Señor Brook's body?"

"Where it fell," Alison told him.

He nodded to the waiting surgeon and to his policemen, and went upstairs. The remainder of the policemen stood in the doorway.

"What's going to happen?" Hugo asked.

"We will have to find that out from Colonel Guimard."

The Colonel came down a few minutes later. He looked grave. "*Señora* . . . you fired all six bullets into Señor Brook's body."

"Yes," Alison said.

Guimard sighed; he had of course long known that if

466

anyone was capable of going over the top it was Alison. "You understand, *señora*, that your tape recording may well stand up in court, and in that case, you were entitled to restrain and arrest a confessed murderer, and to use a weapon for that purpose. Even more were you entitled to use that weapon in your own defence, and the tape reveals conclusively that it was Señor Brook's intention to murder you, and therefore you were entitled to shoot him to save your life. But . . . my doctor says that any one of the six bullets would have rendered Señor Brook incapable of the ability to harm anyone. In fact, every one of the wounds would have been fatal, in a short space of time. Yet you shot him six times."

"I needed all six bullets," Alison explained. "One was for Pat, the second for Sanchez; the third was for Jonny Carter, the fourth for Charlene; the fifth was for Shirley. And the last was for me."

Guimard sighed again, and looked at the ceiling.

"What are you trying to say?" Ben asked.

"That I have no alternative other than to place your mother under arrest, Señor Grange. The charge will be . . ." he hesitated, "manslaughter."

Alison was aware of the strangest feeling of *déja vu*. Not that she had ever been arrested before, but because she had always felt that but for the fact that she was the sole inheritor of Pat's millions she would have been charged as an accomplice in his murder, and thus deep in her subsconscious she had always anticipated being arrested for something, at some time in her life.

Everyone was very charming and as helpful as possible, and yet the essential rules had to be followed. To be searched, fingerprinted, and photographed, to have everything she possessed which could cause the slightest harm to anyone – and most importantly, herself – removed, and then to be locked in a cell . . . it needed very little imagination to shudder at the concept of what this must be

467

like where one was *not* being treated as gently as possible, where the police were really out to get one.

The sort of thing that had happened to Jonny Carter.

But for her, it was of course all a farce. Her millions still protected her. Puig obtained bail within twenty-four hours, and she was home again with the children. They wanted to stay until the trial, but that would not be for several weeks, and so she packed them off to school; she had no intention of calling any of them in her defence.

Ben and Joanne insisted on staying with her, and in fact she was grateful for their company and their unfailing support. If she had to remain doubtful about the prospects of any marriage where the woman was several years the elder, she discovered that she could not fault Joanne as a human being. Nor was her background at all as plebian as Alison had feared on hearing that she was a barmaid. Joanne was well-read and mannered. Her job had simply been forced upon her by the necessity to earn a living after her first husband had abandoned her.

As to her morals in accepting a schoolboy as a lover, and the plain question of who had seduced whom, Alison supposed she was living in a changing world; certainly they seemed passionately fond of each other.

Their support was the more valuable because naturally by the time she got home the media was gathering. She locked up The Keep, with her inside it, but gave an interview from the wall like some medieval chatelaine negotiating with a barbarian army, explaining that she couldn't discuss the case as it was *sub judice*. They were not satisfied, and there were the usual plane swoops over the house, reinforced now by helicopters which could hover only a hundred feet above the fortress, their crews apparently armed with telescopic lenses on their cameras. Alison soon learned to ignore them.

The mail was equally enormous and in many cases horrendous, worse in fact than after Pat's death; the complete reverse of the sympathy she had received after Shirley. Monsieur Dudevant did not write again. But there were also friends. Carlo came down, of course, and was only with difficulty restrained from shooting at the newsmen and their aircraft. Edith Ruthven arrived to lend moral support; Edith had been rather distant since Paul's death, as she had felt at least partly responsible for what had happened, but now she was again her bustling, possessive self.

Carlo was no less possessive. "Whadya gonna do, little lady?" he asked.

"Do? Stand trial, I suppose."

"Oh, sure. No problem there. That rat deserved everything he got. Every last bullet. I meant about, well, everything."

"Just keep on living, Carlo."

"Who's gonna run your business?"

"I am. I did it before, briefly, when David walked out on me." Her mouth twisted. "To arrange Shirley's kidnapping. I only gave it all back to him because I was so upset. As he had planned would happen. But I can do it. I think I'll enjoy doing it. It'll keep me occupied."

"So, no more David Brook, eh?"

"No more men, Carlo."

He peered into her eyes. "Yeah? Not even your friend Jonny? Seems you were right, and he got the rawest of raw deals."

"I know. Carlo . . . can you find him for me?"

"I guess so. With what in mind? You said something about no more men."

"Well . . ."

"I have an idea you really love that guy."

"I gave him as raw a deal as anyone."

"Sure. And you reckon he's gonna forgive that?"

"I'd like to find out."

There were too many ghosts looming out of the past; sometimes she was obsessed with a sense of unreality. She knew why. She had never really accepted the responsibility of being the richest woman in the world. She had not had the mental capability to do so. She had shrunk away from all the varying aspects of her power, save the power itself. And in doing that, she had dug the most colossal pit, into which she had finally tumbled.

Out of it there had come several deaths, and so many tragedies. She did not even know what the final effect was going to be, on her children. She only knew that from here on, she had to lead from the front.

When she was given the right to lead again.

Three weeks later Puig came to see her. By then the media had lost interest, save for one or two diehards, but they were clearly waiting to swoop again when she came up for trial.

"The tape-recording has been examined very carefully, *señora*," the lawyer said. "And it has been determined that it is genuine, and that therefore it can be accepted as a confession of guilt by Señor Brook. This decision has been confirmed by a message from Scotland Yard in London, to the effect that they have located and arrested Señor Linton, who has made a full confession of his part in the kidnapping of your daughter."

Alison waited.

"In all the circumstances, and despite the fact that you used unnecessary force, it has been decided to drop all charges against you."

Alison drew a slow, long breath.

"There are of course, certain conditions."

She nodded. "Don't tell me. Inflation, etc . . ."

"It is a fact of life, *señora*."

"How much?"

"It is felt that perhaps three million a year . . ."

"Okay. But I have a condition of my own."

"*Señora*?"

"You have a confession to the murder of my first

470

husband. I wish the government to issue a full and public pardon to Señor Carter, immediately."

"I think this can be arranged."

"The pardon will of course also cancel the deportation order against him, and enable him to return to Mexico, should he wish."

"Of course," Puig agreed.

"Immediately," Alison reminded him.

By the terms of her new agreement with the Mexican Government, Alison still could not sell The Keep, although as before she had no desire ever to return there. But she decided to stay on for awhile as a stream of congratulations arrived, together, naturally, with the media again.

And now she could begin to live again, as well.

"We stick to the same arrangement," she told Ben. "You will take Business Studies at Cambridge, and in three years time you will take over David's duties as my accountant and business manager."

"And get married," he suggested.

"That too, if that is what you wish."

"Mom . . . you could not have asked for more support than you have had from Joanne."

"Granted.".

"Thank you. But you're still suspicious. Okay, I'll work for you . . ."

"For yourself and the others as well," Alison pointed out.

"Oh, sure. But . . . I'm not going to be replaced."

"Now, who might do that?"

"You tell me."

He knew she was waiting. Which was another reason she couldn't leave The Keep.

He came a month later. Alison was in the study

when he was announced, and she stood up to receive him.

As before, he looked thin and gaunt.

"What kept you?" she asked.

He shrugged. "Brook's confession may have cleared the air, but there are still a lot of people who don't like to have me around. So moving from place to place can be tricky. It was your friend Rubio got me here."

"Good old Carlo."

"He said you wanted to see me."

"Yes."

"You mean you're going to offer me that job again. What was it, exactly?"

"I told you to tell me what you thought you'd be best at."

"I did, and you slapped me down."

"Yes. Well . . . I'm not given to apologies, or looking over my shoulder," she said. "I've made a lot of mistakes, made a lot of very false judgements about people. Including Pat, I may say. Maybe I treated you worse than anyone. But . . . there's always tomorrow. If you'd care to stay."

He went towards her. "I brought a bag. And a toothbrush and razor."

"Welcome home," she said. "Oh, welcome home."